T0122013

Acclaim for Jonathan Coe's

THE CLOSED CIRCLE

"*The Closed Circle* is a satire of a high order. . . . A brilliant (and hugely entertaining) articulation . . . of the myriad forces—personal and political, rational and irrational—that drive us and, occasionally, result in powerful events." —*San Francisco Chronicle*

"The joy of *The Closed Circle* resides in the web of its many characters, the consequences of whose actions undulate throughout one another's lives. . . . Coe persistently tracks England's political and cultural pulse in the aftermath of 9/11, and his ability to layer emotions on each page is, ultimately, delightful from start to finish." —*The Times-Picayune*

"Coe is an artist of character and of his characters' stories, and he is a witty, desolately perceptive observer of the way we live now. . . . Coe develops [*The Closed Circle*] with a sustained, intricate brilliance."
—*Los Angeles Times*

"While social commentary is prevalent throughout, perhaps the greatest success of *The Closed Circle* is its ability to entertain while simultaneously illuminating a period of unrest and uncertainty."
—*The Pittsburgh Tribune-Review*

"[*The Closed Circle*] has an up-to-the-minute topicality that most writers shy away from, but it allows Coe to hone in savagely on his *bêtes noires*. . . . Coe has succeeded in accomplishing that rare feat: a pair of novels that combine the addictive quality of the best soap operas with a basic cultural integrity." —*The Independent* (London)

"The symmetries developed between this novel and its predecessor appear more intricate and abstract the longer you reflect on them, and yet . . . much of the novel has a free-form, improvised quality. . . . Charming. . . . Sublime." —*The New York Times Book Review*

"[Coe is] a very funny satirist and sometimes he's politically incendiary, but he's also an expert plotter who examines individual personalities in depth. As each carefully drawn circle closes in a series of climaxes, he reminds us that both in history and in the history of our private lives, the past has a way of playing pranks on us." —*People*

"A richly comic, entertaining novel. . . . *The Closed Circle* is a masterly portrayal of our ruling classes [and] a fine comedy with a disturbing undertow of menace." —*Literary Review*

"Past and present, personal and political, seep into each other, blurring the lines of meaning and perception in a narrative that nonetheless remains miraculously airy. . . . [Coe is] graceful, constructing a plot that meanders enticingly yet has the pleasing symmetry of a Shakespearean comedy." —*The Boston Globe*

"Jonathan Coe is England's most stylish and amusing social chronicler." —*Philadelphia Weekly*

"The rewards of this novel are as deeply felt as those of the first. . . . [Coe uses] believable dialogue to sketch a convincing inner life while providing flourishes of delightfully Wodehousian humor. . . . *The Closed Circle* finishes on an exceptionally strong note. . . . A wonderful synthesis of Coe's themes." —*The Oregonian*

"Coe is an unusually fine writer who has created the kind of book the reader will want to climb into and relish, hoping it will not end for a long time." —*Deseret News* (Salt Lake City)

"*The Closed Circle* is a wonderfully addictive story. This is a novel meant to be savored." —*Tulsa World*

Jonathan Coe

THE CLOSED CIRCLE

Jonathan Coe's awards include the John Llewellyn Rhys Prize, the Prix du Meilleur Livre Etranger, the Prix Médicis Etranger, and, for *The Rotters' Club*, the Bollinger Everyman Wodehouse Prize for Comic Writing. He lives in London with his wife and their two daughters.

ALSO BY JONATHAN COE

The Rotters' Club

The House of Sleep

The Winshaw Legacy

The Dwarves of Death

A Touch of Love

The Accidental Woman

THE CLOSED CIRCLE

THE CLOSED CIRCLE

Jonathan Coe

VINTAGE CONTEMPORARIES
Vintage Books
A Division of Random House, Inc.
New York

FIRST VINTAGE CONTEMPORARIES EDITION, JUNE 2006

 Published in the United States by Vintage Books, a division of Random House, Inc., New York, and in Canada by Random House of Canada Limited, Toronto. Originally published in hardcover in Great Britain by Viking, an imprint of Penguin Group, London, 2004, and subsequently in the United States by Alfred A. Knopf, a division of Random House, Inc., New York, in 2005.

The Library of Congress has cataloged the Knopf edition as follows:
Coe, Jonathan.
The closed circle / Jonathan Coe.—1st American ed.
p. cm.
1. Birmingham (England)—Fiction. 2. London (England)—Fiction. 3. Legislators—Fiction. 4. Adultery—Fiction. 5. Brothers—Fiction. I. Title.
PR6053.026C57 2005
823'.914—dc22 2004057789

Vintage ISBN-10: 0-375-71395-6
Vintage ISBN-13: 978-0-375-71395-8

Book design by Soonyoung Kwon

www.vintagebooks.com

146122990

For Philippe Auclair

Contents

Author's Note

Among the books which provided background material for this novel were *Labour Party PLC*, by David Osler (Mainstream, 2002), *White Riot: The Violent Story of Combat 18*, by Nick Lowles (Milo, 2001) and *"We Ain't Going Away!": The Battle for Longbridge*, by Carl Chinn and Stephen Dyson (Brewin Books, 2000).

The section of this novel called "High on the Chalk" was inspired by the song of the same name by The High Llamas, from their album *Beet, Maize and Corn* (Duophonic DS45-CD35).

The Closed Circle is a continuation of an earlier novel of mine called *The Rotters' Club*. A synopsis of *The Rotters' Club* is included at the end of this volume, for those who have not read it, or who perhaps—having read it—have inexplicably forgotten it.

J.C.

HIGH ON THE CHALK

High on the Chalk
Etretat
Tuesday, 7th December, 1999
Morning

Sister Dearest,

The view from up here is amazing, but it's too cold to write very much. My fingers can barely hold the pen. But I promised myself I'd start this letter before returning to England, and this really is my last chance.

Last thoughts, then, on leaving the European mainland? On coming home?

I'm scouring the horizon and looking for omens. Calm sea, clear blue sky. Surely that has to count for something.

People come up here to kill themselves, apparently. In fact there's a boy further down the path, standing dangerously close to the edge, who looks as though he may be planning to do exactly that. He's been standing there for as long as I've been on this bench and he's only wearing a T-shirt and jeans. Must be freezing.

Well, at least I haven't got to that point yet; although there have been some bad moments, these last few weeks. Moments when it seemed like I'd lost my bearings completely, that it was all spinning out of control. You must have known that feeling, once. In fact I know you did. Anyway, it's over now. Onwards and upwards.

Beneath me I can see Etretat, the wide curve of its beach, the pinnacled rooftops of the château where I stayed last night. I never did manage to explore the town. Funny how, when you have the freedom to do anything you want, you end up doing so little. Infinite choice seems to translate into no choice at all. I could have headed out for sole dieppoise *and ended up being plied with free Calvados by a flirty waiter; instead I stayed inside and watched some old Gene Hackman movie dubbed into French.*

Four out of ten, for that. See me afterwards. Could do better. Is this any way to begin a new life?

Am I really beginning a new life, in any case? Perhaps I'm just resuming an old one, after a long and finally pointless interruption.

On board the ferry, Pride of Portsmouth
In the restaurant
Tuesday, 7th December, 1999
Late afternoon

I wonder how they manage to make a profit from this line, at this time of year? Apart from me and the man behind the counter—what should I call him, is he the steward or purser or something?—this place is deserted. It's dark outside now and there is rain flecking the windows. Perhaps it's just spray. Makes me want to shiver looking at it, even though it's warm inside, almost overheated.

I'm writing this letter in the little A5 notebook I bought in Venice. It has a silky blue hardback cover with a marbled pattern, and lovely thick, roughly cut pages. When I've finished—if I ever finish—I suppose I could always cut the pages out and put them in an envelope. But there wouldn't be much point, would there? Anyway, it hasn't got off to a flying start. Rather self-indulgent so far, I'd say. You'd think I'd know how to write to you, after the thousands and thousands of words I've written in the last few years. But somehow, every new letter I write to you feels like the first one.

I've got a feeling this is going to be the longest of all.

When I sat down on that bench high on the chalk cliffs above Etretat, I hadn't even decided whether it was you I was going to write to, or Stefano. But I chose you. Aren't you proud of me? You see, I'm determined that I'm not going to go down that road. I promised myself that I wouldn't contact him, and a promise to yourself is the most binding of all. It's difficult, because there hasn't been a day for four months when we haven't spoken, or emailed, or at least texted. That kind of habit is hard to break. But I know it will get better. This is the cold turkey period. Looking at my mobile sitting on the table next to the coffee, I feel like an ex-smoker having a packet of fags dangled in front of her nose. It would be so easy to text him. He taught me *how to send text messages, after all. But that would be a crazy thing to do. He'd hate me for it, anyway. And I'm scared of him starting to hate me—really scared. That scares me more than anything. Silly, isn't it? What difference does it make, if I'm not going to see him again?*

I'll make a list. Making a list is always a good displacement activity.

5

Lessons I've learned from the Stefano disaster:

1. *Married men rarely leave their wives and daughters for single women in their late thirties.*
2. *You can still be having an affair with someone, even if you're not having sex.*
3.

I can't think of a number three. Even so, that's not bad going. Both those lessons are important. They'll stand me in good stead, the next time something like this happens. Or rather, they'll help me to make sure (I hope) that there won't be a next time.

Well, that looks good, on paper—especially this expensive, thick, creamy, Venetian paper. But I remember a line that Philip always used to quote to me. Some crusty old pillar of the British establishment who said, in his dotage: "Yes—I've learned from my mistakes, and I'm sure I could repeat them perfectly." Ha, ha. That will probably be me.

Fourth coffee of the day
National Film Theatre Café
London, South Bank
Wednesday, 8th December, 1999
Afternoon

Yes, I'm back, sister darling, after an interruption of twenty hours or so, and the first question that occurs to me, after a morning spent more or less aimlessly wandering the streets, is this: who are all these people, and what do they do?

It's not that I remember London very well. I don't think I've been here for about six years. But I do (or thought I did) remember where some of my favorite shops were. There was a clothes shop in one of the back streets between Covent Garden and Long Acre, where you could get nice scarves, and about three doors along, there used to be some people who did hand-painted ceramics. I was hoping to get an ashtray for Dad, a sort of peace-offering. (Wishful thinking, for sure: it would take more than that . . .) Anyway, the point is, neither of these places seems to be there any more. Both have been turned into coffee shops, and both of them were absolutely packed. And also, of course, coming from Italy I'm used to seeing people talking on their mobiles all day, but for the last few years I've been saying to everyone over there, in a tone of great authority, "Oh, you know, they're never going to catch on in Britain—not to the same extent." Why do I always do *that?*

Bang on about stuff I know nothing about, as if I was a world expert? Jesus, everybody *here has got one now. Clamped to their ears, walking up and down the Charing Cross Road, jabbering to themselves like loons. Some of them have even got these earpieces which mean you don't realize they're on the phone at all, and you really do think they must be care-in-the-community cases. (Because there are plenty of those around as well.) But the question is—as I said—who are all these people and what do they do? I know I shouldn't generalize from the closure of a couple of shops (anyway, perhaps I got the wrong street), but my first impression is that there are vast numbers of people who don't* work *in this city any more, in the sense of making things or selling things. All that seems to be considered rather old-fashioned. Instead, people* meet, *and they* talk. *And when they're not* meeting *or* talking *in person, they're usually* talking *on their phones, and what they're usually* talking *about is an arrangement to* meet. *But what I want to know is, when they actually* meet, *what do they* talk *about? It seems that's another thing I've been getting wrong in Italy. I kept going round telling everybody how reserved the English are. But we're not, apparently—we've become a nation of talkers. We've become intensely sociable. And yet I still don't have a clue what's being said. There's this great conversation going on all over the country, apparently, and I feel I'm the one person who doesn't know enough to join in. What's it about? Last night's TV? The ban on British beef? How to beat the Millennium bug?*

And another thing, while I remember: that bloody great wheel that's appeared on the side of the Thames, next to County Hall. What's that for, exactly?

Anyway, that's enough social commentary for now, I think. The other things I wanted to tell you are, first of all, that I've decided to face the music, bite the bullet and so on, and go back to Birmingham tonight *(because the hotel prices here are phenomenal, and I simply can't afford to stay here for another day); and also that I may have been back in England for less than twenty-four hours, but already I'm faced with a blast from the past. It comes in the form of a flyer I picked up at the Queen Elizabeth Hall. There's going to be a reading there on Monday, the title of which is "Goodbye to All That." Six "figures from public life" (it says here) are going to tell us "what they most regret leaving behind or what they are happiest to see the back of, at the end of the second Christian Millennium." And look who's number four on the list: no, not Benjamin (although he was the one we all thought would be a famous writer), but Doug Anderton—who we are told is a "journalist and political commentator," if you please.*

Another omen, maybe? A sign I'm not making a bold foray into the future after all, but taking the first involuntary steps on a journey backwards? I mean, for God's sake, I haven't seen Doug in about fifteen years. The last time was at my wedding. At which, I seem to remember, he pressed me drunkenly up against a wall and told me that I was marrying the wrong man. (He was right, of course, but not in the sense that he *meant it.) How weird would it be now, to sit in an audience and listen to him pontificating about pre-millennial angst and social change? I suppose it would just be a version of what we all had to put up with more than twenty years ago, sitting around the editorial table of the school magazine. Only now we're all developing grey hair and back problems.*

Is your hair grey yet, I wonder, dear Miriam? Or is that not something you have to worry about any more?

There's a Birmingham train in fifty minutes. I'm going to make a dash for it.

Second coffee of the day
Coffee Republic
New Street, Birmingham
Friday, 10th December, 1999
Morning

Oh, Miriam—the house! That bloody house. It hasn't changed. Nothing *about it has changed, since you left it (and a quarter of a century has gone by since then: almost exactly), except that it is colder, and emptier, and sadder (and* cleaner*) than ever. Dad pays someone to keep it spotless, and apart from her coming in twice a week to do the dusting, I don't think he speaks to a soul, now that Mum's gone. He's also bought this little place in France and seems to spend a lot of time there. He spent most of Wednesday night showing me pictures of the septic tank and the new boiler he's had installed, which was thrilling, as you can imagine. Once or twice he said that I should go over there some time and stay for a week or two, but I could tell that he didn't really mean it, and besides, I don't want to. Nor do I want to stay under his roof for more nights than I can help it, this time.*

Last night I had a meal out with Philip and Patrick.

Now—I hadn't seen Philip for more than two years, and I suppose it's pretty common, in these circumstances, for ex-wives to look at their ex-husbands and wonder what on earth it was that drew them together in the first place. I'm talking about physical attraction, more than anything else. I remember that when I was a student, and lived in Mantova for the best part of a year, back in 1981 if I can believe myself when I write that (God!), I was surrounded by young Italian men, most of them gorgeous, all of them as good as begging me to go to bed with them. A posse of teenage Mastroiannis in their sexual prime, gagging for it, not to mince words. My Englishness made me exotic in a way which would have been unthinkable in Birmingham, and I could have had my pick of that lot. I could have had them all, one after the other. But what did I choose instead? Or who did I choose, rather. I chose Philip. Philip Chase, whey-faced, nerdy Philip Chase, with his straggly ginger beard and his horn-rimmed specs, who came to stay with me for a week and somehow got me into bed on the second day and ended up changing the whole course of my life, not permanently, I suppose, but radically . . . fundamentally . . . I don't know. I can't think of the word. One word is as good as another, sometimes. Was it just because we were too young, I wonder? No, that's not fair on him. Of all the boys I'd known up until that point, he was the most straightforward, the most sympathetic, the least arrogant (Doug and Benjamin were so up themselves, in their different ways!). There is a tremendous decency in Phil, as well: he is absolutely reliable and trustworthy. He made the divorce so untraumatic, I remember—a back-handed compliment, I know, but if you ever want to get divorced from someone . . . Philip's your man.

As for Patrick, well . . . I want to see as much of Pat as I can, while I'm here, obviously. He is so grown up now. Of course, we have been writing and emailing each other constantly, and last year he came out to Lucca for a few days, but still—it surprises me every time. I can't tell you what a peculiar feeling it is, to look at this man*—he may be only fifteen, but that's what he seems like, now—this tall (rather skinny, rather pale, rather sad-looking) man and know that once he was . . .* inside me, *not to put too fine a point on it. He seems to have a very good relationship with his father, I must admit. I envied them the ease with which they talked to each other, shared jokes together. Blokes' stuff, maybe. But no, there was more to it than that. I can see that they look after him well, Philip and Carol. I have no grounds for complaint there. A little jealousy, maybe. But then, it was my choice, to try my luck in Italy again, and leave Pat with his father. My choice.*

And now to my final piece of news, and in some ways the most momentous—or disturbing, maybe. I saw Benjamin again. About an hour ago. And in the strangest circumstances, I have to say.

I had been given the lowdown on Ben the night before. Still working for the same firm—a senior partner now, and I should think so too, after being there for so long—and still married to Emily. No kids: but, well, everyone has given up asking about that. Phil said that they'd tried everything, and been down the adoption route as well. Medical science baffled, etc., etc. Neither of them is to blame, apparently (which probably means that, deep down, without being able to say it, each blames the other). And in Benjamin's case, as with children, so it is with books: he's been labouring (!) for years to produce some shattering masterpiece, and so far, nobody has seen a word. Though everyone still seems touchingly convinced that it will appear one of these days.

9

*So, that's the story so far. And now picture me, if you will, looking through the History section of Waterstone's on High Street. Only been back here a day and a half and already I can't think of anything better to do. I'm right next to the part of the shop that is set aside for the ubiquitous coffee-drinkers. Out of the corner of my eye I can see a girl who's facing me—*very *pretty, in a paper-thin sort of way—and opposite her, with his back to me, is a grey-haired guy who I assume at first must be her dad. I guess the girl must be about nineteen or twenty, and there's a touch of the Goth in the way she dresses: she has lovely hair, black hair, thick and long and straight, half way down her back. Apart from that I don't take much notice of these two to start with, but when I move over to look at the books on one of the display tables, I notice her reaching down to get something out of her bag, and I notice the way her black T-shirt rides up to expose her midriff, and I notice the way that* he *notices this, quickly, surreptitiously, and all of a sudden I recognize him: it's Benjamin. Wearing a suit—which looks odd, to me, but of course it's a working day for him, and he must just have slipped out of the office for a while—and looking, in that instant, altogether . . . What's the word? I know there is a word this time, a perfect word for the way men look when they're in that situation . . .*

Ah . . . I remember. "Besotted." That's the word, for how Benjamin looks.

And then he notices me; and time seems to slow down—the way it always does, in the moment you recognize someone you weren't expecting to see, and haven't seen for a long time, and something shifts inside you both, some sort of realignment of your expectations of that day . . . And then I'm walking over to the table, and Benjamin is standing up, and holding out his hand, *of all things,* holding his hand out *so I can shake it. Which of course I don't do. I kiss him on the cheek instead. And he looks confused and embarrassed, and straight away he introduces me to his friend; who is also standing up, by now; and whose name, it transpires, is Malvina.*

So, what is *the situation, there? What's going on? After five minutes' broken conversation—not a word of which I can remember—I'm none the wiser. But in what is already establishing itself as a pattern, in the last couple of days, I do have something in my hand that I didn't have before. A flyer. A flyer for* another *event taking place on Monday December 13th. It turns out that Benjamin's band is playing that night.*

"I thought you split up ages ago," I say.

"We've reformed," he explains. "This pub's celebrating an anniversary. Twenty years of live music. We used to have a residency there, and they've asked us to come back and play, for one night only."

I look at the flyer again, and smile. I remember the name of Benjamin's band, now—"Saps at Sea." Named after a Laurel and Hardy film, he once told me. It would be fun to see them again, in a way, although I never cared for his music much. But I'm speaking the honest truth when I say: "I'll come if I'm still in town. But I may have left Birmingham by then."

"Please do," Benjamin's saying. "Please do come."

Then we say the usual awkward stuff about it being nice to see you, and so on, and next minute I'm out of there, with never a backward glance. Well, OK, then—one backward glance. Just enough to see Benjamin leaning towards Malvina—who he introduced to me as his "friend," which was all the explanation I got—and showing her the flyer and telling her something about it. Their foreheads are practically touching over the table. And all I can think of as I hurry away is: Benjamin, Benjamin, how can you be doing this to your wife of sixteen years?

In my old bedroom
St. Laurence Road
Northfield
Saturday, 11th December, 1999
Night time

This trip just gets worse and worse. It happened more than three hours ago, and I'm still shaking all over. Dad is sitting downstairs, reading one of his terrible old Alastair Maclean novels. He wasn't remotely sympathetic. Seemed to think the whole thing was my fault anyway. I don't think I can stay in this house any longer. I shall have to leave tomorrow, find somewhere else to stay for a while.

I'll tell you what happened, briefly. I was longing to see Pat again today, and he was supposed to be playing football for the school in the morning. It was an away game, against a team in Malvern. So I said I'd pick him up from Philip and Carol's house, and drive him over there myself. Much against his better judgment, Dad let me borrow his car.

We went south along the Bristol Road and then took a right turn when we got to Longbridge, through Rubery and along towards the M5. It was pretty weird, being alone in the car with him—weirder than it should have been. He's very quiet, *my son. Maybe he's just quiet when he's with me, but somehow I don't think that's the whole story. He's an introvert, for sure—nothing wrong with that. But also—and this was what really unnerved me—when he* did *start talking, the subject he chose was the last thing I'd been expecting. He started talking about* you, *Miriam. He started asking questions about when I'd last seen you, and how Mum and Dad had coped with it when you disappeared. I was dumbstruck, at first. Simply didn't know what to say to him. It wasn't as if any of this had arisen naturally in the course of conversation: he brought it all up, quite abruptly. What was I supposed to say? I just told him that it was all a long, long time ago now, and we would probably never find out the truth. Somehow we had to live with that, find an accommodation with it. It was a struggle: something we both battled with, me and Dad, in our different ways, every day of our lives. What else could I tell him?*

He fell silent, after that, and so did I, for quite a while. I was a little freaked out by that conversation, to be honest. I thought we'd maybe be talking about life at school, or his chances in the football match. Not his aunt who had vanished without trace ten years before he was born.

I tried not to think about it any more, tried just to concentrate on the road.

Now, there's another thing I've noticed about this country, Miriam, in the few days I've been home. You can take the temperature of a nation from the way it drives a car, and something has changed in Britain in the last few years. Remember I've been in Italy, the homeland of aggressive drivers. I'm used to that. I'm used to being cut up and overtaken on blind corners and sworn at and people yelling out that my brother was the son of a whore if I'm going too slowly. I can handle it. It's not serious, for one thing. But something similar has started to happen here—only it's not that similar really, there's an important difference: here, they really seem to mean it.

A few months ago I read an article in the Corriere della Sera *which was called "Apathetic Britain." It said that now Tony Blair had been voted in with such a huge majority, and he seemed like a nice guy and seemed to know what he was doing, people had breathed a sort of collective sigh of relief and stopped thinking about politics any more. Somehow the writer managed to link this in with the death of Princess Diana, as well. I can't remember how, I can remember thinking it all sounded a bit contrived at the time. Anyway, maybe he had a point. But I don't think he really got to the heart of the matter. Because if you scratch the surface of that apathy, I think what you find underneath is something else altogether—a terrible, seething frustration.*

We weren't on the motorway for long—only about twenty minutes or so—but even so, I started to notice something in those twenty minutes. People on the motorway were driving differently. It's not just that they were driving faster than I remembered—I drive pretty fast myself—but there was a kind of anger *about the way they drove. They were tailgating each other, flashing their headlights when people stayed in the outside lanes for a few seconds longer than they should.*

There seems to be a whole new class of driver who just takes up residence in the middle lane and won't be shifted, and that really seems to infuriate everybody else: people drive about five yards behind them for a while, pressuring them to move, and then, when they don't move, they swing out into the outside lane and swing back in again before it's really safe, cutting into their path. And there were drivers who were happily cruising along at seventy and then, when they noticed that someone was overtaking them, they would accelerate, up to eighty, eighty-five, as if it was a personal affront to suggest that a P-registration Punto might overtake an S-registration Megane, and they weren't going to stand for it; as if it was an insult to the rawest and tenderest part of them. I'm exaggerating, perhaps, but not massively. This was a Saturday morning, after all, and surely most of these people were heading off to the shops, or just out to enjoy themselves, but there seemed to be a collective fury building up on this motorway. It felt tense and pressurized, as if all it would take was for someone to make one really bad mistake and it would tip us all over the edge.

Anyway: we arrived at the school, and battle commenced. Patrick was playing somewhere in midfield, and the game seemed to keep him pretty busy. He was self-conscious with me watching him, and was trying to look tough and grown-up, but then there was also this permanent frown of concentration on his face which wiped about five years off him and almost cracked my heart at the same time. He played well. I mean, I don't know anything about football, but it looked to me as if he was playing well. His team won, 3–1. I almost froze to death, standing there on the touchline for an hour and a half—there was still frost on the pitch—but it was worth it. I've got a lot of ground to make up with Patrick, and this was a start, definitely. Afterwards I'd assumed we would go off and have lunch somewhere, but it turned out he had other plans. He wanted to go back on the coach with his schoolfriends, and then he was going round to the house of this friend of his, Simon, the goalkeeper. I couldn't very well say no, even though it took me by surprise. Within a few minutes the boys had showered and the coach was gone and suddenly I was left in the middle of Malvern all by myself. With the rest of the day to kill.

So: back to my usual state of affairs. The loneliness of the single woman. Too much time, not enough company. What was I going to do? I had a sandwich and something to drink at a pub on the Worcester Road, and in the afternoon I went for a walk along the hills. It calmed me; cleared my head. Perhaps I'm someone who only feels happy inside herself when she's halfway up a hill. Certainly I seem to have spent a lot of time, these last few weeks, climbing up to different vantage points. Maybe I'm at a point in my life where I need that Olympian perspective. Maybe I lost my bearings so thoroughly when I got involved with Stefano that I can only recover them by getting a sense of the bigger picture. The picture today was pretty big, I must say. Would you remember that view, I wonder, Miriam, if you were ever to see it again? We used to go there when we were kids, you, me, Mum and Dad. Freezing cold picnics, ham sandwiches and thermos flasks, the four of us tucked away behind some big rock on the escarpment for shelter, the fields spread out below us, beneath grey Midlands skies. There was a little cave in a hidden part of the hillside, I remember. We used to call it the Giant's Cave, and somewhere I've got a picture of us, standing outside it, in our matching green anoraks, hoods pulled up tight. I think Dad's thrown most of them away, the pictures of you, but I managed to hold on to some of them. Saved from the wreckage. It seems to me now that we were both terribly scared of him, always, and it was that fear that made us so close. But that doesn't make the memories unhappy. Quite the opposite. They're so precious that I can hardly bear to think of them.

I don't believe you could have just walked away from all that. It makes no sense. You wouldn't have done it, would you, Miriam? Left me to fend for myself? I can't bring myself to believe it; even though the alternative's worse.

By half past three, it's getting dark. It's time to gather my strength and go home and spend another evening with Dad. The last one, I've decided. I've been thinking that if things had been better, we might have spent Christmas together, but that's not going to happen. He and I are a lost cause. I'll have to find somewhere else to stay. Maybe Pat and I could go away together somewhere. We'll see.

So, anyway, I'm on my way home. I told Dad that I'd pick up something for us to have for dinner, so I pop into Worcester, and I buy some steak. He likes steak. Considers it his patriotic duty to eat it, in fact, as rare as possible and as often as possible, now that the French have banned it. That's Dad for you. And I'm leaving the outskirts of Worcester and I've already had a bit of a skirmish with someone who tried to overtake me on a roundabout and I'm getting jumpy about it again, getting that sense that everyone behind the wheel of a car these days is for some reason on edge. And as I head further out of the city, there's a car in front of me going very slowly. The streetlamps are lit by now and I can see that the driver is a man, a man on his own, probably not very old; and the reason he's driving slowly is that he's talking on his mobile. Otherwise he would probably be speeding along because he has quite a fancy car—a Mazda sports. But this phone conversation, whatever it's about, is evidently quite distracting. He's driving with only one hand on the wheel and keeps veering over to the left-hand side of the road. We're in a forty-mile limit but he's doing about twenty-six. But it's not the fact that he's slowing me down that's annoying me, so much: it's because what he's doing is so unsafe, so incredibly irresponsible. Isn't it illegal, in this country? (It is in Italy—not that anyone takes any notice.) What would happen if a child were to run out in front of him? He speeds up for a moment and then slows down again, drastically and for no reason, and I almost crash into his bumper. He has no idea that I'm behind him, as far as I can see. I brake sharply and the plastic bag of shopping I've put on the passenger seat next to me shoots off and spills its contents over the floor. Great. And now he's picking up speed again. I think about pulling over and putting the food back in the bag but decide against it. I watch the driver ahead of me, instead, fascinated in spite of myself. He's reached an animated point in the conversation and is making hand gestures to himself. He has no hands on the wheel at all! I decide that I want to get away from this situation as quickly as possible: if there's going to be an accident, I don't want anything to do with it. The road is single-carriageway, at this point, passing through the outer suburbs, and there's a window of opportunity with no other cars in sight. It's not the safest thing to do but I've had enough of this joker: so I indicate, swing out to the right, and try to overtake him. He's slowed right down again so it should only take a few seconds.

But as I'm overtaking, he notices what I'm doing and he doesn't like it. Without dropping the phone, he puts his foot down and starts racing me. I'm the one going faster, still, but Dad's Rover doesn't have a lot of power in it, and it's taking me a lot longer to overtake than I'd like: and now there's a van coming in the other direction. Swearing to myself at the sheer stubbornness of this macho idiot, I change down to third gear, hammer down hard on the accelerator, and rev forward at forty-five, fifty miles an hour, just squeezing in ahead of him as the van closes in, flashing its headlights on to full beam to tick me off.

And that was that. Or would have been, if I hadn't done two really stupid things as I was in the middle of overtaking. I glanced over at the man on the telephone, making eye contact for a second or two. And I pipped my horn at him.

Now, it was only a little, frail, girly sort of pip. I'm not even sure what I meant by it. It was just my feeble way of saying, "You wanker!," I suppose. But it had the most amazing, instantaneous effect. He must have finished that call and chucked his phone on to the passenger seat immediately because a couple of seconds later this car is right *up behind me—about six inches away, I reckon—and his lights are on full beam, blinding me in the rear-view mirror, and I can hear his engine screaming. A real howl of anger. And suddenly I'm scared. Terrified, actually. So I try to accelerate away from him—quickly reaching some ridiculous speed, like sixty miles an hour or something—and he doesn't give any one of those inches. He's still coming up behind me, bumper to bumper. I wonder if I dare try flicking the brakes on, just to give him a shock, just to make him pull back a little, but I daren't do it, because I don't think it would work. I think it just means he would crash into the back of me.*

I suppose this can only go on for a few seconds, although it feels much longer.

Anyway, then I'm out of luck. We come to a set of traffic lights where the road splits into two lanes, and the lights are on red. So I pull to a halt on the inside lane, and Mazda man screeches up next to me and jerks the handbrake on and next thing I know, he's getting out of his car. I'm expecting some lumbering oaf with a neck thicker than his head, but in fact he's a scrawny little thing, only about five foot four. I can't remember anything else about him because what happened next is all a blur. First of all he starts hammering on my window. I glimpse his face for a horrible, stretched moment and then I stare straight ahead, willing the lights to change, my heart pounding as if it's going to burst. Now he's shouting—the usual sort of stuff, fucking bitch, fucking slag, I'm not really taking it in, it all sounds like white noise to me—and then I can't stand waiting for the lights to change again so I go straight across on a red light, thinking that it's clear, only another car is coming at me all of a sudden from the left, and it has to swerve to avoid me and slam on the brakes with a screech and then its horn starts blaring as well but soon that's faded away because I'm driving off like a maniac, no idea what speed I'm doing, and it's not until I've gone about a mile and left the city well behind that I wonder why my side of the windscreen is wet when it's not raining and then I realize it's because the guy managed to spit all over it before I drove off. His parting shot.

There were quite a few lay-bys before I got to the motorway but I didn't stop in any of them because I was scared that he might be following and if he saw me there he'd pull over too and try to complete his unfinished business. So I drove on, which was a crazy thing to do because I was crying and shaking all the way back into Birmingham, and endlessly looking around to see if there was a Mazda sports coming up behind me on the outside lane, headlights flashing, guns blazing for battle.

Maybe some women would have turned around and given him the same treatment in return. But I genuinely think that if I'd wound the window down he would have attacked me. He was beside himself, completely out of control. I've never seen—

I stopped there because I was about to say I'd never seen a man look that way before. But that isn't true. As I said, I only glimpsed his face for a moment, but that was enough to see into his eyes, and yes, I have *seen that kind of hatred in a man's eyes—just one other time. I saw it a few months ago, in Italy. But that's another story, and I should save it for another day because my hands are already stiff from all this writing.*

How quiet this house is. I really noticed it then. I realized that the scratching of my pen had been the only sound.

Good night, sweet Miriam. More tomorrow.

In my old bedroom
St. Laurence Road
Northfield
Sunday, 12th December, 1999
Late morning

So, big sis, can you guess where Dad is, and why I've got the house to myself for an hour or two? Of course you can. He's in church! Making himself a better person. Which would be a wonderful idea, in his case, if there was only the slightest prospect of it working. But he's been doing this, week in, week out for about sixty years now (as he was reminding me over breakfast only this morning), and if you ask me, the results haven't exactly been outstanding so far. To be honest, if that's the best the church can do after sixty years, I think we should ask for our money back right now.

But no—he's not worth thinking about. And besides, I've only got one more meal to sit through with him—the dreaded Sunday lunch—and after that I'm out of here. I've decided to spoil myself, and I've booked in to the Hyatt Regency for two nights. It's the poshest new hotel in Birmingham: more than twenty floors, right next to the new Symphony Hall and Brindley Place. I was walking round that part of town on Friday and I could barely recognize it, it's changed so much since the 1970s. All that area around the canals used to be deserted, a wasteland. Now it's wall-to-wall bars and cafés, and every one of them was jumping. More of that mysterious meeting and talking that I've noticed springing up everywhere.

But maybe you know all this. Maybe you've been there yourself, in the last year or two. Maybe you were there on Friday morning, having a coffee with some friends in All Bar One. Who can say?

Even though I only saw it for a fraction of a second, I keep thinking of the face of that man who swore and spat at me yesterday because I pipped my horn at him. I told you, didn't I, that it reminded me of something that happened in Italy this summer. It was the only other time I've seen a man lose his temper like that. It was a terrible thing to see (in fact I did more than see it, I was caught up right in the middle of it), but in a way the consequences were even worse, because it led directly to me becoming involved with Stefano. And look where that got me.

It seems like a lifetime ago, already.

Lucca is surrounded by hills, but it's the ones to the north-west that are the loveliest, I think. High on a hillside there, in open countryside but with a fabulous view of the city (which is one of the most beautiful in Italy), an old farmhouse was being restored, from top to bottom, inside and out. It was being restored by a British businessman by the name of Murray—or at least, he was the one who was footing the bill. The person supervising all the work was his wife, Liz, and the architect and project manager was called Stefano. Liz didn't speak any Italian and Stefano didn't speak any English and that was where I came in. I was brought in to do all the translating—in person and on paper—and so for six months Liz Murray became my employer.

Now, it's a slightly alarming feeling, to sign a contract with someone and then to realize, about two days later, that you're dealing with the boss from hell. To describe Liz as having a bad temper and a foul mouth doesn't even begin to convey what she was like. She was a stuck-up cow from north London whose basic attitude towards the people working for her—and, as far as I could see, to the whole of the human race—was one of absolute contempt. Whether she had ever worked herself I was never able to find out: certainly she showed no particular talent for anything, apart from scaring people and bossing them around. Luckily, my job was straightforward, and I was good at it, or at least competent; so although I never received a gracious word from her, or was made to feel that I was anything other than her minion, at least I never had her screaming at me. But Stefano had to put up with the most terrible abuse (which I of course had to translate), as did the builders themselves. Eventually, it was more than they could take.

It happened on a Wednesday, I remember, a Wednesday in late August. There was a site meeting fixed for 5 p.m. Stefano, Liz and I all drove out to the house separately. The builders' foreman, Gianni, was already there. He'd been working all day, with four other men, and they were hot and bothered. The job had overrun now by several weeks, and they were probably all wishing that they were on holiday, like everybody else in Italy. The heat was indescribable. Nobody should have to work in that kind of heat. But in the last couple of weeks they had done (I thought) an extraordinary job. A huge swimming pool had been dug out, and almost completely tiled. The tiling alone had taken three days. They had used porcelain tiles in subtly different shades of blue, each one five centimetres square. The effect was magnificent. But there seemed to be a problem.

"What are these?" Liz snapped at Gianni, pointing at the tiles.

I translated for him, and he answered: "These are the tiles you asked for."

She said: "They're too big."

He said: "No, you asked for five centimetres."

Stefano stepped forward, leafing through the thick wedge of papers that made up his spec.

"That's right," he said. "We placed the order about five weeks ago."

To Gianni, Liz said: "But I changed my mind since then. We talked about it."

He said: "Yes, we *talked*, but you hadn't come to a decision. You never came to a new decision, so we just proceeded."

Liz said: "I did come to a decision. I asked for smaller tiles than those. Three centimetres across."

Slowly, as they argued, it must have dawned on Gianni what she was asking him to do. She wanted his men to strip all the tiles out, order thousands of new, smaller ones, and start all over again. What's more, she wanted him to do this at his own expense, because she was adamant that she had given verbal instructions to use smaller tiles in the first place.

"No!" he was saying. "No! It's impossible! You'll bankrupt me."

I translated this for Liz, and she answered: "I don't care. It's your fault. You didn't listen to me."

"But you didn't make it *clear*—" Gianni said.

"Don't argue with me, you fucking idiot. I know what I said."

I translated this, without the "fucking."

Gianni was still furious. "I'm not an idiot. *You* are the stupid one here. You keep changing your mind."

"How dare you! How dare you try to put the blame for your laziness and your sheer fucking incompetence on to me?"

"I cannot do this. My business will go under and I have a family to support. Be reasonable."

"Who cares? Who gives a shit?"

"Stupid woman! Stupid! You said five centimetres! It's written here."

"We changed it, you cretin. We talked about it, and I said three centimetres, and you said you would remember."

"You never put it into writing."

"That's because I was silly enough to think that you'd remember, you big fat fucking moron. I thought that three centimetres would be easy to remember because it's the same size as your dick."

She waited for me to speak. I said: "I'm not going to translate that."

"I pay you," she pointed out, "to translate every word that I say. Now translate it. Every single word."

I dropped my voice, and translated Liz's last comment. And that was when I saw it happen: an astonishing transformation coming over Gianni—this big, kind, gentle man—whose eyes suddenly gleamed with hatred, and who without thinking about it snatched up some tool from the box near to him—it was a chisel, *an enormous chisel—and lunged towards his employer, screaming at her, inarticulate words of fury, so that he had to be restrained by his workmates, but not before he had managed to catch her a blow across the mouth. So that Liz, lips bleeding, had to storm off indoors to the kitchen, which had just recently been plumbed in, and a few minutes later we heard her drive away without another word to any of us.*

After that the men packed up their gear methodically and in silence. Stefano and Gianni had a long conversation in a quiet corner of the garden, beneath the shade of a cypress tree. I had asked Stefano if I could go but he said that he would like me to stay a little longer, if that was possible. I waited for about twenty minutes and then, when he had finished talking to the builder, Stefano came over to me as I sat in what was designed to be the loggia, *and he said, "I don't know about you, but I need a drink after that—will you join me?"*

We went to a restaurant along the main road not far from the farmhouse, up on the hillside overlooking Lucca, and we sat on the terrace and drank wine and Grappa for a couple of hours, and then ate some pasta, and talked until the sun started to go down, and I noticed how handsome he was and how kind his eyes were and what a great, childlike, shoulder-shaking laugh he had, and he told me what a relief it would be if Liz sacked him, because she was the worst client he had ever worked for, and the stress of it was almost giving him a breakdown, and this was the last thing he needed because apart from anything else his marriage was in trouble. And there was a sudden silence after he said that, as if neither of us could understand how it had slipped out. And then he told me that he'd been married to his wife for seven years, and they had a little daughter called Annamaria who was four, but he didn't know how much longer they were going to be together because his wife had been unfaithful to him and although her affair was over now it had hurt him terribly, worse than anything that had happened to him in his life, and he didn't know if he could ever forgive her or feel about her the same way again. And I nodded and made sympathetic noises and spoke comforting words and even then, right at the beginning, I was too blind, too self-deceiving to admit that really my heart was singing when he told me all this, that it was just what I most wanted to hear. And the evening ended with him kissing me in the restaurant car park—kissing me on the cheek, but not just in a friendly way, stroking my hair a little bit as he did so, and I asked him if he wanted my mobile number and he reminded me that of course he'd already got it, it was on my business card, and he said he'd call me again soon.

He called me the next morning, and we went out for dinner again that night.

Living the high life
Hyatt Regency Hotel
Birmingham
13th December, 1999
Late at night

I fell on my feet with this hotel. I'm not quite sure how it happened, because I've never been very good at the fluttering-eyelashes, damsel-in-distress look. But when I turned up here yesterday afternoon, looking pretty downtrodden I suspect, with just a few clothes and things crammed into a holdall (I've left the rest of my stuff at Dad's, for now) the man behind the desk was one of the junior managers and he did me a big *favour. He told me that all of the executive suites were free at the moment and I could have one of those if I wanted. And I can tell you, dear sister, it's been wonderful. After four miserable days in the Amish-style establishment that Dad maintains these days, I've at last been able to* relax *and enjoy myself. I've spent half the time in the bath and half of it raiding the minibar. It will all have to be paid for, of course, but this is going to be my last little fling before I settle down to the serious business of sorting my life out. Meanwhile the lights of Birmingham are twinkling away beneath my feet and all at once the world seems full of possibilities.*

Now: I'm just going to tell you about this evening, and then I shall leave you in peace.

So, just a few hours ago, I decide that I might as well do the decent thing and go to hear Benjamin's band after all. The pub where they're playing, The Glass and Bottle, is only about five minutes' walk along the canal from here. Phil and Patrick will be there, and so will Emily: it's high time that I caught up with her. And there's no danger of running into Doug Anderton, because he'll be in London saying "Goodbye To All That" at the Queen Elizabeth Hall (a marginally more prestigious venue than The Glass and Bottle, I can't help thinking to myself, but there you go). So I have no excuse, really, for not putting in an appearance.

On my way there, all the same, I find myself wondering why it is that I feel so reluctant to be part of the audience tonight. It has nothing to do with musical taste, or my suspicion that I'm in for an evening of slightly morbid nostalgia. I'm trying to be entirely honest with myself, and I know it must be—partly at least—because I had a tiny crush on Benjamin when we were at school, and even now, so many years later, running into him again on Friday at the bookshop felt weird. Not just because of the woman he'd been with, and how obvious they made it that I was interrupting rather more than a meeting between two friends. No, there was something else: I can hardly believe this, because I have hardly given Benjamin a thought (truthfully) in the last decade or more, but it was still there—a stubborn little residue of what I used to feel for him. How annoying—how depressing*—is that? It's the very thing I don't need to know at the moment. I feel that it's now absolutely necessary, to my health, to my mental wellbeing, to my* survival, *that I flush Stefano out of my system as soon as possible: but what if you can never do that? What if those feelings* never go away? *Am I unique in that respect—uniquely hopeless—or does everyone have the same problem, deep down?*

I push open the door to the pub and exchange the black frostiness of the canal-side for a blast of light and warm air and loud, competing voices.

Patrick sees me at once, comes over, gives me a big kiss. Phil is talking to Emily. We fall into each other's arms. Hi, Emily, great to see you, how long has it been, et cetera, et cetera. She hasn't changed. No grey hairs (or at least, she's got a good hairdresser), still with a nice figure, doesn't even look as plump as she used to. (Cruelly, I tell myself that it's easier for women to stay that way when they haven't had children.) I ask for a Bloody Mary and Phil sees to it. (They've already clocked that Patrick is underage—not difficult, to be honest—and are refusing to serve him.) There's a decent-sized crowd in there. "Have they all come for the music?" I ask. Philip nods. He's in a good mood, proud that so many people have turned out for Benjamin. As I said, Philip was always the best-natured of us all. It's not hard to define the crowd's demographic: they nearly all seem to be men on the cusp of early middle age. I see incipient paunches everywhere. But most of the band members have got families by now, as well, so wives are also in evidence, and a few confused-looking teenagers. Altogether there are about sixty or seventy of us, maybe, gravitating in small groups towards the stage, which is in a far corner of the pub, and where the band is setting up. Benjamin is sitting at his keyboard, frowning in concentration, pushing buttons. There are beads of sweat on his brow already: the ceiling is low, and it must be hot up there, under the lights. I look around for his friend, Malvina, and spot her at a table by herself, in another corner. We make eye contact but that's about all: I don't know what the protocol is. She's not socializing with any of the others and my guess is that she hasn't met any of them before tonight. Am I supposed to make introductions? Too risky—I don't want to complicate an already ambiguous situation. I wonder if Emily knows this woman exists, if Benjamin's ever mentioned her. I bet he hasn't. Emily is gazing up at him on stage, now, and her eyes are rapt, hero-worshipping. All he's doing is plugging a keyboard into an amplifier and setting up a piano stool. It's not like he's building a model of Westminster Abbey out of matches or making an ice sculpture or anything like that. But she still adores him, after sixteen years of marriage. I never expected Benjamin and Emily to last that long, I have to say. I suppose in a way it makes sense: Benjamin would always find it hard to split up with anyone, because he hates difficulty, he hates confrontation. Anything for a quiet life, is his unspoken motto, and I imagine that life with Emily must be very quiet indeed. But really, they are not well suited. Benjamin always struck me as rather a self-centred person. I don't mean that he's greedy or (consciously) unkind, I mean that he has a strong sense of self—a good sense of self—and he doesn't really need anybody's company other than his own. He's not very giving *of himself, that's for sure. Whereas Emily gives a lot of herself. She is happy to spread herself around, generously, among her friends, and I expect that within a relationship, or a marriage, she will give herself entirely, hold nothing back: no secrets or no-go areas. But surely there must have come a point where that's started to frustrate her—giving so much of herself to him, and getting so little back? There must have been such disappointments for her, in that time. Not just the children, the lack of children. I mean the small disappointments. The many little ways, the hundreds of ways, in which he has probably let her down. Over the years.*

I know that I'm right. I know that what I'm thinking about Benjamin and Emily is true. I see it in her eyes, later that evening.

The gig (is that the word? It's a word I can never take seriously) goes well. I remember hearing this band play a few times back in the 1980s, and thinking how out of date they sounded. They were doing these long, funky instrumentals, but this was a few years before somebody coined the phrase "acid jazz," and that kind of thing became fashionable again. Back then, what they were doing just seemed perverse and anachronistic. But tonight it goes down a treat. Great rhythm section: I think the drummer used to work with Benjamin in a bank or something, that's how the whole thing got started. Anyway, he knows what he's doing, and so does the bass player: and over this solid foundation Benjamin and the guitarist and the sax player weave sweet, slightly wistful melodies (Benjamin's touch there, I reckon) and improvise cleanly and cleverly: no over-indulgent solos, no blowing endlessly over the same two chords while the audience gives up and drifts back to the bar. After the first two or three numbers, in fact, people have stopped tapping their toes self-consciously and jiggling up and down on the spot. They're dancing! Actually dancing! Even Philip, who may be a beacon of niceness and decency in some ways but is certainly no Travolta in the moves department. Emily's really going for it, too. She's surprisingly nifty on her feet. Really getting down and enjoying herself. She seems to have come along with a whole crowd of friends ("church people," Phil tells me) and in the middle of one piece, after it's reached its first climax and gone quiet again and there's already a smattering of applause and cheering, she turns to one of these people—a tall, narrow-hipped, good-looking guy—and he leans down towards her and puts his hand on her shoul-

ders and she shouts, "I told you they were good, didn't I? I told you they'd be brilliant."

She looks so happy.

Me, I can't quite bring myself to join in. I don't know why. Maybe because the last few days have been so strange and the last few months have taken me on such a long and tiring emotional journey and tonight I can feel the whole weight of that pressing down on me. Anyway. Nothing, nothing on earth is going to get me on to that dance floor. I stand on the edge of the crowd and lean against the wall watching, and after a while I go to the bar and buy myself a pack of Marlboro lights. That shows how bad things are. I haven't had a cigarette for weeks: only took up smoking again when the Stefano business started to get me down, as well—before that I'd been clean for about four or five years. I'm not ready to light one up just yet, but it's nice to have the feel of the pack in my pocket, nice to know it's there. Sooner or later I'm going to want one. I can feel the need coming on.

About half an hour later, the atmosphere changes, and that's when I know it's time to go.

It happens like this. A bright, up-tempo song finishes with a flourish of cymbals and a crashing major chord, and then three of the band members put their instruments down and withdraw to the back of the stage. There are just two of them left—Benjamin and the guitarist—and the guitarist announces the next piece which he says is going to be a duet. He says that it's written by Benjamin and it's called Seascape No. 4. *Then the two of them start playing and the mood changes completely. It's a delicate, sad little tune—almost dangerously fragile—and Benjamin's whole face is transformed when he starts playing it. He's looking down at his keyboard, hunched over it suddenly, tense and introverted, and his eyes are half closed. Although the piece is quite complicated, he doesn't have to concentrate hard on his fingering because you can tell he knows these chords, these patterns, off by heart—they're stamped on his memory like the contours of a love affair that you never forget—so he's free to think about other things, free to fix his gaze somewhere else: backwards, back in time, back to the experience that inspired this heartbroken music, whatever it was. And of course, some of us in this room know what inspired it.* Who *inspired it, rather. And realizing this, I glance across at Emily to see how she's responding to the music; how she's dealing with the change in tone, the change in her husband. And her demeanour has changed, as well. She's no longer staring up at the stage, adoringly. She's looking at the floor. There's a smile on her face, yes, but what a smile! It's the ruin of a smile, a fossilized remnant left over from the exhilaration of the last few numbers; frozen into place now, lifeless and unmoving, a kind of rictus that only spotlights the terrible sadness the rest of her face is betraying. And I can see, with that one glance in her direction, that Benjamin may have had his heart broken, once, many years ago, by the woman commemorated in this music, but Emily's has been fractured a hundred times, a thousand times over in the years she's been married to him, by the knowledge that he has never got over that brief, ridiculous, devastating teenage love affair. Never* tried *to get over it, I would guess: that's the really bruising, the really unforgiveable thing. He has no interest in forgetting her. No interest in making Emily feel anything other than second best. The one he never really wanted. A consolation prize for the inconsolable.*

I look around at the unreadable expressions of the other people in the audience, and ask myself: don't they know what they are witnessing here, what they are listening to? Can't they hear it? Can't they see it in the stricken pallor that Emily's face has been washed in, since this music began?

No. I don't think they get it, to be honest. There's only one other person in the room who seems lost in this music, taken over by it, who seems to know anything about the depths from which Benjamin must once have dragged it: and that, remarkably, seems to be Malvina. She's got her eyes fixed on Benjamin and her *demeanour has changed, too: she's wired, alert. She's been sitting on the sidelines until now, not taking part, observing everything coolly, but I can tell that something about* this *piece of music touches her. She's involved, for the first time this evening—passionately involved.*

Which leaves me wondering, again, the thing I've been wondering a lot over the last few days: what is *going on between those two, exactly?*

I glance at them both again, the two women that Benjamin (obliviously, I'm sure) has started to torment with this music, and I know that I have to get out of this pub right now. I find Patrick and tug on his arm, and when he turns to me I cup my hand around his ear and tell him that I'm leaving, and we make an arrangement that we'll see each other tomorrow in his school lunch hour. Then I'm gone.

I stand by the side of the canal, a few minutes later. Frost is already spreading along the towpath, and the black water ripples sometimes, mysteriously, with the reflections of pale lights splintered into dancing fragments. The smoke from my cigarette coils in the air, and the rough taste of it at the back of my throat is bitter, hot and cleansing.

It feels, now, as if I know everything there is to know about what's happened between Benjamin and Emily in the years I've been away. How easy it is, after all, to read the history of a lifetime in one single unguarded moment. You just have to be looking in the right direction; in the right place at the right time. But I knew that before, if I'm honest with myself. I found it out just a few weeks ago, in Lucca. Not in a pub. Not at a reunion of old jazzers. I was in the local gastronomia *at the time. It was early evening, and I was by myself, and that was when I spotted Stefano and his daughter Annamaria trying to choose between two different kinds of olive.*

Such a banal incident, when you think about it. Nothing unusual about it at all. Of course, my first impulse was to approach him. Why not? There would have been no awkwardness about it. We were supposed to be meeting for lunch in two days' time. I hadn't been introduced to Annamaria before, but it wasn't this that held me back. All that held me back, at first, was my noticing that he was in the middle of trying to call someone on his mobile. I decided to let him finish, before stepping forward, before saying hello.

The relationship between us (right word, again? I don't think there is one, to cover this strange situation) had been going on for three months, by then. Stefano's wife, despite her promises, was still being unfaithful to him. He kept saying that he was going to leave her. Whenever we talked about this, I refrained from giving any advice. I could not trust myself to be impartial. It was in my interest that he left her. No—I'll put that less coldly. I was desperate for him to leave her. I was willing it with every muscle in my heart. But I never said anything. Falsely, our situation had cast me in the role of friend, and the only thing I could do, in that capacity, was remain silent. So we persisted with our lunches, and drinks, and our unspoken desires and the decorous, passionless kisses that marked the beginning and the end of our meetings. And as for the feelings that were giving me such grief, such unassuageable pain, I tried to pretend that they didn't even exist. I tried to be a heroine. Which was stupid of me, really, although I suppose that underneath it all I was kept going by the thought that one day, in the tolerably near future, my patience would miraculously pay off.

The person he was trying to call didn't answer. I heard him say to Annamaria, "No, she isn't there." And Annamaria said to him, "Can't you remember, Papa, which one she likes?" They were looking at two bowls of plump green olives, laid out on a self-service counter, and he was hesitating between them. But this was no ordinary hesitation. Not at all. No—it was really, really *important to him that he bought his wife exactly the olives that she liked best. And I could see at once that it was on little, everyday choices like this that the whole happiness of their shared life was founded. Which means that in that hesitation—*

at that moment—with sickening clarity, I glimpsed it: the unquenchable love that he felt for this woman, that he continued to feel for her despite all her betrayals, the love I had chosen to hope, in the leaden weeks building up to this moment, that he would one day transfer to me. That hope withered and died in a flicker, in the tiniest fragment of time. One second it was there, the next second it was gone. And its leaving felled me. I turned away from Stefano and his daughter, a different person—unrecognizably different from the one who had only just rounded the aisle of the gastronomia *so carelessly and been on the point of greeting them. My identity had crumbled and dissolved in that moment. That's what it did to me, that sudden, terrible gift of certainty: the certain knowledge that Stefano would never leave his wife. Never, for as long as they both lived.*

Olives. Who would have thought it. I wonder which sort he chose, in the end.

Oh well.

The cigarette burns out and I toss it into the marble blackness of the canal. The cold is creeping into my bones and I know it's time to go indoors, back to warmth and comfort.

Enough of thinking, already.

Sitting here at my leather-topped desk on the twenty-third floor of the Regency Hyatt—the last and best of my vantage points!—looking down on the scattered lights of this newly vibrant city which is so busy rebuilding itself, reinventing itself, I'm glad that I went to hear Benjamin play tonight. Do you know why? Because I learned in a priceless instant that he is still lost, still in thrall to the past, and I saw the pain that he's causing because of it, and I realized that I cannot possibly live my own life that way. I'm not talking about Stefano, I'm talking—regrettably, my much-loved sister—about you. You have been my silent companion all these years and somehow throughout that time I have clung to the fantasy that my words might somehow be reaching you, and I feel now that the time has come to let that fantasy go. Tomorrow I shall check out of this hotel and move on to another town and tonight I shall reach the end of this letter, at last—this long, long letter that I will never send because I have no one real to send it to—and when that's done I shall close the Venetian notebook in which I've written it and put it away somewhere safe. Maybe someone else will read it one day. I so wish it could have been you. But that's the very wish, I see tonight, that's been holding me back. My wish that you could hear me. My wish that you could read me. My wish that you were still alive.

I have to start again. Back to the beginning. Which means that I must start by doing the hardest thing of all—the thing I've been resisting all this time—and give up hope.

Can I give it up?
I think so. Yes, I can.
Yes. There. It's done.
And for that, dear Miriam, please forgive
Your loving sister,

Claire.

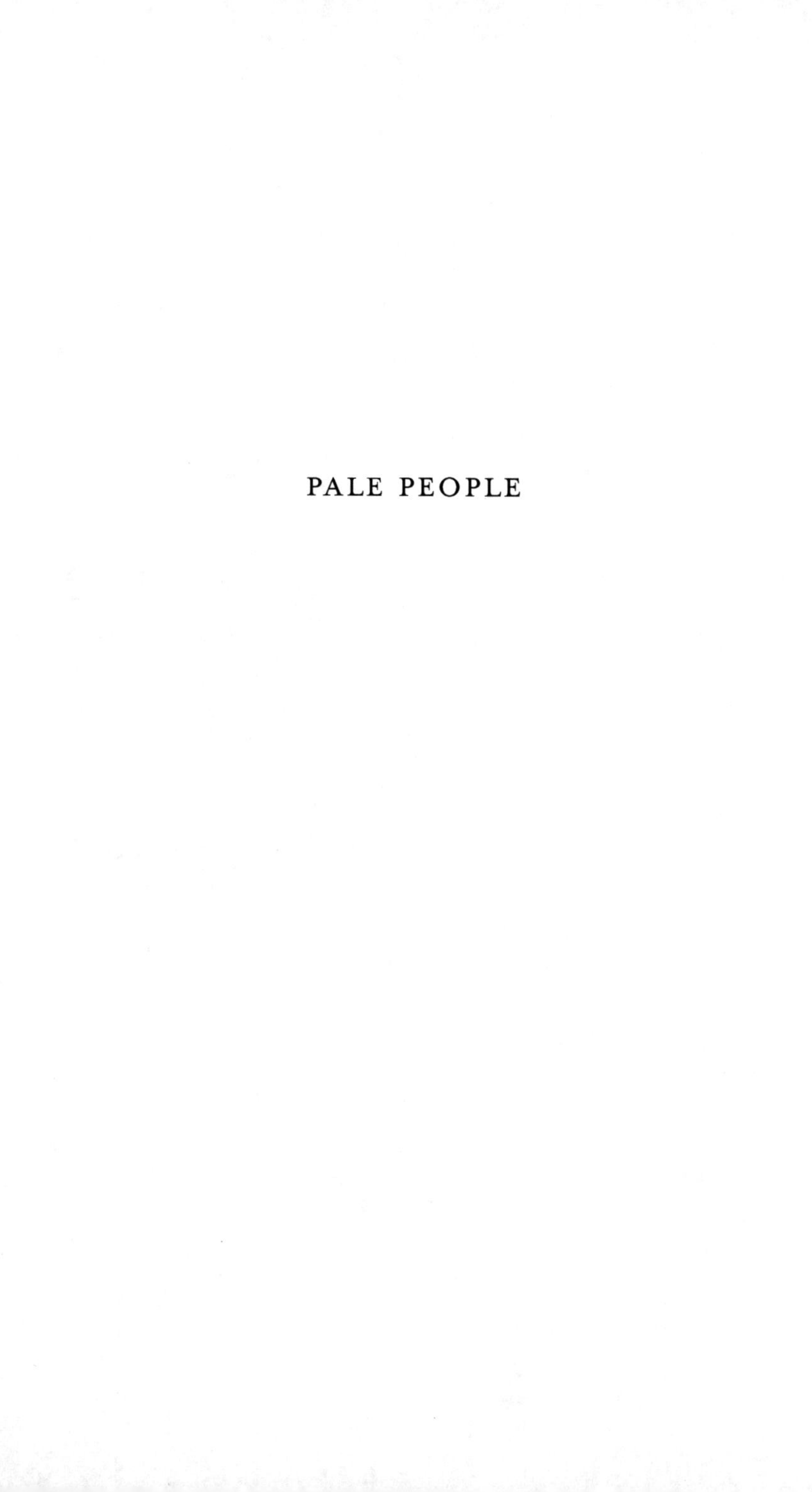

PALE PEOPLE

28

Pale people were filling the streets of London on the last night of the twentieth century. In tightly packed crowds, they pushed and pressed their way down towards the river Thames, to stare in wonder at the new London Eye, and to wait for the astonishing firework display—the so-called "River of Fire"—that the authorities had promised them. It looked dangerous, so many people crammed on to Whitehall and the Embankment at the same time. There had been doom-mongers prophesying for weeks that casualties were inevitable, that the gathering of such large crowds was bound to lead to human tragedy. These same people had, for even longer, been predicting that on the stroke of midnight the world's computer systems would collapse.

"I'm glad I'm here," said Sheila Trotter, "and not there. I wouldn't be there for the world."

Benjamin looked up from his work and glanced at his mother, unobserved. Even in her late sixties, she continued to surprise him. She would prefer *this*, would she, this lifelessness, this deathly quietude, to the party atmosphere of central London tonight? The four of them, sitting in the old living room in Rubery, the house his parents had lived in for the last forty-five years, with not a word to say to each other? Six of them, he supposed, if you counted his sister-in-law Susan, upstairs putting little Antonia to bed: but she was hardly adding to the celebratory mood, anyway. Susan was a conflux of resentments tonight—furious that her husband, Benjamin's younger brother Paul, was not with them. The fact that there was a chance of glimpsing him on television in a few minutes' time only seemed to fuel her rage.

Emily, Benjamin's wife, was offering to pour his mother another half-glass of Cava. "Go on, Sheila love," she was saying, "it's not every day you get the start of a new millennium, is it?"

Benjamin seethed inwardly at the idiocy of this comment, and reached for the pile of CD cases stacked up before him on the dining table. He took out another CD and slotted it into the external CD-writer he had bought a few days ago. He was making back-up files of everything on his computer, and it was a time-consuming business. Most of the music files, for instance (an accumulation of at least fifteen years' composing, sequencing and recording) took up more than ten megabytes, and there were almost a hundred and fifty of them.

"Do you *have* to work, Ben?" his father was saying. "I can't believe you can't take a few hours off, tonight of all nights."

"Give up, Colin," Emily said, resignedly. "He's just doing it to prove a point. He doesn't want to enjoy himself tonight and he's going to make sure that we know about it."

"It's got nothing to do with that," Benjamin said, with controlled insistence, his eyes fixed on the screen of his laptop. "How many times do I have to tell you? I have to back up everything before twelve o'clock."

Susan came downstairs and flopped on to the sofa, looking exhausted and stressed out.

"Is she asleep?" Sheila asked.

"Finally. God, it doesn't get any easier. I've been up there with her for—" (she checked her watch) "—three-quarters of an hour. She just lies there next to you and chatters, and sings. You don't think she could be hyper-active, do you?"

"Here," said Emily, handing her a glass. "Have a drink."

Susan took the glass and immediately got up again, remembering that she had promised to phone her brother Mark before midnight.

"Where did you say he was at the moment?" Sheila asked.

"Liberia." (Mark worked for Reuters, and there was no knowing in what part of the world he was to be found, from one month to the next.)

"Liberia? Just fancy!"

"There's no time difference, apparently. They're on GMT too. I'll only be a few minutes. Don't worry, Colin, I'll reimburse you for the call."

Colin waved his assent, and Susan disappeared to use the phone in the hallway. Meanwhile, midnight approached. At a quarter to twelve, Benjamin took out his mobile and called the office. Adrian, the company's system administrator, was meant to be making back-up copies of every single file on their network: more than 4,000 company accounts, he calculated, and at eight o'clock that evening he had still been working on it. But there was no answer when Benjamin rang, so he assumed that the job had been finished in time. He could always rely on Adrian. Still, as one of the senior partners, it was his responsibility to double-check that the clients' records had been safeguarded.

"Susan, here we are—look! Can you see Paul anywhere?"

The television cameras had moved into the Millennium Dome, where an invited audience of politicians, celebrities and members of the royal family had gathered to await the striking of Big Ben. Nobody was quite sure how, but Paul Trotter had managed to wangle an invitation at the last moment. There had been no tickets available for his wife, or for his three-year-old daughter; but he had not let that deter him. It was too prestigious an opportunity to miss. He was the youngest Labor MP to have been invited, and great emphasis had been laid on this fact in his latest constituency newsletter (to the no doubt considerable bemusement of its readers). His parents had drawn their chairs up close to the television screen, and were straining to identify him.

"Come on, Benjamin, come and look at this. The clock's going to strike any minute."

Reluctantly, Benjamin rose to his feet, wandered over to join the rest of the family, and sat down next to his wife. She put a hand on his knee and handed him a glass. He sipped from it and winced. Ushering in a new millennium with supermarket Cava, for God's sake: couldn't they all have tried a little bit harder, tonight of all nights? He looked at the television and saw the grinning visage of the Prime Minister he had voted for with such optimism two and a half years ago, along with millions of other Britons. He was mouthing the words of "Auld Lang Syne" as he stood next to the Queen, and they were both making rather a poor job of it. Was there anybody who knew the words to that bloody song?

"Happy New Millennium, darling," said Emily, kissing him on the mouth.

Benjamin returned the kiss, and hugged his mother and father, and was about to kiss Susan when she caught sight of something on the television and said: "Look, there he is!"

It was Paul, sure enough, craning forward among the ranks of partygoers, and seizing the Prime Minister by the shoulder as he moved among his political colleagues, backslapping and glad-handing them. Paul managed to hold his gaze for a couple of seconds, and in the Prime Minister's eyes during that time there was visible confusion, not to mention a complete failure of recognition.

"Well done, Paul!" Sheila was calling out to the television. "You got in there. You made your mark."

"Bugger!" Colin shouted, and rushed towards the TV cabinet. "I forgot to put the video on. Bugger, bugger, bugger!"

Twenty minutes later, when the singing was over and the River of Fire had fizzled out in a most disappointing fashion, the telephone rang. It was Benjamin's sister Lois, calling from Yorkshire.

"They've been letting off fireworks in the back garden," Colin reported back to the rest of the family. "They had all the neighbors round. The whole street joined in, apparently." He sank back down into his armchair and took another sip of wine. "Two thousand," he said, wonderingly, sighing and puffing out his cheeks. "I never thought I'd live to see it."

Sheila Trotter went into the kitchen to put the kettle on for some tea.

"I don't know," she muttered as she left, talking to no one in particular. "It doesn't really feel any different to me."

Benjamin returned to his computer, and discovered that, so far, his files were unaffected, and the calendar had clicked over to 01-01-2000 without a murmur of complaint. But he continued with the task of backing up anyway. As he did so, he remembered that, almost thirty years ago, he used to do his homework at this same table, in this same house, with his parents sitting on the same furniture in front of the television. Benjamin's companions then had been his brother and sister, rather than his wife and sister-in-law—but that was hardly a radical change, was it? It was not as if his life had been transformed in the intervening three decades.

He took the mug of tea from his mother's outstretched hand and thought, No, you're right. It doesn't feel any different.

27

Paul Trotter, at this stage in his career, was parliamentary private secretary to a minister at the Home Office. It was turning out to be an ambiguous and frustrating position. Traditionally, it was regarded as a rung on the ladder towards genuine ministerial office; but in the meantime, Paul found himself consigned to an unobtrusive and restricted role, which involved mainly liaising between his minister and the backbenchers. He was not allowed to speak to journalists on matters relating to his department; was not encouraged, in fact, to speak to them at all. But Paul had not entered politics in order to work behind the scenes. He had views—strong views, most of which coincided with the mainstream of his party's thinking—and he was inclined to express them, whenever the opportunity arose. Whereas many of the younger, more inexperienced Labour MPs would scurry away at the sight of a reporter or a microphone, Paul had already acquired a reputation as someone who would talk and more often than not say something quotable. The broadsheet editors had started phoning him with requests for occasional columns, and lobby correspondents would actively seek him out to pass comment on newsworthy topics: even (or perhaps especially) those in which he had no particular expertise.

Paul was not naive about this, all the same. He knew that journalists would like nothing better than to catch him off his guard. He knew that the people who had voted him in had certain expectations of a Labour administration, and that many of his own personal convictions, if he were to state them frankly and publicly, would have shocked them, inspired them with a profound sense of disquiet and betrayal. He had to be careful: and this was already starting to make him impatient. Almost three years into his first term of office, the routine of his parliamentary life (half of every week in central London, and then a long, long weekend at home in his Midlands constituency with his wife and daughter) was beginning to grate. He was getting restless, and hungry for change: rapid, radical change. He could feel himself grow moribund, sink into premature complacence and torpor, and he was looking for something that would shock his whole being into renewed life.

In the event, he found it one Thursday evening in February, 2000, and it came from a most unlikely source: his brother.

Benjamin put up the ironing board while Emily sat watching television. She was watching a team of highly trained celebrity gardeners transform a drab, urban back yard into a verdant oasis, complete with decking, barbecue area and water feature, all in the space of a weekend. Outside, their own garden lay shabby and neglected.

"I'll iron that for you, if you like," she offered.

"Don't be silly," said Benjamin. "I know how to iron a shirt."

His reply was not meant to sound like that: dismissive and ungracious. But that was how it sounded. To be honest, he would have preferred Emily to iron his shirt. He did not like ironing shirts, and he wasn't very good at it. If he had really been going out for dinner *à deux* with his brother Paul, as he had told her, then he would happily have allowed Emily to iron his shirt. But the fact that Malvina was going to be there, and the fact that he hadn't shared this information with his wife, made him feel guilty. Despite his habitually analytical frame of mind, Benjamin did not analyse *why* it made him feel guilty, on this occasion. He was merely aware of feeling guilty, and aware that to have Emily iron his shirt for him before he went out would make him feel guiltier still.

He began to iron the shirt. Every time he ironed one of the sleeves, he would turn it over to find that the other side now boasted two or three obvious creases which hadn't been there before. This always happened; he didn't know why.

The gardening programme finished and was succeeded by a cookery show in which an implausibly glamorous young woman, living in an implausibly elegant house, prepared delicious morsels of food while tossing her hair, pouting seductively at the camera and licking traces of butter and sauce off her fingers in a manner, to Benjamin, so explicitly suggestive of oral sex that he found himself getting an erection while ironing his cuffs for the fifth time. Five minutes into her implausibly effortless concoction of poached pistachio-sprinkled apricots stuffed with crème fraîche he heard the microwave ping: during the commercial break Emily had put on a Marks and Spencer's macaroni cheese, which she now emptied into a bowl and consumed half-heartedly while watching the televised display of erotic gastronomy with beady, envious eyes.

So, why hadn't he told her, Benjamin started asking himself? He cast his mind back three months, to the day in November 1999 when Malvina had sat down at the table next to his in the Waterstone's café on High Street. It had been almost seven o'clock, the end of a long working day. Of course, he should have been at home with Emily by then. But that evening—as on many other evenings—he had told her that he needed to work late. Not so that he could slip away and spend a few hours with his mistress (Benjamin would never have a mistress), but so that he could snatch thirty minutes' solitude, alone with a book, and his thoughts, before coming home to the deeper, more oppressive solitude of his shared domestic life.

He had not been sitting there long before becoming aware that the young, pale, slender woman at the next table wanted to catch his attention. She kept meeting his eye, and smiling, and looking so pointedly at the book he was reading (a biography of Debussy) that it reached the point, soon enough, where it would have been rudeness on *his* part not to say something to her. When they began talking, he rapidly learned that she was a student of media studies at London university, visiting Birmingham for a few days to stay with friends. They must have been good friends, too, for she seemed to come and visit them regularly: after that first occasion, Malvina and Benjamin would meet (at the same place, by arrangement) at least once a fortnight—sometimes more; and before long (for Benjamin, at least) each of these encounters began to feel not like a simple meeting between friends, but a tryst. In the minutes before seeing Malvina he would feel dizzy with eagerness. When they were together, he could never finish the cake or the sandwich he would have ordered. His stomach contracted, turned into a clenched fist. Whether she felt the same way, he had no idea. Presumably she must do, or why would she have approached him like that in the first place? So his hair had gone grey, his jowls were beginning to sag, his midriff had started to expand according to some strange independent timetable of its own, which bore no relation whatsoever to the amount of food he consumed. Did that mean he would never again be attractive to women? Apparently not. There was something that worried him more than that, anyway: the aura of failure, of disappointment, which he could feel clinging to him these days, which he knew his friends had grown accustomed to but which would always, he was convinced, be immediately obvious to anyone new who happened to strike up a conversation with him. And yet—amazingly—Malvina seemed unaware of it. She kept returning to him, again and again. She had never yet refused a single invitation for coffee or a drink. She had even turned up at the reunion concert of his band at The Glass and Bottle, just before Christmas.

What was it about him, he was obliged to wonder, that interested her so much? He was still unable to answer that question, even after the many hours she had spent listening to him, with seemingly unflagging attention, as he talked about his twenty-year career in accountancy, his rather more short-lived part-time musical career in the 1980s, and (the biggest secret of all, in some ways) the novel he had been working on for the whole of that time, which now extended to several thousand pages and felt no nearer to completion than when he had started. It seemed that Malvina had an insatiable appetite for hearing these personal details; and in return, she did let slip the occasional revelation of her own, such as the news that she too was an aspiring writer, with a growing collection of unpublished poems and short stories to her credit. Benjamin had asked—inevitably—whether she would allow him to see any of them; but so far Malvina (just as inevitably, perhaps) had not granted this request. She was probably just being shy; but in any case, curiosity was not Benjamin's motive. He truly wanted to help her, in any way possible. At the back of his mind, all the time—unspoken, unrecognized even—was the fear that these wonderful encounters, which had transformed his life in the last few months, might come to an end at any moment. The more he could help her, the more favors he could offer, the more he might make himself indispensable to her—all of these things, he believed, made it less likely that she might one day grow tired of seeing him. And it was for this reason, finally, that he had offered to introduce her to Paul.

Malvina's second-year project at university was a 20,000-word dissertation on the relationship between New Labour and the media. It was a big subject: bigger than she could manage, he was beginning to suspect. He knew that she was already behind with it; he could hear the edge of panic in her voice whenever it was mentioned; and while it was hardly practical for him to suggest, for instance (as he would willingly have done), that he might write the dissertation himself, he could certainly give her some practical assistance, in the form of direct access to one of New Labour's rising stars.

The kind of first-hand research that none of her fellow students would be able to match.

"Do I have to?" Paul had complained, as soon as Benjamin put the request to him on the telephone.

"No, of course you don't have to," said Benjamin. "But it would only be a couple of hours of your time. I just thought that the three of us could have dinner together, the next time you were both in Birmingham. We could have a pleasant, social evening, that's all."

To which Paul had said, after a short pause: "Is she pretty?"

Benjamin had thought for a moment, and then answered, "Yes." Which was a simple statement of fact. An understatement, actually. It never occurred to him that the question was anything other than casual, offhand: not coming from Paul—a married man, with a young and beautiful daughter.

But then, Benjamin was married himself; and he had never yet mentioned Malvina to Emily. And tonight, as the doorbell rang, it suddenly seemed more important than ever that his wife should know nothing of this new friendship, should not even be made aware that Malvina existed.

With this thought uppermost in his mind, Benjamin rushed to open the door.

"You're not going in that old shirt, are you?" his brother asked, at once. He was wearing a bespoke Ozwald Boetang suit.

"I'm in the middle of ironing one. Come in." As he stepped over the threshold, Benjamin added, in a stage whisper, "Look, Paul, remember: we're not meeting anyone tonight."

"Oh." Paul's disappointment was palpable. "I thought that was the whole point. I thought this woman wanted to meet me."

"She does."

"So when's that going to happen?"

"Tonight."

"But you just said we weren't meeting anyone tonight."

"We're not. But we are. D'you see what I'm getting at?"

"I haven't got a clue."

"Emily doesn't know."

"Doesn't know what?"

"That she's coming to dinner with us."

"Emily's coming to dinner with us? Great. But why doesn't she know?"

"No—Malvina's coming to dinner with us. Emily isn't. But she doesn't *know* that."

"She doesn't know that she isn't coming to dinner with us? You mean—she thinks that she is?"

"Listen. Emily doesn't know—"

Paul pushed his brother aside irritably.

"Benjamin, I don't have time for any of this. I've just spent forty-five excruciating minutes with our parents and it becomes more and more obvious to me that there is a streak of insanity in our family, which you seem to have inherited. Now are we going out for dinner or not?"

They went into the sitting room and Benjamin finished ironing his shirt. Paul attempted a few moments of broken small-talk with Emily and then sat wordlessly beside her on the sofa, watching the cookery goddess unpeeling a banana with languorous fingers and then nuzzling abstractedly at its tip with her pulpy lips. "God, I'd like to fuck her," he murmured after a while. It wasn't clear whether he knew he'd spoken the words out loud or not.

In Paul's car on the way to Le Petit Blanc in Brindley Place, Benjamin asked him, "Why was it so excruciating seeing Mum and Dad?"

"Have you been to see them lately?"

"I see them every week," said Benjamin, catching the self-righteous note in his own voice and wincing at it.

"Well, don't you think they're becoming odd? Or were they always like that? When I told Dad we were driving into town tonight, do you know what he said to me? 'Watch out for gangs.'"

Benjamin frowned. "Gangs? What sort of gangs?"

"I have no idea. He didn't say. He was just convinced that if we went into the center of town on a Thursday night, we'd be set upon by gangs of some description. He's losing his marbles."

"They're old, that's all," Benjamin said. "They're old and they don't get out much. You should give them a break."

Paul grunted, and then fell silent. Normally he was an impatient driver, prone to jumping across traffic lights and flashing his headlamps at anyone who wasn't going fast enough, but tonight he didn't seem to be concentrating. He drove with one hand on the steering wheel, and kept the other one close to his mouth, biting on it occasionally. Benjamin recognized the gesture from their childhood: it was a sign of nervousness, preoccupation.

"Is everything OK, Paul?"

"What? Oh yes, everything's fine."

"Susan on good form?"

"She seemed to be."

"I only thought that . . . something seems to be bothering you."

Paul looked across at his brother. It was hard to tell whether he was grateful for Benjamin's concern, or annoyed that his own unease should prove so visible.

"It's just that I was cornered by a journalist in the members' lobby this afternoon. He asked me a question about Railtrack and . . . well, I didn't think hard enough before answering. I think I may have put my foot in it."

That afternoon, it had been announced to the press that responsibility for safety on the railways was going to be handed over to Railtrack—a privately run company—rather than to an independent and publicly accountable body as many critics had been demanding. Paul basically approved of this idea (all of his political instincts inclined him towards the private sector) and had been happy to say so on the record, believing that this would make him popular with the party leadership. However, it appeared that he may have overstepped the mark.

"It turns out," he said, "that the people who are really up in arms are the ones who lost relatives in the Paddington rail crash. They say it's not good enough."

"As you'd expect."

"Well, of course they're *grieving*. That's entirely understandable. But that still doesn't make it helpful to blame every little thing that goes wrong on the government. We're starting to live in a culture of blame, don't you think? It's like the very worst side of America."

"What did you actually say?" Benjamin asked.

"It was a guy from the *Mirror*," Paul explained. "He said to me, 'What would you say to the families who were bereaved in the Paddington rail crash, who are describing this decision as an insult to their loved ones?' So first of all I said that I respected their feelings, and so on, but of course that's just the kind of thing he'll cut out. I know exactly what he's going to quote. It was the thing I said last of all. 'Those who seek to make capital out of human lives should look to their consciences.' "

"Meaning the relatives?"

"No, not at all. Meaning the people who are going to hijack the relatives' emotions and use them to score political points. *That's* what I meant."

Benjamin tutted. "Too subtle. People are just going to think you're a heartless, uncaring bastard."

"I know. Fuck it," said Paul, to himself, looking out of the window at what used to be the ABC cinema on the Bristol Road, but had now for many years been a large drive-thru McDonald's. "Tell me about this woman we're meeting, anyway. Is she going to cheer me up?"

"Her name's Malvina. She's very bright. Divides her time between here and London, from what I can make out. Just wants to talk to you about your relationship with journalists, I think. A bit of background to help with her dissertation."

"Well," said Paul, grimly. "She could hardly have chosen a better day."

Looking back on that evening, some time later, Benjamin realized that it had been foolish of him not to have anticipated the change he saw in Malvina. He was so familiar—so wearily familiar—with his younger brother that he could never quite get used to the idea that nowadays Paul was a star, to most people, and meeting him was an event: something you dressed up for. When they arrived at Le Petit Blanc, and found Malvina already waiting for them at their window table for three, Benjamin lost his breath for a moment, startled by her loveliness into awestruck silence. He had seen her wearing make-up before, of course, but never quite so lavishly or artfully applied; never with her hair teased into quite such calculated disarray; and never, unless he was much mistaken, wearing a skirt *quite* as short, quite as indecent as this one. Benjamin kissed her on the perfumed cheek—how intently he anticipated that moment, and how quickly it was gone—then turned to make the introduction to his brother and saw that Paul had already taken her hand so reverently, so tenderly, that Benjamin thought at first he was going to kiss it rather than shake it.

He watched the way their eyes met, and how abruptly they both looked away. He watched the way that Paul straightened his tie, and Malvina smoothed down her skirt as she sat down. His heart sank. He immediately found himself wondering whether he had just made one of the worst mistakes of his life.

While Benjamin toyed with his first course—Thai chicken salad with green papaya and rocket—Paul began telling Malvina, in a likeable, self-deprecating way, about the foolish remark he had made to a journalist that afternoon; and soon he was talking more generally about the uncomfortable co-dependence, as he saw it, between the government and the print and broadcast media. Benjamin had heard much of this before, but was struck, tonight, by how knowledgeable Paul sounded, how authoritative. There was also, he realized, a *glamour* that attached to his brother these days: a glamour that derived from power—even the limited power that he was able to wield in his current position. Malvina listened, and nodded, and sometimes wrote things down in her notebook. She said very little herself, at first, and seemed rather humbled by the thought that Paul was taking time out to explain these matters to her. By the time of his second course—panfried seabass fillet with courgettes, fennel and sauce verge—Benjamin could see that the balance had started to shift slightly. Malvina had become more talkative, and Paul was no longer just imparting information: he had begun to ask questions, soliciting her opinions, and it was clear that she was both surprised and flattered. Benjamin himself had lapsed into a morose silence, which persisted into dessert. Picking unenthusiastically at his passion fruit brulée, he watched as they polished off a single dish between them: chocolate mi-cuit, smothered in warm crème anglaise, which they shared with one long-handled spoon. By now he knew, with a lumpy certainty in the pit of his stomach, something that would have seemed inconceivable a couple of hours ago: he had already lost Malvina. Lost her! In what sense had he ever possessed her? In the sense, he supposed, that while those ambiguous weekly meetings had continued, he had at least been able to sustain a fantasy about her, a fantasy that this friendship might, through some miracle (Benjamin was a firm believer in miracles) mutate into something else, something explosive. He had not bothered himself, so far, with the details; had not got as far as contemplating the pain he might cause to Emily—and himself—by proceeding further down this treacherous path. It had begun as a fantasy, and would probably have stayed that way: but Benjamin lived for his fantasies—had done all his life: they were as solid to him as the contours of his working day or his weekend trip to the supermarket; and it seemed cruel, bitterly cruel, to have even these pale imaginings snatched away from him. He felt coils of despair beginning to wrap themselves around him, and at the same time a familiar hatred for his brother crept into his bones.

"So what you're trying to argue, as I understand it," Paul was saying, "is that political discourse has become a kind of battleground, in which the meaning of words is disputed and fought over, every day, by politicians on the one hand and journalists on the other."

"Yes—because politicians have become so careful about what they say, and political utterances have become so bland, that journalists now have the task of *creating* meaning out of the words that they're given. It's not what you guys *say* that matters any more, it's how it's *interpreted.*"

Paul frowned, and licked the last traces of liquid chocolate off the back of their spoon. "I think you're being too cynical," he said. "Words have meanings—fixed meanings—and you can't change them. Sometimes I wish you could. I mean, look at what I said to the *Mirror* guy this afternoon: 'Those who seek to make capital out of human lives should look to their consciences.' There's no getting out of that, is there? It's going to sound nasty, however it's presented."

"OK," said Malvina, "but supposing you claimed that you'd been quoted out of context?"

"How could I do that?"

"By saying that you weren't talking about the victims' families at all. What you were doing—as someone who supports railway privatization, by and large—was firing a warning shot at the new railway companies, telling them not to make 'capital' out of human lives by putting profit above safety. So that *they're* the ones who should be looking to their consciences." She smiled at him: a quizzical, challenging smile. "There—how does that sound?"

Paul looked at her in astonishment. He didn't quite understand what she was saying, but somehow she had already made him feel better about this afternoon's gaffe, and he could feel a huge burden of anxiety starting to slip from his shoulders.

"That's what's so clever about the word you used," Malvina continued. "'Capital.' Because that's the danger, isn't it? That people start to see everything in terms of money. It was such a smart use of language. So ironic." That smile again. "You *were* being ironic, weren't you?"

Paul nodded, slowly, his eyes never leaving hers.

"Irony is very modern," she assured him. "Very *now*. You see—you don't have to make it clear exactly what you mean any more. In fact, you don't even have to mean what you say, really. That's the beauty of it."

Paul remained silent and immobile for a few moments, mesmerized by her words, her certainty, her stillness. By her youth. Then he said: "Malvina, will you come and work for me?"

She laughed incredulously. "Work for you? How can I? I'm just a student."

"It would only be for one day a week. A couple of days, at the most. You could be my . . ." (he searched his mind for a suitable phrase) ". . . media adviser."

"Oh, Paul, don't be silly," she said, looking away, and blushing. "I've got no experience."

"I don't need someone with experience. I need someone with a fresh pair of eyes."

"Why do you need a media adviser?"

"Because I can't do without the media but I don't understand them. And you do. You could really help me. You could act as a sort of—buffer, a conduit, between . . ."

He tailed off, and Benjamin muttered: "They mean the opposite of each other."

Paul and Malvina both looked at him—it was the first time he had spoken in about twenty minutes—and he explained: "Buffer and conduit. They mean opposite things. You can't be a buffer *and* a conduit."

"Didn't you hear?" Paul said. "Words can mean what we want them to mean. In the age of irony."

Paul offered to drive Malvina to New Street Station, in time for the last train to London. He picked up the bill for dinner himself, and paid it discreetly and quickly while Malvina went to the toilet.

"What exactly are you playing at, Paul?" Benjamin hissed, as they waited for her outside the restaurant. "You can't *employ* her."

"Why not? I get an allowance for that sort of thing."

"Do you know how old she is?"

"What's that got to do with anything? Do you?"

Benjamin had to admit that he didn't: it was one of the many things he didn't know about her. In any case it occurred to him, as he watched Malvina climb into the front passenger seat of Paul's car, that the age difference between them didn't seem so great after all. Paul looked a good deal younger than his thirty-five years, and Malvina looked . . . well, ageless, tonight. They made a handsome couple, he conceded, through gritted teeth.

The passenger window of Paul's shimmering black BMW glided noiselessly open, and Malvina looked up at him.

"See you soon," she said, fondly: but they had not kissed, this time.

"Keep your pecker up, Marcel," said Paul, who for some years had delighted in annoying his brother by introducing him to people as "Rubery's answer to Proust."

Benjamin glared at him and said balefully, "I will." His parting shot—the best he could manage—was: "Remember me to your wife and daughter, won't you?"

Paul nodded—inscrutable, as always—and then the car was gone, with a squeal of rubber against tarmac, and Malvina with it.

Rain started to fall as Benjamin set off on his slow walk to the Navigation Street bus stops.

26

Half way across Lambeth Bridge, Paul braked to a halt, steadied himself with one foot on the kerb, and rested a while to recover his breath. His thigh muscles pulsed with dull pain from the unaccustomed effort of his one-and-a-half mile ride. After a few seconds, he swung the bicycle through ninety degrees and pedalled over to the eastern side of the bridge. Just as he was dismounting, the driver of a huge bottle-green people-carrier, a vehicle more suited to transporting essential food parcels along the treacherous supply roads between Mazar-e Sharif and Kabul than taking—as seemed to be the case this evening—a rather comfortably-off family of three down to the local Tesco and back, honked her horn angrily as she swerved wildly to one side, mobile phone in hand, and avoided killing Paul by about three inches. He took no notice, having quickly come to realize that such near-death experiences were a daily occurrence in central London, where car drivers and cyclists lived in a permanent state of undeclared war. And besides, it would make a good episode for his new column, "Confessions of a Cycling MP," which Malvina was planning to pitch next week to the editor of one of the free magazines that got distributed on the underground every morning. She was taking her new appointment seriously, and this was just one of a string of ideas she had presented to him a couple of days ago. Another was that he should make an appearance on a high-profile satirical television quiz show: she knew one of the producers, apparently, and was planning to broach the subject with him as soon as possible. Already she was proving far more efficient, and far more useful, than he would have believed possible.

He lifted his bike on to the pavement and leaned it against the railings of the bridge. Elbows on the parapet, chin cupped in his hands, he gazed for a while at the view that never failed to entrance him: to his left, the Palace of Westminster, floodlit and buttery, its shimmering reflection throwing a golden light on to the black metal surface of the sleeping Thames; and to his right, the new upstart, the London Eye, bolder, sleeker, bigger than any of the buildings around it, patterning the river with pools of neon blue, transforming the whole cityscape with casual impudence. One of them represented tradition and continuity—the things Paul was most suspicious of. The other represented—what? It was sublimely purposeless. It was a machine, a flawless machine for making money and for showing people new vistas of something that they already knew to be there. The Wheel and the Palace squared up to each other, co-existing for now, sharing their ascendancy over this part of London in a surreal, uneasy, beautiful truce. And Paul stood on the bridge between them, feeling a shivery exhilaration, an overwhelming sense of the rightness of a life that had led him, finally, to this place, and this time. It was where he belonged.

Doug Anderton was waiting for him at a corner table of a Westminster restaurant specializing in Anglo-Indian cuisine. The restaurant building had until recently housed a lending library, and the walls of the galleried mezzanine area were still lined with books, so that the diners, already cushioned by the air of exclusivity generated by the extravagant prices, could experience an extra illicit *frisson* at the thought that they were eating in a space which had once opened its doors to the general public, in accordance with a now comically outdated democratic ideal. Doug was studying the op-ed pages of one of his broadsheet competitors, with a frown either of concentration or rivalrous contempt—it was hard to tell which—while sipping on a pineapple Bellini. His studiedly proletarian uniform of denim jacket, T-shirt and jeans did not detract at all from the impression that he looked very much at ease in these surroundings.

"Doug," said Paul, holding out his hand and smiling warmly.

Doug folded up his newspaper and gave him a curt handshake. "Hello, Trotter," he answered.

"Trotter?" said Paul, sitting down opposite him. He seemed determined to keep things good-humoured. "That's not very friendly, is it, after twenty-one years?"

"You're ten minutes late," Doug pointed out. "Did you have trouble parking?"

"I cycled," said Paul, helping himself to a large glass of still water, from a bottle for which they would later be charged more than the hourly minimum wage recently introduced by New Labour. "I cycle everywhere these days. Malvina thought it would be good for me."

Doug laughed. "Got you on a health kick already, has she? I thought your wife was called Susan, though."

"She is. It's got nothing to do with health. Malvina's my media adviser. You spoke to her on the telephone."

"Ah, yes. Of course. How could I forget. Your . . . *media adviser.*" He stretched the words out as thinly as he could. "Well, look, shall we order something, and get the preliminaries over as quickly as we can—what have you been doing for the last twenty years, all that sort of bollocks. Then we can at least get some food down our necks."

"Not much need to catch up, is there?" said Paul, picking up a menu. "I've followed your career with close attention. And vice versa, I'm sure."

"Well, I did refer to you, obliquely, in a little talk I gave on the South Bank a couple of months ago," said Doug. "But I'd hardly say that you've been uppermost in my mind over the last few years. In fact I don't think I'd given you a moment's thought till you popped up on election night, 1997, knocking a very distinguished Conservative minister into political oblivion and looking like you'd just had the shock of your life."

"You don't still believe that hoary old crap, do you, about me not expecting to get elected? I know you wrote it at the time, but . . . come on. Give me a little bit more credit than that."

"How's your brother?" Doug asked, by way of reply.

"Oh, Benjamin's fine." (It was hard to tell whether Paul really believed this, or he was just trying to convince himself of it.) "You know—his real trouble is that he's perfectly happy, but he won't allow himself to admit it. Being unpublished suits him. Being unperformed suits him, too. He actually loves being an accountant. Nothing could please him more than being able to think of himself as the Emile Zola of the double-entry system. The fact that the rest of the world refuses to recognize him just adds to the piquancy."

"Hmm . . ." Doug didn't seem very persuaded by any of this. "Well, I don't know him as well as you do, of course: but I would have said he was unhappily married, hated being childless, and was completely unfulfilled in his professional and creative life. What about Lois?"

Paul reeled off some details quickly—that Lois was still living in York, still a university librarian, still married to Christopher—making it more and more clear as he did so that his brother's and sister's lives bored him almost to the point of disgust. When he noticed that Doug himself was doing his best to suppress a yawn, he said: "I know. They haven't exactly set the world alight, have they, my siblings? Sends you to sleep just thinking about them."

"It's not that," said Doug, rubbing his eyes. "We've got a new son. Ranulph. Five months old. I was up half the night with him."

"Congratulations," said Paul, dutifully.

"Well, you know, Frankie wanted another. That's my—"

"Your wife. I know. The Honourable Francesca Gifford. Daughter of Lord and Lady Gifford of Shoscombe. Cheltenham and Brasenose College, Oxford. I looked her up in Debrett's this afternoon." He glanced at Doug, with an indefinable slyness in his eyes. "Married before, wasn't she?"

"Uh-huh."

"Amicable break-up?"

"What is this, an interview?" Doug had been pretending to study the wine list. Now he laid it down, seeming to conclude that if he had landed himself with the task of spending two or three hours in Paul's company, he might as well make a go of it. "Basically, she only left *him* because he didn't want any more kids. He'd had enough of the whole child-rearing thing: whereas she loves it, for some unknown reason. Loves the whole business. Loves being pregnant. Doesn't even seem to mind the labour too much. Loves everything that comes afterwards. The visits from the midwife. The bathing, the nappy changing. All the paraphernalia—the slings, the push-chairs, the cots, the Moses baskets, the bottles, the sterilizers. She *loves* all that. Spends half her waking hours expressing, these days—hooked up to this milking machine that makes her look like a prize Jersey." He blinked, apparently having some difficulty getting the image out of his head. "Gives me a completely different attitude to her breasts, I must say."

"How many does she have now, then?"

"Just the two—same as everybody else."

"Children, I mean."

"Oh. Four, altogether. Two boys, two girls. All living at our place. Plus the nanny, of course." Reflecting upon his current *ménage* like this never failed to depress Doug, or at least to make him feel obscurely guilty. Perhaps it was the thought of his mother, now widowed and still living alone in Rednal, and how small and lost she appeared whenever he managed to persuade Francesca to allow her to stay with them for a few days. He shook the thought away impatiently. "And Antonia must be—what? She must be three by now."

"Yes, absolutely. What a retentive memory you have."

"Hard to forget a baby who was named after the party leader, and managed to play such a big role in an election campaign when she was only a few months old. She must have visited more doorsteps than the postman that month."

Paul sighed tiredly. "She was *not* named after Tony. That's another stupid myth you journalists have dreamed up." He added: "Listen, Douglas, if you're just going to be cynical and hostile to me all evening, I don't know that there's much point in continuing with this."

"I'm not entirely sure that I could see the point in the first place," said Doug. "Why *did* you invite me here, exactly?"

And so Paul attempted to explain. Malvina had made him realize, he said, that in order to raise his media profile, he would have to start cultivating friendships with well-disposed journalists. What could be more natural, then, than a desire to renew his acquaintance with someone who had made a name for himself as one of the most highly regarded political commentators in the country, and who had been such an important figure to him throughout their schooldays together, back in the far-off, touchingly innocent days of the late 1970s?

"But we hated each other at school," said Doug, smartly putting his finger on the only flaw in the proposal.

"I don't think so," said Paul, frowning and looking shocked. "Did we?"

"Of course we did. Well, for a start, everybody hated you—you must remember that."

"Really? Why?"

"Because we all thought you were a creepy little right-wing shit."

"OK, then—but it was nothing *personal.* So that means we can still be friends, doesn't it, twenty years on?"

Doug scratched his head, genuinely baffled by the direction the conversation was taking. "Paul, the years haven't made you any less weird, you know. What do you mean, 'friends'? How could we ever be friends? What would this friendship consist of?"

"Well . . ." Paul had already worked out the answer to this. "Malvina thought, for instance, that since you and I had children of about the same age, we could maybe introduce them and see if they wanted to play together."

"Let me get this straight," said Doug: "your *media adviser* is suggesting that your children and my children should play together? I've never heard anything so ridiculous."

"It's not ridiculous at all," Paul insisted. "You and I have far more in common than we used to."

"Such as?"

"Well, politically, for instance. We're both on the same side now, aren't we? We both agree, by and large, that the best hope for the prosperity of Britain and its people lies with the Labour party."

"What on earth makes you think I believe that? Don't you even read my stuff in the paper?"

"Oh, I know you have a few criticisms to make, here and there—"

"A few—?" Doug sputtered, brokenly, scattering the remnants of a pickle-laden poppadom over the tablecloth.

"—but on the whole it's true, isn't it? You subscribe, as I do, to the core beliefs and ideals of the New Labour revolution. Don't you?"

"Well, I suppose I might," said Doug, "if I could work out what the fuck they were."

"Now you're just being silly," Paul muttered, sulkily.

"No I'm not." Warming to his theme, Doug dismissed the waiter who was hovering at their table and continued: "What *are* your 'core beliefs,' Paul? Tell me. I'm curious. Genuinely."

"Do you mean mine, personally? Or the party's?"

"Either. Anyway, I'm assuming they're the same."

"Well . . ." For the first time that evening, Paul seemed to be lost for words. He hesitated for a moment and then said, "What did you send that guy away for? I was just ready to order."

"Don't change the subject."

Paul wriggled in his seat. "Well, look here, Doug, you're asking me to reduce a very broad, very complex set of beliefs to some easy formula, and it just can't—"

"The 'third way,' for instance," Doug prompted.

"What?"

"The 'third way.' You're always banging on about it. What is it?"

"What is it?"

"Yes."

"How do you mean?"

"I mean, 'What is it?' It's a simple enough question."

"Really, Douglas," said Paul, dabbing at his lips with a napkin, even though he hadn't eaten anything yet, "I can't help thinking you're being very naive about this."

"*What is it?* That's all I want to know."

"Well, OK." He wriggled a little more, then sat up straight, then drummed his fingers on the table. "Well, it's an *alternative*. An alternative to the sterile, worn-out dichotomy between left and right." He looked to Doug for some sort of reaction, but saw nothing. "That's a good thing, isn't it?"

"It sounds like a very good thing. It sounds like something we've all been trying to find for years. And you guys managed to come up with it in a weekend, as far as I can see. What are you going to turn up next? The philosopher's stone? The Ark of the Covenant? What else has Tony got hidden down the back of a sofa at Chequers?"

For a second or two it looked as though Paul was finally going to lose his temper. But all he said was: "Are our children going to play together or not?"

Doug laughed. "OK, if you want." He caught the waiter's eye and called him back again. "Do you want to know why? Because I reckon that one of these days, there's going to be some story about you, and it's going to be so huge, so fucking *scandalous* . . . And I want to be around when it breaks." He smiled combatively. "That's it. That's the only reason."

"Good enough for me," said Paul. "And it proves my point, after all." When Doug looked at him in surprise, he explained: "We do have something in common—ambition. You don't want to stay in the same job all your life, do you?"

"No," said Doug, "I suppose I don't. But a little birdy tells me I've got a promotion coming up anyway."

And then, having at last reached an understanding of sorts, they moved on to the more pressing business of ordering food.

Paul returned to his flat in Kennington shortly after eleven. During the week, he lived on the third floor of a converted terrace a few streets away from the Oval cricket ground. This meant that Susan and Antonia were left alone, four nights out of seven, at their country home—a barn conversion on the semi-rural outskirts of his Midlands constituency. This arrangement caused him some pangs of guilt, occasionally (the house was fairly isolated, and he knew that Susan had not yet managed to make many friends in the area), but otherwise it suited him very well. Essentially, he lived like a bachelor, but with the added safety net of a welcoming family life, in which he could take refuge whenever he started to feel stressed out or lonely. The best of all possible worlds.

Susan did not have a key to his London flat. A few days ago, however, he had arranged to have one cut for Malvina. She had seemed nonplussed when he presented it to her, and had asked, "What's this for?" "You might need it," Paul had answered, meaninglessly, and had then kissed her on the cheek, for the third time in their friendship. As before, she had not recoiled from the kiss; nor had she returned it, exactly. He could not imagine what she made of these gestures—either the kiss, or the gift of the key—and he was not sure, for that matter, whether he really understood them himself. He had not yet admitted to himself how attracted he was to Malvina, or what a large part that attraction had had to play in the decision to employ her. None the less, this attraction was real, and it determined much of his recent behaviour, however incapable he was of owning up to it. In truth Paul would have liked nothing more, now, than to feel the responsibility for his actions being taken out of his own hands, to allow himself to be swept away on a wave of passion that someone else had set in motion. In short, he was waiting for Malvina to do something that she would never do: to throw herself at him.

As he opened the door to his flat that night, therefore, Paul felt a tingle of anticipation: for, ever since he had given Malvina the key, he had been half-expecting to encounter what he liked to call a "James Bond moment." By this he meant something approximating the scene in countless James Bond films where the hero returns to his hotel room late at night in an exotic foreign location, and turns on the light only to find that his bed is already occupied by a naked *femme fatale*, who stirs languidly between the sheets and invites him to join her by purring some sleepily seductive line. Being blessed, in his more alcohol-fuelled flights of fancy, with something of the suave sexual magnetism of Ian Fleming's legendary creation, Paul continued to hope that it was only a matter of time before something similar happened to him.

Tonight, however, he was again disappointed. His bedroom remained inexplicably Malvina-less, and when he texted her to ask where she was and what she was doing, he received no answer. There was nothing for it but to phone Susan, listen impatiently to her long narrative of the minutiae of her day, and ask her to kiss Antonia for him. Then, after reflecting that his dinner with Doug had been much more successful than he had expected, he fell into a deep and self-satisfied sleep.

25

A little over two weeks later, on the afternoon of Wednesday, March 15th, 2000, the first edition of the *Evening Mail* hit Birmingham's streets bearing the stark headline, "STABBED IN THE BACK."

The accompanying story made for grim reading. It appeared that the car manufacturer Rover was to be sold off by its German owner, BMW, resulting in huge job losses at the Longbridge factory just outside Birmingham. This in spite of the fact that its future had recently been assured—so everybody thought—by a grant of £152 million from the government the previous year, and in spite of repeated promises from the BMW management that they had every intention of keeping the ailing company afloat. The Labor MP for Northfield, Richard Burden, was promptly quoted as saying: "It would be a gross breach of faith if BMW deviates from its stated plans for Longbridge. This has been a bolt out of the blue. This is playing with the lives of the 50,000 people whose jobs depend on Longbridge. BMW has made a commitment to the British people and the British people have made a commitment to them. It is up to both sides to keep those commitments."

Next day, towards the end of the afternoon, Philip Chase logged off his computer at the *Birmingham Post* early and drove out to Longbridge, wishing to gauge for himself the mood of the workforce and the local residents. His colleagues on the Business Desk had flown over to Munich that morning, to be present at a press conference with the BMW management team. The news being sent back simply got worse and worse. It seemed that even

Land Rover, the most prestigious part of the Rover empire, was to be disposed of, while the Longbridge plant itself was being offered for sale to a small venture capitalist firm called Alchemy Partners, who had already announced their intention to lay off the vast majority of workers, retaining just enough to keep the company going as a small-volume producer of specialist sports cars. The rest of the factory site was to be completely redeveloped, probably as residential property: but who was going to want to live in that community any longer, if there was no industry to sustain it?

There was not much activity at the gates to the South Works that afternoon. A keen March wind was blowing, the sky was grey and puffy with clouds, and the few departing workers Philip managed to detain all had more or less the same thing to say: they were "gutted," or "devastated"; the decision was a "slap in the face" from those "German bastards." Within a few minutes, Philip's job was done: these quotes would serve his purpose, even if he could just as easily have made them up at his desk. He didn't want to leave, though. It felt as though history was unfolding here: dismal, melancholy history, to be sure, but still something that demanded to be witnessed, and recorded. Pulling his raincoat tightly around him against the encroaching cold, he began to walk uphill along the Bristol Road. Shortly before reaching the 62 bus terminus, he turned right and made for The Old Hare and Hounds pub, pushing open its doors and, at first, not recognizing the interior: for the place had been redesigned, since he had last been there, to attract a middle-class clientele, and instead of ancient oak tables and an almost impenetrable half-light, he found a number of smaller, more welcoming seating areas, with books on the walls and fake log fires in every corner.

Squeezed into one of these corners was a group of at least twenty men, all discussing the latest developments from Munich in tones of subdued but palpable fury. Philip wandered over and introduced himself. Many of them knew his name and, as he had expected, they were more than happy to talk to a local journalist. Before long they were discussing the initial responses of the media and the Labour party to the evolving crisis, and a good deal of approval was voiced for the comments already made by Richard Burden. At which point somebody asked: "What about Trotter?"

"Who?" said at least four or five voices around the table.

"Paul Trotter. What's he got to say about it?"

"His constituency's miles from here."

"Yeah, but he's a local lad, isn't he? Grew up round here. I can remember when his dad worked at the factory. What's he got to say about it?"

"Well, we can find that out easily enough," said Philip, taking out his mobile. "I'll give him a call."

He retrieved Paul's number from the SIM card memory and hit the dial button. On the fourth or fifth ring, a female voice answered. Philip introduced himself as a journalist from the *Post* who had once been at school with the MP, and after a certain amount of confusion he was put through.

"I was just wondering," he said to Paul, "what your reaction was to the news from Birmingham yesterday."

There was a short silence in the pub, while the men round the table leaned forward, attempting vainly to hear Paul's words. Philip's expression was neutral at first, then puzzled.

"Can I just get things clear, Paul?" he asked, before hanging up. "You're saying that you're happy about this announcement, are you?" There were just a few more loud, decisive words from the other end of the line; after which, there was a decidedly quizzical note in Philip's voice as he said: "OK, Paul, thanks for your comments. Good luck for tonight. 'Bye now."

He clipped the phone shut and laid it on the table in front of him, frowning deeply.

"Well?" someone asked.

Philip looked around him at the circle of attentive faces, and told his listeners, in a tone of wonderment. "He said it was good news for the industry, good news for Birmingham and good news for the whole country."

When Philip phoned, Paul was sitting in the dressing room of a television studio on the South Bank in central London, his cheeks pink with newly applied blusher. Longbridge was the last thing on his mind, as it happened. He was actually practising the delivery of a joke about chocolate.

It had begun the day before, with a phone call from Malvina.

"You're on," she said. "This week. They're recording tomorrow afternoon."

"On what?" Paul asked, and she reminded him of her promise to secure him an appearance on a satirical TV show: a weekly panel game on which young comedians would sit around making scathing jokes about the news, sometimes joined by a high-profile politician. It was considered a great *coup* for an MP to be invited on to this programme, even though he (it was rarely she) would often find himself subjected to a barrage of mockery from the other guests, and could sometimes scarcely be expected to leave with his reputation intact.

Paul could hardly believe it.

“They want me? You talked them into it? How on earth did you do that?”

“I told you—I know one of the people who works there. He was my mother’s boyfriend for a while.” (Malvina’s mother had, by the sound of it, lived with a good many different partners during the last few years, so this explanation sounded plausible enough.) “Remember? A couple of weeks ago I told him you’d be available at short notice, in case someone else dropped out. You know, someone they really wanted to have on.”

“That’s fantastic,” said Paul—who, upon hearing any piece of good news, seldom noticed if there was an insult buried in it. But almost immediately afterwards he became nervous. “Hang on, though—am I expected to be funny?”

“It is a comedy programme,” Malvina pointed out. “It wouldn’t do you any harm to make a joke or two.”

“I don’t really do jokes,” Paul admitted. “I mean, what other people find funny . . . I can never quite see it.”

“Well, you’ll just have to develop a sense of humor,” said Malvina, pragmatically. “You’ve got about twenty-four hours. I should start working on it if I were you.”

“How am I going to do that?”

“Go home tonight,” she said, “with all of the newspapers, sit down and read them, and see if you can think of anything funny to say. Try and choose a story that has something to do with you, some personal connection. Don’t be shy, go in for a little bit of self-advertisement. And try to be irreverent. That’s what it’s all about.”

“But everyone at Millbank watches that show. I think even Tony watches it. They might not like it if I’m irreverent.”

Malvina told him not to worry. She had noticed, by now, that humour was not Paul’s strong point. And yet his tendency to take everything seriously was one of the very things that most endeared him to her. It made him so easy to tease.

Back at the flat, Paul spent all evening reading through the newspapers and flicking through the satellite channels from one news station to another. There wasn’t much that caught his eye. The Northern Ireland secretary, Peter Mandelson, had announced that 500 troops were to be called back to the mainland, and British Aerospace had been given a £530 million grant to develop a European “superjumbo” to be introduced in 2007. BMW were selling off the Rover factory at Longbridge—which was all very sad, of course, and a Birmingham story of sorts, but hardly the stuff of comedy.

The only item that struck Paul as at all promising was the news that EU ministers had at last agreed to allow the sale of British chocolate in other European countries: previously it had been ruled that it contained too much milk and vegetable fat, and not enough cocoa solids.

He mulled over this last development and had cautiously begun to feel, by the time he went to bed, that here was a story that might well suit his purposes. For one thing, the main beneficiary of the ruling would be the Cadbury factory in Bournville: by mentioning it, then, Paul would appear to be speaking up for Birmingham, his home town, where he generally seemed to be regarded with suspicion and almost invariably got a bad press. Also, it was a positive, upbeat story about a much-loved British product, so he would certainly endear himself to the party leadership by bringing it up. (Much more so than by dwelling on that miserable Longbridge business.) All he needed to do, then, was to think of a joke on the subject, and to make sure that somehow or other he was able to shoehorn it into the programme.

"And what did you come up with?" Malvina asked the next day, as their taxi stopped and started its bottlenecked journey through the central London traffic in the direction of the South Bank.

"Nothing much so far," Paul admitted. "The only thing I could think of was—isn't there a sort of . . . old cockney expression, or something, 'I should coco'?"

Malvina nodded solemnly.

"What does it mean?" he asked.

"It means, 'I should say so.'"

"Well, perhaps I could say that." In response to her blank stare, he added: "It would be a pun, you see. A pun on 'cocoa.'"

"Yes." She nodded again, seeming to weigh his words with uncommon seriousness. "And when are you going to bring this up, exactly? How are you going to . . . drop it into the proceedings?"

"We could be talking about the EU story," Paul explained, "and one of the other guests could say to me, 'What about you, Paul? Do you like British chocolate?' And . . ." his voice faltered, losing all confidence, in the face of Malvina's unwavering stare, "that would be . . . when I said it . . ."

"From what I've heard," she replied, after a significant pause, "they have gag-writers on the set. They can supply you with material if you get into trouble."

Paul looked away, glancing out of the taxi window, offended. "It'll be funny in context," he said. "Wait and see."

And he was still turning the joke over in his mind as he sat in his make-up chair later that afternoon. The last two hours, which had been taken up with rehearsals and awkward small-talk with his fellow-panellists, had done nothing but make him even more nervous. He didn't understand any of these people, didn't speak their language, couldn't even tell half of the time whether they were trying to be funny or serious. Having been provided with a list of the questions that were supposed to provide a springboard for the televised banter, he was alarmed to see that the subject of European sales of British chocolate was not mentioned anywhere. He had raised this issue with one of the producers, run his "I should cocoa" joke past him, and been rewarded simply with incredulous silence.

"He just ignored me," Paul complained to Malvina. She was sitting in the chair beside him as he waited in front of a brightly lit mirror for the return of the make-up girl, who had been called away to the telephone. "Just looked at me and didn't say a word."

"I wish he'd ignore *me*," Malvina answered. "He had me pressed up against a wall for most of that rehearsal. You'd think it was enough that he'd already shagged my mother."

"You know what's the matter with all these people, don't you?" Paul leaned in towards her and lowered his voice to a whisper. "*They're all on drugs.*" He directed her gaze to a large bowl of white powder which stood on the shelf in front of him. "I was offered that, you know. By the make-up girl, if you please. Brazen as anything. 'Do you normally use this, Mr. Trotter?' she said. Can you believe it? Can you imagine if I had, and she'd blabbed to the newspapers? That almost amounts to entrapment, don't you think?"

Malvina got up and inspected the contents of the bowl. She dipped her finger in, took a lick and grimaced.

"Paul, calm down, can't you? It's loose powder, for God's sake. You put it on your face. It covers up the sweat."

"Oh."

Paul's mobile rang, and, while Malvina was answering it, he carried on thinking about his joke. To him it seemed every bit as funny as some of the wacky flights of fancy invented by his team captain (a popular TV comedian), or the cynical point-scoring of his opposite number (the smart-arsed editor of a satirical magazine). And besides, it was important that the public knew about this. Chocolate was of interest to everybody. Cadbury's was a great British company. Why shouldn't this story be given a bit of prominence?

Malvina tapped him on the shoulder at this point and handed him the phone.

"Have a word with this guy," she said. "Philip Chase. From the *Post.*"

Paul didn't recognize the journalist's name and his first response—thinking of a conversation he'd had with Malvina almost a week ago, about starting to build up a media profile in America—was to grab the phone and yell excitedly: "Hello, Washington!"

"Philip Chase here," said the nasally accented voice at the other end. "Calling from Birmingham. Sorry if you were expecting Woodward and Bernstein. Is that Paul Trotter?"

"Speaking," said Paul, flatly.

Philip reminded him that they had been at school together—information in which, at that moment, Paul was not the slightest bit interested. He told Philip about the television programme he was about to record—information by which Philip, for some reason, did not appear to be remotely impressed. Philip, sensing that Paul was not in the mood for a lengthy conversation, asked him what he thought of yesterday's news from Birmingham. Paul, his mind still running on chocolate exports rather than motor industry redundancies, replied that it was good news for the industry, good news for Birmingham and good news for the whole country. There was a shocked pause at the other end of the line: obviously, Philip had not been expecting him to express himself quite so pithily.

"Can I just get things clear, Paul?" Philip asked. "You're saying that you're happy about this announcement, are you?"

Paul glanced at Malvina joyfully and took a deep breath before saying, as loudly as he could—and in a horrific mockney accent—"I should coco!" Then, reverting to his own voice—but even now barely able to keep a tremor of excitement out of it—he added: "And you can quote me on that!"

After which, it hardly mattered whether he managed to say it on the programme tonight or not.

A chauffeur-driven car took them back towards Kennington. It was more comfortable than a black cab. The seats were deeper, plusher, upholstered in some sort of yielding imitation leather that swished arousingly whenever the sheerness of Malvina's black tights shifted against it. Streetlamps spotlighted her face at amber intervals. The arresting, beckoning action of traffic lights—a set every few yards, it seemed—rocked her body backwards and forwards beside him. Paul's thoughts were fuzzy with the vodka he'd knocked back in the hospitality room after the recording. He was elated, borne aloft by the realization that his first brush with show business had been so successful. (By which he meant that it hadn't been a disaster.) He wanted to show his gratitude to Malvina, the woman who was bringing him all this. The woman who had stood constantly beside him, smoothing things over—intervening, expertly, whenever he had tried to communicate with all those baffling media types. The woman who had phoned Philip Chase as soon as Paul had been called on to the set—sweating with the knowledge that he had just committed another outrageous gaffe (would those rivulets of panic show up on camera?)—and had managed to resolve the whole situation in a few moments, explaining what Paul had really meant to say, showing it up for the comical misunderstanding it was. How had he ever managed to do without her? What would happen if she abandoned him now? He wanted to hug her: but the thin tautness of her body—always wired, never relaxed—forbade him. He wanted to kiss her, too. Perhaps that would come later. For the time being he merely said:

"Do you think it went well tonight?"

"What do you think?" she answered, turning her head a fraction, brushing away the hair that fell over one eye.

"I think it went well. I think I was on pretty good form, actually. That's what your friend said, isn't it?"

"Well, not exactly. What he said was, 'It's OK, we can probably edit around you.'"

Paul looked downcast for a moment. Then thought about it a little longer, and burst into tipsy laughter. "Jesus. I was *shit*, wasn't I?"

"No," said Malvina, kindly. "All they said was, they could edit around you."

She brushed the rogue strand of hair away again, and allowed her eyes to meet Paul's briefly—having carefully avoided doing so, for the last few minutes—and Paul seized upon this crumb of intimacy, resting his hand on her lean, nylon thigh, stroking it, caressing her knee, as she looked down at his hand impassively, with what looked like almost out-of-body detachment.

"You're the best thing that's ever happened to me," he blurted out.

Malvina smiled and shook her head. "No I'm not."

Paul pondered his own words. "You're right. I suppose winning that election was the best thing that ever happened to me."

"What about your wife? Your daughter?" He didn't answer, so she continued: "Paul, you're going to have to get real."

"Real?" He sounded as though the word was new to him. "About what?"

"About everything. You're living in a fantasy world at the moment. You're so screened off from what's happening in the real world, it's frightening."

"Are you talking about Longbridge?" he asked, with a curious frown.

"Partly I'm talking about Longbridge, yes. I mean, I may not be the most politically . . . *conscientious* person in the world, but even I can see that thousands of people losing their jobs is more important than how much cocoa they have to put in a chocolate bar before they can sell it in Antwerp, for God's sake . . ." She took hold of his hand and removed it from her knee, which it had still been clasping limply. "But that's not all. You have to get real about me, as well."

"Meaning . . . ?" said Paul, leaning closer, and beginning to think, with a shift in his heartbeat, that the moment he had been anticipating for so long was about to arrive.

"Meaning, that sooner or later you have to decide, Paul, what it is that you want from me."

"That's easy," he said, and stroked her hair gently, two, three times before putting his lips to the tiny, immaculate curve of her ear and whispering: "I want to make love to you tonight."

It may only have been a whisper, but it was still loud enough to make their driver switch his car stereo on. His radio was tuned to some late-night AOR station, playing the theme song from the film *Arthur*.

Malvina drew away. She said nothing, for some time, merely fixing Paul with a look that seemed at once to convey rejection, sadness and even (unless he was just deluding himself) a little bit of reluctantly suppressed desire. But then all she said was: "I don't think you've really thought this through."

24

This was only the second time Benjamin had visited Doug's house. Doug and Frankie's house, he supposed he should call it. Or perhaps just Frankie's house, since it had been in her family for two or three generations, and Doug had simply married his way into it. After his first visit, Benjamin hadn't wanted to come again: it had been too upsetting. He didn't want to have his nose rubbed in it any more, the knowledge of all that Doug had won for himself. But Emily had enjoyed her weekend down there, and Doug and Frankie had invited them again, and Benjamin, besides, ended up finding himself unwillingly drawn to the place: realizing that he had finally reached the point where the most he could ask was to be allowed—if only for a couple of days—to scavenge like a starveling cat for whatever scraps he might find of the life he had once imagined himself leading. That life—only ever conceived by Benjamin as an abstract ideal, but now concretized by Doug, with his skyrocketing career and fortuitous marriage—included (among many others) the following elements: a house worth something in the region of two or three million pounds, spreading over five floors, tucked away in a hard-to-find backwater between the King's Road and Chelsea Embankment, as pretty and quiescent a spot as you were ever going to find in central London; four implausibly attractive, good-humoured and cherubic children (two of them not Doug's own, it must be said); and an extended household which seemed to be populated almost exclusively by young, desirable women—au pairs, child-minders, home-helps, twentysomething East European refugees of every description who judging by their looks could just as easily have found employment as high-class escorts or porn stars; and to top it all, of course, Frankie herself. The Hon. Francesca Gifford, a former catwalk model (with an old black and white portfolio to prove it), and now something big in charitable fund-raising on the Chelsea circuit, a somewhat ill-defined and mysterious occupation (profession?), but one which certainly seemed to keep her busy between pregnancies.

Frankie was blonde, slender, probably in her late thirties but looking about ten years younger, with the sing-song voice and slightly terrifying smile of the devoted Christian, which is exactly what she was. Her Christianity, at least, gave her something in common with Benjamin and Emily, whom she liked but appeared to regard—collectively—as little more than another charitable object deserving of her compassionate attention. Benjamin sensed this and resented it deeply, but was annoyed to discover that it didn't stop him from fancying the pants off her. Merely being in her presence gave him a secret thrill; and that, perhaps, was the last and most decisive reason for agreeing to come down for the weekend.

When he wandered into the kitchen early on Sunday morning (three days after the recording of Paul's television triumph), Benjamin found that Frankie was the only other adult to have risen. Her five-month-old, Ranulph, was jigging up and down on her lap, the traces of some unidentifiable mucus-like baby food smeared over most of his face, his hands, his upper torso and his mother's white towel dressing gown. Frankie herself was attempting to drink some coffee but every time the cup got anywhere near her lips the baby's jigging would upset it, and mostly it ended up either on her lap, her feet or the floor. There was a brushed steel, digital radio on one of the shelves, tuned quietly to Classic FM, and—as usual—Benjamin could recognize the music: it was Ravel's *Introduction and Allegro*, a work which for him always seemed to evoke images of an unattainable paradise and so felt particularly appropriate in this setting.

"You're up early," said Frankie; and her second thought was, "Gosh, I must look simply terrible."

Benjamin was never able to say anything gallant if he thought it might make him sound lecherous or sexist. This was a failing to which he had been prone for more than twenty years. So instead of protesting, "No, you look fantastic actually"—as perhaps he should have done—he merely asked: "Did you sleep well?"

"So-so," said Frankie. "But it doesn't help when there's a certain gentleman who won't leave your nipples alone all night."

It flashed through Benjamin's mind for a second that she was talking about Doug, so acute was his current tendency towards sexual envy; but then

Frankie smiled sweetly down at her baby son, just in time to put him right. Benjamin went over to put the kettle on, in order to hide his confusion.

"Emily needs a cup of tea before she can face the world," he explained. "We thought we'd get up and go to the ten o'clock service."

"Oh good, I'll come with you," said Frankie. "It's so nice to find a couple of Duggie's friends who don't regard going to church as some sort of perversion."

They went to the morning communion at St. Luke's Church in Sydney Street, and here, for a brief hour, Benjamin was able to immerse himself in ritual and forget the pressure of dissatisfaction which at all other times he felt mounting up and threatening to overwhelm him. Leaving the church he made eye contact with Emily—even that was rare enough, these days—and they smiled warmly at each other, drawn into temporary closeness. After which, they loitered outside in the sunshine, having nothing much to say to each other, while Frankie busied herself talking to other members of the congregation. Most of these people, presumably, she saw every week or so, but upon meeting it still seemed necessary to hug them with tremulous passion, like old friends from whom she had been separated for long, lonely decades. She appeared to know everybody, and to be regarded on all sides as some kind of saint: people clustered around her, hovered on the fringes of her conversations, as if purely to have the privilege of touching her. Her two older children had stayed at home, but she was carrying Ranulph in front of her in a baby-sling—his face pressed smotheringly into her bosom—while Coriander Gifford-Anderton, her two-year-old daughter, clutched Emily's hand and waited in patient silence, sometimes looking up and down the sunlit street warily; gloweringly sceptical of the world she was in the process of having bequeathed to her.

"OK," said Frankie, rejoining them, the breathless social round completed. "Where to next?"

"I was hoping to look at some shops," said Emily.

"Oh, Mummy!" Coriander protested, hearing this. "You promised the tarousel."

"It's *carousel*, darling. *Ka, ka*. She has trouble with her *c*s, for some reason," she explained.

"Where's the carousel?" Benjamin asked.

"Oh, she just means the little roundabout in the park down the road."

"I don't mind going there," said Benjamin—seizing what he thought would be a chance to spend more time alone with Frankie and her daughter. "You can spare me for a bit, can't you, Em?"

"Gosh, that's nice of you!" said Frankie. At once she took Emily by the arm and began steering her hurriedly away. "You lucky girl," she added to Coriander, "getting Benjamin all to yourself." And to Emily: "Come on then, I'll show you that new fabric shop I was telling you about."

Coriander felt for Benjamin's hand and clasped it uncertainly as they watched the two women walk off together in the direction of the King's Road. It was hard to tell which of them felt more shocked or abandoned.

On the way to the shops, Frankie made a quick call to Doug, who was still in bed. The conversation was short, flirtatious, enigmatic, and had something to do with swearing. Afterwards she explained to Emily: "Duggie's been in a shocking mood all week because I'm on a sex strike."

"A sex strike?" said Emily, swerving off the pavement to avoid a crazed middle-aged platinum blonde on roller blades who appeared to be jabbering to herself, although it turned out she was just negotiating some kind of flight deal on her hands-free mobile phone. The "day of rest" thing didn't seem to have caught on in Chelsea.

"To stop him swearing all the time," Frankie explained. "You know, I've only just noticed how much he does it. In front of the children, as well, that's the problem. Not Hugo and Siena so much—I mean, for goodness' sake, they hear worse at school already—but Corrie's been coming up to me recently and saying things like, 'Mummy, what's a dickhead?' and 'What's a wanker?' and—well, much worse, actually, so I've told him that it's got to stop. Every time he swears in front of the kids he misses out for another day. Two days for the F-word, and three for the C-word. Access denied."

"Aren't you punishing yourself as well?"

Frankie laughed. "Not really. It's never much fun, is it, having sex only five months after you've given birth? You probably remember."

She realized her mistake as soon as the words were out of her mouth. But then, people always seemed to forget that Emily and Benjamin didn't have children of their own. Perhaps because they were so good with everybody else's.

"Look at me, Benjamin, look at me!"

Coriander stood triumphant at the top of the highest slide—the one that was only supposed to be for children older than five—and waited until Benjamin had come closer, until she could be certain that she was the focus of his adoring, undivided attention. Then she launched herself down the slope, her eyes even then never leaving him, checking that not for a moment should he allow himself to be distracted. She didn't notice that a toddler was already sitting at the bottom of the slide, not quite knowing how to get off, and there was a brief, spectacular collision as she crashed into him with outstretched legs and kicked him off on to the rubberized asphalt. Benjamin rushed over, picked him up and dusted him down. He cried a bit but didn't seem too upset, and his father, sitting on a nearby bench reading the business section of the *Sunday Telegraph*, didn't even notice.

There were lots of fathers in the playground that morning, and lots of children seeking attention and not getting any. Coriander, despite the absence of her parents, was not doing badly in that respect. Most nannies, it would appear, had the day off on Sundays, and the deal was that fathers got to spend quality time with their children in the playground while the mothers stayed at home and did whatever it was they couldn't do during the rest of the week when their nannies were looking after the children. In practice this seemed to mean that the children were left mainly to their own forlorn, bewildered devices while the fathers, heavily freighted not just with newspapers but also pint-sized paper cups from Starbucks and Coffee Republic, attempted to do on the playground benches exactly what they would have done at home, given the chance.

Coriander wanted to go on the see-saw next. While he was pushing her up and down, Benjamin looked across at a pair of diminutive swings in the corner and watched a curious drama unfold. There were two little girls on the swings, but neither of them was doing any swinging. One of them, a grave-looking toddler with pale eyes and brown ringlets, was sitting bored and motionless while her father leaned against the metal frame of the swing and scoured the pages of the *Herald Tribune*. The other girl—not at all dissimilar in looks and colouring—was trying to give her swing some much-needed momentum with thrusts of her own body, but hadn't got the hang of that move yet. "Daddy, Daddy!" she started calling, but her father didn't hear her, and besides, he had a cappuccino in one hand and, in the other, a mobile phone on which he seemed to be talking to a business colleague in Sydney. Pushing the swing in these circumstances was clearly out of the question. Both the girls' swings were completely at rest when this second father, concluding his call, took a final swig from the coffee cup, tossed it in the rubbish bin, lifted one of the girls into his arms and headed off in the direction of the playground gate. What interested Benjamin about this situation was that he had *not* picked up the girl who had addressed him as "Daddy." She remained in one of the stationary swings, staring with mounting distress at the receding figure of the man who was presumably her father. Meanwhile the *Herald Tribune* reader read on, happily unaware that his own daughter was in the process of being benignly abducted.

Neither of the adults seemed likely to notice the mistake, and the little girls seemed to be too stunned to say anything, so Benjamin ran over and intercepted the cappuccino-drinker at the playground gate.

"Excuse me," he said. "It's really none of my business, but—I think this girl might not be your daughter?"

The man glanced down at the toddler in his arms. "Shit," he said. "You're right. This isn't Emerald." He hurried back to the swings and accosted the other father just as he was folding up his *Tribune*. "Is this yours?" he asked.

"Daddy!" Emerald held out her arms, her cheeks glistening with tears. There was a hasty swap-over, much shamefaced laughter, and then, just as Benjamin was returning to the see-saw, the playground gate squealed open again and a familiar, unexpected figure burst in, pulling a visibly reluctant three-year-old girl behind her.

"Susan!"

"Benjamin? What on earth are you doing here?"

"I'm here with Doug's daughter. We're staying down here for the weekend."

"Is this her?" Susan asked, looking down at the little girl sitting in mute bewilderment at the bottom end of the see-saw. "This is Lavender, is it, or Parsley or whatever she's called? Right." She picked up Antonia and plonked her at the other end. "Go on, then, you two—play. That's what you've been told to do, so get on with it. Bloody hell, I sound like Miss Haversham, don't I?"

She sat down on a bench and patted the space next to her.

"What are you doing in London, though?" Benjamin asked.

"We've driven down for the day. Took us two-and-a-half hours. And all because of your *bloody* brother. Jesus, I don't know why I even listen to him. Yesterday afternoon he suddenly *announces*, completely out of the blue, that we all have to come down today so Antonia can be dragooned into playing with Doug Anderton's children. Apparently it's important that they become bosom buddies—never mind the little fact that they live 120 miles apart. Everything has to revolve around him and his *bloody* career . . ."

"So where is Paul?"

"Oh, *he* hasn't come along. He's gone straight off to Kennington to have a post-mortem about that stupid programme he was on. With his *media adviser*, if you please. Did you see it on Friday?"

"I did."

“What a prat. He never said anything funny from start to finish. Well, how could he, he had his sense of humor surgically removed at birth. No, he just abandoned me on Chelsea Bridge, jumped out of the car, gave me their phone number and left me to get on with it. So I phoned up the house and got some dippy girl who hardly spoke a word of English—”

“That would be Irina. She’s from Timisoara.”

“—and she told me that everyone would probably be here. So here I am. And here they are.”

She looked over at the two children, who were still sitting in the same positions on the unmoving see-saw, staring at each other with horrified antipathy. Benjamin wandered over to say, “Come on, you two, what’s the problem here?,” and pushed the see-saw up and down a few times, after which they carried on by themselves, albeit rather half-heartedly. Susan got up to join them, and pinned a rogue strand of Antonia’s hair back with a butterfly hairclip.

“Are we going to see Daddy again soon?” the little girl asked.

“That,” said Susan, “is anybody’s guess. He’s supposed to be joining us for lunch, but I wouldn’t like to bet on it. Not when there’s a choice between us and his media adviser.”

The words were spoken brightly; but Benjamin knew—from the way she then took his arm and squeezed it—that the brightness was forced. He tried to think of something consoling to say, but couldn’t.

23

When they arrived at Pizza Express on the King's Road, they found that Emily, along with Frankie and Doug, their three other children, Ranulph, Siena and Hugo, plus Irina, the Romanian nanny, were all waiting for them at one of the large, round, marble-topped tables. The children, under the guise of doing some drawing, writing and coloring, were in fact poking each other in the eyes, ears and various other body parts with a selection of crayons and pencils, while the grown-ups were smiling the tight, eyes-on-the-horizon smiles of people who really wished for nothing more dearly than to be transported away from this place and back to a time before they had children. The noise level was deafening, and indeed you could have been forgiven for thinking, at first, that you had wandered not into a restaurant but a terminally short-staffed crêche for under-disciplined and over-privileged children. Everywhere you looked, blond-haired boys and girls with names like Jasper, Orlando and Arabella were wreaking havoc, hurling fragments of half-chewed pizza and dough balls at each other's French and Italian designer outfits, fighting for possession of their state-of-the-art Game Boys and shrilling across the room in perfect BBC English: beginning even now to master the braying accents of the ruling class with which, in twenty years' time, they would no doubt be filling the pubs of Fulham and Chelsea. A lone childless couple sat together at one small table in the corner, occasionally ducking to avoid the flying foodstuffs, sometimes looking up and glancing around in wordless horror, clearly desperate to leave and bolting their pizzas down as if aiming for a world record.

Susan and Benjamin made sure that the two new friends were placed side-by-side (for Antonia and Coriander, against all the odds, had already become inseparable, little more than an hour after meeting each other), then squeezed in and picked up their menus. Benjamin leapt up almost immediately, with a mingled cry of revulsion and pain, having sat on a half-chewed piece of bruschetta which was mysteriously impaled on the detached arm of a Barbie doll. Irina took it off him and spirited it away, defusing the crisis with the silent, inscrutable efficiency that appeared to be her hallmark.

Doug was in an expansive mood. He had spent all morning reading the Sunday papers and was apparently satisfied that this week he had beaten off the competition, as far as his rival commentators were concerned. He had written an impassioned polemic about the threatened closure of the Leyland plant, drawing heavily on memories of his late father's days as a shop steward there. Nothing else he had read that morning had been written with such feeling, or imbued with such a strong sense of personal experience. Now he felt ready to relax, and play the role of charismatic father-figure to this chaotic, extended family.

Fully within the earshot of his children, and mischievously conscious that he was being transgressive, he began to tell Benjamin the full story of Frankie's recent refusal to have sex with him.

"She's told you about this system she devised, has she? One day without sex for an ordinary swear word. Two days for F and three days for C?"

"Ingenious," Benjamin conceded, glancing across at Frankie and noticing that she was listening to every word of the conversation, grinning broadly, clearly doting on her husband and enjoying the power she had over him.

"Well," said Doug, turning in her direction, "do you realize that I haven't sworn for more than a week? And do you know what it means?"

"What does it mean?" she asked. (And there was, to Benjamin's ears at least, a kind of flirtatious tenderness to her voice even in apparently bland phrasings like this.)

"It means that tonight's the night," said Doug, triumphantly. "I've paid off my debt to society. Balance repaid, account closed. And I fully intend—" he took a meaningful sip of his Pinot Grigio "—to claim my reward."

"Duggie!" she reprimanded. "Do you have to share the details of our sex life with everyone at the table?" But she didn't really seem to mind. Benjamin and Emily were the ones who shifted in their seats and looked uncomfortable and avoided each other's eyes.

A few minutes later, Paul arrived.

"Bloody hell," he said, kissing Susan functionally on the top of the head, "it's like the third circle of hell in here." He ruffled Antonia's hair and she looked up—briefly—from her drawing, dimly registering the fact that her father had appeared. He ignored Benjamin altogether and merely said: "Hello, Douglas—are you going to introduce me to your beautiful wife?"

As Paul drew up a seat next to Frankie and embarked upon what he fondly believed to be the process of charming her, Doug stared across the table at him darkly. "I hate being seen out in public with that twat," he whispered to Benjamin, sawing into his Four Seasons pizza. "Let's get out of here as soon as we can."

And indeed, the parliamentary private secretary and his would-be ally in the quality press said almost nothing to each other over lunch, except for one moment when Doug made a point of catching Paul's attention, and raised the subject of his television appearance.

"Can I just ask you, by the way—if you can prise yourself away from my wife for a second, that is—what happened to you on television the other night? I mean, were you under written instructions from Millbank not to say anything? Because I don't think I've ever seen a guest on that programme who remained completely silent before."

A look of fleetingly murderous anger passed across Paul's face; but he quickly composed himself and said (following the line he had agreed with Malvina a few hours earlier), "Do you know what? They cut my contributions out. Every single one—I don't know why. I said some terribly funny things, as well. There was this brilliant line about chocolate . . ." He tailed off, and shook his head regretfully. "Ah well—what's the use? I'll know next time. They just edit these things to make themselves look good, don't they?"

Doug pondered this explanation for a moment, before snorting in thinly veiled disbelief and getting to his feet.

"Anyway," he announced, "Ben and I haven't had much of a chance to catch up so far, so we're just going to take a walk. See you all back at the house."

They cut through the back streets until they had reached Chelsea Embankment, where an unbroken stream of cars and trucks roared back and forth, and the clouds of carbon dioxide hung heavy over the little village of millionnaires' houseboats moored in a crook of the river Thames, and the postmodern grandiosity of the Montevetro building gleamed back at them from the other side of the river and shimmered in the pale March sunlight.

Benjamin thought of home: not the city centre, where he worked every day—and where buildings not unlike this one were beginning to spring up, as well, on a smaller scale—but the house he shared with Emily, off King's Heath high street, the little world they had built for themselves there, extending to not much more than a few shops, and a couple of pubs, an occasional foray into Cannon Hill Park . . . The difference seemed immense, suddenly. He couldn't get his head around it.

"Do you like it here?" he asked. "I mean, do you feel . . . comfortable?"

"Sure," said Doug. "What's not to like?" Anticipating his friend's answer, he added: "If you're comfortable with yourself—inside your head—then you can feel at home anywhere. That's what I reckon, anyway. Stay true to yourself."

"Yes, you've done that," said Benjamin, pursing his lips doubtfully, "I suppose."

"Just because I've married into a posh family," (Doug's voice was rising in exasperation), "doesn't mean I've forgotten where I came from. Where my loyalties lie. I haven't given up on the class war, you know. I'm behind enemy lines, that's all."

"I know," said Benjamin. "I wasn't implying anything. Anyone can tell that about you—you only have to see what you write for the paper. It must be great," he went on, more quietly (envy creeping into his reflections again), "having that kind of platform. You must feel . . . you must feel you're doing exactly what you want to do."

"Maybe." They had been leaning against the low wall close to Battersea Bridge, looking out across the water. Now Doug straightened up and began to walk downriver, breathing deeply on the noxious fumes pumped out by the ceaseless traffic. "I've reached a bit of a ceiling there, I think. I've been writing those pieces for about eight years now. A few months ago I started telling people I was feeling ready for a change. You know, putting the word around the office. Well, now they've sat up and taken notice, apparently. They're planning a big reshuffle. Been planning it for weeks, in fact."

"Sounds good," said Benjamin. "What do you think's going to happen?"

"Well, I know the editor's PA a little bit—Janet, her name is. Nice girl: she's only been there since just before Christmas. We kind of hit it off, and now she's always feeding me bits of gossip. And she heard—well, she *over*heard him talking on the telephone, and it seems my name came up, in connection with a job."

Benjamin waited. Then had to ask: "Yes? Which was?"

"She wasn't sure," Doug admitted. "She couldn't hear properly. But she said it sounded definite; and this was just a couple of days ago. And she was sure—well, ninety per cent sure, anyway—that he either said it was political editor—which would be brilliant—or deputy editor. Which would just be . . . fantastic."

"Deputy editor?" Benjamin repeated, obviously impressed. "Wow. Do you really think that's what it's going to be?"

"I'm trying not to think about it," said Doug. "Political editor would be great. That would be just fine. I'd settle for that."

"Would it mean more money?"

"They both would. Lots more money, potentially. Which is going to make Frankie happy, for a start. Someone's probably going to phone me up today to let me know which one it is."

"Today? On a Sunday?"

"Yep." Doug started rubbing his hands together at the thought. "Today's the day, Benjamin. Maybe we can have a bit of champagne before you drive off this evening. Followed, in my case—after a whole week's abstention from oaths, profanity and all manner of filthy language—by what I can only imagine is going to be an *epic* shag. The mother of all shags."

They crossed the road effortfully, threading their way through the four lines of traffic, heading back towards the picturebook enclave where the Gifford-Anderton residence lay hidden.

"I thought you weren't in sympathy with the other people on the paper," said Benjamin. "Politically, I mean."

"Ah, but that's my trump card," Doug pointed out. "It's true, they're all fucking Blairite idiots. But the bottom line is, they have to cater for the readers: and most of the readers are still Old Labour. So they need to have someone like me on board, even though they don't like it. I give those people a voice. The kind of people who think we should make some sort of an effort to keep Longbridge open even if it isn't making any money. The kind of people who are actually in their forties and fifties and sixties and have been reading the paper for years and don't give a fuck about what kind of eyeliner Kylie Minogue uses, which is the kind of story our esteemed editor seems obsessed with . . ."

"Do you not get on with him too well?" Benjamin asked.

"We get on fine," said Doug, "but he's a man of no scruples. Completely opportunistic. A few months ago, for instance, they shot some particularly under-nourished looking model for a fashion piece in the magazine, but she looked so ill and scrawny that they couldn't use the pictures. Then last week he dug them out and put them in the main paper after all—to illustrate a story about anorexia nervosa. Didn't seem to think there was anything wrong with it."

He chuckled sourly as they reached the garden gate and squeaked it open. Doug had forgotten his house-keys, so he pressed the entryphone button and they waited for a while, admiring the trails of ivy around the door lintel and the mullioned windows. Frankie was always too busy to do any gardening, Doug explained, so they had a man come and do it for them, three mornings a week.

Soon the front door was opened by a breathless Irina.

"Ah—Doug—come in, quickly. Someone phoned for you."

"Who is it?" he said eagerly, following her inside.

"There—in there."

She gestured towards the downstairs sitting room, which ran the length of the house and ended in a conservatory twice the size of Benjamin's back garden. Doug and Benjamin hurried in and found that everyone was there: Paul, Susan, Emily, Frankie, all of the children. They stared at Doug excitedly, smiling with anticipation, while Frankie spoke to someone on a cordless phone.

"Yes—he's here. He's just literally come through the front door. I'll hand you over. Here you are."

Doug grabbed the phone off her and retreated to a corner of the room.

"Is it about his job?" Benjamin whispered, and Frankie nodded.

At first it was hard for the others to tell what was happening, just listening to one side of the conversation. Doug said very little, apart from occasional grunts of assent. Everyone started to notice, however, that these changed in tone as the exchange went on. Doug's silences became longer and longer: the voice at the other end of the line seemed to be building up to some sort of revelation. And when it finally came, Doug went deathly quiet. So did the rest of the room.

It felt as though whole minutes had ticked by before Doug said, "What?," very quietly; and immediately afterwards shouted "*WHAT?*," again, only this time at the very top of his voice, in a bellow of thunderous fury that had the children glancing at each other in frightened apprehension.

Now the voice at the end of the line was raised too, and could be heard saying, "Doug—please think about it. Don't ring off. Whatever you do—"

Doug pressed a button to end the call, took the phone over to the mantelpiece and laid it there in a gesture of preternatural calm.

"Well?" said Frankie, unable to bear the suspense any longer.

Doug was staring at his own face in the gilded mirror.

"That woman," he said at last, his voice hoarse, and strangely remote. "That woman Janet. She's going to have to get her hearing tested." He turned to look at the circle of bewildered faces. "Political editor? No. Deputy editor? No." Then, gathering breath, he bellowed: "*LITERARY* editor. Do you hear me? *LITERARY—FUCKING—EDITOR.* They want me to commission book reviews. They want me to spend every day putting novels into fucking jiffy bags and sending them out to . . . to . . ." He spluttered, lost for words, and then started reeling around the room in a frenzy, yelling as he did so: "The *cunts.* The fucking, fucking, fucking, fucking, fucking, fucking *CUNTS*!"

In the absolute silence that followed, Benjamin almost imagined that he could hear the words echoing around the room and dying away. Nobody could think of anything to say, until Coriander turned to her mother and gravely whispered: "What's a tunt? What's a futting futting futting futting tunt?"

It was the longest sentence she had ever spoken. But Frankie did not think it was the moment to remark on this; or to mention the fact that her husband had just disqualified himself from sex again, for at least the next three weeks.

22

Claire, who could be more or less garrulous in the right company, sat at the kitchen table opposite her son and tried to think of something to say.

It was becoming obvious to her that she was out of practice at motherhood. Ten years ago, when Patrick was just five, she wouldn't have believed such a thing to be possible. It was not just that loving him, in those days, had come as naturally to her as breathing: of course she still loved him, as much as she ever had. The difference was that she no longer knew how to behave around him. The process had begun, she knew, even before she had left for Italy. Already, when he was only nine or ten, she had felt herself losing her footing, not knowing quite what tone to strike: she hadn't understood his burgeoning obsessions, the sports he became fixated on, the clothes he felt compelled to wear. She could see that this wasn't happening between him and Philip; not to the same extent; and that was one of the reasons she felt it was sensible—or at least permissible—to let him move in with his father and stepmother, while she set off on her Italian adventure. By the time that was over—by the time she arrived back in Birmingham five years later (homesick, absurdly, for a place she didn't even like that much)—an even greater distance had opened up between them. That was inevitable, she supposed: he had visited her, in that time, and she'd come back to England at least twice a year, but still, he had changed, grown away from her, immeasurably, almost beyond recognition. The wordlessness she had already been starting to feel in his presence became more and more acute.

It was the first time she had been back to her father's house since December. On that occasion, she had moved out after only four days, then stayed two nights at a hotel in Birmingham and spent Christmas with friends in Sheffield, friends from her university days. There was no way she could have lasted a minute longer. This weekend, however, Donald Newman was safely out of the country: living it up in the second home in France that he was always bragging about, these days, and which she had no intention of ever visiting. It sounded as though, since retirement, he spent more and more time there: but then she knew little about his current arrangements, and cared less. Some clever stockbroker friend had made him a few thousand in the nineties, apparently, and that had enabled him to pick up this picturesque ruin somewhere outside Bergerac. Bully for him. He was welcome to it.

It was Patrick who mentioned him first, as it turned out.

"Grandad keeps this place pretty well, doesn't he?" he remarked, looking around the orderly kitchen. "For a bachelor, I mean. An old geezer like him."

"Nothing else to do, I suppose. Anyway, I think he gets some skivvy in to do it for him. I'd be very surprised if he knew one end of a vacuum cleaner from another."

Her son smiled. She wanted to say something nice to him—how good his hair looked, now that he was wearing it a bit longer, how glad she was that he didn't seem to have had any body parts pierced yet—but the phrases wouldn't form. Instead she thought about the evening ahead, the two places she was going to have to lay at that table, the meal they would later be eating in thick suburban silence, and felt suddenly afraid that she couldn't go through with it.

"Look, Pat, shall we go out tonight? Drive out to the country, find a pub or something?"

"Why? I thought you'd bought some food."

"I have, but . . . you know." She gestured with her eyes. "This place."

"We can liven it up," said Patrick. "Put some candles on the table. I brought some music."

While Claire rummaged in drawers to find a tablecloth, her son took a ghetto blaster out of his holdall and connected it to a wall socket. He flicked through a wallet of CDs and clicked one into the machine. Claire braced herself, anticipating some monstrosity, but heard instead a piano figure in a minor key, pulsing, insistent, tango-like, surrounded soon by cunningly woven lines for violin and cello and bandoneon.

"That's nice," she said. "What is it?"

"Astor Piazzolla," said Patrick. "Thought you might like this one." And then, with a short laugh: "Of course, it's not what I listen to by myself. Normally I only ever listen to big black gangsters singing about raping their bitches and being strung out on crack. I just keep this one as a standby, for the old folk."

"You watch what you're saying," Claire warned. "You're treading on sensitive ground, there. I shudder to think what the other people in that house say about me."

It was March 31st, 2000, and Claire had come to Birmingham that weekend to take part in tomorrow's protest against the Longbridge closure: a huge, city-wide demonstration, which was to begin with a march from the centre of town, with more crowds joining along the way to converge, finally, on a rally in Cannon Hill Park. Claire's home, at this time—not that she thought of it as home, or as anything other than a momentary staging post—was a house in Ealing, west London, which she shared with three graduate students in their early twenties. She'd found a temporary job as a sort of glorified accounts clerk, processing invoices for a firm which imported Italian furniture. The whole set-up was decidedly grim. She felt as though her life was a tape which someone had just rewound by about fifteen years.

"They take the piss out of you, do they?" asked Patrick.

"It's not quite as blatant as that. They're much too polite. But you can tell from the way they look at me that they're wondering if they should get a Stannah stair-lift installed one of these days, or buy me one of those foot-spas for my birthday."

She put a saucepan on to the hob for the pasta, and started chopping onions and tomatoes. Patrick poured her some wine and asked if he could have some.

"Of course you can. You don't have to ask that."

Patrick wandered out into the living room and was gone for a few minutes. Claire peeped through at one point and saw that he was looking at the family photographs on the mantelpiece. Except that "family" photographs was not the right word for them. There were no pictures of Mr. Newman's daughters, there: no mementoes of the missing Miriam, or the errant Claire. Just photographs of Donald and Pamela, a tracking of their life together, their ageing: the wedding picture, the holidays in Scotland and the Scilly Isles; the two of them outside the Bergerac cottage, Pamela looking bowed, shrunken. She'd surrendered to cancer just eight months after they bought it. In the centre of the mantelpiece was a silver-framed portrait of her, A4 size. It must have been taken some time in the fifties, before the children came along. Dark hair, pearl necklace, a cocktail dress in black or navy blue. She was smiling the unknowable smile that people wear for the camera. Patrick lifted the picture, tilted it away from the light, appraised it intently; as if it was going to yield up some family secret.

"So," he said, returning to the kitchen, wineglass in hand, "are you actually speaking to Grandad at the moment?"

"There's been no official declaration of hostilities," said Claire. "It's just that I never phone him, and he never phones me. Or almost never. I mean, he was perfectly civil when I asked if I could stay here for the weekend. Though he thought my reason for coming to Birmingham was ludicrous."

"Well, he never was much of a revolutionary, was he? Can you imagine Grandad going on a demo? It would have to be in favour of bringing back hanging for people who hold hands in public before marriage."

"Or making fox-hunting part of the National Curriculum." She smiled, not so much at the jokes as at the warmth they were promising to generate between them. "Anyway, what about you? Are you going to come along tomorrow?"

"Yes. 'Course I am. It's important, isn't it? A lot of people's jobs are at stake."

"Is your dad going?"

"Yep."

"Your step-mum?"

"I should think so. Carol's pretty worked up about Longbridge, like everybody else. You going to be OK with that?"

"Oh, sure. I've got a lot of time for Carol."

"Some of Dad's friends'll be there, too. Doug Anderton? D'you remember him? He's coming up from London. And Benjamin's tagging along, I think."

"My God," said Claire, "that really *will* be weird. A proper little King William's reunion. I haven't seen Doug for donkey's years. And I think the last time we were all together was at our wedding."

"Benjamin was best man, wasn't he?"

"That's right. He made an absolutely disastrous speech. Full of quotations from Kierkegaard—which might have meant more to the audience if he hadn't insisted on reciting them in the original Danish—and then some elaborate joke which hinged on a confusion between Rimbaud the poet and Rambo the Sylvester Stallone character. Nobody had the faintest idea what he was talking about." She sighed, fondly. "Poor Benjamin. I wonder if he's changed."

"I thought you saw him just before Christmas."

Claire resumed chopping, and said merely, "We didn't get much of a chance to speak," in a tone which implied—to her son, at least—that there was nothing more to be said on that subject.

The evening went well. Patrick managed to dig out three more CDs that met with his mother's approval, and there seemed no need to resort to her fall-back plan, which had been simply to cut their losses and watch television when they ran out of things to say to each other. In fact—perversely—Claire ended up feeling that it had gone almost too well. Which is to say that tonight, for the first time, she started to notice something strange about Patrick's behaviour: that it was too thoughtful, too considerate, too much predicated on her own needs and responses, which he was adept at second-guessing. There was a curious stiffness, a curious unease, about the way he carried himself, she realized—almost as if he believed himself to be role-playing, an actor in somebody else's script. Perhaps this was just the characteristic self-consciousness of adolescence; but there seemed more to it than that—there was an extraordinary *watchfulness* about Patrick, a sense that he was waiting for the world to show him how to behave, to disclose his own personality to him before he could begin to inhabit it. Was this what they—she and Philip—had done to him, by splitting up when he was just three, and then shunting him backwards and forwards from parent to parent for years afterwards? He was *missing* something, she was beginning to see that now, missing some vital component. Something she couldn't yet identify, although she knew it was more than a question of family stability.

Patrick poured her a last glass of wine and brought it to her on the living-room sofa.

"Here you are," he said. "I'm going to bed, now. Don't sit up all night getting pissed."

"I won't."

He leaned down to kiss her. His cheeks were downy, with the first traces of a baby beard.

"It's been nice tonight, hasn't it?" she said.

He folded her in a hug. "Yes, it has."

As he straightened up again, she let the wine give her courage and asked: "You're OK, are you, love? Phil and Carol look after you well, do they?"

"Of course they do. Why, don't I look OK?"

They were too vague, too complicated, the anxieties that had been stirring within her for the last few minutes. All she could say was: "You look pale, that's all."

Patrick smiled defensively. "We all do," he said. "Me and all my friends. It's all that junk your generation keeps feeding us." In a quieter voice, he added: "We're the pale people."

Without explaining what he meant, Patrick blew his mother one last goodnight kiss; and then she noticed, before he went up to bed, how his eyes lingered again on the mantelpiece photographs.

After her shower the next morning she came out of the bathroom to find that he had opened the door of Miriam's old bedroom, and was standing inside.

She followed him in.

"Not much to see, is there?" she said.

It was just as she had last found it: no furniture, bare floorboards, white-washed walls. Not a room at all, but a statement: a statement of absence. She imagined her father coming in here every day, standing quite still in the centre, breathing in the nothingness of it. Thinking about Miriam, as he must have thought about her every day, unmoving, inscrutable. Why else would he keep the room this way? It was spotless, too: as conscientously dusted and hoovered as every other room in the house. She could see his logic, even as it repelled her. This was a missing person's room.

"Where's all her stuff?"

Claire shrugged. "I don't know. I've got some of it: you know, the pictures you've seen, a few other bits and pieces, bracelets, a hairbrush, that sort of thing. Some toys—" (she thought her voice was going to crack, but recovered herself) "—from when she was little. I think Dad threw the rest away. Gave away all her furniture, I know that. There were a lot of other things—photograph albums, all her diaries. I don't know what became of them. They've gone for good." She paced the length of the forlorn, tiny room in three short steps, and stared out of the window at the back garden, frugal and obsessively tidy like everything else at this house. "Do you talk about her much?" she asked. "I mean, do they ever mention her—Philip and Carol?"

"No."

"But *you* think about her, don't you? I can tell that you do."

Patrick said, "She may still be alive." And all at once his voice was pleading.

Claire turned on her heel and left the room. "Let's not go there, OK?"

They were out on the landing together now. Patrick pointed up at the trap door in the ceiling.

"How do I get up there?"

"You can't."

"All it would take is a ladder."

"There's nothing there. Just junk."

She stared at him, willing it not to happen. She didn't want this to be his mission. *She* couldn't go through it all again, for one thing; and it was dangerous for him, too. He was too young, too vulnerable to take on something like this.

"I'm going out to the shops," she said. "We can have fish tonight, is that OK? And I'm going to get some more wine. Have a bath or something. We've got to leave in about an hour if we're going to get to Cannon Hill on time."

He nodded, but didn't move. Finally she said: "There's a ladder in the garage. At least there used to be." She touched his shoulder. It felt bony and thin. "Why do you want to do this, Pat? What's it all about?"

He removed her hand; but gently. "I don't know. It's to do with you and Dad, and why you split up, and . . ." He turned away, heading down the stairs. "I don't know. I just want to."

"You won't find anything," she called after him. "He threw everything away."

But Claire was wrong.

When she came back from the supermarket half an hour later, she found Patrick—still unbathed, still wearing the T-shirt and boxers in which he had slept—sitting on the bare floorboards of Miriam's old room. Somehow he had managed to carry a massive, old-fashioned leather trunk down from the loft, and he was sitting beside it. The trunk had been padlocked, but he had wrenched the lock apart with a pair of pliers. He had removed about half the contents of the trunk, which lay scattered on the floor around him. Claire stared at them, unbelieving. Her mouth dropped open and she was drained of breath.

Here were things she had not seen for more than twenty years. Her sister's clothes. Her books and ornaments. A little treasure box she had brought back from John O'Groats, filled with plastic jewellery. Old magazines, copies of *Jackie*, with pictures of seventies pop stars clipped out and dotted with holes where Miriam had drawing-pinned them to the wall. David Bowie and Bryan Ferry. A man's purple shirt which had once been one of her most precious possessions, although no one had ever learned why. And diaries. Two or three volumes of diaries, written in blue biro in her looping, girly handwriting.

Claire reached for these first.

"You haven't looked at these, have you?" she said. She had remembered that they would be meeting Doug Anderton at the rally. She didn't want Patrick to know that Doug's father had been involved in the disappearance.

"No," he answered. He had found dozens of photographs of Miriam—Miriam and Claire—slides mainly, and he was holding them up to the grey light framed by the uncurtained windows.

"Good," said Claire, and opened the diary for 1974, flipping the pages, too shocked to read anything properly, and dropping the book altogether, letting it fall to the floor with a slap, when she came upon pages brown with fingerprints—the prints of her own, fourteen-year-old Bovril-stained fingers—and her eyes filled with acid tears, tears like needles, the kind she thought she had forgotten how to cry.

21

—— Original Message ——
From: Malvina
To: btrotter
Sent: Thursday, March 30, 2000 3:38 p.m.
Subject: Rally for Longbridge

Hi Ben

Yes, I think I've persuaded your brother to come—though of course he is terrified of doing anything which might be seen to be critical of the party, and Tony in particular—so shall certainly be there myself.

It would be lovely to meet up. Waterstone's café, for old times' sake? I could probably be there by ten.

See you there, unless I hear to the contrary.

Love
Malvina XoX

Benjamin arrived first, inevitably. He bought himself a cappuccino and a pain au chocolat, and a large mocha for Malvina, because he remembered that that was what she liked.

He was ten minutes early; she was five minutes late. He filled in the time by reading two Inland Revenue leaflets: one about changes in the way that consolidation adjustments were to be recorded, the other about how to recover advance corporation tax by way of offset against mainstream corporation tax liability. It was as well to keep up with these things. By the time that Malvina arrived, her mocha had gone cold, and she had to order another one. Her cheeks were icy to the touch when he kissed her. He prolonged the kiss for as long as he could, breathing in her perfume, which instantly brought back to him the memory of all their earlier meetings, and the weird, vaporous hopes he had built around them.

Once they were seated opposite each other, he found that he could think of nothing to say to her. His embarrassment seemed to be contagious, and for a while they sat in clumsy silence.

"So," Malvina said at last, after two or three sips of her warming drink, "what do you think will happen today? D'you think it's going to achieve anything?"

"Well—I don't know . . ." Benjamin seemed nonplussed by this question. "I just thought it was a sign that we could . . . you know, carry on being friends."

Malvina held his gaze for a moment, then smiled. "I didn't mean that. I was talking about the rally."

"Oh. Oh—that." Benjamin looked down at the frothy surface of his coffee. Was there no end to the ways in which he could humiliate himself? "I don't know. I think it'll be a memorable day. I think people will feel inspired, and encouraged, probably. It won't change anybody's mind, though, will it? The powers that be."

"No. Of course not." More brightly, she said: "And what about your work? How's that going? Have you written much, in the last few weeks?"

Malvina was one of the few people in whom Benjamin had confided any details of his *magnum opus*. Even then, he had not been able to talk about it to any depth. He had told her the title—*Unrest*—but as soon as he began trying to explain what he hoped to achieve with it—why he considered it to be unique, and groundbreaking, and necessary—words became inadequate; he could hear himself speaking, but the phrases issuing from his mouth seemed to bear no relation to the ideal, pristine form which the work continued to take inside his head. He wanted to tell her that it was the most important thing in his life; that it was driving him mad; that it was an unprecedented marriage of old forms and new technology; that it would change the relationship between music and the written word for ever; that he hadn't written a word or composed a note for months; that sometimes he felt it was the only thing that was keeping him alive; that he could feel himself losing faith in it, as in so much else . . . But there seemed no point, no point in expressing any of that to this beautiful, unfathomable woman who was sitting opposite him licking traces of coffee from her fine, wine-dark upper lip.

"So-so," he ended up saying, lamely. "I keep plugging away at it."

Malvina smiled, and shook her head. "What are you, Benjamin—the king of understatement? You've been writing this thing for *twenty years.* Are you ever going to allow yourself a little pat on the back? It's incredible, the way you've stayed with it. God, if I write just five lines of a poem and then get stuck for an idea, I usually give up and throw it away." She sat back and looked at him, beaming, almost with pride. "How do you do it? What keeps you going?"

And after a moment Benjamin answered, quietly: "I've told you that before. The very first time we met."

Malvina glanced down into the depths of her coffee cup. "Ah, yes—the mysterious *femme fatale.* The love of your life. What was her name again?"

"Cicely."

"And the idea behind this book is . . . Can you remind me?" Benjamin said nothing, so she continued: "That's right—she's going to read it one day and realize that you're a genius and she was crazy to leave you, and then she'll come running back. Something like that, wasn't it?"

"Something like that," said Benjamin, his face suddenly grim, withdrawn.

"Benjamin," Malvina said—urgently, now—"I may not know what I'm talking about here, but has it ever occurred to you that being abandoned by her was the best thing that could have happened to you? That you may have had a narrow escape?"

Benjamin shrugged, and sipped the dregs of his cappuccino.

"I mean, if it makes you carry on writing, all well and good—that's probably the only thing that keeps you sane, anyway—but otherwise, I wish you'd forget this stupid business. There comes a point where you just have to draw a line. And in your case I'd say you'd passed it about two decades ago."

It was impossible to say whether Benjamin was even hearing this advice or not. He simply changed the subject, by asking: "What about you? Getting anything written at the moment?"

"Oh, yes, I'm still . . . 'plugging away,' as you'd put it."

"I don't know how you find the time," said Benjamin, "with everything else that's going on in your life." (Although he did know how she found the time, really: it was because she was young.)

"Well, you know," she answered. "Late nights. Black coffee. I'm trying to write more stories, but I can never seem to manage more than a few pages. They're just fragments. I don't know what I'm going to do with them."

"Have you shown them to anyone?"

"No. I'd be too embarrassed."

"Maybe you should."

What Benjamin still wanted, of course, was to read them himself: anything to bring himself back into a kind of closeness with her. But he could tell that she would never agree to this. He clutched, instead, at the thought that he might be able to help her in some more practical way, even though a few moments' clear-eyed reflection would have told him that this too was impossible.

"I know someone you could show them to," he said. "A friend of mine: Doug Anderton."

"Yes, I know Doug. At least, I've spoken to him on the phone. He just got a new job, didn't he?"

"That's why I mentioned him. He's literary editor now. Why don't you send your stuff to him?"

Malvina frowned. "What would be the point? He just commissions articles and book reviews, doesn't he? They wouldn't publish stories or anything like that."

"Sometimes they do," Benjamin insisted. "And besides, he told me that publishers keep phoning him up and asking him out to lunch, now. So if he liked your stuff, he could mention it to them, couldn't he? And they're always going to want to do him a favour, to make sure they get good coverage. The whole business is a racket. You might as well take advantage of it."

It came out sounding pretty plausible, he thought, considering that he didn't really know what he was talking about. And Malvina—who was always swift to believe that the world operated in this way—looked more than half convinced.

"Maybe . . ." she murmured.

"Anyway," said Benjamin, "you'll be seeing Doug in a minute."

"Really? He's coming on the march today?"

"Of course he is. His dad was a shop steward at Longbridge, remember? I was going to meet him at New Street Station in about twenty minutes. Can you come along?"

"I don't know yet. I don't know where I'm meeting Paul."

The answer to that came quickly enough. Malvina and Benjamin finished their coffees, stepped out into the damp, bone-chilling morning and joined the thickening crowd as it headed out along New Street in the direction of the Bristol Road. Already the human river was busy and fast-moving, even though this was just a tributary to the main current. There were banners everywhere you looked ("Don't Let Rover Die," "Save Our Jobs," "Blair Doesn't Care"), and all of the city's life seemed to be here: pensioners were walking with teenagers, Bangladeshis alongside whites and Pakistanis. It was a good atmosphere, Benjamin thought, even if everybody did look decidedly cold. He kept close to Malvina, partly for fear of losing her in the crowd, partly because he wanted to; so she was not able to hide her reaction when a text message from Paul came through. She seemed irritated, even a little hurt, but not in the least surprised.

"Oh, *Paul*," she said to the phone, slapping it shut and putting it back in the pocket of her leather jacket.

"What's up? He hasn't bottled out, has he?"

"Says he's got too much paperwork to get through." She looked away, biting her lip. "*Shit.* It would have done him so much good to be seen here. Why couldn't I get him to believe that?"

"My brother's a coward," said Benjamin, as if to himself.

She looked at him sharply. "Do you think so?"

Benjamin shrugged. "Sometimes." Then he added: "I know I shouldn't say that to you." And, more quietly: "I know you're fond of him."

"Yes," Malvina admitted. "Yes, I am. That doesn't mean he can't be a complete arsehole sometimes."

"So he's staying down in London, is he?"

"No," said Malvina. "He's at home. I'm going to join him there later."

"Oh." Benjamin was taken aback. "And what does Susan think about that?"

"She doesn't know. She's gone to her parents' for the weekend. With Antonia."

"You're staying the night?"

"Yes."

"Cosy," said Benjamin, investing the word with a good deal of meaning.

"You think it looks bad?"

"Don't you?" He gave a short laugh. "You're supposed to be the one who understands how the media works. Can you imagine what would happen if the papers found out?"

Malvina turned and looked at him earnestly. There was a sudden intensity to her voice, and in her eyes, that struck Benjamin as almost comical. "I'm not having an affair with him, you know. I'm not sleeping with him. And I never will."

He couldn't think of anything to say. Except, after a brief pause: "I believe you."

"Good," said Malvina. "Because it's God's own truth."

There were five of them, in the end, marching together towards Cannon Hill Park: Benjamin, Doug, Malvina, Philip Chase and his second wife Carol. They kept an eye out for Claire and Patrick, but so far there was no sign of them. There were tens of thousands of people, now, walking solemnly along the Pershore Road, the mood of the crowd defiant, resolute, rather than noisily militant. Benjamin had been expecting it to be a mainly local demonstration, but there were Trade Union banners from all over the place: Liverpool, Manchester, Durham, York. The groundswell of support for the saving of Longbridge was clearly massive and widespread, even though some attempt seemed to have been made—by the usual suspects—to hijack the demonstration: every so often the air would ring with that ubiquitous cry of street protest, as English as the first cuckoo of spring: "*SO*cialist Worker! *SO*cialist Worker!" Leading Doug to exclaim, gleefully: "This is *fantastic*, isn't it? It's just like being back in the 1970s."

Phil and Carol walked arm in arm, with Phil carrying a "Keep Rover Running" banner high above his head. Malvina gravitated towards Doug, and after a while began a low, confidential conversation with him: Benjamin assumed that she was bringing up the subject of her writing. Somehow, once again, even in the company of two of his oldest friends, he found himself excluded, consigned to another, private universe, thrown back on his own imaginative resources. He could never work out how it happened, but it always did. If Emily had been there, he supposed, he could have talked to her, or at least held her hand. But she was tied up with work at home: the church-warden, Andrew, was coming round that morning, and they were going to deliver copies of the parish newsletter together. She had considered coming to the rally instead, but Benjamin had managed to talk her out of it. He didn't want her to meet Malvina.

"What was she talking to you about?" he asked Doug, as soon as Malvina was out of earshot, and he had regained his friend's attention about three hundred yards from Cannon Hill Park.

"Oh, this and that," said Doug. "Your fuckwit brother, mainly. I told her he needn't bother cosying up to me any more. Appearing on the books pages is hardly going to raise his profile. Only about ten people read them, and eight of those are the people who write them, as well."

"Did she mention her short stories?"

"She said something about that, yes. I wasn't really listening."

Not for the first time, Benjamin was disturbed to see that Doug wasn't making the slightest attempt to appear interested in his new job. He never spoke about it except with contempt. It was starting to feel as if it might only be a matter of time—and not much time, either—before he walked out on it altogether.

"They're crazy," he said, "to have sidelined you like that. I mean, you could have written something great about this rally. Did they send anyone else to cover it?"

"They're letting me do it. Allowing me a swansong. Phil said I could go back to his place afterwards and use his computer. I'm not sure I can be bothered, to be honest." He sighed, his breath steaming in the drizzly air. "I don't know what I'm going to do about this, Ben. Make the best of a bad job, I suppose. Which reminds me—do *you* want to review something?"

"Me?" said Benjamin, incredulous.

"Well, why not? If I'm going to get any benefit at all out of this shitty job I might as well use it to do my friends some favours."

"But I've never reviewed anything before. Let alone for one of the nationals."

"Doesn't matter. You couldn't write anything worse than some of the rubbish the regulars send in. Anyway, I've got something that's right up your street."

"Yes?"

"D'you remember that doddery old queen who came to read his poetry to us at school? Francis Piper, his name was."

Benjamin nodded. That day was, in fact, imprinted upon his memory with indelible force. It was the same day he had forgotten to take his swimming trunks to school, and had been threatened—under the brutal, arcane rules of King William's PE department—with the possibility of having to go swimming in the nude in front of all his classmates. God had come to his rescue that day; and it was upon this incident (although hardly anybody else knew it) that Benjamin's entire system of religious belief was founded. It was not the kind of day you forget in a hurry.

"Yes, I remember him. Nice old bloke: I bought all his poems after that. Haven't read them for years, mind you. You're not telling me he's still alive, is he? He must have been about ninety when he came to read to us."

"Died about five years ago, apparently. And now there's a biography coming out. Massive great thing—about eight hundred pages. What do you reckon? Do you think you could write something about it?"

"Yes, of course—I'd love to."

"We should be getting a copy in about two or three weeks. I'll send it straight on to you."

Philip had been walking only a few paces behind them during this conversation, and now, drawing level, he said: "I remember that guy. He had this sort of . . . angelic look about him, but his poems were absolutely filthy when you realized what he was going on about."

"Which none of us did, at the time."

"Except for Harding," said Phil. "Don't you remember? He put his hand up in one of Fletcher's lessons and asked him if Piper was gay."

"Only he didn't put it quite that nicely, did he?" Doug smiled, and wondered aloud: "Ah, Harding, Harding . . . whatever happened to you? Where are you now that we need you?"

"He could be anywhere," said Benjamin. "We don't know that he even left Birmingham. He could be here today."

Phil shook his head. "Sean? No. This was never his style. He wouldn't go in for solidarity with the workers, or with anybody else. Anarchy was more his thing."

"Well, it'd be a let-down to meet him again anyway," said Doug. "As I've said before, he probably became a quantity surveyor or something. He's probably turned out more boring than any of us."

"Who are you talking about?" Malvina asked, drifting back towards them after spending the last few minutes on the fringes of the march.

"Just someone we used to know," Doug answered. "Three middle-aged farts reminiscing about their schooldays. Stuff that happened before you were born." And then he asked, as an afterthought: "When were you born, anyway?"

"1980."

"Jesus." They all looked genuinely incredulous at this information, as if what Malvina was claiming was a biological impossibility. "You really are one of Thatcher's children, aren't you?"

"Well, don't worry about having missed the 1970s," said Phil. "I think you're just about to enter a time capsule."

. . .

Warning for Blair as 100,000 Rally for Rover

Doug Anderton

The chanting never seemed to stop, and after a while it became hypnotic, like a classic piece of trance: "Tony Blair, Shame on You! Shame on You for Turning Blue!"

Whether the Prime Minister is listening or not is another matter. But the people of Birmingham left the government in no doubt about their feelings yesterday, as the city saw not only its own biggest demonstration since the 1970s, but one of Britain's most significant expressions of mass protest since Mrs. Thatcher's confrontations with the striking miners.

BMW's decision to abandon Rover cars has stirred the city into action. In an angry but good-natured display of public feeling, Rover workers, union leaders and tens of thousands of ordinary citizens marched side-by-side through the Birmingham streets yesterday, converging on Cannon Hill Park to hear a number of defiant speeches, preceded by a short set from local band UB40.

In terms of age, class and ethnic grouping, the rally was a fine demonstration of the city's broadness and diversity. Eighty-four-year-old Joe Davenport carried a banner offering a new spin on the initials BMW: "Betrayed Midland Workers." Meanwhile, children as young as three or four milled around the grown-up feet, sporting balloons and candy floss from nearby stalls. There were no incidents and no arrests.

During the speeches there was some heckling from far-left groups. Richard Burden, the Labor MP for Northfield, had to bear the brunt of the crowd's anger at what many people see, at the very least, to be inertia and lack of foresight on the government's part. (His parliamentary colleague Paul Trotter, incidentally, was conspicuous by his absence.) Other speakers elicited a powerful response. Albert Bore, the leader of Birmingham City Council, got the biggest cheer for describing the Longbridge sell-off as "the rape of Rover." The TGWU's Tony Woodley also pulled no punches, insisting that BMW had behaved "dishonestly and dishonourably," and that the government has "a responsibility to Rover, to Britain and to British manufacturing industry."

> Probably the biggest hit of the afternoon, however, was radio celebrity and self-styled "community historian" Dr. Carl Chinn, who proved himself a compelling orator and drew unashamedly on a wealth of references to working-class and trade union traditions of protest: the sort of rhetoric that, were it to come from a member of his inner circle, would have the current Prime Minister choking on his Chardonnay.
>
> But with memories of the Chartists ringing in their ears, most of the crowd seemed to go home invigorated and fired up for battle. What form that battle takes, and who will be enlisted, now depends—like everything else, it seems—on occult discussions which will no doubt be taking place behind the closed doors of Millbank over the next few days.

Carl Chinn's speech ended with the words: "We serve warning—if they do not hark to our voice then we will march through the streets of London and take our fight to the doors of Westminster." And when the cheering had died down, Tony Woodley returned to the rostrum to add: "There has been a clear message to BMW today. We are not going quietly." He was repeating the phrase, to even louder cheering and swelling applause, when Philip felt a tap on his shoulder and turned to see his son and his ex-wife standing behind him, smiling warmly in greeting.

"Hi, Claire," he said, and embraced her tightly. He clapped Patrick on the back while Claire and Carol also managed to do the decent thing and greet each other with a short, functional hug.

Then Claire found that Doug was looking at her. It was their first meeting in more than fifteen years. He took her by both hands and in his eyes she could see the same hunger, the same curiosity she remembered seeing even longer ago: back when they were schoolchildren, and had travelled home together every afternoon on the number 62 bus. It was not as if the decades since then had simply dissolved. The moment was more troubling than that, because it impressed upon her, again, the truth of what she had realized at Benjamin's concert in December: there were some feelings that never faded, no matter how many years intervened, no matter how many friendships and marriages and relationships came and went in between. It was true, she thought, glancingly: he will always feel the same way about me; and I will always feel the same way about Benjamin; and Benjamin will always feel the same way about Cicely. Twenty years on, and deep down, nothing has changed. Nothing ever changes.

She didn't say any of this. She just smiled when Doug said, "You're looking fabulous, Claire," and answered back: "You're looking great, too. I hear you've joined the aristocracy now. Hanging out with the upper classes obviously agrees with you."

Before he could think of an answer, Doug became aware that the person standing behind Claire wanted to speak to him. He was a tall, slightly diffident-looking man, wearing a navy blue anorak, his hair thinning and greying, perhaps in his late sixties, clinging on to the arm of his wife, who seemed stouter and fitter and more assertive. Doug knew that he should recognize them, but he couldn't put a name to their faces. Claire noticed his uncertainty and turned to make introductions.

"Oh, I'm sorry—you do know each other, don't you? This is Mr. and Mrs. Trotter. Benjamin's mum and dad. We ran into each other just outside the cricket ground."

"Hello, Doug." Colin Trotter shook his hand, then held on to it, having apparently forgotten to let it go. "Doing very well for yourself now, I see. Sheila and I are so pleased. What would your dad have made of all this, I wonder?"

"He would have been glad to see you here, I can tell you that," said Doug, meaning it.

"Well, we had our differences. We all did, in those days. But this is a great factory, that's the truth of the matter. Nobody wants to see it being tossed on the scrapheap like this."

"Are you still working there, Colin?"

"No. I retired four years ago. Not a minute too soon, I have to say. We were sorry to hear about your father, Doug. Very sorry. He never got to enjoy his retirement much, did he?"

"Well, it was quick. He would have hardly known what was happening to him. It's not such a bad way to go."

"How's Irene coping?"

"Battling on. She would have loved to come today, but she's only just had her hip done. I had to come up last week, take her to hospital and all that. We went private in the end."

"Well," said Colin, "there's no point having money, is there, unless you spend it?"

"Seems to be the way things are going," Sheila Trotter added. And then said—perhaps to change the subject—"We thought Benjamin would be with you."

"He should be." Doug looked around, suddenly realizing that he hadn't seen his friend for about fifteen minutes. "He went off to say goodbye to someone, but he said he was coming straight back." He turned to Philip and Carol, and although there was surprise in his voice, it was tinged with a familiar exasperation. "Has anybody seen Benjamin recently?"

Malvina had soon grown bored of the speeches: Benjamin could see that clearly enough. That wasn't why she was here. She had come to be with Paul; partly to make sure that Paul was present, and seen to be present, but also from sheer longing to be in his company. Benjamin hated having to admit such a thing to himself, but there was no avoiding it. And the worst of it was, it didn't seem to change his own feelings for her at all. When she turned to him in the middle of Tony Woodley's speech and said, "I think I'm going to head off," he followed her unthinkingly, and walked with her all the way to the Cannon Hill car park, clearing her path through the jostling crowds. "Don't miss the rest of this," she said to him, at the main gateway. "You should go back and join your friends." He nodded, helpless. He was ashamed of himself, for feeling so drawn to her, but nothing could be done about it. It couldn't be shifted. And Malvina must have sensed it, too, because just before leaving, she said an odd thing, a wonderful thing, something he would never have expected. She said: "You know, Benjamin, whatever happens, however any of this pans out . . . I shall always be glad that I met you. I'll never regret it." Then she kissed him quickly, fiercely on the cheek and darted away, like a fish making a sudden bolt for safer waters. Benjamin watched her disappear.

He began to wander back towards the stage at the far end of the park, where Doug, Phil and Carol had taken up prime position. The speakers' rhetoric had started to sound like meaningless shouting, a barrage of hectoring noise in some language he had long forgotten—although it still seemed to be remembered by the crowd, whose waves of cheering and heckling now felt to him entirely predictable, entirely robotic, a response only to the tone and rhythm of the voices from the stage, not to anything that was being said. He had started out this morning feeling engaged, politicized, and was now consciously slipping into a kind of melancholy inertia: the very opposite of what the rally was hoping to achieve. It wouldn't do. He would have to rejoin them all, go to the pub with them afterwards, talk about how inspiring the day had been and how they could keep its momentum going. Perhaps his parents had shown up by now and they would want to come along too. This was where his obligations lay. This was the sane and proper thing to do.

He walked back through the car park and reached the fringes of the crowd. A hot-dog stall filled the air with the smell of meat and onions, and a white-haired, ruddy-faced man with union jacks emblazoned on his top hat and waistcoat was selling balloons to children. Benjamin watched as two little girls—aged about five and three, at a guess—clutched the strings of their balloons solemnly while their mother wrestled with the lid of a Tupperware lunchbox and took out a little pile of jam sandwiches wrapped in clingfilm.

The five-year-old took her sandwich and bit into it; but her younger sister's co-ordination was not equal to the task. She reached out for a sandwich and in doing so let slip the string attached to her yellow balloon. Instantly it floated up into the air. She looked up and for a moment her face was wiped clean of all expression; then it froze into wide-eyed horror. "*Mum-my,*" she shouted, and made a grab for the string but already it was too high. "*MUMMY!*" she shouted again, and to Benjamin's ears her voice seemed far louder, far more affecting than the guttural ranting coming from the stage. He saw what was happening and ran forward; heard himself calling, "I'll get it, I'll get it!," as if from a great distance, and ran past the girl's mother who was watching him in complete bewilderment, convinced he was a madman. The girl stared after him, too, but he took no notice: his gaze was fixed on the balloon as it drifted determinedly in the direction of the horse chestnut trees towards the edge of the park. It picked up speed and so did he, jostling the tight bunches of demonstrators and catching the shoulder of one woman who shouted after him, "*What the FUCK . . . ?*" Emerging from the crowd into more or less open ground he broke into a sprint, but it was much too late. The yellow balloon rose higher and higher, caught itself briefly on a branch but wrenched itself free, then took flight, spiralling into the grey April sky with innumerable loops and turns until it dwindled and faded, melted slowly into the infinite distance, leaving nothing behind but a yellow dot burned on to the retina and an aching, insupportable sense of loss . . .

Benjamin stumbled back to the mother and her young children and said, struggling for breath: "I couldn't get it. I tried, but it was too fast for me."

"It's all right," the mother said, coldly. "It was only a balloon. I'll get her another one."

He looked at the little girl. Her eyes were filled with tears but she was still staring back at him fixedly; cautious, bewildered.

"I'm sorry," said Benjamin. "I'm really sorry."

And he turned and walked away from the crowd for the last time.

20

—— Original Message ——
From: Malvina
To: Doug Anderton
Sent: Wednesday, April 19, 2000 1:54 a.m.
Subject: Story

Dear Doug

I thought long and hard about sending you this and have finally decided to take my life in my hands.

Please don't read too much into it. It is a piece of *fiction* although of course we all have to write about people we know, and things we've experienced. I had lots of fragments to choose from—have been doing this on and off for about three years now—and couldn't decide what to send so in the end I just chose the most recent thing I've written. I finished it just a couple of weeks ago.

I'm not expecting you to publish it or anything like that. I know you don't have the space or the inclination (or the editorial freedom?). It's just that I would value your opinion, as I have always found you *simpatico* and you are the only person I know who has anything to do with the book world in any shape or form. If you think it's worthless (as you probably will), please just delete it and PLEASE don't show it to anybody else.

Seems ages since the Longbridge rally. Paul sends his regards, and his congratulations on the new job, which he hopes you are enjoying.

Love
Malvina x

——TEXT FOLLOWS——————————————————————————

DEMONSTRATIONS

1.
She loses her way.

She takes the wrong exit out of the station and walks for almost a mile in a mist that turns to dusk.

Her hair is damp, bedraggled. Her stockings cling wetly to her legs.

She left early for this. She could have stayed longer, one of the crowd, listening to the speeches, with the people she is starting to think of as friends, with the man who stares at her longingly, the man she keeps secrets from, the man she feels unimaginably close to.

She does not want to be one of the crowd. That is one of the facts of the matter. There are not many others (facts), she sometimes thinks.

Clouds part. A creamy moon rises. She turns, retraces her steps.

There is a hunger in her, as she walks. It grows stronger, more painful, as she nears the house. She feels this hunger, in his presence. It is a new feeling, for her. It is what draws her back, she supposes, against all her better instincts. Sometimes it is a tightness around her heart, sometimes an emptiness in her stomach, sometimes a sweet nothingness between her legs, aching to be filled. Why it should be him, of all people, who makes her feel this hunger is one of the bigger, better mysteries.

Because they are kindred spirits? Surely not.

2.
It is not a house, it is a barn. Nobody wants to live in houses any more. They want to live in barns, warehouses, mills, churches, schoolrooms, chapels, oasthouses. But especially barns. Houses are not good enough any more, not for these people, not for the people our prosperity has turned us into. As she thinks this, she is obliged to add: I am not distancing myself, not holding myself aloof. We are all in this together. I would like to live here myself.

She would like to live here herself but unfortunately, somebody else seems to have got here first. Goldilocks (with jet-black hair), she bites her lip and gazes at the pictures of his wife, the pictures of his child. The Barbies on the floor and the teddy bears on the bed and the little trampoline out in the garden. And it will amaze her, later tonight (after more wine, and a supper that she will have cooked herself—bouillabaisse, her mother's favorite, heavy on the saffron and the garlic, the one that never fails to pacify her), that he wants her to sleep in his daughter's bed. He wants her to sleep beneath a duvet embroidered with flower fairies, in a room with posters of Tweenies on the wall. In a bed so small that her feet stick out at one end. Perhaps he is a foot fetishist, and intends to come and stroke them in the night. Or perhaps (aha!) he is sulking, because she would not sleep in a bed with him, and this is her punishment. He would never admit as much. He just says, The spare bed mustn't look slept in. That would arouse suspicion.

She thinks it is a little late, personally, for such niceties.

But that is still to come. In the meantime she sips her sour, lemony wine and watches as he squats on all fours and builds a pyramid of wood in the fireplace, then takes a match to it and almost howls with satisfaction as the flames catch and rear on their hind legs, dancing upright in the hearth. A few minutes later, when the fire has already withered, fallen in upon itself, dwindled to a heatless flicker, he will sulk again and blame the dampness of the wood.

3.

Shapeshifting, she splits herself in two. It is a knack she has. One of several.

They sit together on the sofa, six decent inches apart, and cradle their drinks in silence. They have worked—work is her excuse for being here—and now the traitorous time before bed must be filled. She looks at the fire and looks at the rug in front of the fire and knows that he would like her to be lying there, looking up at him. She would like to be lying there too. She would like to be lying there, looking up at him, feeling her veins tingle with the knowledge of the power she has over him, touching his leg with the tip of her stockinged foot, teasing his legs apart, moving her foot upward, up towards his thighs, up towards the weak and pliable heart of him.

And while she is teasing his legs apart and moving her foot upwards, she would look at herself, this other person sitting beside him on the sofa, six decent inches away, and she would say to her: What are you doing here? WHAT IN GOD'S NAME are you doing here? And the woman on the sofa would look down at the woman on the carpet, this wanton, aroused woman, letting her skirt ride up around her thighs, exposing the luminous pallor of her skin, and she would explain:

All my life, it has been my role to look after people. For as long as I can remember. I am twenty years old and I have never been taught how to love people, only how to look after them. That was the role I was assigned by my parents. My parent, I should say. In my short grownup life I have been fucked by two men and shortly after they fucked me they left me because they did not want to be looked after by me. I pissed them off by wanting to look after them but I cannot help it because it's all I know. And in this man I sense a need. A need that I think I can satisfy and I don't think anybody else can. And that is what draws me to him and that is what makes me desire him and I believe that this is the only kind of desire that I know and will ever know.

And the woman on the carpet sits up and she pulls her skirt down primly over her knees and she says:

I think you are a fool.

And she also says:

I think you are looking for a father.

4.

It is early in the morning, maybe half past one, maybe two o'clock. She cannot sleep and his daughter's room feels stuffy so she has opened the window and she's smoking a cigarette, looking out into the night, making fireflies in the dark.

This is a black place. It scares her. Foxes howl in the night, but it is neither city nor country. She has lived in the city and she has lived in the country, she has lived in many different places and even different continents, but this is the place that scares her most. The scattered lights in the distance. The long, indifferent, absolute silence of this Midlands night.

Middle England.

The door hushes open and he stands before her, framed by the doorway, lit from behind by the dimmed landing light. She stubs out the cigarette, turns, walks towards him. She is wearing only a singlet and white cotton panties and although these clothes do not feel at all sexual to her she can tell that he is excited by the sight of her. She can feel his eyes drawn to her tiny breasts and her nipples that are hardened by the cold of the night. He steps forward and puts his hand to her cheek, traces the line of her jaw, the curve of her long neck. She wants to respond, wants to purr and return his caress with her cheek like a voluptuous cat. But something prevents her. She tells him no and he asks her for the fiftieth time Why Not, and all she can say is:

Because I cannot be the person who destroys all this.

And she adds:

It has to be you.

19

Doug read Malvina's story, bleary-eyed, at about 2:30 in the morning, some forty minutes after she had sent it to him. Ranulph had just woken up for the third time and he had carried the grizzling, sleep-hungry infant down to the kitchen, retrieved a bottle of Frankie's expressed milk, and then sat at his desk checking emails while his son sucked noisily at the teat until his eyes closed tight shut and his breathing metamorphosed into the slow, regular ebb and flow of baby-snores. With the child cradled heavily on his left arm, Doug proceeded to carry out a number of laborious, one-handed tasks at the computer. He created a folder called "Trotter" and saved Malvina's story to it. Then he created a blank document called "Malvina notes," saved it to the same folder, and typed a few sentences:

M slept overnight at PT's house, April 1 2000

Feels damaged in some way. Is he taking advantage of someone young and naive and confused?

Relationship = Career-wrecker, at this rate?

After that he could feel himself falling asleep, too. He shut down the computer, carried Ranulph back to his cot, then padded back to his own bedroom, slotted his body lovingly around the curves and corners of Frankie's, and gave the story no more thought for the next few days.

He was still expected at the editorial meetings, but was beginning to wonder, now, whether there was any point in turning up. Usually he was the last person to be invited to speak. Sometimes they ran out of time and the books pages weren't even discussed at all.

Next Tuesday morning, for instance, industrial news was first on the agenda. The editor arrived late, as always, threw himself into his swivel chair and found the usual circle of faces awaiting his attention with varying degrees of nervousness, according to age, experience and temperament. "OK—James," he began. "What have you got for me?"

James Tayler, the new business editor, was eleven years younger than Doug. He was an economics graduate from King's College, Cambridge and had been working at the paper for less than two years.

"Crunch day for Rover," he announced, in his frank, confident way. "Alchemy Partners have got until Friday to finalize their bid. We can expect an announcement that day. I thought we should do a profile of their boss—the man who's going to run Rover, that kind of thing."

"It's a done deal, is it?"

"Looks that way."

The editor never smiled. Very rarely, however, a malicious twinkle would light up his eyes, and it appeared now. "You mean to tell me," he said (not looking at Doug, or even anywhere near him, but somehow making it clear that he was the one being addressed), "that that wonderful, epoch-defining demonstration in Birmingham has not made the slightest bit of difference?"

"Apparently not," said James.

"What's the matter, don't they read the *Evening Mail* over in Munich? We even put something on our front page, didn't we? Remind me, somebody—who was it who wrote that piece?"

There was embarrassed silence around the table; a few half-hearted giggles.

"There's a rival bid," Doug pointed out, quietly.

The editor turned to him. "Excuse me?"

"It's not a done deal yet. There's a rival bid on the table."

Feigning shock, the editor asked: "Did you know about this, James? Surely you must have heard, if the news has even reached our correspondent from the world of *belles lettres*."

"Yes," James conceded, "there's a group of local businessmen, calling themselves the Phoenix Consortium. They reckon they can keep the firm going as a mass producer. Pretty heavyweight bunch, actually. Headed up by John Towers, who used to be Rover's chief executive."

"So we should take them seriously?"

He shook his head. "It's not going to happen. They haven't had enough time to prepare their bid, they haven't had proper access to BMW's books. And at the end of the day they probably haven't got enough money."

"Stephen Byers supports them," Doug said.

The editor swivelled again. "Pardon?"

"The Secretary of State for Trade and Industry supports them. Rumour has it."

"That's true," said James. "But Blair's made it clear that they're not going to get any help." He consulted his notes. "Monday April the third, quote: 'If governments in the past, of both major political parties, have been drawn towards "rescuing" a company in difficulties, we see our role now as helping to equip people and business for the new economy, as encouraging innovation and entrepreneurship, as improving education and training and as broadening access to new technology.'"

"The usual New Labour bollocks, in other words," said the editor. "Which translated into English means Fuck off, No cash. Good. So Alchemy has it, and we run this week with a profile of their boss."

"I wouldn't be too sure—" Doug began.

"Douglas, let's break with tradition and do your pages next, shall we? I don't want to detain you any longer than necessary. You have hotly awaited contemporary novels arriving by every post, I imagine. What are you leading with this week?"

Doug took a deep breath, trying to calm himself. He was beginning to feel in the mood for some physical violence. He knew that his time was up, that he couldn't tolerate this any more, that he would only be here for a few more days. But it was the end of an eight-year working relationship and he was going to do it properly, with dignity. He would get through this meeting, leave the building and then consider his options.

"Michael Foot," he said, with perfect composure. "Michael Foot on Jonathan Swift."

The editor was staring at him blankly.

"Eighteenth-century writer," Doug explained. "*Gulliver's Travels.*"

"That's going back a bit, isn't it?"

"It's a timeless classic."

"No, I mean back to the days of Michael Foot. *Michael Foot?* He was *born* in the fucking eighteenth century, wasn't he? He could barely stand up when he was leader of the Labor party, and that was twenty fucking years ago! What the fuck are we doing on the music pages this week—the rise of skiffle? *Michael Foot?* You've got to be taking the piss. What else have you got?"

"There's a biography of Francis Piper. I'm waiting for the review to come in."

"Never heard of him. Or her. Tell me she's a woman. Tell me she's still in her twenties and drop-dead gorgeous and we can run a half-page picture."

"Poet. Male. Dead. White. Generally considered to be pretty good."

"'Generally considered to be pretty good.' Now there's a headline we can use. Let's add fifty thousand to the print run this week, shall we? Who's reviewing it?"

"Benjamin Trotter."

"Never heard of him."

"Paul Trotter's brother."

The editor began to speak, then thought better of it. He picked up a pen and sucked on it for a moment or two. Finally he said: "You know, Doug, just for a minute there, I thought you were telling me something useful. I thought you were going to tell me that *Paul* Trotter had written something for you. Now *that* would have been interesting. We've all heard of Paul Trotter. We've seen him on the television, we've heard him on the radio. He's young, he's sexy, he's got a buzz around him. He's *news*. Can I just run a little concept past you? Paul Trotter's *brother*—" (he smiled his politest, most dangerous smile) "—is not news. On the other arts pages this week, we will not be reviewing a show by Damien Hirst's sister. We will not be reviewing any films directed by Quentin Tarantino's aunt. The news pages will not be dominated by Gordon Brown's nephew's views on the British economy. Do you get the picture?" His voice rose almost to a shout: "We want public figures in this newspaper. We want well-known people, not their family members. OK?"

Doug stood up, gathered the few pieces of paper he had brought with him, and said: "I know them both. Benjamin's one of the cleverest and most talented people I've ever met and it just so happens that he's never had a break in his life. Paul Trotter is a nonentity. A famous nonentity, admittedly, but if the people who voted for him knew what his real opinions were he wouldn't even be that for long. And Jonathan Swift is one of the greatest writers in the language and Michael Foot knows more about him than almost anybody so as far as I'm concerned that piece is *news*. And believe it or not, that also happens to be the kind of news *your* readers are interested in: not the news that some pubescent pop singer's got herself up the duff or Paul Trotter might be shagging his assistant."

And suddenly, all the eyes that had been averted from Doug were upon him at once, from every direction.

"I didn't say that," he backtracked, after a stunned pause.

"What did you just say?" the editor asked.

"I didn't say it."

"Did you just say that Paul Trotter was shagging his assistant?"

"No."

The editor swivelled in his chair and looked straight at his chief political correspondent.

"Laura, does Paul Trotter have an assistant?"

"He has a media adviser."

"Have you met her?"

"Yes."

"Is she young? Is she pretty?"

"Yes."

"Find out if he's shagging her."

"OK."

"Excellent. Douglas," said the editor, swivelling back, "you've just made my day."

But Doug was no longer there to receive the compliment.

It turned out, rather to his surprise, that Malvina was a near-neighbor. He phoned her that afternoon and while they were trying to think of a suitable place to meet for a drink, she revealed that she lived in Pimlico, not much more than a mile from his house in Chelsea. How could a student afford to live in an area like that? Everything he found out about Malvina, it seemed, just piqued his curiosity even further. They agreed to meet that evening, anyway, in the basement of the Oriel café on Sloane Square. All he told her was that he wanted to discuss her story; he didn't want to give any more specific reasons for the meeting. Indeed, Doug himself wasn't entirely sure what they were.

He arrived early, and ordered a double whisky to supplement the six or seven he'd already had that afternoon. Not that he was drunk, or anywhere close. Nobody had ever seen him drunk. He didn't get drunk, and he didn't get hangovers. Never had; not even as a schoolboy. Although alcohol did loosen his tongue, and made him bolder in conversation than he might normally have been.

"I have to ask you," he said, almost before Malvina had had a chance to take off her coat. "Why did you send me that story? What on earth possessed you?"

At which words her face, long and thin and somewhat melancholy at the best of times, was suddenly all dejection.

"Was it really that bad?" she asked. "Is that what you think?"

"Look, Malvina: I know fuck all about writing. I'm only doing this job because it seems to be the editor's way of punishing me. I'm not talking about the style, the way you wrote it. I'm talking about the content. It was so . . . revelatory."

"It was a story. I made it up." But she could see at once that he didn't believe her. "Anyway, isn't writing meant to be revelatory? Aren't you meant to be expressing yourself? Otherwise, what's the point?"

"The point is that I'm a journalist. If you're having an affair with Paul, I should be the last person you tell about it."

"But I'm not," she protested.

"Yeah—well, we'll come on to that." He watched as she screwed up her face at the tartness of her drink. She had chosen to join him in a whisky. "Did anyone from the paper phone you this afternoon?"

"Yes."

"Who? Laura?"

"How did you know? She's a nice woman, I've had dealings with her before."

"What did she want?"

"Rather like you, she wanted to meet for a mysterious drink. I'm seeing her tomorrow."

"Uh-huh." He put his face in his hands, unable to think, for a moment, how he was going to handle this. The direct approach seemed the only way. "Malvina—there are rumors going around about you and Paul. That's why she wants to see you."

"Oh." She paused in mid-sip, put her glass down. "Shit."

"Shit. Exactly."

"How did that happen?"

Even with the whisky inside him, Doug found that he couldn't bring himself to admit the part he had played. "Are you surprised?" was all he said. "Journalists have got a radar for this kind of thing. You've raised Paul's profile—very successfully, it has to be said. Unfortunately, there's a pay-off for that. People start . . . ferreting around."

"But we're not having an affair."

"You slept at his house. You slept there while his wife and daughter were away, when they didn't know anything about it."

"*Slept. Slept* being the operative word. We haven't done anything wrong."

"Oh, come on . . ."

He left her with a look of reproach and went to get two more drinks.

Malvina couldn't hold her alcohol the way that he could. After a few more glasses, her speech was starting to slur and she was staring dully past him, somewhere into the middle distance, unseeing. Her chin was cupped in one hand and she had a cigarette in the other. The noise of the partying Sloanes all around them was now so great that they were almost having to shout to make themselves heard. The only alternative, when they wanted to talk, was to sit forward and lean in to each other, affecting a kind of lovers' intimacy. Which is what they found themselves doing.

"How did it all start, anyway?" Doug asked her. "How did you end up as his media adviser, at your age?"

"It's all a joke," said Malvina. (Though not a very funny one, judging from her tone of voice.) "It's all a terrible mistake. What's that song? 'This Wasn't Supposed to Happen.' Who was that, Björk? That's what it's like, anyway. None of this was supposed to happen. And I'm not his 'media adviser.' He shouldn't be paying me a penny. I got him on to one quiz show, because I happened to know some sleazebag producer. The rest has just been common sense."

"Well, that's a pretty precious commodity, as far as Paul's concerned. He certainly hasn't got any of his own. How did it start, though? How did you meet him?"

"Through Benjamin." She took a drag on the cigarette, rubbed one tired eye with her thumb. "I was staying . . . I was going up to Birmingham . . . pretty regularly . . . staying with friends. I started going to the café in Waterstone's and I kept seeing him there and in the end . . . we just got talking. We started talking about books, and then he told me about this thing he's writing, and I told him about the stuff I write, and . . . He just mentioned one day who his brother was, and . . . I'd seen Paul's picture in the paper, or something . . . seen him on the TV, and . . . I suppose I fancied him a bit even then, already . . . And Benjamin . . . Benjamin kept trying to do things for me . . . *keeps* trying, actually . . . He thinks that if he helps me, he'll . . . Well, I don't know what he thinks. Benjamin seems to be going through a little . . . crisis . . . all of his own."

"Benjamin's in love with another woman. Has been, sadly, all his married life. Someone he knew at school."

Malvina's eyes came into focus and she looked directly at Doug, as if this was the first truly interesting thing he'd said all night. "He told you that? He told me that as well."

"Well, it's no secret, unfortunately. Benjamin was on the rebound when he married Emily. In fact he's still on the rebound. He'll be on the rebound when he's seventy, the poor bastard. If he ever gets that far without topping himself." He smiled, mirthlessly, knowing at once that he shouldn't have said this. "Go on."

"So, he offers to introduce me to his brother . . . as some kind of favour. I don't think I even asked him to do that for me. Though I liked the idea, as soon as I heard it. It was to help with my dissertation . . . which I'm still trying to write. Didn't help at all, as it happened. It's held me up, if anything . . . Anyway, so then Paul and I meet, and . . . *bingo* . . ."

She smiled a loopy, embarrassed, what-can-you-do sort of smile. Doug couldn't quite return it.

"I suppose," said Malvina, working herself up to a seismic declaration, "I suppose I'm in love with him."

"Shit."

"Shit. Again. That's turning out to be a pretty useful word tonight, isn't it?" She appeared to have shocked Doug into temporary silence. "I don't suppose you think much of my taste."

"Hey," he said. "Everybody's got to love somebody. The heart has its reasons, et cetera, et cetera. And I suppose he's not bad looking."

"Yeah, but . . . none of you like him, really. Admit it."

"I don't like his politics, that's all. And I think he's allowed himself to become dishonest, because of this . . . weird situation we've got ourselves into in this country at the moment."

"What do you mean?"

"I mean if the public ever got to hear what he really thinks—well, they'd realize. Because most of them still believe that they've voted in a left-wing party. Whereas really they've just voted for another five years of Thatcherism. Ten years. Fifteen, even." He laughed quietly at the irony of it, which seemed to pass Malvina by. "Anyway, that's why he never knows what to say when someone puts a microphone in front of his nose. And that's why he needs you. He does. You've transformed him. Turned him around."

"Oh, he *needs* me all right. He needs my . . . *services.* And he's desperate to sleep with me, into the bargain. But that's not what I want."

"You want a hell of a lot, actually, don't you?"

Malvina tried to drink from her glass, not noticing that it was empty. "That woman's not good for him. Not right for him. Don't you agree?"

They looked at each other for a few silent seconds.

"I don't have an opinion about that," said Doug. "And I don't think you should, either."

He tried to read the expression in her eyes, which seemed blank. Her eyelids were drooping. Then, all at once, he saw tears welling up, and Malvina was quivering with sobs.

"I'm so fucked," she kept repeating. "I'm so fucked."

"Malvina . . ."

"You're right. I shouldn't have shown you that story. It was a stupid thing to do."

"Never mind about the story. The story's . . ."

"Get me another drink."

"I don't think that's a good idea."

"One more. Please. Then I'll go home."

He sighed, and said, against his better judgment: "One more. A single."

"Thank you. I'm going to pull myself together now." She took a Kleenex from her handbag, and started dabbing at her eyes and the running mascara.

Doug returned with two more drinks.

"Where are your parents?" he asked.

"My parents? What have they got to do with anything?"

"Maybe you should go home for a bit. Have a break from Paul. Do a bit of thinking."

"I am having a break from him. We've hardly seen each other in the last couple of weeks."

"Still. You could probably do with some home comforts."

Briskly, Malvina said: "One: where my parents live—or rather, where my mother lives, with her fifth or sixth or ninety-seventh or whatever the fuck it is partner—is not my home. Two: there's nothing comfortable about it."

"Where are they?"

"Sardinia. He runs a hotel there. Five stars—the kind of place movie stars stay. We were staying there ourselves, in fact. That's where she met him."

"Can't you afford the air fare to get out there?"

"Oh, I dare say he'd pay for that, if necessary. It's his flat—*one* of his flats, I should say—that I'm living in these days, after all. But I'm not going. No fucking way."

"What about your dad—your real dad?"

Malvina shook her head. "Never met him. All I know about him is what my mother told me. He worked in the theatre: he was a set designer. Complete genius, according to her. They split up even before I was born and then she heard he died of AIDS, some time in the eighties." Already she had finished the latest whisky. She gave the empty glass a puzzled sort of look, as if she couldn't remember drinking it. "Why am I getting through this stuff so much quicker than you? Are you one of those men who pretends to be drinking but really he's just waiting for the woman to get pissed so he can take advantage of her?"

"I'm not the one who's taking advantage of you."

She looked at him sharply and he thought, at first, that she was going to start crying again. Instead she slumped across the table and rested her head on his shoulder. He had no idea whether she was being flirtatious or was simply exhausted.

"Malvina . . ." he said. "What do you think you're doing?"

"That," she murmured, forming each word with a drunkard's care, "is the fifty—million—dollar—question."

"OK. I'm going to take you home now."

"Good. You're a gentleman. There are very few of them left."

He stood up with some difficulty while Malvina continued to lean heavily against him. He grabbed both their coats and then, with his arm around her narrow, almost skeletal shoulders, he did his best to propel her up the stairs. She stumbled at the top and fell flat on her face. Doug picked her up and dusted her down, muttering apologies to the other drinkers and diners and praying that none of his wife's friends were there that night.

Outside, mercifully, he was able to find a taxi within seconds.

"Pimlico," he told the driver, and once they were sitting inside he managed to prompt Malvina into whispering the full address in his ear.

It was only a five-minute journey. As they climbed out of the taxi Doug looked around to see if the place was being staked out by any journalists: but no, they didn't seem to have reached that stage yet. He paid the driver and gave him an outrageous tip, then draped the now semi-conscious Malvina in her coat and fumbled through the pockets for her keys.

She lived, as he had expected, in a portered and well-heeled mansion block. Doug did his best to avoid the porter's curious eye as he guided her past the desk and towards the stairs. The porter called, "Goodnight, miss!" as they started climbing the first flight, but Malvina didn't answer.

The flat's main room was decorated neutrally, expensively, with only a few of her own books, and some teetering piles of newspapers and magazines, to indicate that they were anywhere other than some bland intercontinental hotel. Malvina was saying nothing by now so Doug had to guess for himself where the bedroom was. It was much smaller, more homely and chaotic. A desk in the corner was submerged beneath papers, floppy disks and a laptop which was still switched on: multicolored cartoon fish were criss-crossing the screen in random formations, with bubbly sound effects.

"You should drink some water," Doug told her, but in an unannounced and surprisingly violent movement Malvina withdrew her arms from around his neck and threw herself on to the bed. Her eyes were firmly shut and she closed herself into a foetal ball and that was that. She was out for the night.

18

For the next few days, Doug and Frankie had guests at their house.

Malvina phoned him the next morning, to apologize for her behaviour and to thank him for looking after her so kindly. He repeated his suggestion that she should go and stay with someone for a while: what about her friends in Birmingham, for instance? She told him that they didn't live there any more: they had left the country. There was no one, really no one, she felt she could impose upon. So Doug invited her to stay with them. She arrived with a small holdall and stayed for two nights, spending most of the time in the kitchen sipping hot coffee, and watching Ranulph and Coriander wreak their infant havoc. She talked a lot to Irina and the other, more transient members of the Gifford-Anderton staff; less to Doug and Frankie themselves. On the afternoon of Thursday, April 27th, learning that Doug's mother Irene was coming down for the weekend and would ideally like to sleep in her bedroom, she thanked them fulsomely, presented them with a beribboned cellophane package containing twelve absurdly expensive cardamom-scented chocolates from a local shop, and left. She seemed in good spirits. She had not mentioned Paul throughout the whole of her stay.

Doug met his mother at Euston station on the Friday afternoon. It was four weeks since her hip operation and she was determined to show that she could be mobile again. Normally they would have taken the tube back to Chelsea but this time Doug insisted on getting a taxi and she kept a shocked eye on the meter, wincing with alarm every time another pound was clocked up.

"Seventeen pounds!" she repeated, over and over, as Doug carried her case up the garden path. "I used to get a week's family meals out of that when you were at school!"

The preposterous expense of living in this part of London remained, as always, a recurring theme of the weekend. All of the pubs where the elderly locals used to go and drink in familiar surroundings had been tarted up over the last few years, dividing walls smashed down and their interiors turned into vast open-plan spaces where young stockbrokers and estate agents could drink imported Dutch and Belgian beers at four pounds a pint. It was no use taking her to one of those. There remained a handful of unpretentious cafés scattered around the area, serving fry-ups and mugs of instant coffee; but Irene could still surprise him, sometimes, with a sprightly appetite for new experiences, and when she saw that a branch of Starbucks had recently opened on the King's Road, she asked if they could give it a try.

It was Saturday afternoon, one day after a strange and unexpected development in the Longbridge saga: the day before, flying in the face of all predictions (including James Tayler's) Alchemy Partners, without any forewarning or explanation, had pulled out of its negotiations to buy the troubled Rover group from BMW. Workers and campaigners, who had opposed the Alchemy bid from the start, had been jubilant when the news broke: there had been riotous celebrations outside Longbridge's Q gate on the Friday afternoon. Already, however, a new mood of uncertainty had settled in; it was by no means clear that the rival proposals from Phoenix were being taken seriously; and that was now the only other bid on the table. The alternative was simple, and terrifying: outright closure.

There were free copies of some of the day's newspapers scattered around the café, and while Doug queued at the counter, his mother picked up *The Sun* and scowled over its business pages.

"Disgusting rag," she said, tossing it over to her son as he handed her a mug that was almost too big for her to hold. She gazed at the drink in stupefaction. "What's this?"

"It's a tall latte," Doug explained.

"Didn't they have any coffee?"

He smiled and started reading the *Sun*'s article.

Fifty thousand jobs were doomed last night as all hope of rescuing car firm Rover vanished. In a day of industrial disaster for Britain, the Alchemy group **SCRAPPED** its deal to take over the company from BMW.

> Workers **CHEERED** as the news broke—because they believed the rival Phoenix bid for the firm would resurface, saving more jobs than the Alchemy plan. *But last night the cheers had turned to tears as the bleak reality sank in at thousands of Midlands homes—there will be* **NO** *Rover rescue and many families are set to face life on the dole.*

"What right," Irene was saying, indignantly, "what right have they got to publish something like that? Nobody knows what's going to happen. What are people's families going to feel when they read that this morning? They have *no right* to say it." She took the paper back from him and flicked through its front pages, tutting over everything, especially the Page Three girl. "This used to be a socialist paper," she said. "Until Murdoch got his hands on it. Look at it. It's a disgrace. Soft pornography and . . . tittle-tattle."

"Spirit of the times, Mum. Spirit of the times."

"Yes, but you don't write stuff like that, do you? Nobody *has* to write it."

Doug thought for a moment, then drew closer to her and said: "Can I ask you something, Mum?"

"Of course you can."

"The thing is—well, I've found something out. Something about a Member of Parliament."

"Yes?"

"It's to do with his marriage, and sex, and . . . you know, the usual sort of stuff."

"Yes, I know."

"I'm not sure if it's big enough to finish off his career—maybe it isn't—but it would certainly do a lot of damage. What do you think I should do?"

Irene said, without hesitation: "Politicians should be judged on their politics. Anything else is just gossip and nonsense." She pointed at the newspaper lying on the table between them. "You don't want to end up like them, do you?"

"Of course not."

"Anyway. People can be weak, in their personal lives. Especially men. It makes no difference." Matter-of-factly, she added: "Your father was no saint."

Doug was amazed. He had never heard her say anything like this before. "What do you mean?"

Irene weighed her words carefully, her fragile hands cradling the enormous coffee mug. "I had a lot to forgive him for. But he was a good man. He had strong principles, and he stuck to most of them. Nobody sticks to them all." She looked around her and said, brightly: "After all, as socialists, we shouldn't really be drinking in a place like this, should we? Isn't globalization meant to be the new enemy?"

"Apparently," said Doug. "It's May Day on Monday. There are going to be demonstrations all over London. They'll probably be targeting this place."

"There you are, you see: the people are on the move again. It was bound to happen, sooner or later. Will you be joining in?"

"Maybe." He smiled and leaned across to her, squeezing her hand. It lightened his heart to see her looking so well. "How's your coffee, anyway?"

"Delicious. How much did it cost?" And when Doug told her, she said: "I hope they put a big brick through the window."

In the event, it was not Starbucks that came under attack from the protesters on Monday, but McDonald's: a small branch in Whitehall (a branch that was closed for the day) next to a *bureau de change* which was also smashed up and looted. Until then, the demonstration had been relatively peaceful: although the sight that greeted Doug when he jumped off the bus near Parliament Square was certainly bizarre.

It was not long after midday, and the Square had been taken over by about one thousand protesters. Drums were pounding, people were sitting up trees, and a statue of Winston Churchill had now been augmented by an upturned policeman's hat with a geranium planted in it. As for the Square itself, people had started digging it up, tossing the turf on to the road and embarking upon an impromptu gardening session which involved planting everything from lemon balm and rosemary to sunflower and rhubarb. Doug stood and watched for a while, thinking back to the rally for Longbridge just over a month ago and reflecting that what was happening here was very different in spirit. He moved on when he saw that a maypole was being raised into position and dancing had begun.

He had arranged to meet Paul in the members' lobby at 12:30, but in fact he didn't have to walk that far. He caught sight of him standing on the Green—the ritual gathering-point for representatives of the media who wanted to waylay any passing MPs and solicit their views—sounding off about the May Day protests to a couple of cameramen from Sky News and BBC News 24. Doug hovered in the background until the interview was over (it only took a couple of minutes) and then attracted Paul's attention with a wave.

"Been giving them the benefit of your wisdom, have you?" he asked, as they struck off on foot in the direction of Downing Street, dodging the swelling groups of anarchists, environmentalists and riot police gearing themselves up for a skirmish. "Come on, then: what was your line this time?"

"I told them that these people weren't to be taken seriously. If they want to contribute to the political process, then they have to renounce violence and they have to work within the existing structures."

"Brilliant, as always," said Doug, "except for the tiny fact that *you're* the people who've shut them out of the existing structures in the first place."

"What on earth do you mean?"

"I mean that the entire system nowadays is only geared to accommodating a tiny minority of political opinion. The left's moved way over to the right, the right's moved a tiny bit to the left, the circle's been closed and everyone else can go fuck themselves."

"Just from your vocabulary, Douglas, I can tell that you're mired in the past," said Paul, as they cut down Horseguards Avenue, and into Whitehall Place. "That's your basic problem—mired in the past. As I seem to remember telling you more than twenty years ago, one bonfire night if I'm not mistaken. Where are we going, anyway?"

Doug took him to a vaulted, subterranean wine bar called Gordon's on Villiers Street. It was a narrow, tunnel-like space where neither of them could stand up straight as they made their way to a table: Doug explained that this was once a riverfront warehouse, and they were sitting in one of the vaults where the Thames barges would have come in.

"Very intimate, anyway," said Paul, approvingly. He had not known about this place before, and had already got it marked down as somewhere he could safely bring Malvina.

"Well, I didn't want us to be overheard," said Doug. "I wanted to talk to you about something private. Some*one*, I should say."

Paul looked at him evenly. "Go on."

"I think you probably know who I mean."

"Probably," said Paul. "What about her?"

"Well . . ." Doug swilled his orange juice around in his glass. He had decided to stay completely sober for the purposes of this conversation. "I think you should . . . consider . . . very carefully . . . where you're going on this one, in terms of both your . . . working and personal relationship."

"OK." Paul mulled these words over, and confessed: "I don't understand that. What exactly are you trying to say?"

Doug didn't know exactly what he was trying to say, in all honesty. Having considered, carefully and at some length, what he was hoping to achieve by meeting Paul this afternoon, he had come to only one conclusion: for both Malvina's and Susan's sake, he wanted to provoke Paul into taking some action, initiating some change. And the only way he could get him to do that, as far as he could see, was by scaring him.

"Paul," he said. "I've got good news, and bad news. I went out with Malvina last week and after she'd had a few drinks she started talking to me about her feelings for you and she said . . . Well, she told me that she loved you."

"Fuck." Paul gulped down half the contents of his wine glass. "OK. Fine." He had gone pale. "That's bad—I mean, that is *seriously* bad—but thank you for telling me. I'm . . . very grateful."

"As it happens," said Doug, "that's the good news."

Paul's eyes began to flicker with anger and panic. "Are you taking the piss? How can that be the good news?"

"She's a very attractive woman. Beautiful, you might even say. Very intelligent. Nice disposition, from what I've seen. Any man would be proud to have a woman like that fall in love with him."

"But I'm *married*, for Christ's sake. I've got a daughter."

"Arguably, Paul, you should have thought about that before you started doing things like inviting her to spend the night at your family home."

Even though Doug was speaking quietly, almost in a whisper, Paul instinctively looked around to check that no one could have heard.

"How the fuck do you know about that?"

"That," said Doug, "brings me on to the bad news. I was at an editorial meeting last week and your name came up and it looks as though there are people on the paper—probably other papers as well—who've started to get interested in you and Malvina."

"Shit," said Paul, paling still further. "Shit shit *shit*. How much do they know?"

Doug changed the subject abruptly. "How's your relationship with Tony, these days? Close? Polite but cordial? Indifferent?"

"Just come out with it, Anderton. Just tell me what you're driving at."

"I was only thinking that political parties, and prime ministers, react to these kinds of situations quite differently. Some people are considered indispensable, for instance, and even when they've disgraced themselves, party leaders will stand by them through thick and thin. Others are—well, more dispensable, to put it bluntly. I was just trying to work out which category you fit into."

"I haven't *disgraced* myself."

"Well, that all depends on how it's presented in the media, nowadays, doesn't it? Everything seems to depend on that."

Paul ignored his enigmatic teasing, for the time being, and mused aloud: "Tony likes me. I'm pretty confident of that. Always smiles at me in the corridor or the tea-room. And he sent me a very nice note after the question I asked a few weeks ago."

"The one about British chocolate and the European union?"

"Yes."

"Well, that's good, Paul, but I wouldn't say that you've quite put yourself into the 'indispensable' bracket yet. Not only is it widely known, these days, that you and your minister don't get on—" (Paul started to deny this, but Doug kept talking) "—but even apart from that, one profoundly unmemorable appearance on a TV quiz show, a short-lived column on cycling for a freebie newspaper and a blatant piece of public arse-licking disguised as a question about cocoa solids isn't going to do the trick, I'm afraid. If any of this comes out, you may be for the chop."

"I'm a rising star, though. It said so last week in the *Independent*."

"Words, words, words," said Doug, dismissively. "Words mean fuck all in a scenario like this. People are still judged by their actions, just about: which is the only thing that gives me any hope, actually. Anyway . . ." He was starting to feel almost sorry for Paul, who already had the look of a condemned man. "What I was going to suggest—which I'm sure will appeal to a man as firmly attached to traditional values as yourself—was a good old-fashioned piece of blackmail. Are you up for it?"

Paul eyed him warily, although there were also traces of relief on his face. "What's your price?"

"Well, I've no intention of spending any more time on the books pages, thank you very much, so in a few days' time I'm going to start offering my services to other newspapers as a political editor. And if I can offer them this story as part of the package, then I reckon they're not going to be able to resist."

"You'd do that, would you?" said Paul, his voice pulsing with contempt. "You'd sink to that level? Common . . . *decency* means that little to you?"

"Ah—now I'm glad you've brought up the subject of decency. Because, actually, that unassuming, much-maligned little word means a lot to me.

Which is why I'm prepared to keep this whole thing to myself. On condition that *you*, Paul, do the decent thing."

"Meaning?"

"Meaning that you put Malvina out of her misery. And Susan, while you're about it. I mean, I don't *know* that Susan's miserable too, but I would have thought it was a fair guess."

This was not at all what Paul had been expecting to hear. "How am I supposed to do that?"

"Up to you."

"You think I should break it off with her?"

"That's one option. Probably the best option. What would *you* like to happen, Paul? What are your . . . feelings in this matter?"

Paul drained the last of his wine, rested his chin in his hands and stared thoughtfully ahead of him. Now that Doug had posed this question, it seemed ridiculous that he had never tried to answer it before. He had been content for the relationship with Malvina to proceed as it did, unresolved, directionless; little more, really, than a titillating adjunct to his marriage, one which didn't impinge on his work or disrupt his career in any drastic way. Even the lack of sex, he realized now, had been part of the attraction: it had stopped things from ever getting too intense, too real. How was he supposed to know that Malvina, meanwhile, had been starting to take it all so seriously?

"I'm not sure," he said at last, mutedly. "I'm going to have to think about this for a little while."

"She's in love with you, Paul: that's all I'm saying. Do something about it. Fix the problem. The message I'm picking up from her at the moment is that she's had a pretty shitty life. She's looking to you for a way out, into something better. Don't become one more thing that she has to survive."

Paul stood up. He felt suddenly claustrophobic. "OK. Point taken, Doug. I'll do something about it." He reached for his overcoat. "Can we get out of here, now? I could do with some fresh air."

"I'm giving you two weeks. After that I go public."

Paul thought about this, weighed up his options. "That's fair," he said, and made for the staircase.

They walked together up towards the Strand. Doug wondered what Paul was thinking. He had just presented him with a potentially momentous decision: either he was engaged in profound contemplation, or the implications of it hadn't sunk in yet, or there really was an emotional vacuum where his heart should have been. Could anyone be that unfeeling?

In the time they had been sitting in Gordon's, the demonstration had clearly moved on. All the roads into Trafalgar Square were now blocked by rows of riot police. There seemed to be several thousand protesters hemmed into the square, with no apparent means of exit. Elsewhere, gangs of protesters ran through the streets, dodging the police batons and shouting abuse at anyone who got in their way. Small-scale fights and scuffles were breaking out all over the place. There were rancorous arguments taking place between the environmentally minded protesters and the more confrontational ones. "Plant your fucking veggies, fucking hippies, see what good that'll do," Doug heard somebody shouting.

"What sort of country are we living in?" Paul muttered bitterly, as they surveyed the mayhem from the relative safety of a shop doorway. "Who *are* these people? What do they want?"

"They probably don't know. Nor do you, it would seem. Nor do any of us, when it comes to the crunch."

"The *Guardian* have given me a slot on their op-ed page this Friday. Twelve hundred words, about anything I want. I'm going to write about this. Say what a disgrace it is. That ought to go down well, don't you think?"

"With your constituents? What do they care? They're a hundred miles away."

"No: I meant with Tony."

Doug turned to him and said, with some impatience: "Paul, just because I've let you off the hook, it doesn't mean that other people are going to. I told you, something about this business with you and Malvina is going to come out in the next week or two. It won't be much—it'll just be some offhand, anonymous comment in a gossip column or something—but after that it's going to be out there, and it's going to snowball, and you're going to have to deal with it. And sucking up to Tony isn't going to be enough. I told you—only the indispensable survive this kind of thing."

"You keep saying that," Paul protested. "I can hardly make myself indispensable in a week or two, can I?"

"No. Of course not," said Doug; and decided not to labour the point any more. "Write something about Longbridge, anyway. Your silence on that subject has been positively deafening. It's more than a local issue, you know. Fifty thousand people's lives are hanging in the balance."

Paul nodded: "Maybe I will," he said, without much obvious conviction. At which point, a wine bottle was hurled forcefully in their direction, shattering against the shop door just above their heads, and they made a run for it.

. . .

Back in his Kennington flat, Paul sat in an armchair, quite unmoving, for several hours.

When the daylight faded he sat in the dark. He sat in the dark and thought about Susan, and how she would react when the story started to leak out.

He thought about Malvina, too, how thoroughly he had come to depend on her. How fond of her he had grown, in the last few weeks. More than fond, in fact. Much more.

These thoughts were only interrupted by the periodic ringing of the telephone. There were messages from all the usual people: his minister, journalists, lobbyists, Susan, his friend Ronald Culpepper, the Whips. In the middle of these came a call from Benjamin, which was fairly unusual. But Paul still didn't pick up the phone.

At ten o'clock he turned the lights on and phoned for a pizza. He ate about half, threw the rest away, and drank most of a bottle of Chablis to wash it down. All at once he felt incredibly tired. He stripped off down to his underpants and sat on the bed, running his hands through his hair.

He got into bed and was about to turn off the light when he suddenly asked himself: "Why did my brother phone?"

He went to the answering machine, scrolled without curiosity through the first nine messages, and then heard Benjamin's voice.

"Hi Paul, it's big brother here. I was just calling to . . . well, to find out how you were, and also to ask if you'd seen the *Telegraph* today. Have a look at the picture on page seven. If you don't recognize the face, read the caption underneath. Might jog a memory or two, you never know. Small world, isn't it? Take care, and send my . . . send my best to Malvina."

Paul could scarcely be bothered to go into the kitchen and look at his unread copy of the *Telegraph*. What arcane fragment of their shared history was his nostalgia-prone brother getting excited about now? Some long-forgotten schoolfriend, maybe. Some relative last glimpsed at a dismal family Christmas party . . .

Reluctantly, annoyed that he was falling for this one, Paul opened the paper at page seven, saw the picture, and indeed—just as his brother had predicted—failed to recognize the face. At first, he didn't even know which face he was supposed to be recognizing. There were four men in business suits, standing outside the main offices of BMW in Munich. None of them looked remotely familiar.

Then he read the caption; and when he saw one of the names, he stared again at the photograph in wonder. Could that be him? That balding man of about forty, holding a pipe, with a thick, well-trimmed beard and a clearly discernible paunch?

The caption identified him as Rolf Baumann, and gave his job description as "Head of Corporate Strategy, BMW."

Paul took the newspaper into his sitting room, collapsed back into the armchair where he had already sat for so many hours that day, and let a tidal wave of remembrance break over him. That holiday in Denmark—the only foreign holiday his parents had ever taken them on . . . The beach house at Gammel Skagen . . . The two feral Danish boys, Jorgen and Stefan . . . The two ungainly sisters Ulrike and Ursula, and clumsy, floundering Rolf, who had almost drowned trying to swim out to sea at the point where the waters collided . . .

And then, feeling that he, too, was almost about to drown in this whirlpool of memory, Paul resurfaced blinkingly into the present as the full meaning of tonight's discovery broke upon him. Rolf was a powerful man, now. He sat on the board of BMW—the same firm where his father Gunther used to work. BMW was on the point of selling Rover. The destiny of the Longbridge factory lay in its hands.

And it was here: it was Paul's for the taking. He had found a way to make himself indispensable, and not even in a week or two: it could be done in a matter of days. Salvation—his own salvation—was waiting for him at the other end of a telephone line.

It was time to call in a twenty-three-year-old favour.

17

Finally, it felt to Paul as though he were driving through a lunar landscape. Sandy flatness stretched out on either side of him. The intervals between the trim, unassuming villages became longer and longer. He passed a sign saying that Skagen itself was only seven kilometres away.

It was getting on for six o'clock in the evening: but there were still many hours of daylight left, and the sky was an extraordinary, pellucid grey-blue. It was this light, this gentle but somehow overpowering light that he remembered best, better than the dunes and the low-roofed houses painted fawn and lemon-yellow. He knew that it was created, in part, by the reflection of sunlight off the waters of the two seas that rushed together at the tip of the peninsula. It filled him with an indescribable admixture of excitement and serenity. It made him realize that in London there was no light to speak of. Not like this. You had to come here to discover what light was really made of. He hugged this knowledge to himself and felt that he was the keeper of a proud secret.

It seemed to Paul that in the space of a few hours he had made a journey not just to a different country, but to a different consciousness, a new condition of the heart. His was the only car on the road. There was no sound, other than the almost inaudible purr of the engine as he cruised along in fifth gear. The smooth brush of the tyres against the tarmac. A soundless wind was blowing, driving the turbines dotted in groups of three and four all over the countryside, their huge propellers rotating in stately unanimity. The whole world seemed hushed, utterly placid and self-contained, as if there had been no news here for a thousand years, and no more was ever expected.

He passed the sign to the sand-filled church, and remembered having cycled there one day with Rolf. It was the first landmark he recognized. They must have travelled this road dozens of times, then, and yet this evening it all seemed uncannily new; it was impossible to imagine his twelve-year-old self in these surroundings, pedalling along behind the German boy, red-faced and struggling for breath; or was it Paul who had made all the running, in fact? Now that he thought of it, he could remember being pretty fit in those days—he must have been, to have pulled Rolf out of the water on that last afternoon. And hadn't he taken a bullworker to Denmark with him, packed carefully into their suitcase alongside Benjamin's A-level set texts? It was astonishing how little thought he had given to the past in recent years—to any part of it, let alone an episode as fateful as this one now seemed. He had lived by discontinuities.

After a few more kilometres, the sharp left-hand turn to Gammel Skagen presented itself. Paul swung the car around and as he drove down the long, straight approach road, he slowed to little more than the speed of the three elderly cyclists who shadowed his progress in the bicycle lane. In a minute or two he would be arriving at the very house they had shared with the Baumanns. Nine of them, there must have been altogether. Or had Lois come with them? No, of course not: she had been hospitalized, that summer. That had been one of her worst times. It had taken her years—three, was it, or could it even have been four?—to recover fully from the shock of seeing Malcolm die. Sheila hadn't wanted to leave her behind: there had been several arguments about it. And it had, he supposed, been a long time to go away without her, two whole weeks, but there had been no question of Lois coming—she wouldn't even have been able to get on the plane—and her grandparents were there, the whole time, just a few miles from the hospital. But Sheila had been anxious, and preoccupied. She hadn't really enjoyed the holiday, because of worrying about Lois. He remembered that now. It was all coming back.

The road brought him at last to the tiny hamlet of Gammel Skagen, and he followed its last, unexpected coils as it wound past some tourist shops and a hotel before depositing him in the car park above the beach. There were only two other cars there, and the little hut selling coffee and snacks was already closing down for the evening. Paul had more than an hour to wait. He had flown to Aarhus that morning on a low-cost flight, and allowed himself four hours for the drive up to the very tip of Denmark: in the event it had taken less than two and a half. He had forgotten that this was a small country.

Before getting out and walking down to the sea he took one more look at yesterday's fax from Rolf Baumann's assistant.

3 May 2000

Dear Mr. Trotter,

Mr. Baumann asks me to tell you that he was both delighted and astounded to receive your telephone message.

He notes with pleasure your request to visit him in Munich later this week, but he has an alternative suggestion to make. He asks if it would be convenient for you to meet him in Denmark tomorrow evening (4 May). He proposes that you meet on the beach at Gammel Skagen at 19:30 hours local time.

Please let me know if this is convenient for you. If your answer is affirmative, I will make a booking for both yourself and Mr. Baumann to stay at an hotel locally tomorrow night, for one night.

Mr. Baumann hopes that you will agree to his suggestion and tells me that he is looking forward very much to meeting you again.

Sincerely.

Paul locked the car and walked the sandy path down to the beach. His mind should have been racing with thoughts of what he was going to say to Rolf that evening, how exactly he was going to phrase his request, but all the concerns he had left behind in London—even though they were his pretext for coming here—had begun to seem irrelevant. His eyes were drawn, instead, to the distant trawlers he could see silhouetted on the horizon, while he listened only to the wash of waves against the shore. Walking north along the beach, Paul could already discern the outline of the house where they had once stayed. It pulled him up short, and he stopped in his tracks, rendered suddenly breathless by memory. Wanting more than anything else to savour this moment, he swore under his breath when the double beeping of his mobile announced the arrival of a text message. But habit got the better of him, and he could not resist taking the phone out of his pocket.

The message was from Malvina.

Sorry if went OTT last nite—u have this effect on me. Missing u badly, dont think ill of me txt when u can. M xxx

He sat down awkwardly on a rock a few feet away from the breaking waves and, without thinking too hard about what he was doing, keyed in a quick reply.

Will never think ill of you P xxx

He continued his walk towards the house.

Paul had never read Benjamin's account of their Danish holiday; the account that had won him King William's Marshall Prize for creative writing in 1976. He'd felt no curiosity about his brother's writing as a teenager, and felt even less now. Benjamin had written about the "silver breakers which pounded the length of the seemingly endless strand," and had described the "angry roar" of the waves. Paul, a stickler for detail, might have taken issue with this. As he made his way across the yielding sand, he could feel no anger, either in the ocean or in himself. All had subsided into calm, into a sense of rightness, into a gladness that he had found himself in this place, on this day. There were lights coming from the windows of the house, so he didn't approach too close. It had been painted pink: or had it been pink before? He couldn't remember. The smaller house next door—the one where Jorgen and Stefan had been staying with their grandmother Marie—seemed to be unoccupied. He trudged up to it and tried to peer through the windows, shading his eyes with his hands; but the glass would show him nothing, merely reflected back to him the undulating, sun-speckled water. He walked around the back, looked at the sandy patch of grass where he had played so many games of football with the other boys. All of them, had it been? No, Benjamin had almost never joined in. He had sat in the window seat, reading his novels, having his great thoughts, occasionally glancing out at them with that annoying, fey, unguessable look in his eye. It had taken them all in, that mysterious-genius act of his. And now look at him! Fifteen years, or something, working for the same firm, and not so much as a haiku to show for it. It was sad, really: the way he kept up this pretence, the way he took so many people in, all convinced that he was one day going to fulfil his promise—Emily, Lois, their parents. Sad, too, the way he drooled over Malvina still, refused to accept defeat gracefully . . .

Paul walked back to the edge of the glimmering ocean and thought again about Malvina. Had he been right to say what he'd said to her last night? The question skimmed across his consciousness, barely impacting, barely sending out a ripple. These things could not be rationalized. He had spoken from the heart, that was the only thing that mattered. God, it was a long time since he'd done that, after all. It was about time his heart was allowed a voice, for a change—managed to catch the Speaker's eye, as it were. And it was not as if he had *promised* her anything. He hadn't really committed himself in any way. He had simply told her—honestly—what he felt for her, and in the process, he had made her happy: transcendentally happy, it seemed. That in itself was an achievement, wasn't it? When was the last time he had made anybody happy? When was the last time he had seen a look on anyone's face like the one he had seen on Malvina's last night, and known that he was responsible for it?—a look of gratitude, and love, so penetrating and so powerful that it had burned itself on to his memory, lingering there even now with a clarity that made him scarcely able to believe she was not standing next to him on the beach, her hand reaching out to touch his. That was something. Whatever else happened, he had the memory of that look, to carry with him. Surely that meant that he had done the right thing?

Paul continued to walk north along the beach, away from the houses he had come to revisit. He had been alone with his thoughts, now, for seven or eight hours—on the taxi ride to Stansted, the flight to Aarhus, the drive to Jutland—and they were beginning to exhaust him. He tried to let his mind go blank.

At exactly half past seven, he returned to the car park and found that his was the only car there. He waited there for a few minutes, half-sitting on the bonnet, looking out at the approach road. Seagulls swooped low over the beach, alighting on the rocks, keening. Only a few yards of the road were visible to Paul before it curved away out of sight, so any car that arrived would appear quite suddenly. But nothing came. A quarter of an hour passed.

Finally he heard a noise. It was not the engine noise that he had been expecting. In fact it came from the sky, not from the road. It was a distant buzz that rapidly grew louder. Looking up, Paul saw a winking light against the pale blueness, and a black, amorphous, moving object which, as it came closer, assumed the shape of a helicopter. Within seconds the noise was overwhelming, and the long grass behind him was flattened by the helicopter's air-stream as it hovered over the dunes, looking for a place to land.

Even before it touched the ground a door was flung open, and a middle-aged man in a dark business suit stepped out, bent double against the force generated by the whirring blades, a lightweight attaché case his only baggage. He saw Paul approaching him from the car park, and when they had reached each other and were shaking hands, the first words he shouted, above the scream of the engine, were: "I'm so sorry, Paul. Seventeen minutes late. A nasty spot of turbulence over Lübeck."

Then the helicopter rose into the air again and was gone. And Rolf Baumann laughed delightedly to find himself in the presence of the man he had not seen for twenty-three years, and clapped him on the shoulder and said: "I take it you've got a car?"

16

Rolf's assistant had booked them both single rooms at the Brøndums Hotel, on Anchersvej. Downstairs, it was a quiet, old-fashioned, elegant place: upstairs, where the bathrooms and showers were shared, it turned out to be rather more spartan. They both remembered it as a place where their families had come for an *al fresco* evening meal in the summer of 1976, and had sat at a large table in the leafy garden, and felt slightly intimidated by the formality of the service and the elaborate detail of the menu which had had Colin Trotter flicking frantically through his English–Danish dictionary beneath the cover of the white tablecloth.

"What *naïfs* we all must have been, in those days," Rolf said, chuckling, as they left the hotel later that evening and struck out towards the harbour in search of dinner.

"Well, *my* family were, that's for sure," said Paul. "My God, that was the only holiday we took in the whole bloody decade that didn't involve sitting in a caravan in North Wales in the pouring rain. It was an incredible adventure for us."

"And yet you, personally, took it in your stride. I remember thinking that you were completely . . . unflappable. I don't think I'd ever seen such self-possession in a young boy."

"Benjamin and I are both self-possessed," Paul mused, "in our different ways. In his case, it's turned out to be his downfall. In mine, it's been my strength. At least, I used to think so. Now I'm beginning to wonder. What about . . . allowing yourself to be possessed by somebody else? I'm beginning to think there's something to be said for that."

Rolf looked at him keenly, but did not ask him to explain.

"And your sister," he began, instead. "She was not with us that summer. She was very ill, I remember. None of you talked about it much: it was rather peculiar. She had received some injury—there had been a violent incident. Something about terrorism comes back to me. Am I right?"

Paul told him the story of Lois and how she had witnessed her boyfriend Malcolm's death. As he did so, they walked along Østre Strandvej, the quiet, verdant back roads having given way to an uglier, more commercial part of town, where the street was flanked by massive grey warehouses and the air smelled overpoweringly of fish. Rolf listened to the narrative gravely and did not speak for some time; he had no words of consolation to offer.

"And now she is well?" he said finally. "She leads a normal life?"

"More or less," said Paul. "She works in a university library, these days. Married to a nice lawyer. One daughter, Sophie. I think there are occasional . . . relapses, but I don't hear about them much. We've never been close, Lois and I. I haven't seen her all year."

They arrived at the harbour. It was after nine o'clock by now but the sky was still a luminescent eggshell blue. Rolf and Paul walked in silence. The tourist season had not started yet and all was quiet: the wooden huts selling beer and fish and chips to the early holidaymakers were already closed, the car parks were empty and the only noise was the subtle, irregular tinkle of rigging from the dozens of yachts and fishing boats moored by the quayside.

The receptionist at their hotel had recommended that they try eating at the Pakhuset restaurant, which did indeed appear to be the busiest and most welcoming spot in Skagen that night. A blonde waitress in her early twenties led them up a staircase, past captains' wheels, rudders, chronometers and nautical decorations of every description, towards a scattering of tables arranged on the wooden gallery, overlooking the downstairs bar which was thronged with two dozen or more young men and women, apparently celebrating a birthday party. Paul and Rolf sat opposite each other at a tiny table, their knees almost touching, and frowned with pointless intensity over the Danish menus.

"Let's ask that cute waitress for advice when she gets back," Rolf suggested. "It will give us a good excuse to get talking to her."

Paul nodded, although he had failed to notice, on this occasion, whether the waitress was cute or not. His head was still full of Malvina—from whom he now received another text message, just as he was gearing himself up to start talking to Rolf about his reasons for wanting to meet again.

Hope not interrupting vital discussions. Just wanted to say am still thinking of u. Always always always. Call later 2nite if u can? xxx

Paul put the phone away in his pocket after reading this and hoped that his smile had not betrayed too much.

"*Friske asparges* means fresh asparagus, presumably," said Rolf, looking down at the menu over the top of his glasses. "With *rødtunge*, which can only be some kind of red fish—I suppose a snapper?" He gave the menu another brief glance and then laid it down. "What proportion of text messages, I wonder, are on a sexual or romantic theme? Ninety or ninety-five per cent, would you think? I wonder if there's been any research done into the subject yet."

Paul laughed uneasily. "I hope you don't think—"

"I imagine that Mr. Tony Blair himself is texting you on a matter of state. Either that or your wife still harbours enough romantic feelings to send you virtual *billets doux* during your business trips abroad. How long have you been married now?"

"Five years. Yourself?"

"Twelve."

Rolf added nothing to this bald information, and began spreading butter thickly on to a chunk of rye bread.

Paul hovered for a moment on the edge of the precipice—no more than that; it was really an easy leap to make—and then blurted out:

"I'm in love with somebody else."

Rolf bit into his bread, leaving a perfect semi-circle of teeth marks in the butter. "Ah, yes. Well, that happens. That certainly happens."

"You don't sound very surprised," said Paul, rather offended to find this momentous confession being received with such insouciance.

"Who is she?" Rolf asked.

"Her name's Malvina. She's my media adviser."

"Is that the same as a research assistant?"

"I suppose so, more or less."

"Hm." Rolf grunted. "No marks for originality, Paul. How old is she?"

"Twenty."

He raised his eyebrows, tutted, and chewed on some more bread. "Dear me."

"I know how that sounds," said Paul. "But it's the real thing. It really is . . . the real thing."

"Oh, I can see that," Rolf assured him.

"You can? How?"

"It's in your eyes. They look desperate. The look of a man experiencing temporary euphoria, when underneath he doesn't have the faintest idea what he's going to do." Paul was regarding him disbelievingly, so he added: "I know what I'm talking about, Paul. I've seen that look before."

"Really? Where might that have been?"

"In the mirror. Twice."

The waitress came to take their order, and Rolf got to work on the serious business of ordering food and the even more serious business of flirting with her. Within a few minutes he had established that she was a student at the university in Aalborg, reading biological sciences, that she had spent three months last summer in the United States, that she had two brothers and no boyfriend, that she kept in shape by doing yoga three times a week and she thought that Radiohead were overrated. She also persuaded them to try a house speciality called *Hvidvin med brombærlikøk*, which she explained was a white wine supplemented with redcurrant liqueur. She brought them two tall glasses and after drinking his down within a few seconds, Rolf demanded that she bring them two more.

When they were both thoroughly drunk and thoroughly well fed, Rolf said to Paul: "A case can be made for saying that a male is simply a defective female. What do you make of that?"

"I'm not familiar with that theory," said Paul, frowning.

"Well, you can look at it from a biological point of view," said Rolf. "The presence of the Y-chromosome itself is a sign of deficiency. But you don't even have to be so specific about it. It's just common sense. Look at that waitress, for instance."

"Lise."

"Lise. Is her name Lise? Did she tell us that?"

"She did. A number of times."

"Well. Look at her, anyway—trotting up and down that staircase, being so effortlessly charming to everybody. What is she, twenty-one, twenty-two? Look at the way our eyes follow her. What do we know about her? Only that she's young, and she has a body that we both crave. Apart from that, nothing. She could be a serial murderer, for all that we know. And yet either one of us, after a couple more drinks, would put our family lives at risk if she asked us to come back to her room. Wouldn't we? It's a pathological disorder of the male sex. We have no loyalty—no nesting instinct—

none of the healthy, natural things women are born with. We're defective. A man is just a defective woman. It's as simple as that."

"I think you're talking rubbish," said Paul, "with the greatest respect. For one thing, why would she ask one of us back to her room? We're old men, as far as she's concerned."

"You say that, Paul. But you have won the heart—apparently—of a beautiful twenty-year-old woman. So it can happen."

"That's different. What's happening between me and Malvina has been building up for a long time. Last night it just came to a kind of crisis."

Rolf laughed quietly. "The crisis has not yet begun, Paul. It hasn't even begun."

"I know, it'll probably get into the papers. Nearly has already, in fact. But I can handle—"

"That's not what I mean," said Rolf. "That's nothing. Nothing at all." They had moved on to brandy by now: he swirled the ochre liquid around in its bell-like glass, his face souring into depression as he did so. "Anyway," he said, snapping out of it with a willed effort, "talking of *crises*, isn't it about time we got down to business? Or am I expected to sit here all night waiting for you to tell me what it is you want from me?"

"What makes you think I want anything from you?"

"You didn't contact me this week in order to reminisce, Paul. Credit me with a little knowledge of human nature. Almost the last thing I said to you when we saw each other all those years ago—I don't remember the exact words, perhaps you do—was to thank you for saving my life and to assure you that I would always be in your debt. It's not the kind of thing you forget easily, is it? And now suddenly, out of the blue, you call me, after more than twenty years. *This week*, Paul. Now why would a British Member of Parliament, with a constituency in the West Midlands, contact a member of the board of management of BMW *this week*, of all weeks? Hm? It's a real puzzle, isn't it?"

Paul looked away, unable to meet his eye. But Rolf insisted: "I don't mind, you know. I wouldn't have come here if I hadn't wanted to help you. But I'm not sure there's much I can do."

"If I . . ." Paul began, with some difficulty; then floundered and tried again. "If you and I can just . . . discuss some options. It's just that—the thing is, I may have got myself into a bit of a spot with the party, and I've been a bit inactive on the Longbridge front over the last few weeks, a bit preoccupied. If I could just show them, somehow, that I was . . . on the ball."

"And this 'spot' you're in—it has something to do with your media adviser?"

"Possibly."

"Well then. It's always best to be direct, Paul. We save so much time that way. Just tell me what it is you want. No embarrassment. Straight to the point."

"All right then." Paul laid down his brandy glass, and clasped his hands together, almost in an attitude of prayer. Waves of throaty laughter reached them from the party downstairs. He waited for the noise to subside. "You shouldn't be selling Rover. BMW shouldn't be selling Rover. You should commit yourself to the Longbridge plant, and make a go of it."

Rolf seemed genuinely taken aback, for the first time that evening. "But what you are proposing, Paul—or suggesting, rather—flies in the face of your own government's policy. Correct me if I'm wrong about that. But since the Alchemy bid failed, we are in talks with another buyer: the Phoenix Consortium. The talks are going well. And your Mr. Byers supports the Phoenix bid. In fact I was talking to him about it only this afternoon."

"That's true. But my information is that the Phoenix bid is not realistic."

"And where does this information come from? The newspapers, I suppose."

"Mainly," Paul was forced to admit.

"Well, as we know, you shouldn't believe everything that you read in the newspapers."

"You mean, you're considering it?"

"What's the alternative? That we make thousands of workers redundant, and create a public relations disaster for ourselves?"

"There's a much simpler solution. Keep Longbridge going."

Rolf gave a short, dismissive laugh. "And lose millions of pounds every week?"

"The losses aren't nearly as high as you've been making out. A lot of those figures are down to your own accounting methods."

Whether because this was true, or whether because he was impressed by the sudden passion and sincerity with which Paul seemed to be arguing his point, Rolf fell silent for a while. He appeared to be considering the matter seriously.

"Well, let me get this clear," he said at last. "You want me to persuade the board to change their minds about this—to perform a complete U-turn, in effect—so that you can go home and tell the news to your Mr. Blair and present yourself as a hero. The man who saved Longbridge."

"Put like that—"

"Be honest with me, Paul. However much that goes against your training. Is that what you want me to do?"

Paul could see no point in dissembling. "Yes, I suppose it is."

Rolf looked at him, now, as if it had finally occurred to him that he might be someone to reckon with. Otherwise, his expression gave nothing away—any more than his words. "Very well," he said, scraping back his chair. "I'll sleep on it." And signalled across the room to Lise for the bill.

Paul awoke the next morning with a severe hangover and didn't make it down to breakfast. Rolf, however, must have arisen early, for it was only just after nine o'clock when he knocked firmly on Paul's door and said: "Are you awake? Hurry up! I have to leave in an hour and a half—and we have a journey to make before then."

Paul ran his head under the cold tap, swallowed two paracetamol and shuffled downstairs. Rolf was waiting for him in the street, wearing a pleased expression and standing beside a shiny, lightweight bicycle: a tandem, to be precise.

"What do you think?" he said. "It's a nice one, isn't it?"

Paul walked around the bicycle, inspecting it from every angle with the air (not entirely affected) of an expert.

"Not bad," he said. "Not bad at all. Where did you get this from?"

"There's a hire shop in the town. I thought it would be the simplest way to get there."

"Where are we going?" asked Paul.

"To where the seas meet, of course. Climb on—you're going to be steering. I've got to take my luggage with me."

And so they set off, turning right along Oddevej and then continuing past the Grenen *Kunstmuseum* on to Fyrvej and up towards the tip of the peninsula. There were few people around to take notice of them at this hour, but they must have made an incongruous couple, all the same. Paul, at least, was dressed for the part, in the standard New-Labour-MP-off-duty uniform of open-necked shirt and crisply ironed pale blue jeans. Rolf was not only still wearing his dark business suit, but he also had his attaché case carefully balanced on the handlebars in front of him as he rode. Neither of them cared what they looked like, anyway. They were enjoying the sensation—which came back to them as soon as they left the town behind and set out on the long, unswerving road to Grenen itself—of being twelve- and fourteen-year-old boys again.

"This takes you back, doesn't it?" Rolf shouted; and when Paul turned to look at him he saw that Rolf's face, besides turning slightly red even after these moderate exertions, was none the less suffused by a kind of boyish exhilaration which seemed to have wiped it clean of frown-lines and all the other signs of incipient middle age.

After that they said nothing, and Paul savoured once again the absolute silence: a silence which seemed to mark the suspension of time; so that it seemed not only possible, while he was here, to live in the moment (which he could never do in London, so *temporal* was his existence there, so thoroughly comprising plans, forethoughts, survival strategies), but possible, too, to conceive of that moment as being stretched, eternal. This realization, fleeting as it was, gave him a feeling of delicious luxury; and as he pedalled through the featureless landscape, the kilometres falling away behind him, he saw a vision. A memory rose up before him: Marie, the Danish boys' grandmother, reaching for the cord of the Venetian blind at the end of her long story, raising the blind to the very top of her high sitting-room window so that the room was suddenly flooded with the afternoon sunlight, grey-blue like her eyes . . . The vision was fugitive, evanescent, but while it hovered before him it seemed so vivid, so real that it took his breath away and he forgot everything else: where he was, who he was with, what he was still hoping to gain from this strange and wonderful reunion.

"Hey, Englishman!" Rolf called suddenly. "No slacking at the front there! This is a two-man job, remember."

Paul realized that he had stopped pedalling.

"Sorry!" he called, and went back to work with redoubled energy.

The road hugged the shoreline for a while and then curved away, in a slow, graceful arc, past a festively painted lighthouse, until it dropped them gently into the car park at the northernmost point of the peninsula. They left the tandem, unlocked, in one of the many bicycle racks (nobody seemed to give very much thought to crime in this part of the world) and completed the journey to the beach on foot, taking off their shoes and socks as they made their way through the soft rise and fall of the dunes.

"Ha! Remember that?" said Rolf, pointing behind them. And there in the distance was an odd sight, a single railway coach being towed by a tractor, taking the first handful of early-morning tourists to the furthest part of the beach, the very tip of Denmark where the Kattegat and the Skagerrak seas ran into each other.

"Yes, I remember," said Paul; and stopped, after a few more steps, to read the prominently displayed notices, in English, Danish and German, which warned visitors that the welcoming, unpretentious nature of this landscape concealed hidden dangers.

"*Livsfare*," he read, aloud. "Were these here before?"

"Oh yes," said Rolf. "I believe so."

"Didn't your mother manage to drive her car on to this beach somehow? And didn't the fire brigade or someone have to come and dig her out?"

"That's right. Poor Mutti—she died two years ago, and she was the world's worst driver right up until the end. That was the day . . . that was the thing that made Jorgen, or whatever his name was, tease me so badly. What I said to him in response was very insulting, I think. I still blush when I think of it."

"It was a long time ago," said Paul, as they started to walk on. "We were all very young."

Rolf shook his head. "I should not have said it."

They walked close to the water's edge, where the sand was dark and firm. It was getting on for ten o'clock, now, and the tourists were swelling in number, larking about in groups of three and four, endlessly taking photographs of the beach from every conceivable angle. The barefoot businessman and his politician friend seemed more conspicuous than ever.

At last they reached the end of the peninsula and, shielding their eyes against the morning sunlight which the water was now throwing back at them with dazzling intensity, they stared in renewed wonderment at the two sets of waves which ran together, forming strange triangular patterns as they did so, mingling and coalescing in what the teenage Benjamin had once described as "foamy, promiscuous couplings." They smiled at each other, wanting to share the moment, but neither of them said anything at all for many minutes. The beeping of Paul's mobile told him that another text message had arrived, but he didn't look at it yet. He would save that for later.

When Rolf spoke, at last, it was very slowly, as if dredging up the words from some deep ocean of thought. "Strangely . . ." he began, "strangely, I have no memory of what it felt like, to be lost out there in the water, dragged down towards the sea-bed by some elemental force. I must have believed that I was dying. I don't even remember you saving me. I mean, I know that it happened, but I cannot picture it: I can't . . . bring the sensation to mind." He looked towards the horizon and his eyes narrowed further against the blinding sun. "The mind has fuses, I suppose. Yes, I know that to be the case."

"I don't remember it too well, either," said Paul. And he added, sensing the banality of his own words: "We've both come a long way since then."

"I wonder if you were right to save me," said Rolf, unexpectedly.

"What do you mean?" asked Paul, genuinely shocked.

"The absolute sanctity of human life," Rolf mused, half to himself. "I've never really understood that concept. Or subscribed to it, I should say. I suppose that, in my moral philosophy, I've always inclined towards the utilitarian. When you ran out into that water and saved me it was an unthinking act, an animal impulse. I wonder whether I would have done the same thing."

"When you see somebody drowning," said Paul, "you don't think about whether their life is worth saving. You don't stand there for ten minutes weighing up their contribution to humanity. There isn't time, for one thing. You just dive in and do it."

"Of course," Rolf answered. "I understand that. I simply mean that, from a rational point of view, I believe you may have done the wrong thing."

"The *wrong* thing?"

"If I had drowned that day . . . Well, my parents would have grieved, that goes without saying. But after that—" he shook his head "—my wife would have met somebody else, who would not have made her as unhappy as I have. That's for certain. My love affairs, which caused nothing but pain to everyone concerned, would not have occurred. My employers could easily have appointed someone else to their board, someone just as capable." He turned to Paul and there was an edge of anger to his voice now, almost violence. "You see, I am under no illusions about myself. I've realized that I am a selfish man. I care very little about the happiness of others."

"I was right to do it," said Paul quietly, "and nothing you can say will persuade me otherwise."

Rolf put his hands in his pockets and strolled away towards the water's edge. For a long while he stood with his back to Paul and did not move. Eventually Paul came and stood beside him, prompting Rolf to say, at last: "You realize, don't you, that I cannot possibly do what you're asking of me? Some things are not worth saving. Even if you don't believe that applies to human beings, it certainly applies to ailing companies." He laid a hand on Paul's shoulder, but the gesture felt awkward, and he let it fall. "I know that I'm in your debt. And I will help you, in any way that I can. I'll give you money. I'll lend you my summer house on the coast—somewhere to take your mistress this summer. I'll give you the phone number of the best prostitute in the world, who lives in London, incidentally. But I cannot do this for you. I'm not strong enough. You're asking me the impossible."

"All I'm asking you to do is put it to the other members of the board—that they reconsider their options . . ."

"I already know what they would say. We're not talking about pulling somebody out of the sea, Paul. We're talking about something stronger than that, actually, something even more elemental. The market. Which can also be ruthless, and also be destructive. You believe in the market, don't you? You and your party? Then you should be honest with people. You should make them aware that sometimes it sucks men under and tosses them back lifeless on the shore and there's nothing that you or anybody else can do about it. Don't lie to them. Don't encourage them to believe that you can have it both ways."

And then, behind them, in the distance, came the noise of an approaching engine. Both men turned and saw, as Paul had seen the previous evening, a black dot in the sky, growing bigger and bigger. Rolf glanced at his watch and nodded with satisfaction.

"Ten-thirty. Not a minute behind schedule. Come on, Paul, and wave goodbye to me if you will."

He ran towards the helicopter, which was now landing on the western beach and attracting much interest from the tourists. They gaped at this portly, ungainly figure in his dark bespoke suit, running across the sand with his attaché case in one hand and his shoes and socks in the other, closely pursued by Paul. Some of them even started taking photographs.

They had to shout their farewells.

"It's been wonderful seeing you again, Paul," Rolf roared, his hair billowing in the tail wind. "And to see this place. Thank you so much for coming. Let's not leave it another twenty years, yes?"

"We won't," Paul answered.

"I'm sorry," Rolf said. "Sorry that I couldn't do what you asked. But don't worry. That situation will resolve itself."

"I hope so."

"I know it will. It's your other situation I'm worried about."

"It's under control. Don't worry."

Rolf threw his things into the cabin, and clasped Paul in his arms. They embraced fervently. Then Rolf was about to climb into the helicopter when he turned, put his mouth to Paul's ear, and said:

"All I would say, Paul, is—it's an unusual woman who likes being a mistress. You are not a cruel man, so remember that: they find it a very uncomfortable role to play. One of mine committed suicide." Finally he kissed Paul on both cheeks, in a most non-Germanic way. "I'm still not convinced that you were right to save me."

After which, in a confusion of noise and movement and flurries of sand flung into the air, stinging Paul's eyes, the helicopter leapt into the sky and was gone.

15

Benjamin sat in his office, on the seventh floor of a tower block overlooking St. Philip's Place. He had worked at the same desk for more than ten years now, and he had always relished the view from here, this grey panorama of the city he still loved, despite all his cravings to break free from it. But today, he didn't look at the view. Instead, for the second time, he picked the book up from his desk, read disbelievingly through the last sentences, and then let it fall from his hands.

It was lunchtime, and he had with him a large mocha from Coffee Republic, and a comically overpriced feta cheese and black olive ciabatta from the new sandwich shop in Piccadilly arcade. The biography of Francis Piper had been open on his desk and he had reached page 567. Doug wanted the review by the end of the week at the latest so Benjamin really needed to finish reading the book some time today. He was conscientiously taking notes as he went along.

Piper's biographer had obtained access to the poet's private diaries and was threading his narrative around quotations from these original sources. The diaries were extensive (interminable, some might say), and no very strong editorial hand appeared to have been exercised by the publisher. It had taken 550 pages, therefore, to reach the year 1974, and there were still a good 200 pages to go. Benjamin had got the hang of things by now: by this stage in the story, Piper's greatest, most productive days as a poet were some thirty years behind him, he was writing nothing of any substance (apart from those endless diaries), and—having been sexually inactive for the best part of a decade—he had become prey to sexual fantasies and obsessions of a tiresomely morbid cast. The litany of somewhat pathetic non-encounters (builder's mates followed forlornly for miles along suburban streets, incipient gropes in public toilets abandoned in fits of panic) was becoming frankly tedious.

Francis Piper's income, at this time, seemed to have derived entirely from his occasional public appearances at schools and universities around the country, or the odd visit to some barren British Council outpost in Bucharest or Dresden. On March 7th, 1974, he had come to talk and read from his work at King William's School, Birmingham. Benjamin himself had been in the audience. He had noticed that the school was mentioned in the index, but had not wanted to read any parts of the book out of sequence, and assumed—in any case—that it would be the subject of no more than a glancing mention. Thus the description of that visit, when it came, caught him completely unawares.

It was after reading this passage for the second time that he dropped the book to the floor and staggered out of his office, without saying a word to any of his colleagues, or to Judy, who sat at the receptionist's desk. She looked at him strangely, but did not realize—why should she?—that the very foundations of his life had been blown asunder in the last few seconds.

Benjamin stepped out into the fast-moving traffic along Colmore Row—prompting a symphony of angry car-horns—and then wandered trancelike around the periphery of St. Philip's, only dimly registering the headlines that were going up on the *Evening Mail* placards outside the newagents: "*It's a Deal! Phoenix Victory Saves Longbridge.*" What did it matter to him, if hope and meaning had returned to the lives of tens of thousands of strangers, when they had abruptly, brutally, been snatched away from his?

His mobile rang. It was Philip Chase.

"Hello, Ben—have you heard the news? Rover's been saved. BMW have accepted the Phoenix bid. It's fantastic, isn't it? I'm going to drive out to Longbridge, see what's going on outside Q gate. Do you want to come? I could give you a lift." There was no answer to any of this—prompting Philip to say: "Hello? Benjamin? Are you there?"

After a second or two, with what felt like a great effort of will, Benjamin said: "I can't, Phil. Thanks, but I've got to work."

"Oh. All right." And Phil hung up, sounding puzzled and disappointed, not by the excuse, but by the tone of voice in which it was made.

But Benjamin did not go back to work. At least, he went back to his office, briefly, to retrieve his copy of the biography, but then he half-walked, half-ran all the way to New Street Station, and got there just in time to board the delayed 13:48 to London Euston.

Irina answered the door and looked embarrassed when Benjamin asked, "Are they in?"

"Well," she said, "they are in, but I don't think they are quite—"

"Who is it?" It was Doug's voice, as he came down the stairs, trouserless, out of breath, and fumbling with the buttons on his shirt.

"Benjamin—is that you?" This time it was Frankie calling down. She was leaning over the bannister, wrapped in a sheet but otherwise naked. Her hair was fabulously tousled and had Benjamin not been in a state of such blind panic he would doubtless have felt the usual hot waves of desire course through him. From the kitchen Ranulph could be heard, his screams growing louder and more indignant.

"I'll go and see to him," said Irina, turning on her heel.

"Benjamin?" said Doug, now at the bottom of the stairs. "What are you doing here?"

"Don't tell me," said Benjamin, "I've come at a bad moment."

"Not really. It's just that—you know—I haven't been swearing much lately." He took Benjamin's arm and steered him in the direction of the downstairs sitting room. "Come on, come and sit down. You look shattered. What's happened?"

"I'll be right down!" Frankie called after them, and disappeared to get dressed.

"What are you doing in London?" Doug asked, as Benjamin collapsed on to one of the sofas. "Why aren't you at work?"

"Something's happened," Benjamin said. "Something . . . terrible."

"You and Emily have split up," Doug said—instinctively, before he'd had time to check himself.

Benjamin stared at him. "No."

"No. Sorry—I don't know why I said that. Would you like a cup of tea or something? I'll get Irina to put the kettle on."

"I wouldn't mind something stronger, actually."

"OK." This request was very out of character—it was only 4:15 in the afternoon—but Doug poured him a large Scotch anyway. "There you go. Get it down you, and tell me all about it."

Benjamin drained most of the whisky in one gulp, winced as the acrid burn hit the back of his throat, and said: "It's about the review."

Doug let out a sigh of both incredulity and relief. "You came all the way down here," he exclaimed, "to talk about that *review*? For Christ's sake, Benjamin, what do you think telephones are for?"

"I can't talk about this on the telephone."

"Look—you don't have to worry about it. If you write it, fine. If you don't, it's no big deal, I'm only going to be in that job for a couple more weeks anyway. You won't be letting me down or anything."

"It's not that. There's something in that book. Something about me."

"About *you*?"

"Well, not directly. I mean, I'm not mentioned by name. But there's a story about something in there and—it's about me, I know it is."

Doug was alarmed to hear Benjamin talking like this. Years of writing for a national newspaper and receiving dozens of readers' letters every week had taught him—among other things—that mental illness, of varying degrees of severity, was more widespread than most people realized, and could take the most surprising forms. He was familiar with the concept of "delusions of reference," which could cause people to become convinced that perfectly ordinary articles on matters of general interest were in fact full of hidden meanings intended only for them. These delusions could turn sinister. Not long ago a man in Chalfont St. Giles who had attempted to murder his wife had pleaded in mitigation that he was being instructed to do so by coded messages embedded in the TV listings.

He sighed again, and ran a hand through his hair. Had he been stupid to give Benjamin this commission in the first place?

Fortunately—for Doug had no idea what to say next—two things happened at this point. Frankie came into the room, and the telephone rang.

She leaned over Benjamin, kissed him on the cheek and hugged him. "It's so nice to see you!" she said, and gave the impression—as always—of really meaning it. She had slipped on a V-neck cashmere sweater with no blouse or bra underneath, and Benjamin could smell on her neck the warm odour of recent arousal. She sat down beside him and they both listened to Doug's half of the telephone conversation.

"I know, David, it's fantastic news. They can hardly believe it down at Longbridge, apparently. No one in the London press was taking that bid seriously. They didn't give a fuck about the factory—fifty thousand jobs lost made too good a story. That's all they were interested in. Of course I will. How much do you want? Fifteen hundred words? I'll do it now. You'll have it by six o'clock. OK, leave it with me."

Hanging up, he turned to Benjamin and said, apologetically: "I've jumped ship, as you may have gathered. Back writing the real stuff again. Technically I'm still on contract to the other lot, but—fuck 'em." Seeing Frankie's reproving glance he corrected himself: "I mean—they'll just have to put up with it. Anyway—you've heard the news from Longbridge, have you? Amazingly, your brother has already managed to get himself on the radio saying that this was what he'd been hoping for all along. Which comes as a surprise to many of us, I must say." He looked at his watch. "I'm sorry, Ben, I've got to start work. They want this thing by six. Can we talk about it over dinner?"

"Sure," said Benjamin, glumly.

"Don't worry," said Frankie, "I'll look after him." And then, after Doug had run upstairs to his study, she refilled Benjamin's glass and sat in the armchair opposite him, leaning forward attentively, her hands clasped together. "Now," she said, her voice almost trembling with kindness (the sincerity of which Benjamin could never quite bring himself to doubt), "tell me what's wrong."

Benjamin wondered where to begin. In the end, there seemed only one way of putting it:

"I don't believe in God any more."

Frankie took some time to digest this. "Wow," was all she could say, at first; and sat back as if impelled by a physical force. "But how . . . I mean—since when?"

"Since about ten past one this afternoon."

"Wow," she said, again. "I'm sorry, I'm not being very articulate about this, but really, Benjamin, this is . . . Well—surely you can't be serious, can you?"

"No, I'm serious. Completely serious." He stood up, paced the room a couple of times, then took the biography from the coffee table where he had laid it, and showed Frankie the portrait of Francis Piper on the front cover. "Do you know anything about this guy?" he asked her.

"No," she admitted.

"Well. He is—or was, before he died—a poet. Pretty well known. He was famous in the 1930s and progressively less famous after that, and when he came to talk to us at school in 1974, none of us had really heard of him. And now someone's written this book about him and Doug asked me to review it. And today, I got up to the bit where he came to our school. March the seventh, 1974."

Benjamin sat down again, and tried to compose himself. The story he had to tell Frankie was long and complex, and probably worlds removed from her own experience. Could she really be made to understand the kinds of anxieties that gripped a thirteen-year-old boy, standing on the threshold of puberty, terrified of losing the fragile, capricious respect of his friends? Anxieties that seemed, now, to belong to an almost prehistoric era: although sometimes (and never more so than today) it felt to Benjamin that he was still trapped there, while the rest of the world had moved on . . .

"Well, in those days," he began, with a deep breath, "I was pretty shy, and not very confident about things—physically—and fairly . . . ashamed of my own body, I suppose." He smiled a grim smile. "No change there, then." He waited for a smile of agreement—or perhaps contradiction—but Frankie's face remained solemn and expectant. "And at King William's they had this rule—I don't know if Doug ever told you about it—that if you forgot to bring your swimming trunks to school, you still had to go swimming. Naked."

"Gosh," said Frankie. "That must have been cold."

"Well yes—there was the temperature factor to take into account, obviously, but more important than that was the *shame* of it. Boys at that age, as you probably know, are very cruel, and very . . . *competitive*, in certain areas. And very self-conscious, as I said, about their own bodies. So really it was the worst punishment they could possibly devise. And I lived in terror—literally sheer, mind-numbing, daily terror—of this ever happening to me."

"And one day it did?"

"One day it did. My dad gave me a lift to school and I left my kit bag on the back seat of his car. And I don't know how it happened, but within minutes, it was all over the school that Trotter had forgotten his swimming trunks. It was like it was the joke of the century. There was this kid in our year called Harding, Sean Harding, and he was probably the one who started it. It's funny, he was my friend—one of my best friends, actually—but he wanted to humiliate me. How do you explain that? I don't know. There's a weird kind of mixture in kids. Cruelty and friendship—there doesn't seem to be any contradiction between them."

"I know all about Harding," Frankie said. "When Duggie gave his talk last year, at the Queen Elizabeth Hall, that was who he talked about. Him, and your brother."

"Yes." Benjamin laughed. "Two of a kind, in many ways. Though we didn't think so at the time. Anyway. I went to pieces. This guy—this poet—Francis Piper was coming to the school that morning, to give a reading in Big School, and there was a brief moment of respite when I thought that meant the swimming lesson was going to be cancelled. But it wasn't. So during break that morning, just before the lesson was due to start, I went off to the locker room by myself and I had a sort of . . . breakdown, I suppose you'd call it. And that's when it happened."

"I know what you're going to say," said Frankie, her voice throbbing with feeling now. "You prayed, didn't you? You turned to Christ."

"How did you know that?" Benjamin asked.

"It's what I would have done."

"Well, I'd never given God much thought before," said Benjamin. "But suddenly—almost without thinking about it—I got down on my knees, and I started praying to Him. Bargaining with Him, to be precise."

"Bargaining?"

"Yes. I struck a deal. I said that if He sent me some swimming trunks, I would believe in Him. For ever and ever."

Frankie looked impressed by the audacity of this tactic. And asked, inevitably: "Did it work?"

"Yes." Benjamin stared ahead of him, mesmerized by the clarity with which the events of that day never failed to recur to him. "The locker room was absolutely silent. Then I heard the noise of a locker door, opening and shutting. I got to my feet, and walked towards the noise. The door of the locker was open. And inside was . . ."

". . . a pair of swimming trunks," said Frankie, her voice hushed to a whisper. "It was a miracle, Benjamin! You witnessed a miracle."

She came closer, knelt before him, put her hands on his knees. More than anything, at that moment, he would have liked to kiss her. But it didn't seem to be what the situation required.

"And after that," she asked "—did you keep your side of the bargain?"

"Yes, I did. I started going to church, and I continued going to church, in the face of much derision from my friends and contemporaries. Twenty-six years, I've kept that up. And when at last I found someone who shared my beliefs, I . . . well, I don't think I fell in love with her, exactly, I kind of . . . gravitated towards her. I mean, I'd known Emily at school and we'd talked about religion a little bit but actually it wasn't until I went and spent a weekend with her at university—some time in our third year, I think it was: I was at Oxford, she was at Exeter—well, that was when we first got talking seriously about it. That was also the first weekend we slept together, I seem to remember. She was a virgin. I wasn't, because a couple of years before, upstairs in my brother's back bedroom . . ."

He tailed off, and noticed that Frankie was trying to get his attention.

"Too much information, Benjamin. Too much information."

"Yes. OK. Well then—what I'm trying to say is that faith—or what I've always taken to be faith—is at the centre of my life and also the centre of my marriage. And today, as of—" (he glanced at his watch) "—three hours, twenty minutes ago, I've lost it. My faith has gone."

"But why?" said Frankie. "God's kept His side of the bargain, hasn't he?"

"I always thought so. Listen to this." He took up the biography, and walked over to the front bay window, where the light was better. "'It was at this point that Piper's sexual career seems to have reached its absolute nadir. The turning point came, according to his diaries, during a two-day trip to Birmingham to give a reading at King William's School. It was from this day on that he realized he could not continue with the habits to which he had become wearily accustomed, while still retaining any vestiges of self-respect.'"

He looked across at Frankie, to check that she was listening—which she was: although without, at this point, very much comprehension.

"You'll understand in a minute," he assured her. "Just listen: 'Piper recorded his impressions of Birmingham in his characteristically unsparing style: "An unspeakable excrescence of a city," he wrote, "as if God had unwisely partaken the night before of a divine Vindaloo of horrific pungency, and promptly evacuated his bowels over the West Midlands the next morning. The people pallid, corpse-like, moronic; the buildings so ugly as to induce a state of actual nausea in the hapless onlooker." After a few more observations like this, Piper noted that, after spending the night in the Britannia Hotel (where "the food would have disgraced the standards of a soup kitchen in the vilest slums of Victorian London"), he made his way shortly after breakfast, on the morning of his reading, to the municipal swimming baths for his daily constitutional.

"'This custom, as we know, had less to do with the provision of healthy exercise than with the opportunity it offered him to ogle the bodies of the other swimmers with relative impunity. And on this occasion, he was certainly not disappointed. "I had only been in the water a few minutes," he wrote, "when the rank hideousness of the baths themselves—apparently designed by some aesthetically bankrupt mediocrity in a fit of vindictive hatred against his fellow-citizens—was suddenly transcended, *brought to life*, by a *vision*, an *apparition* of manhood in its most magnificent, supra-natural form. A young negro of no more than twenty years, his thigh muscles as solid as young saplings, his buttocks tauter than the skin on a—"' Well, there's quite a lot more in that vein, anyway. I won't bore you with all the details." He flicked over to the next page, noting that Frankie was now following his every move with rapt, wide-eyed captivation. "He follows this guy up and down the baths for a few lengths—though he can't keep up with him very well, obviously—and then trails after him as he heads off back to the changing rooms. Lots of self-loathing stuff about his own body here—'the mottled skin hanging off my powdery bones like the scrotum of a senile and disease-ridden roué in the final stages of decrepitude,' et cetera, I'm sure you don't need to know all that—and then we come to the crunch. The other guy strips off and gets into the shower—'disclosing to my ravished eyes an organ of pleasure so heavy and cumbersome that I was put in mind of a prodigious Milanese salami I once saw hanging from the rafters of a trattoria high in the mountains above Bagni di Lucca . . .'—Jesus, he does go on, doesn't he?—and then Piper succumbs to his moment of weakness: 'Suddenly, it seemed to me intolerable—unbearable—that this God-like being should pass in and out of my life so fleetingly, without leaving the smallest trace except the memory of his unattainable loveliness stamped on to my aching consciousness. I had to have—at the very least—a souvenir. It was an impulse, an instant of lunatic audacity, no more—but that was all it took, to snatch his navy blue swimming trunks from the bench where he had left them, wring them out on the floor, allow my questing nostrils (yes, I admit it!) to inhale for just a second the intoxicating smell of those dark, mysterious regions with which the cloth (o happy fibre!) had recently been in contact, and then to cram them into the briefcase where I had stored not only my own bathing things, but also the very volumes of poetry with which I was vainly hoping to impress the doubtless cow-like and torpid pupils of King William's school later that morning.' "

Benjamin closed the book slowly and thoughtfully, then sank down on to the sofa again. He stared at the window for some time, with sightless eyes, while Frankie—utterly lost for words, for the time being—waited to hear if he would complete the story.

"So that's where they came from," he said at last. "By the time he arrived at the school, the lust had worn off and all he felt was shame, self-hatred and fear at the thought that he might be found out. So before going off to see the Chief Master, he dashed into the locker room, and chucked them into the first locker he could find. And that was where *I* found them, a couple of seconds later." Benjamin shook his head, overwhelmed by bitterness at his own credulity. " 'The breath of God!' *The breath of God*, I called it! Some raddled, disappointed old man grabbing the spoils of his latest debacle and shoving them out of sight as fast as he could. *The breath of God . . .* What a fiasco. What a joke."

He had nothing more to say. In the long, miserable silence that followed, the distant howls of Ranulph could be heard from the kitchen, protesting loudly at Irina's latest attempt to feed or dress him.

Finally, Frankie came over to sit beside Benjamin again, and took both of his hands in hers.

"Benjamin, God works in many ways, you know. Many and mysterious ways. Just because there turns out to have been an explanation for what happened, that doesn't make it any less . . . meaningful."

"I thought it was a miracle," said Benjamin, as if he hadn't heard her. "But there are no such things as miracles. Just random sets of circumstances, intersecting in ways that make no sense."

"But it *did* make sense, for you . . ."

"Just chaos," he continued, rising to his feet. "Chaos and coincidence. That's all it is."

And nothing that either Frankie or Doug could say would change his mind, either for the rest of that day or during the middle of the night when, on three separate occasions, they found him pacing from room to room in their house with the soundless tread of a sleepwalker.

14

A visitor to the tiny Cotswold village of Little Rollright on the hot afternoon of Monday, May 22nd, 2000, would probably have been drawn there, like many of its visitors, by an interest in church architecture. She (let us suppose it is a she) would have driven the winding single-track road up to the fifteenth-century church, with a copy of Pevsner in hand, hungry for a feast of ogee heads, corner buttresses, cusped arches and embattled cornices. On her way into the church she might have noticed that, sitting on a bench against its southern wall, looking out over the village's golden cluster of houses, sat a man in his mid-thirties, and a woman in her early twenties, and that they were talking together, earnestly but brokenly, in low, murmurous voices. Supposing that her interest in church architecture was more than casual—supposing, in fact, that she could simply never get enough of niches, quatrefoils and crocketed canopies—she might have spent up to an hour in the church itself, notebook in hand, sketchpad at the ready, and when she emerged, blinking, into the afternoon sunlight which by then would only have increased in ferocity, she would have noticed that the man and the woman were still there, and still talking. Sitting slightly further apart, perhaps, and looking both a good deal hotter and a good deal more melancholy than when she had last observed them. But still there. And as she left through the churchyard gate, she might have glanced back at them for one last time, and noticed that the man was leaning forward, with his head in his hands, and was muttering some despondent words which there was no breeze, that sweltering day, to carry over to her suddenly curious ears. And then she would have walked back to her car, never to learn anything more about the drama that was being played out in the churchyard that afternoon, never to know that as she was closing the gate behind her with a squeak and a click, Paul Trotter was saying to Malvina: "I can't believe we're going to do this. I can't believe we're really doing it."

Paul had not known what to expect of this meeting. All he knew was that he was longing to see Malvina again. They had not seen each other for almost three weeks, since the night before his trip to Skagen. While he had been away—on the morning of his conversation with Rolf on the beach at Grenen—a story about him and Malvina had appeared in the diary column of one of the broadsheets. It was couched in terms careful enough to skirt the libel laws, but the implications were plain to anybody who happened to read it; and unfortunately, this had included Susan.

She had not actually kicked him out of the house when she learned that Malvina had spent a night in the family home without her knowledge, although for a while she had threatened to do so. But Paul had been made to promise that he would not see her again, and from that day on Malvina had ceased working as his media adviser and he had stopped paying her a wage. In an email on May 8th, he had written:

Not to see you at all is unthinkable. That simply isn't an option, as far as I'm concerned. But you had better lie low for a while, maybe. And we had probably better not meet up for a week or two.

Malvina had answered:

Not sure I like the idea of being hidden. Though I can see your logic, I guess. I'm scared, probably, of the thought that everything between us might suddenly go pear-shaped, that feelings we worked hard to bring out into the open are going to be strangled at birth by complications, the whole nightmare of keeping the rest of the world at bay . . .

Since then, Paul had been circumspect, to put it mildly. He had told Malvina not to email him, not to text him, not to visit him. He never wondered how she might fill her time during those days, with nothing to occupy her but course-work and thoughts of their possible future together; that was not his problem. For his own part, he immersed himself in parliamentary business, volunteering for so many research assignments and social duties on his minister's behalf that relations between the two of them (which had been at breaking point for months) became—briefly—almost cordial. He spent more time at home, playing with Antonia, until he found that ten minutes was about the most he could manage without dying of boredom. For the first time in years, he contacted his brother of his own accord, and spoke to him on the telephone after hearing reports from Susan that Benjamin had started to behave oddly: he was not going to church any more, it was rumoured, and had been arguing bitterly with Emily. (Paul failed to elicit much information on this point, however, and didn't carry his concern for Benjamin's welfare to the extreme of actually going to see him.) And he wrote a number of articles for the papers about the Longbridge crisis, how successfully it had been resolved, and how adroit was the government's handling of it. He even invited himself to the factory for a photocall with the victorious directors of the Phoenix consortium—although, in the end, he only got to meet their PR spokesman, and the picture was not taken up by any of the press agencies.

In the midst of this activity, anyway, all he really wanted to do was to see Malvina again.

At last, the time came when he judged that it was safe for them to meet. He did not want it to be in London; he was convinced that his every move there was being shadowed by the press. But he was going to drive down that day from his constituency, and he suggested that Malvina take a train from Paddington and meet him half way, at Moreton-in-Marsh. They could spend a few hours together, have lunch in a pub, take a country walk. It would be quiet, and discreet, and they would both get a much-needed change of scene. The weather forecast was good. Paul looked forward to it all weekend.

He didn't like the idea of meeting her off the train—too many people around—so he waited for her in his car, parked outside the White Hart Hotel. Fifteen minutes later than expected, she knocked on his driver's window and when he opened it, bent forward to kiss him. The very smell of her, at that moment, was wonderful. Why did he always forget to ask her what perfume she wore? If he knew what it was he would buy a bottle himself, keep it by his bedside so that he could smell her whenever he wanted. He felt himself enfolded by her, tangled up in her hair, her arms reaching forward to clasp his neck. His mouth made as if to touch hers but at the last moment some uncertainty interposed itself, some register of ambiguity about their relationship—friends? colleagues? lovers?—and they ended up kissing on the cheek. But neither of them seemed to mind. They laughed and as Malvina held on to him tightly she said, "Hello. I've missed you," and then she climbed into the car.

They talked about nothing very serious over lunch. There were dozens of well-known pubs in the area, recommended in guide books for their rich and varied menus and their old-world charm, but Paul didn't want to go to any of those: at this time of year, they would be crammed with tourists, and he might be recognized. So they went to a place on one of the A-roads, with an ugly pebbledash exterior and food straight out of the 1970s. As she struggled with her burger, Malvina was girlish, nervously chatty, seemingly as reluctant as he was to broach the subject of their shared future, if any. She talked instead about her course, the impending delivery of a long end-of-year assignment, and how one of her tutors had made a diffident but unmistakable pass at her during a recent supervision.

"Poor you," said Paul. "That's the last thing you need—some lecherous old sod drooling all over you."

"He's younger than you, actually," said Malvina. "And almost as good-looking." And her eyes laughed as she said it, thrilled by the intimacy which gave her licence to tease him.

After that they drove east, along the road towards Banbury, but after only a few minutes Paul noticed a sign to a public footpath, and pulled over into a lay-by.

"Where is this?" Malvina asked. "It looks vaguely familiar."

Paul had no idea where they were. There were two or three other cars parked in the lay-by, from which a gate led through a patch of rough hedgerow towards some tourist attraction beyond. Malvina walked over to the gate and read the notice attached to it, which told her that these were the famous Rollright Stones, a prehistoric stone circle probably marking an ancient burial spot—but also associated, in local legend, with stories of witchcraft.

"I think I've been here before," she said. "In fact I'm sure of it. Can we go inside and have a look?"

Paul wasn't keen. There were at least a dozen people wandering around the site already, taking photos of the weirdly shaped, pockmarked and lichen-encrusted stones.

"Sorry," he said. "It's too risky. Let's walk somewhere instead."

"Oh, come on—please. Just for a few minutes."

"We'll leave the car here. We can come back later, when it's a bit less crowded."

They set off down the main road and then took a left turn down the footpath. Soon the ground had started to shelve, and the village of Little Rollright disclosed itself before them, nestled furtively in the valley formed between swathes of hilly pastureland. The squat tower of its church shone brazenly in the afternoon light. All was quiet, now, and deadly still. No traffic noise, no tourists. They had the world to themselves.

There was a bench next to the church door, facing out over the village. After looking in a desultory way around the interior (which at least had the effect of cooling them down after their walk), and inspecting the gravestones—which were nearly all too weathered to read—they took refuge here, and steadied themselves for the conversation that could no longer be put off.

"Well," said Malvina—who had known all along that she would have to be the one to get it started—"things have moved on a bit, haven't they, in the last few months? The balance has shifted. When we started out, I got the impression—I mean, I might be wrong about this—that all you wanted to do was sleep with me. And that gave me a feeling of control over you and I suppose I liked that, I enjoyed it. But it started to feel different for me . . . when was it? . . . on the day of the march. That night, I mean. The night I stayed at your house. I remember . . . just sitting with you on the sofa, after dinner, in front of the fire, before we went to bed. We couldn't bear even to touch each other and in a weird sort of way that's what made it feel so intimate to me: or at least, that's what made me admit to myself where we'd got to. That we'd got to the edge of a cliff, without realizing it. And then . . . Then I suppose we have Doug to thank for the rest. He told you what I was going through. And then you came round to see me, the night before you went to Denmark. And . . . well, I was surprised, I must say. Absolutely amazed, in fact. You really let yourself go that night. You said a lot of things—"

"I meant them," said Paul, quickly. "I meant them all."

"I know you did," Malvina answered. "I don't doubt that for a minute. All the same, I'm not going to hold you to anything." She glanced at him. "You know that, don't you?"

Paul said nothing. The sun was making his eyes ache and he was conscious that his shirt was becoming sticky with sweat. He was going to have sunburn by the end of the day, if he wasn't careful. How would he explain that to Susan when he next saw her?

"I was on cloud nine for a day or two after that," Malvina continued. "Till that thing in the paper brought me down to earth, I suppose. And now it doesn't look quite so rosy. The last few weeks have been just awful. I feel I've lost all control over my life. I feel completely powerless. Do you know what that's like? Probably not."

Paul laid his hand on hers, and tried to sound reassuring. "I know things are difficult," he said, "but it won't be for much longer . . ."

"What do you mean?" said Malvina, suddenly angry. "How can you say that? Why won't it be for much longer?"

"Because after a while the press will lose interest."

"Never mind about the press. What about *you*? What are *you* going to do? What are you going to do about me? *That's* the question, isn't it? Not the fucking newspapers."

"Yes," he said, sighing deeply, and beginning to get a sense for the first time of what she was talking about. "Yes, you're right. That is the question."

He fell gloomily silent, then. It was not even that he was lost for words: he was lost for thoughts. All at once he was quite anchorless, adrift, with no idea at all of what he was supposed to be thinking or feeling.

"I can't have an affair with you," said Malvina, when it began to seem that he was never going to speak again. "I can't handle it. I don't want to hurt Susan, for one thing, or your daughter. And I can't walk on eggshells all the time, never knowing when I'm allowed to phone you, never knowing when I'm going to see you next. That doesn't seem to bother you. You almost seem to thrive on it. But . . . we can't spend the rest of our lives meeting up in country churchyards, with you looking over your shoulder every five minutes to see if there's a photographer behind you, or checking your mobile to see if Susan's called." Her voice was shrill with exasperation. "Can we?"

"No, I told you—I told you in an email, this is just a phase, until things quieten down, until they . . . sort themselves out."

"But they're not going to sort *themselves* out, Paul. *You* have to sort them out." In a different voice—quieter and sadder—she added, "I know that's asking a lot. And it's not me that's doing the asking, actually. You're asking it of yourself, if you think about it. All I'm saying is, it's got to the point where we have to make a choice."

"Between?"

"Between being friends, and being lovers."

Of course, it was just what he had been expecting to hear. But the starkness of the phrase rocked him, even so.

"Ah," was all he managed to say, at first.

But then it started to dawn on him that the choice was not so brutal after all. What did "friendship" mean, anyway? Friendship was what they had already. An unusually intense, passionate friendship, certainly, but that was the best thing about it: that was what made it so new and exciting for him. So they hadn't slept together: well, they could congratulate themselves on that, on their self-control. He and Malvina were doing something radical, actually—what they were experimenting with was a *new kind* of friendship, and one which (he was only dimly starting to intuit this) happened to satisfy his emotional needs rather well, when placed into the context of his secure marriage and family life. He saw no need to rock any boats, for the time being. What he had with Malvina was enough. And perhaps, even, as the friendship evolved, they would find a way of adding a sexual dimension, they would feel ready for it, after a while . . . Anything was possible. Anything was possible as long as they kept seeing each other, and took things slowly.

"Well then," he said. "It has to be friendship. If that's all we can have, then . . . that's what it has to be."

The words did not sound as triumphant, spoken out loud, as he had hoped they would. And they did not have the expected effect on Malvina. He felt a force-field go up around her, a protective wall of energy. Her whole body tightened. She didn't move, but it seemed as though a physical distance had immediately opened up between them.

Her voice cracked as she said, after what felt like aeons: "Then why did you say those things to me? The night before you went to Skagen? What was the point?"

"I . . . had to," Paul answered, helplessly. "It was what I was feeling. It was the truth. I couldn't keep it inside me any longer."

"I see."

She stood up, and walked slowly to the other side of the churchyard. She stood there for some time, with her back towards him, looking out over the parched and baking fields. She was wearing a pale blue, sleeveless summer dress and once again Paul was struck by the *thin*ness of her, the startling weightlessness of her bones, her terrible fragility. For an instant he felt as fatherly and protective towards her as he had ever felt towards Antonia. And in the same instant he remembered, with a rush of guilt, that he had had a ludicrous fantasy in the car on the way over, which had involved bringing her to some secluded churchyard just like this and making exalted love somewhere among the gravestones. It didn't seem very likely, on the whole, that this was now going to happen. He wondered if he should go over and put an arm around her, say something to her. But now she was blowing her nose, and turning, and coming back to him. She sat beside him on the bench and sniffed a few more times. The sun passed behind a tall yew tree which folded them both in cooling shade.

At last she was able to say:

"OK, then. Friendship it is. But there's something you have to understand."

"What's that?"

She swallowed and announced: "We can't see each other any more."

These words, when he first heard them, made literally no sense to Paul. He wondered if she had simply spoken them by mistake.

"What do you mean?"

"I mean that we cannot have a friendship—a successful, normal friendship—until these feelings have gone away. Not until we've got each other out of our systems."

Paul's stomach was churning now. He could feel himself starting to panic. "But—how long is that supposed to take?"

"How should I know?" said Malvina, rubbing her eyes and exposing their bloodshot rims. "I can't speak for you. A long time. A hell of a long time." She looked away, and twirled a strand of hair around one finger. In the sunlight it didn't look so black any more: it was auburn, almost. "Anyway, I'm the one who's in deepest, here. Deny that if you like, but it's true. So it has to be me who decides when we get back in touch. When I feel ready to be friends with you again. I don't want you contacting me in the meantime. I can't cope with that."

Still bewildered at the speed with which this was happening, Paul asked: "Are we talking . . . weeks? Months?"

"I don't know. As I said: I think it'll be a long time."

"But—" Now it was his turn to get up and start pacing between the crooked gravestones. "But this is crazy. Not long ago we were—"

"No. It isn't crazy. The way we've been trying to live the last few weeks is crazy. Think about it, Paul. I'm right. It's horrible, but I know I'm right."

He did think about it. And they talked about it, too, for much longer, the conversation never going anywhere now, turning round upon itself in endless loops, oscillating and repeating itself, always coming back, in the end, to the central fact of Malvina's proposal, which even to Paul seemed to have taken on a dreadful, unarguable necessity. So that finally, browbeaten into a kind of paralysis, he could only sit forward on the bench with his head in his hands and repeat the same exhausted phrase:

"I can't believe we're going to do this. I can't believe we're really doing it."

"Neither can I, to be honest," Malvina said. "But there you go."

"I just think . . . there *has* to be some other route we could go down, some other—"

"Paul, listen to me." She looked him directly in the eye. "When it comes to a situation like this, *there is no third way*. Do you understand? Do you get it? Stop trying to convince yourself that there is." She stood up, and he could see that her eyes were glistening with tears again. "Right," she said, her voice shaking. "Walk back to the car now?"

They walked back up the hill in near-silence. At first they held hands. Then Paul put his arm around Malvina and she leaned into him. They walked like that for five or ten minutes; it was the closest they had ever come to physical intimacy. Then Malvina detached herself, and for the last few hundred yards she strode on ahead. She was waiting for Paul at the gate beside the car.

"I'm going to have a look at the stones," she said. "Do you want to say goodbye now?"

"No, I'll come with you," said Paul, and followed her through the gate.

There was nobody else there anyway. Despite the windlessness of the afternoon, it was not completely silent, for the stones were sited next to a main road, and every few seconds a car would speed past. None the less, as soon as they stepped inside the circle, they were both newly conscious of a great stillness; derived from nothing more, perhaps, than a sense that they had found themselves in a very ancient space, created for some sacred but now unfathomable purpose.

They stood very close to one another, not talking, not moving.

"I have been here before," Malvina said at last. She wandered a few steps away from him. "My mother brought me here. I don't know what we were doing in this part of the world. She'd just split up from her husband; her first husband. He was Greek, he had nothing to do with this area, I can't explain it. Anyway: I remember it now, very clearly. My mother was weeping. She was doing this terrible histrionic weeping, clinging on to me, telling me what a dreadful person she was and how she was ruining my life. I must have been . . . six, maybe? Seven? No—six. That's right. I can still remember this couple staring at us, this middle-aged couple, staring at us and wondering what the hell was going on. The woman was wearing a green headscarf. It was winter." She looked around her at the corroded, misshapen stones, as if she hadn't noticed them before. "Funny to be here again."

Impulsively, Paul said: "Malvina, I don't know what's going to happen between me and Susan. I don't even know if we're going to survive this. Some time in the future, if I come looking for you . . ."

She smiled. "Well, of course you can do that. But I don't know where I'll be."

"You'll stay in London, won't you?"

"I meant where I'll be emotionally. Somewhere else, I hope. Somewhere new." Kindly now, she added: "Paul—you had a choice to make, and you made it. That's the important thing. Well done. Now go. I'll make my own way back to the station."

"Don't be silly—it's not safe."

"It's a beautiful afternoon. I'll walk. Let's get this over with."

He could see that she was determined, even on this point.

Then Malvina took his hands and drew him towards her.

"Come on, then," she said. "*Ae fond kiss,* as Robbie Burns would put it."

But they didn't kiss, even now. They merely held each other, and Paul breathed in the scent of her hair, the warmth of her skull, and that perfume whose name he still didn't know, and the uncanny stillness of the circle reminded him of Skagen, with its unbroken silences, and he realized that he was being offered another of those moments that would never end, that would always be with him. He clung on to it fiercely, willing himself into a sense of timelessness. But he could feel Malvina pushing, pushing him gently away from her. And at last he released her and broke away.

Paul looked back only one more time as he made for the gate. It occurred to him, in a spasm of despair, that this might be his last ever sight of Malvina. Standing with her back towards him again, looking out over the fields, alone, in a pale blue summer dress, at the center of the circle; the circle of stones which watched over her, closed in on her, like the demons she had been fleeing all her life and whose nature he had never, he now realized, even begun to understand.

He turned on his heels and walked back towards the car.

He was still in a state of shock when he arrived back at the flat in Kennington. He drank the last two-thirds of a bottle of whisky and then every other drop of alcohol he could find in the kitchen. At ten o'clock he passed out on his sofa, fully clothed. He woke up again at three in the morning, with a raging thirst and an aching bladder. His head throbbed like the thumb of a cartoon character after it has been caught in a mousetrap. He wanted to be sick. Then he realized what had woken him up, and he almost shouted for joy. It was the double beep of a text message on his mobile phone. She had contacted him again. Of course she had. She couldn't go through with it, any more than he could. It was all a terrible mistake and in the morning they would see each other again. He opened the message and found that his service provider was telling him he had won a £1000 prize draw. He would have to dial a special number to claim his prize and calls were charged at 50p a minute.

13

Paul's resolve held firm. He was never quite sure if Malvina was doing this to punish him, or whether it was truly the only course she felt they could take, if she was to survive with her sanity and her sense of self intact. Either way, he respected her wishes, and made no attempt to contact her. The days without her were long and agonizing. He checked his answering machine messages obsessively, his emails every few minutes. Nothing came.

In time the days came to seem shorter, and the agony came to be less.

He acted swiftly to stop the gossip about his private life, and on June 1st, 2000 issued a statement to the press: delivered, as tradition demanded, in front of his family home, with Antonia clutching at his knees on the doorstep, and Susan standing beside him, smiling a tight, furious smile.

"After acting foolishly and wrongly," he said, "I have made a strong decision to commit myself to my marriage, and my family . . ."

Malvina read these words in the newspaper the next day, while sitting in her college library. Feeling sick, she hurried to the toilets, but collapsed on the way and had to be taken by the assistant librarian to his office, and revived with a glass of water.

Just over a year later, in the early hours of June 8th, 2001, she was watching the television coverage of the general election results when the cameras went live to Paul's constituency. He had been re-elected, with a slightly reduced majority. His beaming, gratified face filled the screen for a moment, and Susan, who was standing by his side, leaned in to kiss his cheek in close up. The sound faded as he stepped forward to make his victory speech, and his voice was drowned out by that of the TV pundit, commenting on the strength of the challenge Paul had faced from the Liberal Democrats. The camera pulled out for a long shot, and Malvina noticed that Susan was not only clasping Antonia's hand in the background, but cradling a baby—probably another girl, judging from her pink sleep-suit—who seemed to be little more than two or three months old. So that was how they had resolved it, then. Why not? Who could say how other people's relationships worked? A phrase came to her, suddenly, out of nowhere: *You've been dead a long time* . . . It was from a song, maybe, a song she'd heard some time last year, when she'd still been working for Paul. That was how she felt; and saw no prospect of ever feeling any different. Fuck it. She wished them well, anyway: then decided she didn't want to watch any more, poured herself another Diet Coke from the fridge and started flicking between channels.

12

12 June, 2001

Dear Philip,

I don't know if you remember me, but we were at King William's School together back in the 1970s. All seems like a very long time ago now!

I'm writing to you out of the blue like this because sometimes I get to see the Birmingham Post *and I like your journalism.*

I live in Telford now—with my wife Kate and two daughters, Allison and Diane—and work in the R&D department of a local firm specializing in plastics. (I never did get anywhere with physics, after messing up that exam. Ended up doing chemistry at Manchester. Polymers are my thing, these days, if that means anything to you. It probably doesn't.) We've been here for just over nine years and we're doing fine.

Telford has been in the news a bit lately. I'm sure you know all about the Errol McGowan case, which has been in a lot of the national papers. Errol was a doorman at the Charlton Arms hotel and pub. He fell out with a white guy who had been barred from the pub and started getting a lot of racial abuse—through the post, on the telephone. Anonymous stuff. It started to turn really nasty and Errol became convinced he was on some kind of Combat 18 death list. In the end it gave him a kind of nervous breakdown and just over two years ago he was found dead in somebody else's house, hanging from a door knob. He was thirty-four.

The police decided straight away that it was suicide and basically weren't interested in hearing any other explanation. Not even when his nephew, Jason, was found hanging from railings outside another pub six months later! People were pretty angry about this and eventually there was an inquest. It happened last month and you probably read about it. The coroner decided it was suicide again. The police admitted Errol had contacted them about the death threats but they hadn't done anything about it.

I'm writing to you because I've been sent a few things in the post here myself in recent weeks. Two letters, and a CD—a really horrible CD, which I only put on for about ten seconds. (And then only in the car, because I knew what it was going to be like and I didn't want my family to hear it.)

I'm not scared about any of this. I just think there's a story here, which nobody is telling. Sure, we live in a successful multicultural society. A tolerant society. (Though what have I ever done, that people have to "tolerate" me?) But these people are still out there. I know they're a minority. I know they're just jokers and tossers, most of them. But look at what's been going on, the last few weeks, in Bradford and Oldham. Race riots—proper race riots. Black and Asian people being made the scapegoats, again, for something that has gone wrong in white people's lives. So I'm thinking that maybe this "tolerance" is just a mask for something ugly and rotten which is going to flare up at any moment.

I won't go on. I expect journalists don't like people telling them what pieces they should write. I just think it says something when people like me aren't allowed to get on with their lives peacefully. Even now—in the twenty-first century! In Blair's Brave New Britain.

Ah well. Get in touch if you can, if only for old times' sake.

All the best,

Steve (Richards). (Astell House, 1971–79)

Two days later, at around seven o'clock in the evening, Philip drove out to Telford. Traffic on the northbound M6 was dreadful, as always—there always seemed to be at least one lane coned off to make way for non-existent roadworks—and it was after eight by the time he parked at the bottom of Steve's drive. The houses here were even newer than most of the houses in Telford: this was a New Town, after all, one of the great experiments of the 1960s, but the estate where Steve lived must have been finished only two or three years ago. The houses were spacious, comfortable-looking, neo-Georgian. Fiats and Rovers and sometimes BMWs were parked in the driveways. It did not feel soulless, exactly: just placid, and somehow unambitious, and very, very quiet. Philip could imagine that it wasn't such a bad place to live. It just felt odd, to him (and had always felt odd, ever since he had come to know this part of the world as a boy, visiting his grandparents) that this militantly new, characterless town had so recently arrived, unannounced, without preamble, without *history*, and simply dumped itself into the middle of one of the oldest and least-known, most mysterious and recondite counties in the whole of England. It didn't belong there, and it never would. It was a breeding ground for displacement and alienation.

But Steve, it had to be said, looked neither displaced nor alienated when he opened the door with a broad smile and beckoned Philip inside. He was greying around the temples, and he wore glasses now, but the smile had not changed, and there was a youthfulness, a boyish delight about the way he tugged Philip into the living room to introduce him to his two daughters, who turned the television off without complaint and seemed genuinely intrigued by the appearance of this unassuming phantom from their father's past.

"The girls have already eaten," Steve explained. "It's no good trying to get them to wait. Come on now, you two, get upstairs. No more telly till your homework's done. You can come down and have something to drink with us after."

"Wine?" asked Allison, the elder of the two, who looked to be about fourteen.

"Maybe," said Steve. "Depends how good you've been."

"Brilliant."

They both ran upstairs; after which, Steve took Philip through into the kitchen, to meet his wife, and to eat.

Kate had baked two pizzas—hot ones, with ground beef and chilli peppers—and dressed a crisp green salad of watercress and rocket leaves. From a wine rack under the stairs Steve chose a rich and velvety Chilean Merlot, although Philip had to switch over regretfully to mineral water after only one small glass.

"Now, Kate is going to find this really boring," Steve said, throwing her an apologetic glance, "but I have to ask you—are you still in touch with any of those guys from school?"

"One or two of them," said Philip. "Claire Newman, for instance—remember her?"

"Yeah, I remember. Nice girl. She used to work on the magazine with you."

"That's right. Well, I married her, a few years after we left school."

"You did? That's fantastic! Congratulations."

"OK, but don't get too excited. Then we got divorced."

"Oh."

"It's all right. Everything worked out fine. It was just one of those . . . bad decisions. We've got a son called Patrick. He lives with me and my second wife, Carol, for various complicated reasons. Claire was in Italy for quite a few years but just recently she's moved to Malvern, so maybe we'll see a bit more of each other now. We were talking about having a few days in London together soon, going down with Patrick."

"All sounds very grown-up and liberal to me," said Steve. "Not sure I could handle that."

Teasingly, Kate said: "Steve's getting more and more conservative in his old age. I've been trying to persuade him to have an open marriage for years, but he won't listen."

He laughed this away. "But what about Benjamin? Did you ever hear what happened to Benjamin? I mean, I know this sounds crazy, but every so often I go into a bookshop, into WH Smith or something, and I go and look at the 'T's in the paperback section, 'cause I'm still expecting something by him to pop up there any minute. I mean, we all thought he would have won the Nobel Prize or something by now."

"Oh, I'm still in touch with Ben. See him every couple of weeks, actually. He's still in Birmingham. Works for a company called Morley Jackson Gray."

Steve speared some rocket and said, "Sounds like a firm of accountants."

"That's exactly what it is."

"He became an *accountant*?"

"Well, T. S. Eliot worked in a bank, didn't he? I dare say that's the kind of precedent that goes through Benjamin's mind."

"I remember now," Steve said. "Benjamin worked for a bank, didn't he? Just for a few months, before he went up to university."

"That's right. And then . . . Well, after he graduated, he'd just started this novel, and he wanted to get it finished, so he didn't want to get a proper job at first. The bank said they'd take him back for a few months, and that must have sounded like the ideal way to buy himself a bit more time for writing. But—I don't know, the novel never quite seemed to get finished, and meanwhile he got friendly with this other bloke from the bank and they formed a band—you know how Benjamin always used to write music, as well—and that started to take up more and more time, and somehow in the middle of all this, he must have got some kind of taste for all that number-crunching, because the next thing I hear, he's doing his accountancy exams and saying that the novel's gone on hold and he needs a long period of stability to get his head around it." Philip took a sip of water and added: "And then, of course, he goes and marries Emily."

"Who?"

"Emily Sandys. From school. Don't you remember? From the Christian Society."

Steve shook his head. "Not my scene, really. I always assumed he was going to marry . . . you know . . . Cicely."

His voice dropped as he spoke this name: leading Phil to wonder whether, even now, Steve still suffered from some sort of sexual guilt about the time he and Cicely had been in the school production of *Othello* together, and afterwards had had a quick fling (though fling was too strong a word for it—nothing more than a teenage grope, really, at the after-show party) which had led to the break-up of his first serious relationship. It never ceased to surprise Philip that even after two decades there were some people who could not pronounce that name without it producing a kind of *frisson:* Benjamin was one of them, obviously, but so was Claire, for some reason, and now (apparently) Steve as well. How could anyone have left such a legacy behind her, such a trail of energy, generated so unthinkingly and in such a short time?

"No one really knows what happened to Cicely," he said, guardedly. "She went back to America and kind of . . . left Benjamin in the lurch. Took him a long time to recover from it."

"*Has* he recovered from it?" Steve asked, after a pause.

Philip mopped up some salad dressing from his plate with a scrap of bread, and said: "Benjamin told me once—I don't know if this is true or not—that she went back to America to be with this woman Helen, and they became . . . you know . . . lovers."

Steve's eyes widened. "*Cicely?* A dyke?"

"As I said, I don't know if it's true or not."

Kate stood up and began to clear the plates away.

"Maybe we should change the subject," Steve said, when she was over by the sink, out of earshot. "But there's one more thing: what happened to Benjamin's sister? The one with the boyfriend who died in the pub bombings."

Now it was Philip's turn to look suddenly wistful.

"Yeah . . . Lois . . . Well, Benjamin doesn't talk about her much. Doesn't see her much either, I don't think. As far as I know she lives up north somewhere—York or something. I think she was ill, for quite a long time, after that happened. And then she met this guy and sort of . . . threw herself into it. Got married, had a daughter . . . Can't remember her name now."

"Did Benjamin have kids?"

"No. They couldn't. I don't know why. Don't think they do either." Philip was remembering, now, the last time he had actually spoken to Lois. "There was this dinner party," he said, reminiscing aloud, while Steve frowned, doing his best to follow the rambling train of thought. "And Lois was wearing this dress. She could only have been about sixteen. I fancied her something rotten. We had this terrible food—God, can you remember what we used to *eat* back in the seventies . . . ?"

"I know." Steve laughed, and gestured at the debris on the table. "We're all such sophisticates now."

". . . And that was the night . . . I suppose that was the night I got my first clue, that my mum was thinking of starting an affair with Mr. Plumb—Sugar Plum Fairy: d'you remember him?"

"I certainly do. The horny old sod."

Philip smiled, and shook his head. "My parents nearly broke up over that. Can you imagine? It did my head in, for a while." Steve offered to pour some more wine, and he pushed his glass forward, not caring, for a moment, that he had a long drive ahead of him later that night. "Thanks."

"He and your mum, though: they never . . . *did* anything, did they?"

"Depends what you mean," said Philip, swirling the wine around in his glass. "She died five years ago, and afterwards, I cleared out some of her old stuff. Dad didn't want to do it. And there were all these letters. Letters he'd written to her. They were very passionate—even if you did need a bloody dictionary to understand them. And she hung on to them, all that time. I don't know what to make of that. Don't know what it tells me . . ."

"She stayed with your dad all that time, as well," Steve reminded him. And when Philip didn't respond, he asked: "Is he coping OK—with being on his own?"

"Well . . ." Philip smiled again; a private smile this time. "He's a great reader, that's the thing you have to remember about my dad. Always has his nose in a book. His eyesight's going, but he still reads. Every day. Novels, history—anything he can get his hands on."

Kate came back to the table carrying a plate of strawberry cheesecake, and for a while the two old friends forced themselves to stop talking about their schooldays. Philip learned, instead, how Kate and Steve had met in their last year at Manchester university, how Kate had interrupted her career to bring up the girls but was now looking for a way to get back into teaching as soon as she could, and how Steve had found himself a niche working in the research laboratory of a local firm, based on an industrial estate just outside Telford, trying to make advances in the field of biodegradable plastics.

"I *am* the R&D department, basically," he explained. "Me and a part-time assistant. It's frustrating that we don't have many resources, but they're a good company—really into what I'm trying to do."

"Unfortunately," said Kate, spooning out the cheesecake, "they can only afford to pay him peanuts. That's the real problem."

"I didn't think plastics *were* biodegradable," Philip said, feeling rather simple-minded as he did so.

"Well of course they're not," Steve said. "They're synthetic. But we might be able to *make* them biodegradable, or photodegradable, in time. They've developed some plastics that are soluble in hot water, for instance. Cellophane is biodegradable—did you know that? The trouble at the moment is that the degradation takes such a long time."

"What about recycling? Isn't that the answer?"

"Well, it's not easy, because people chuck all their plastic stuff away together, but then it all has to be recycled in different ways. So someone has to sort it all. Thermoplastic polymers and thermosetting polymers can't be recycled in the same way, for one thing."

"I've got a feeling," said Kate, "that Philip doesn't know what you're talking about. Any more than I do, to be honest."

"No, but I can tell that what you're doing's important," said Philip.

"It's too important, actually, for the place where I'm working. Too big, in a way."

"Do you think you could move on to somewhere else? A bigger firm, with more money for that sort of thing?"

"These people have been great, but . . . yeah, it's crossed my mind." Steve reached for the cafetière and started pouring coffee. "I'm keeping my eye on the job adverts, put it like that."

Just before Philip left, Steve handed him a large jiffy bag. Inside were some sheets of handwritten paper, and a CD. The handwriting was ragged and erratic—a mixture of lower-case letters and capitals, scrawled with a blotchy blue biro. The CD seemed to have been manufactured on the cheap: the black-and-white cover looked as though it had been reproduced on a photocopier, and featured the usual neo-Nazi iconography of skulls and swastikas. The title was *Auschwitz Carnival* and the band was called "Unrepentant."

"Lovely," said Philip, scanning the song titles briefly.

Conscious that Allison and Diane were lingering in the hallway, looking on with some curiosity, Steve said: "Look, Phil, it's been a great evening. Fantastic to see you again. Don't let's spoil it by talking about stuff like that."

"OK," said Philip. "I'll check it out in the next couple of days."

"Be good if you could write something."

"I'll see what I can do."

They smiled at each other, now, and Philip offered to shake Steve's hand; but Steve embraced him instead, and clapped him gently on the back.

"Let's stay in touch from now on—yeah?"

"Will do."

Philip kissed Kate goodnight, and kissed both of Steve's daughters, and looked back at them as they stood waving in the doorway when he walked down to his car. It had a good feeling about it, that family, he thought on the drive home; and this made him even sicker with fury the next day when he read the letters Steve had been sent, with their references to his "white slut wife" and his "deformed children, half-white and half-nigger." He only listened to a few minutes of the CD, turning it off in the middle of the second track. Without having to reflect for a moment longer, he knew that he owed it to Steve to find out more about this. He would have to write a piece. A series of pieces. Maybe something even bigger.

II

MINUTES
of a meeting of
THE CLOSED CIRCLE
held at Rules Restaurant, Covent Garden
Wednesday 20 June, 2001

Strictly Private and Confidential

An inaugural meeting of THE CLOSED CIRCLE was held at the above venue on the above date. The members present were:

Paul Trotter, MP
Mr. Ronald Culpepper, MiF, EMBA
Mr. Michael Usborne, CBE
Lord Addison
Prof. David Glover (London Business School)
Ms. Angela Marcus

Drinks were served in a private room at 7:30 p.m. All the members being well known to each other, no introductions were considered necessary. Dinner was served at 8 o'clock and the business of the meeting began at 9:45 p.m.

It having been previously agreed that the nature of the CIRCLE's business, and the manner in which it was to be conducted, required that there should be no chair, informal opening remarks were addressed by Mr. CULPEPPER.

These remarks were brief, and consisted principally of congratulations directed towards Mr. TROTTER on his recent re-election as a Member of Parliament. A toast was proposed to Mr. TROTTER's continued parliamentary success. Mr. CULPEPPER's sentiments were warmly echoed by the other members of the CIRCLE.

The remainder of the business consisted largely of an address by Mr. TROTTER.

In his address, Mr. TROTTER proposed to lay out the principal aims and undertakings of THE CLOSED CIRCLE. In doing so, he paid warm tribute, first of all, to Mr. CULPEPPER, with whom he had enjoyed a long friendship and association for more than twenty years. He informed the other members that the name, "THE CLOSED CIRCLE," had been chosen as an act of remembrance, in memory of a society to which he and Mr. Culpepper had both belonged when they were at school, and where they had first met.

He then recalled the circumstances which had led him to found the Commission for Business and Social Initiatives (CBSI) earlier in the year, beginning with his grave decision to resign as Parliamentary Private Secretary to a Minister of State in January. Mr. TROTTER dismissed press speculation that his working relationship with said Minister had degenerated beyond repair. He insisted, rather, that after more than three years he had begun to find the role of Parliamentary Private Secretary increasingly constricting, and had resolved to find a more fruitful outlet for his ideas, which had always tended towards the more radical fringes of the party's thinking.

Once freed from the restrictions imposed by his responsibilities towards his Department, the setting up of a Commission had seemed an appropriate way to proceed. Although he was at pains to remind fellow-members that the CBSI had the full support of the party leadership (by which he meant both its wings—or, as some preferred to call them, factions), Mr. TROTTER reiterated that his intention had always been for the Commission to remain totally independent and totally free-thinking. Only in this way, he remained convinced, could it hope to achieve its aim: which was, he reminded them, to find ways in which the involvement of the business community in the provision of public services could be promoted to a greater extent even than the Labour party had achieved in its first term.

The purpose of THE CLOSED CIRCLE, Mr. TROTTER maintained, was to support the work of the Commission, not to undermine or circumvent it. Nonetheless, the six members of the CIRCLE had been chosen from the eighteen members of the Commission for a specific reason. The Commission was essentially a public body, whose membership details were in the public domain and whose proceedings were being documented by the press. It had been necessary, therefore, to draw its membership from the full spectrum of political opinion. Obviously, this made it a lively forum for debate, and there was no question that any member of the CIRCLE might wish to stifle such debate. However, it could be—and indeed had been—argued that there was scope, within the bounds of the Commission itself, for a further forum: a sort of circle-within-the-circle, in which those members who were attuned to the most progressive currents of policy-making could express their views freely, in an informal and unguarded manner, knowing that their remarks would be addressed only to like-minded thinkers, and that their words would not be open to misinterpretation or censorship.

The aim of the CIRCLE, then, was to create a space within the Commission where the most radical and far-reaching ideas could be floated for the first time. It would remain clandestine only so that its members had more freedom to speak their minds, not less. Mr. TROTTER reminded his fellow-members that private finance initiatives had now made their way into the public sector in ways which would have been unthinkable ten years ago, under the Conservative government. Responsibility for substantial areas of health provision, state education, local government, prison services and even air traffic control were now in the hands of private companies whose duty of care lay towards the interests of shareholders rather than the general public. In order to advance this programme even further—to "roll back the frontiers of the state" to a point which even the author of that phrase (Margaret Thatcher) would not have recognized—members of the CLOSED CIRCLE were going to have to think the unthinkable, and imagine the unimaginable. His own task, as an enabler, was simply to provide them with a context in which this could be possible.

Mr. TROTTER concluded his address at this point and asked the other members if they had any questions.

Ms. MARCUS asked if the existence of the CIRCLE was known to the Prime Minister. Mr. TROTTER replied that it was not. The Prime Minister was keenly interested in the work of the CBSI, but was not aware that some of its members had formed themselves into a supplementary body. Nor was there any intention to make him so aware.

Lord ADDISON inquired as to the proposed frequency of the CIRCLE's meetings. Mr. CULPEPPER offered his suggestion that the CIRCLE should meet twice as often as the Commission itself: viz., once shortly after each meeting of the Commission, to share responses to the meeting, and once shortly before the next meeting, to discuss strategy. This proposal was generally approved.

Mr. TROTTER reminded the other members of the CIRCLE that the next meeting of the Commission would concentrate on the subject of the railway network, in view of the current crisis at Railtrack. Loss of public confidence in the wake of a series of fatal rail accidents had resulted in an operating loss of £534 million. There had been speculation that the government might renationalize the railways in response to public opinion, but Mr. TROTTER insisted that this was not an option. It was more likely, he said, that the company would be put into administration, although no detailed plans for a replacement had as yet been drawn up. Lord ADDISON voiced the opinion that this was an "extraordinary" state of affairs. He asked if Mr. USBORNE, one of whose companies was contracted to maintain large sections of track in the south-east, had received any confirmation of this information. Mr. USBORNE replied that he was somewhat "out of the loop," having resigned his position as CEO of Pantechnicon some two months earlier, following concern over breaches of safety regulations, mounting redundancies and falling share prices.

Professor GLOVER asked Mr. TROTTER to clarify his own position on this subject, since he remembered reading remarks attributed to him in the newspapers last year, which could have been interpreted as critical of the management of the privatized rail companies. Mr. TROTTER replied that his remarks had been taken out of context and did not represent his real views.

At this point Mr. TROTTER was called away to receive a fax. He explained to the other members that he had recently secured a contract to write a weekly column for a national newspaper, recounting his experiences of fatherhood, and the writer who composed the column for him had agreed to fax it over to the restaurant this evening for his approval prior to publication. He apologized to the other members of the CIRCLE and told them that he would return in a few minutes.

Meanwhile Mr. CULPEPPER expressed his commiserations, belatedly, to Mr. USBORNE on his enforced resignation from Pantechnicon. Mr. USBORNE thanked him for his concern, and admitted that he had been disappointed that his efforts on behalf of the company had been undervalued, and his conduct misrepresented in parts of the financial and popular press. For his own part, he was proud of the way he had streamlined the company and made considerable savings in human capital. However, he was able to reassure Mr. CULPEPPER that he had received, on the whole, satisfactory compensation for his distress, and had subsequently been offered a range of other chairmanships and executive posts, from which he was currently in the process of choosing. Ms. MARCUS expressed the hope that he had invested his compensation payment wisely and Mr. USBORNE informed her that he had used it to add to his private property portfolio.

There followed an informal discussion on the subject of remuneration packages, and the meeting broke up in great good humour at 10:55 p.m.

It was agreed that the next meeting of THE CLOSED CIRCLE should be held on Wednesday, 1 August 2001 at the same location.

IO

Claire was crouched to one side of the garden path when Benjamin arrived, snipping away decisively at the offshoot of some prickly, grey-green plant which, as usual, he was completely unable to identify. The squeak of the garden gate made her look up. She smiled and rose to her feet in a lithe, youthful movement. The evening sun was low and shone full on her face, exposing crows' feet and laughter-lines. But her skin—tawnier, more Mediterranean than Benjamin remembered it—was pulled tight still over strong cheekbones, and the cut of her greying hair was neither severe nor merely sensible: it followed the curve of her cheek in a fashionable bob, and made her look young—eight, ten years younger than he knew her to be.

"Hi, Ben," she said, briskly, and gave him a short kiss on the cheek. He tried to hold her in a hug as she did it, but the embrace dissolved rapidly, after a second or two. They both took a half-step back.

Claire shielded her eyes and regarded him coolly, appraisingly.

"You're looking good," she said. "Filled out a bit. You used to be a skinny thing."

"It happens," said Benjamin. "You look good, too. Very good, in fact."

The compliment provoked a smile that was half gladness, half politeness. "Come on in," she said, and turned to lead the way back towards the house.

It was a tiny, redbricked cottage, part of a modest row which nestled against the shoulder of the hill beneath the Worcester Road, the houses staring down with practised indifference over the rough expanse of parkland that lay beneath them. The front door gave directly on to a sitting room filled with unsorted clutter, through which it was just possible, with a bit of ingenuity, to trace a path through to the kitchen and finally towards a paved yard and small, as yet untended patch of back garden.

"Must've been a hassle," Benjamin said, "moving in here, all by yourself."

"I did have removal men to help me. Besides, I do everything by myself, these days. You soon get used to it."

"Still—" he looked around at the half-dozen or more packing cases that filled the sitting room and threatened to spill their contents on to the floor—"you need a day or two, don't you, to get your breath back, after something like that? Before you start putting everything in order."

"I moved in four months ago," said Claire. "Don't you remember? I always was an untidy cow." She cleared a space on the sofa for him by removing a plate of half-eaten toast and a week-old copy of the *Guardian*'s "Society" supplement. "Luckily," she added, "I live with someone who's pretty tolerant about that sort of thing."

"I thought you lived on your own," said Benjamin.

"That's what I meant." That taut smile again. "Now—tea, coffee?—Or shall we just go to the pub?"

As they began the steep climb up Church Street towards Great Malvern, Benjamin said, musingly: "I'm trying to remember when it was that we last clapped eyes on each other."

"It was in Birmingham, about eighteen months ago," Claire reminded him. "We ran into each other in the Waterstone's café."

"That's right. I'm sorry I didn't have much to say for myself. To be honest, it was such a surprise, seeing you there, that . . . well, I didn't know what to say, really."

"You had the presence of mind to give me a flyer for your concert, anyway."

He didn't seem to notice the cutting edge to this remark. "That was a good evening, too. It was a shame you couldn't come."

"I *was* there actually, for a while."

"You were? But I never noticed you."

"No, I just sort of—lurked in the background." She glanced at Benjamin, who seemed hurt by this revelation. "Sorry, Ben, I should really have come over and said something to you. But I was feeling a bit strange—I'd only been back in the country a few days—and . . . oh, I don't know. It was a weird evening. You looked as though you were in another place."

"It was a big night for me."

Benjamin frowned, readjusting his memories of that bitter-sweet occasion.

"Try not to judge me, Ben. It was very, very peculiar seeing you again like that. I probably shouldn't have gone."

"What was so peculiar about it? I haven't changed that much, have I?"

"Jesus," said Claire, exhaling deeply. "If you really can't work that one out, then . . . Well, in that case—" (and now there was real amusement in her smile, as well as fondness) "—in that case, no: I can honestly say that you haven't changed at all."

As they neared the top of the street—Benjamin complaining all the way ("Couldn't we have brought the car?")—a pub called The Unicorn loomed into view, and beyond that the dramatic, almost vertical rise of the bracken-clad hillside. Benjamin, who had not been to Malvern since he was a child, was moved by the sight of the grey escarpment silhouetted against a pale blue, cloud-scattered, early evening sky. For a moment—having been depressed, at first, by his glimpse of Claire's new living conditions—he felt strangely envious to think that she had chosen to make this place her home.

"I like it here," he said. "There's something quite majestic about it, in fact. In a small, West Midlands sort of way."

"It's not bad." Claire conceded, taking Benjamin's arm to steer him away from the pub and along the curve of the Worcester Road. "I can't say this was where I was planning to end up. Milan, maybe. Prague. Barcelona. That was the sort of thing I always had at the back of my mind. Maybe tonight we could be having a drink at the . . . Café Alcantara in Lisbon—fabulous place, I went there once with a would-be boyfriend—all done up in art deco—the café, I mean—just a few steps away from the Atlantic waterfront. Instead, here we are." She stopped outside a doorway. "The Foley Arms Hotel in Malvern. Just about sums us up, doesn't it, Benjamin? Just about what we deserve."

They sat on the sun terrace, which offered a vertiginous prospect of the Severn valley, heat-hazed, limitless, drenched in evening sunlight, and Benjamin thought that he would be hard pressed to exchange this view even for the best that Lisbon had to offer. But he kept this reflection to himself. Instead, when Claire returned from the bar with a bottle of warmish white wine and two glasses, he said (unable to keep a note of irritation out of his voice): "Anyway, how can you say that I'm looking good? I'm in a terrible state. For more than a year now I've been going through the most dreadful crisis."

"Benjamin, your whole life is a dreadful crisis. Always has been, probably always will be. Nothing new there, I'm afraid. And you're looking good. Sorry about that, but there you are." She handed him a full glass and added, more kindly: "OK then, what's the matter? What is it this time?"

"Me and Emily," said Benjamin, sipping his wine and looking away from her, gazing abstractedly at the view.

Claire drank too, and said nothing.

"My marriage is falling apart," he added, in case she hadn't caught his drift. But there was still no answer. "Well, aren't you going to say anything?"

"What is there to say?"

Benjamin stared at her in exasperation, then shook his head. "I don't know. You're right. Probably nothing."

"I went through all this with Philip, you know. I do know what it's like. It's bloody horrible. And I'm sorry, Ben—really, really sorry. But I'm not going to tell you that I couldn't see it coming."

Benjamin leaned forward, his gaze becoming more and more doleful. "I just feel so . . . so . . . what is the word?"

"Guilty."

"Yes." He glanced at her, surprised. "I feel guilty. I spend every minute of every hour feeling guilty. How did you know that?"

"Because, as I said, you haven't changed a bit. And I always knew that when something like this happened, guilt would be the thing you did. The thing you were best at. You have a talent for guilt, I reckon. Which has lain dormant, for quite a while, but now you're probably going to make up for it."

"But what have I got to feel guilty about? Why should I feel guilty?"

"You tell me."

"I haven't been unfaithful to Emily."

"No?"

"I haven't slept with anybody else, at any rate."

"That's not quite the same thing." She sighed. "What happened? When did it start?"

"It started last year," Benjamin said, and then told her the story of Francis Piper's diaries, and how they had revealed to him the prosaic truth about the "miracle" in which he had believed, fervently and secretly, for twenty-six years.

This was a lot for Claire to absorb. "You mean—you don't believe in God any more?"

"No," said Benjamin, emphatically.

"Well, *that's* a bloody relief for a start. Come on, I'll drink to that!" And she tried to clink glasses, but Benjamin would not return the gesture.

"You don't seem to understand," he said. "It's not just the shattering of an illusion—though that's bad enough, I have to say. It's what this means for me and Emily. We don't have it in common any more. She believes. I don't. But that was the only thing that was keeping us together."

"But you're still together. Aren't you? A year down the line. That has to count for something. That has to mean that you've got other things to build on."

"You'd have thought so. But it hasn't been like that. It's been a terrible year. Awful. We hardly speak to each other any more. At home we can just about cope because we're both out at work all day, and then, you know, there's the telly, and I can go upstairs to write, and so on. But next month we're going to Normandy for a couple of weeks and I'm *dreading* it. Trying to share your life with someone when you feel no . . . closeness, no intimacy—there's nothing worse than that."

"Nothing?" said Claire, archly. "Famine, maybe? Getting blown apart by a suicide bomber?" She looked down, with a quiet smile. "Yeah, I know. Self-righteous. I haven't changed that much either."

Benjamin reached out to touch her hand; but the attempt, as usual, was fumbled, and she didn't really notice.

"So why are you still with her?" she asked.

"That's a good question."

"I know. It's not as if . . . I mean, it's not as if there are children to worry about."

"True." He shook his head. "I don't know the answer to that one, Claire. Why am I still with her?"

"I'll tell you if you like," she said, topping up his glass. "Because you're scared, maybe? Because you've been with her for eighteen years and it's the only way you know how to live? Because it suits you, in lots of ways? Because you've got your own little room at the back of the house with your desk and your computer and your recording stuff and it's all too nice to leave? Because you can't remember how to use a washing machine? Because watching some crappy programme about gardening with someone else is not quite as depressing as watching it by yourself? Because you're fond of Emily? Because you feel loyalty for her? Because you're afraid of ending up sad and lonely?"

"I wouldn't end up sad and lonely," Benjamin insisted, defensively. "I'd probably find someone else, anyway."

"What—just like that?"

"I don't know . . . In a few months, or something."

Claire looked impressed; or pretended to. "You sound very confident about this. Anyone in mind?"

Benjamin hesitated for a moment, then leaned forward. "There is someone," he confided. "She works quite near our house. She's a hairdresser."

"A hairdresser?"

"Yes. She's gorgeous. She has this really . . . angelic face. Angelic and sophisticated at the same time, if that makes any sense."

"And how old is she?"

"I don't know—late twenties, maybe, something like that."

"Name?"

"I don't know. I haven't actually—"

"—spoken to her," said Claire, finishing off his sentence with the weariest of inflections. "Christ, Benjamin, what are you *like*? You're in your forties, for fuck's sake—"

"Only just."

"And you've got a crush on a bloody *hairdresser* who you've never spoken to? This is who you're seriously considering as your future life partner?"

"I didn't say that." Claire noticed that he was having the decency to blush, at least. "And you shouldn't prejudge people, anyway. She looks very intelligent. I reckon she's probably a Ph.D. student, doing it to make money or something."

"I see. So you envisage having a few serious conversations about Proust and Schopenhauer between shampoos, do you?"

If she was expecting Benjamin to rise to the bait, she was disappointed. He merely looked more and more downcast. "What's the point?" was all he muttered, bitterly, after a while. "I'm so bloody out of practice. I wouldn't even know how to get into conversation with someone like that."

"It's not difficult to get into conversation with a hairdresser," Claire pointed out. "All you have to do is go in there and ask for a cut and blow dry."

Benjamin spent an unexpectedly long time pondering this phrase, as if Claire had just revealed to him some secret password that would unlock a hidden door on to a world of unimagined possibilities.

"Just a thought," she felt obliged to add, somewhat embarrassedly. "You look as though you could do with a trim, to be honest." Then she hesitated, feeling that it was time to shift things on to a more serious plane. "Benjamin . . ." she began, tentatively. (This was going to be difficult.) "You know what the problem is, don't you? I mean, the real problem."

"No," he answered. "But I'm sure you're going to enjoy telling me."

"I'm not, actually." She took a long, anxious sip from her glass. "The thing is . . . you're not over her, are you? Twenty-two years later, and you're still not over her."

Benjamin looked at her intently. "By her, I take it you mean—"

Claire nodded. "Cicely."

There was another long silence, as her name—the forbidden, never-to-be-spoken name—hung in the air between them. Finally, Benjamin enunciated one word, with great emphasis and feeling.

"Bollocks."

"It's not bollocks," said Claire, "actually. And you know it isn't."

"Of course it's bollocks," Benjamin counter-argued. "We're talking about something that happened when we were at *school*, for Christ's sake."

"Exactly. And you're still not over it. You're still not fucking over it! And what's more, Emily knows that, and she's known it all your married life, and it's probably torn her apart in that time."

And she told him what she had noticed at the concert, about the change that had come over him when he sat at his keyboard and played the opening bars of *Seascape No. 4*, how a different look had come into his eyes, remote, unseeing, an intensity of gaze directed not at anything in the room but into his own self, into the past, and how the look in Emily's eyes had changed with that music, too, how she had stared at Benjamin for a moment and then down at the ground, all her enjoyment in his performance, all her pride, suddenly evaporating, leaving her bereft, her eyes hollow with loneliness and regret.

"And incidentally," Claire added, "whatever happened between you and that woman?"

"Woman? What woman?"

"The one you were with when I saw you at the café. The one you introduced to me as your 'friend.'"

"Malvina? What about her?"

"Well, you seemed pretty intimate with her, I thought. And she had a touch of the Cicelys about her, I couldn't help noticing."

"What are you talking about?" Benjamin was incredulous. "She's got black hair!"

They lapsed into silence for a few seconds, both trying to regain some poise.

"I wasn't . . . criticizing you or anything," Claire began, apologetically.

Benjamin muttered: "Nothing came of it," and there was no mistaking the ruefulness in his voice. To him, this transient friendship was still one of the defining emotional events of his recent life.

"So what did happen? Did you stop seeing her?"

"Not just that. She started having an affair with Paul."

Claire winced and shook her head. "That's rough."

"I know," said Benjamin, drinking again, consciously allowing his self-pity to be fuelled by the wine.

"No," said Claire. "I mean—that's rough on *her*. Jesus, that's not something I'd wish on my worst enemy." She paused, and then made a decisive pronouncement: "You need to say something to Emily about this."

"About Malvina? What's the point? It was nothing. I haven't seen her for ages."

"Not about that, necessarily. About why it started. What made you do it. I mean, clearly you have some need, some emotional need, that Emily isn't satisfying at the moment and that's . . . well, that's something you should talk about, isn't it? Because she probably feels the same way anyway. Will she be awake when you get home tonight?"

"Probably. She usually sits up and reads."

"Well then, promise me this, Ben. Promise me that when you get home tonight, before you go to sleep, you just say to her, 'Emily, we have to talk soon.' That's all it takes. Do you think you can do that?"

Benjamin shrugged. "I suppose so."

"Promise me you'll do it?"

"Yes, I promise."

And after that, they talked about other things. About Claire's decision to go freelance as a technical translator, what a relief it had been to get out of that student house in London, and how there was more call for business Italian in the Worcester and Malvern area than you would imagine. About how, in any case, most of her work could be done over the internet now, so that the contacts she'd made in London and Lucca were still useful to her, and she was already making more than enough to cover her tiny mortgage payments: which meant that she still felt a little precarious now and again, and sometimes woke up in the middle of the night having the odd panic attack, but things were all right really. And they talked about her son Patrick. How quiet he was, how introverted. How Claire was starting to believe he was far more damaged by her divorce from Philip than she had ever imagined. How he talked incessantly, obsessively, about his aunt Miriam whom he had never met because she had disappeared in 1974, at the age of only twenty-one, never to be seen again, despite the best efforts (apparently) of the West Midlands police force. It was as if, Claire surmised, the separation of his parents had left him with some void, some obscure but bottomless void in himself, which he was trying to fill by seizing on this mythical, lost figure from recent history, and making her some kind of totem of everything that was absent from his own experience of family life. He collected photographs of her, pumped his mother for memories and anecdotes whenever they talked.

"How old is he now?" Benjamin asked.

"Seventeen. Takes his A-levels this year. Then he wants to do biology at university. I've no idea whether he'll get the grades."

He caught the undertow of anxiety in her voice and said, "Don't worry. I'm sure he'll be all right."

"I know," said Claire, who was hardly likely to be reassured by anything that Benjamin said, on this or any other subject. They were standing by the gate to her little front garden, and it was getting on for midnight. An almost-full July moon hung in the sky. Benjamin looked at it and remembered, as he always remembered, that there had been a full moon that night, too, the night after he had made love to Cicely in his brother's bedroom. A yellow moon, like the yellow balloon of his childhood memory. He had sat out in the garden and looked at the moon and tried once again to savour his moment of perfect happiness and had already, in some obscure way (or was this just the wisdom of hindsight?), felt it slipping away from him. He had never seen Cicely since then, never once set eyes on her since she had left him sitting alone in The Grapevine with Sam Chase, after she had just spoken to her mother on the telephone and heard that there was a letter from America waiting for her, a letter from Helen. The next day he had phoned her mother himself and learned, incredibly, impossibly, that Cicely was already on a plane to New York. What could have been in the letter? He didn't know, preferred not to think about it, could not bring himself to remember anything more about that conversation with her mother, so that his last real memory of Cicely, relating to Cicely, was of the half-hour or so that he had spent sitting outside in his parents' garden, looking at the yellow moon, and ever since then he had measured his life in full moons, had never been able to look at a full moon without thinking of that night, and he now calculated, swiftly, without really having to think about it, that this was the 265th full moon since then. And he couldn't decide whether that made it feel like a long time, or no time at all, or both . . .

"Benjamin?" Claire was saying. "Are you OK?"

"Mm?"

"I seem to have lost you."

"Sorry." He became aware that they had been on the point of saying goodbye, and gave her another of those brief, botched kisses.

"Good boy," she said. "Now have a lovely time in Normandy. It might be just what you both need. It might work wonders."

Benjamin was unconvinced. "Maybe," he said. "But I don't think so."

"Go to Etretat," said Claire.

"Where?"

"It's on the coast, next to Le Havre. There are these fantastic cliffs. I was there two winters ago: just before I came back home. It was bloody freezing, but the view is something else. I stood there for hours, high on the chalk . . ." She tailed off, remembering. "Well. It's just a suggestion."

"All right. We will."

"And don't forget—don't forget what I told you. What you've got to say to her."

"Yes, I remember," said Benjamin. "'Cut and blow dry, please.'"

Claire assumed he was joking, at first. Then sighed when she realized that he wasn't, and decided that there was no point in putting him right.

"Do you ever wonder why I bother with you, Ben?" she asked. "I do, sometimes."

There was no answer to that, of course. But even Benjamin had noticed, and been touched by, the self-mocking sincerity with which Claire had said it, and a few minutes later, as he drove away from Malvern, towards the midnight lamps of the M5, he experienced a small epiphany. He tuned the car stereo to Radio 3, and recognized the music they were playing: it was the "Cantique des Vierges" from Arthur Honegger's oratorio *Judith*. Of all the useless gifts with which life had lumbered him, none was more useless, he sometimes thought, than his ability to identify almost any snatch of music by a minor twentieth-century composer, and yet he was glad, on this occasion, because he realized that he hadn't listened to his ancient cassette of this work for ten years at least, and although most of it was pretty unmemorable, this passage had once been one of his favourites, something he would turn to when he felt that he needed consolation, which the ethereal simplicity of its gossamer, child-like melody never failed to afford him. And now, looking into his passenger wing-mirror and seeing the yellow moon reflected, and beneath it the lights of Malvern (one of them, he knew, the light from Claire's sitting-room window), and hearing this tune, again, this tune which had once been so familiar and important to him, he felt a glow of pleasure, of comfort, at the thought that he and Claire remained friends even after two decades. But there was more than that: for at this moment he admitted to himself, for the very first time, that there had always been a desire on Claire's part for something bigger than friendship, a prospect which must have scared him, before now, else why would he have denied it for so long, suppressed the knowledge so ruthlessly? But tonight, suddenly, he didn't feel scared by it. Nor did he want to turn the car around, drive back towards Malvern, and spend the night with her. The feeling which came over him wasn't as simple as that. It was merely that the combination of Honegger's limpid melody and the yellow moon which was so much an emblem of his most primal wishes seemed tonight to take on the aspect of a sign: a pointer towards his own future—at the centre of which, distant but ever-present, ever-dependable—was the gleaming lamplight from Claire's cottage. As the radiant certainty of this swept over him, Benjamin found himself shivering, and having to pull over to the side of the road to brush hot tears away from his eyes.

He sat by the roadside until the music had finished, breathing deeply, before swinging out again on to the carriageway and resuming his north-bound journey; back to the city, the house, the bedroom where Emily would be sitting up, yawning over an unread novel; her whole being—every look, every movement—a lexicon of unspecified reproach.

9

18 July, 2001
Etretat

Dearest Andrew,

I promised you a postcard from Normandy. Well—lucky you, you are going to get rather more than that. I'm booked home on a ferry which doesn't leave for another two days and quite frankly I have had enough of driving around the countryside looking at monasteries and cathedrals so I am just going to sit in the hotel until then, and try to think things through, and calm myself down. I've got a lot of stuff to sort out in my head, but don't worry about me: I'm fine. Whatever else happens—and I know there's going to be a lot of pain to get through in the next few days and weeks, a lot of "difficulty" as my beloved counsellor would call it—I've come to a decision and I'm going to stick to it.

And in case you're wondering why the whole of that paragraph was written in the first person singular, the answer is easy: I'm here by myself. Benjamin has gone. He went yesterday. I think he's gone to Paris, but I'm not sure about that and to be perfectly honest I couldn't care less. He's turned off his mobile and that suits me fine as well. I'm cross with myself for trying to ring it yesterday, in fact. What would we say to each other anyway? I have nothing to say to him at the moment. Absolutely nothing at all.

Our marriage is over.

Meanwhile—let me tell you a little bit about the holiday from hell.

Perhaps "hell" is putting it a bit strongly—as far as the first ten days were concerned, anyway. "Purgatory" probably gets it about right, though. Then again, the whole of the last year has been a kind of purgatory for me—longer than that, even. I suppose the pain has just been building up and intensifying to the point where it became unbearable. Unbearable for me, at any rate. Sometimes I wonder whether Benjamin ever ***feels*** *any pain: real pain, I mean. No, that's not true—he has felt it, in the past, I know he has, because of what he told me, years and years ago, when we were still at school, about the thing that happened to Lois and how he helped her to recover from it. I don't doubt that he suffered over that, that he shared her suffering, very deeply. Every week, he used to visit her, I remember, without fail, and that must have marked him. So he* ***can*** *feel things deeply, he is just good at masking it: he has a lot of self-control, Benjamin—a very British quality, some people might say, and probably one of the things that drew me to him in the first place. (Benjamin thinks that our whole relationship is based on religion but it's not, that's just nonsense, it's a convenient story he likes to tell to himself to explain why things have gone wrong.) But anyway, something has changed about Benjamin, since that day down by the canalside, when he told me the story of Lois and Malcolm. (You remember me telling you about that? God, I feel I have told you my whole life story—and the life stories of practically everyone I know—during the last year or two, and you have been so patient, listening to every word. You are such a good listener, dear Andrew. There aren't many of them around!) It's as if something has frozen him in time, so that he's stuck at one particular moment and he can't move on, he can't shift himself. I even think I know what did it—or* ***who*** *did it, more to the point—but that can wait for another time.*

Now, if this was one of my emails (and how many emails have I written to you in the last eighteen months or so? My guess is more than a hundred) I would delete most of what I've written so far and try to focus on what I wanted to tell you. The crux of the story. But instead I have gone back to the steam age of pen and ink and it constrains me to do my thinking on paper—which I have to say feels more like a luxury than a constraint. Writing this is probably good therapy for me—that's what I mean to say. I could always call you on the telephone after all; and we're bound to see each other in a few days' time, aren't we? So I don't even need to post this, really. But I'm pretty sure that I will.

So: my final week in purgatory, by Emily Trotter. Or Emily Sandys, as it looks like I shall soon be calling myself again. Where to begin?

The first ten days, as I said, were bearable at least. I can't tell you much about them because they all start to blur into one. Car journey followed by sightseeing followed by car journey followed by lunch followed by car journey followed by walk followed by car journey followed by check into hotel followed by dinner, and so on and so on and so—endlessly!—on. I think it was all the driving I hated the most because the roads here are pretty quiet and straight and there is something uniquely desolate (you've never been married so you wouldn't know this) about the knowledge that you're turning into one of those middle-aged married couples you always swore you wouldn't turn into, driving for hours side by side, eyes fixed on the road, without a word to say to each other. "Ooh look—cows," I would almost find myself shouting out, just to break the ghastly silence. I mean, it wasn't quite as bad as that, but you get the general idea.

Anyway, we did Rouen, we did Bayeux, we did Honfleur, we did Mont-St-Michel and along the way we had it up to here with bouillabaisse and brandade de morue and chateaubriand. Not to mention vin rouge because it became increasingly obvious as the week went on that it was only the prospect of getting drunk as a skunk every night that was stopping us both from giving it all up as a bad job and going home. Or strangling each other, for that matter. And all the time—this was what made it all so incredibly tiring, for me—I was trying my hardest to jolly things along in my jolly, Emily-ish sort of way. I suppose I've spent most of the last eighteen years trying to do that, one way or another, and where Benjamin's concerned it's bloody hard work at the best of times. Well, these aren't the best of times. In fact the last twelve months have been the worst of times, and here it was just the same. Those long, miserable silences of his. Eyes fixed on the middle distance, thoughts fixed on . . . what? I don't have the faintest idea—even now, even after eighteen years of marriage! Every so often I would find myself asking, desperately, "Are you depressed about something?" To which he would inevitably reply, "Not really." And I would ignore that and say, "Is it your book?," and then more often than not that would make him fly off the handle and start shouting, "Of course it's not my book!," and so it would go on . . .

I'll tell you what made me so angry this time. It was the realization that it was only towards me that he ever behaves like this. If you see him with his other friends—like Philip Chase, or Doug and Frankie—he suddenly comes to life, suddenly seems to remember, for some reason, how to be funny and how to be sociable and how to have a conversation. Just in the last few weeks, that's really started to annoy me. As a small illustration of this—why am I in Etretat at all? Because Benjamin wanted to come here. And why did he want to come here? Because Claire told him all about it, when he went for a cosy little tête à tête with her a few weeks ago; from which he returned at about one in the morning, the worse for drink, and looking all pleased with himself. Now Claire is my friend, as much as his. More than his, in a way. Did he invite me along? No. And they must have talked for about five hours. When was the last time he talked to me for five hours—or one hour—or five minutes? It's things like this that have made me realize that a lot of the time I don't even seem to exist for Benjamin any more. I don't even make it on to his radar.

Maybe this sounds petty to you. But when it's been going on for months, when it's been going on for years, it stops being petty. It becomes huge—the biggest thing in your life. (And it's got nothing to do with whether he believes in God or not, whatever he likes to say.) And the day before yesterday, I suppose it just got too big for me to handle.

This was what sparked it off.

Ironically, it had probably been the best day of the holiday so far. Or at least, for me it had: until I realized I'd been deluding myself. We'd had lunch in Le Bec-Hellouin, which was nice enough (actually more than that—the apple tart was to die for), and then we'd driven up to St. Wandrille, which is a beautiful little village in the Seine valley, with a famous old tenth-century Benedictine monastery. We parked the car in the village and had a long walk up the river—about three hours altogether, I should think. And half way through the walk we found this simply magical-looking old building. It was some kind of old farm outbuilding, but the rest of the farm seemed to have gone ages ago, and it was standing by itself only about twenty yards from the banks of the river. It was almost completely derelict and frankly looked a little bit dangerous, but still, we poked our heads through the windows and then found that the door wasn't locked or anything, so we stepped inside and had a little look around. It was full of weeds and stinging nettles but you could still get a sense of what it might be like if someone came along and did it up. I looked at Benjamin and could have sworn that he was thinking the same thing. We'd always talked (or had until recently) about getting a place in France or Italy, escaping from the big city, somewhere he could find peace and quiet and at last get this wretched book of his finished. And although this building was an absolute ruin, you could tell that once it had been restored, it would be simply perfect. We even talked about where the dining room would go, and where he could put all his computers and recording equipment and that kind of stuff. It was a proper conversation, for once. And afterwards, when we walked away from it, back down the river towards St. Wandrille, we looked back at the house (I'd started to think of it as a house), and the sun was just sinking behind the roof, and the water looked all cool and glimmery in the twilight, and it just looked the most wonderful and romantic place, and I took Benjamin's hand and then—a real miracle, for a change—he held on to me for a good five or ten minutes, before he sort of let my hand slip and drifted off on a path of his own. (He always does that.)

It was about eight o'clock when we got back to the village, too late to have a look around the monastery except from the outside. Benjamin was all excited because he'd read in one of the guide books that you could go on retreats there, but the office was all closed up and there was no one he could ask about it. But we were still in time for Complies, *at nine o'clock. I didn't think Benjamin would want to come with me, because as you know he hasn't been anywhere near a church for more than a year, but much to my surprise he was up for it. Maybe (this is what I thought at the time) seeing that magical house and talking about maybe trying to find out who owned it and buying it and doing it up had made him feel closer to me, at last.*

Anyway, we went inside the chapel and took our seats. It's a beautiful chapel, I have to say, converted from an old tithe barn, with a fabulous beamed ceiling and everything arranged with absolute simplicity. There was no artificial lighting of any sort and although it was still quite bright outside, the chapel itself was full of shadows now, with just the palest, goldest, reddest traces of sunshine glowing around the windows. (No stained glass here.) There were about thirty of us in the congregation and after we had all been sitting there for about ten minutes the monks filed in. They were totally absorbed in the ritual, totally intent, didn't seem to register that we were there at all. Perhaps that was just my impression. Their cowls were grey and the hoods were up so you couldn't see their faces most of the time. There were probably more than twenty of them. When you did see their faces they looked somehow both very serious and very cheerful at the same time. And they had the most wonderful voices. When they started chanting, these long, beautiful lines of melody just seemed to flow out of them, rising and falling, almost as if they were improvising until you listened closely and realized there was a wonderful logic to it. It was the most restful and most spiritual and the purest*-sounding music I think I've ever heard. Benjamin said afterwards that it made even Bach and Palestrina sound decadent! I took away a leaflet with some of the words on it and this was one of the hymns they sung. (They sung it in Latin, of course.)*

Before the day ends, we ask you
Creator of all things,
In your endless goodness,
Watch over us, guard us.

Keep far away from us
The dreams and nightmares of the night,
Enslave our enemies
So that nothing may sully the purity of our body.

Exalt us, all-powerful Father,
Through Jesus Christ our Master,
Who reigns for ever, with You,
And with the Holy Spirit. Amen.

And all the while they were singing this I could feel Benjamin leaning in even closer, and when the service was over and we left the chapel in the dusk, we held hands again as we walked back to the car. And I was sure that everything was going to be all right.

So, we got back to the hotel—this hotel, the one that Claire recommended—and went down to dinner, and while we were waiting for the first course to come I looked at Benjamin and I could see that his face was transformed since the morning. There was a light in his eyes now, some sort of sparkle of hope, and I realized then how dull his eyes had been looking for months, how dim and lifeless. I wondered whether it was the service that had done it—whether it had done anything to re-kindle his faith at all, because I can't believe that anyone could hear that singing and not feel some kind of intimation, not catch some little glimpse of divinity behind it. But I didn't say anything about that. I just said something bland like, "Did you enjoy yourself today?," and that was all he needed. He started to open up at last.

"I'm sorry," he said. "I've been so depressed lately." And he said that for months he hadn't been able to get any sense of the future, couldn't find anything to look forward to. But today, he said, he'd seen something: something he knew he'd never be able to have, but at least he knew it was real, at least he knew it existed, and that gave him hope, somehow, made the world seem more bearable to him, now that he knew it was there, even if it was out of his reach.

"Like a kind of symbol?" I asked.

He looked doubtful about that, but said: "Yes."

So I leaned forward and I said, "Ben, it doesn't have to be just a symbol. It doesn't have to be a pipedream. Anything's possible, you know. Really."

And I meant it. I mean, just on a practical level, we paid off our mortgage in Birmingham years ago, and we could sell our house for a fortune now. We could have bought that ruin, done it up, and still had enough money to live on for years. That's what I was thinking.

But Benjamin said, "No. It could never happen."

And I said: "Well come on, then. Think about it—step by step. What would it involve?"

"Well," he said. "I'd have to learn French, for one thing."

"Your French is pretty good," I told him. "And it'd soon get better if you had to use it all the time."

"And I'd have to do a hell of a lot of training."

It's true that Benjamin is useless at DIY. He can tell César Franck from Gabriel Fauré after a couple of bars, but he can't put up a coat rack to save his life. But I wasn't going to be defeatist about that. Like I said, it felt as though anything was possible today.

"You could do a course," I said. "There are evening classes in that sort of thing."

"What, in Birmingham?"

"Of course there are."

He thought about this for a while, and then he started to smile, and the gleam in his eye started to get brighter, and he looked at me, and he said: "Right now, I can't think of anything that would make me happier."

"Right then," I said, and my stupid heart was almost bursting. "Let's do it."

And he stared at me, and said: "What, both of us?"

"Of course both of us," I said. "You don't think I want you to live in that house without me, do you?"

And then he stared at me some more, and said: "I'm not talking about the house."

I waited a second or two and said: "What are you talking about, then?"

And he said: "I'm talking about becoming a monk."

Sorry, I had to break off from writing for a minute then. I've been scribbling this down like a madwoman for about two hours, and I needed to take a break.

Just then, when I put it down on paper, it almost seemed funny to me. I promise you, it didn't feel that way at the time.

What did I say? I can't really remember. For a while I think I must have been too shocked to speak. In the end my voice was just very quiet—that happens to me, I've noticed, when I'm angry about something—I mean really angry—and I just said something like: "I might as well not be here, mightn't I, Benjamin? In fact, you'd prefer it that way." Then I got up, threw a glass of water over him—that was surprisingly satisfying—and went upstairs to our bedroom.

He followed me up and knocked on the door about two minutes later. And that was when the fight began. And it was a fight. I don't mean we attacked each other, physically, but there was a lot of shouting—enough to get someone from the hotel staff running upstairs and asking if everything was all right. I told Benjamin everything that I'd wanted to tell him for years: that he showed me no respect, that he paid me no attention . . . At one point he even had the nerve to drag you *into it, saying that he thought we saw too much of each other, and I just had to yell at him, Well what do you expect, when my husband looks right through me every day as if I'm invisible, when he just acts as though I'm not even there?*

It ended with me telling him I didn't want to see him again. He packed some things and I think he checked into a single room for the night. When I went to bed myself I imagined that in the morning I would maybe want to speak to him, try and find a way of making things better. But as soon as I woke up, I realized that I didn't. It was true: I really didn't want to see him again. Anyway he wasn't down at breakfast and after breakfast the receptionist told me that he'd checked out and he'd left a message to say that he was going to Paris. Where he can stew, as far as I'm concerned. At least he had the decency to leave me the car so I've got a way of getting back home.

Home. For which I suddenly feel a great longing.

It will be nice to see you when I get back, dear Andrew. At least I won't have to tell you this whole sorry story face to face.

I used to think it would be different if we'd had children, or if we'd pushed our case a bit harder at the adoption agency, but I don't even think that now, I think they would have just got caught in the crossfire and the poor little things have had a narrow escape.

What a mess. Eighteen years—eighteen years of life together and it ends like this.

I suppose it's always a mess. Perhaps this isn't even as messy as most.

Will you take me out for a drink some time very soon and make sure I get totally sloshed, please?

Sealed with a kiss.
In friendship,
Emily
xxx

8

Wednesday, August 1st, 2001 was the thirteenth anniversary of Claire and Philip's divorce. It was not normally an occasion that they celebrated, but this time, since they were down in London anyway—staying at a hotel in Charlotte Street with Patrick for two days—they decided to make an exception. Neither of them knew the names of the London restaurants that were considered fashionable these days, so they chose Rules in Covent Garden, which was mentioned in several of the tourist guides. At eight o'clock they settled into the heavy velvet banquettes, studied the menus, and prepared themselves for an evening of red meat, winter vegetables, rich, dark sauces and rust-colored claret. Outside, on the streets of London, it was a thick, sultry evening, and the evening sunshine was still warming the flagstones of the piazza and the tables of the pavement cafés. Inside the restaurant, with its dimmed lighting and atmosphere of careful formality, they might have been dining at a gentlemen's club one autumn night back in the 1930s.

Patrick had chosen to stay in the hotel watching television. They were not used to talking together without him, or having the luxury of being able to choose any topic of conversation that happened to present itself; and they responded in the way that many married—and indeed divorced—couples respond to this situation.

"Do you think Patrick's OK?" Claire was the first to ask. "I mean, he doesn't seem to be working very hard. He's very laid back about these exams."

"That's because he's on holiday! And anyway, he's got months and months to get ready for them."

"And he looks so *thin*."

"We do feed him, you know. Have been doing for some considerable time." Philip added, more earnestly: "Don't look for a problem, Claire, when there isn't one. Life's complicated enough as it is."

Claire pondered this advice doubtfully, before asking: "Does he ever talk to you about Miriam?"

Philip was scanning the wine list. "He doesn't talk to me much at all, to be honest."

"I think he has a thing about her."

"What sort of thing?" asked Philip, looking up.

"Well, last year—the morning of the Longbridge demonstration—he insisted on getting all her stuff out of the attic at Dad's house. And after that we talked about her . . . disappearance. Talked about it for ages, actually. Of course, I didn't tell him everything about who she'd been seeing—" She broke off. "I'm sorry, Philip, is this subject boring you?"

Philip's attention had wandered. He was looking at the receding figure of a youngish, dark-haired man in a sharp tailored suit, who had just breezed through the restaurant purposefully and disappeared upstairs in the direction of the private rooms.

"That was Paul," he said. "Paul Trotter. I'm sure it was."

Claire did not seem very interested. "This is probably the kind of place he comes to all the time. Do you want to go and say hello? *I* certainly don't want to speak to him."

"No," said Philip, turning round to face her again. "Sorry—carry on with what you were saying."

"I was just saying," Claire resumed, rather testily, "that we talked about her disappearance that morning, and—well, it reopened a whole lot of stuff, as far as I'm concerned. Stuff which I've been trying not to think about, since then—for the sake of my sanity as much as anything else, because I went down that road a long time ago, and all it achieved was . . . Phil, are you *listening* to any of this, or not?"

"Of course I am," said Philip, snapping to attention again.

"What's your problem, then? Your eyes keep glazing over."

"Sorry. It's just that . . ." He took his glasses off, and rubbed his eyes in a distracted gesture. "Seeing Paul just now . . . And hearing you talk about Miriam . . . I don't know, it sparked something off. There's something at the back of my mind—some connection between those two. It keeps coming and going—you know, like *déjà vu*?"

"What sort of connection?" Claire asked. Her voice was eager, suddenly.

"I don't know," said Philip. "Like I said, it keeps coming and going." He picked up the wine list again. "Don't worry, I'm sure it'll come back to me."

"I've nearly finished the article," Philip was saying, a couple of hours later. "But really I've only just been scratching the surface. The thing about these neo-Nazi organizations is . . . you *can* just dismiss them as the lunatic fringe: you know, Holocaust deniers and that sort of thing—nutters, basically. But then, look what's been going on in the north these last few months. Not just the race riots, but the number of council seats the BNP has been winning off the back of all that unrest. Now, the way the BNP's marketing itself at the moment is very interesting. They've been watching New Labour, I reckon, and they're targeting women voters, and middle-class voters. Half their candidates seem to be women, these days. What's different is that you only have to peel back the marketing and you come bang up against something *really* ugly—like that CD. But the white voters in Burnley and Bradford aren't doing that. We've all become too used to taking things at face value, you see. There's no spirit of inquiry any more, we're just *consumers* of politics, we swallow what we're given. So it's actually about the way the whole country is going, the whole *culture*. Do you see? That's why it has to be a book. I can take the far right as a starting-point, but it's going to be about much more than that."

"Sounds fascinating. Have you got the time to do it?"

"I'll have to make the time. I've got to move on, Claire. I can't go on writing 'About Town with Philip Chase' for the next twenty years. Everybody's got to move on some time."

"We're all so restless now, aren't we?" Claire said, almost crossly, as if the whole of her generation had just at that moment started to irritate her. "Our parents stayed in the same jobs for forty years. Nowadays no one can sit still. Doug's changed jobs. I've changed jobs—and countries. Steve wants to get a new job, by the sound of it." She thought for a moment, and added: "D'you know, I can only think of one person who never seems to move on."

"Benjamin," said Philip, without needing to be asked.

"Benjamin," she repeated, quietly, and sipped at her coffee.

"Well," said Philip. "At least he's moved on from his marriage, now."

This provoked a curt laugh. "But he hasn't *moved on*, has he? He's been kicked out. That's just so typical of him. He creates an impossible situation and then he just . . . *festers* in it until somebody else does the dirty work of putting it right." Her anger—if that's what it had been—was quickly spent, and now she asked in a more kindly vein: "How is he, anyway?"

"Oh, all right," said Philip. (Benjamin had moved in with him three days ago.) "Out at work most of the time, which is a great relief. Predictably, he's gone a bit bonkers, but I imagine that's only a short-term thing. He keeps talking about becoming a monk."

"A monk? He hasn't got religion again, has he?"

"No—I think it's more of a lifestyle choice."

"Poor Benjamin. How long's he going to stay with you? Is Carol OK about it?"

"Well, not over the moon, exactly. But he can stay as long as he wants, I suppose."

"I worry about him," said Claire; which, as far as Philip could see, was merely stating the obvious. "Do you think he's *ever* going to finish this book?" she asked; and then voiced an even more dangerous question. "Do you think it even *exists*?"

"Well, let's ask his brother," said Philip, and stood up to waylay Paul, who was passing through the restaurant again on his way out. "Paul!" he called out, cheerily, offering his hand. "Philip Chase. *Birmingham Post*—and, indeed, King William's School. We spoke on the phone last year. How are you?"

Paul shook his hand limply, thrown into visible confusion by this chance encounter. He was flanked by two other men, at this point. One of them was tall, grey-haired, imposing: he was dressed like a businessman but his weathered features, paradoxically, suggested a predilection for the outdoor lifestyle. He looked as though he was no stranger to yachting clubs and Jamaican beaches, and seemed to be a good twenty years older than Paul. The other man not only looked older still—being almost completely bald, for one thing—but was massively corpulent, with a stomach of kingly girth and darting, watchful eyes made apparently tiny by the fleshiness and jowly rotundity of the face in which they were deeply sunk. Philip would never have recognized him in a million years. But it was this man who happily exclaimed:

"Chase! Philip Chase, as I live and breathe! What the hell are you doing here?"

Realization dawned slowly, and Philip again held out an uncertain hand. "Culpepper?" he said, tentatively. "It *is* you, isn't it?"

"Of course it is. Good grief, I haven't changed that much, have I?"

Could this be the same person who had once competed with Steve so fiercely for the title of *Victor Ludorum*, the top athletics trophy in the school? The transformation was bewildering.

"Not really, it's just that you've . . ."

"Oh, I know. I've put on a few inches round the midriff, over the years. Who hasn't? Mind if we join you for a minute or two?"

The other man was introduced to them as Michael Usborne, but before anyone had had the chance to sit down, Paul Trotter—looking more uncomfortable by the minute—glanced impatiently at his watch and announced that he had to leave. Culpepper, meanwhile, suggested that instead of ordering more drinks at the table, they should all move on for liqueurs at the bar of his hotel, which was only a few minutes' walk away. Claire and Philip agreed—impelled (as they admitted to each other later) almost entirely by morbid curiosity to find out what had become of this legendary *bête noire* from their schooldays.

Paul said goodbye to them in the street, and saved his final words for Culpepper. "Well, enjoy having a drink with your *journalist* friend, won't you?" he said.

If there was a hint involved, Culpepper seemed to take it. He shook Paul's hand solemnly.

Afterwards, as they were walking up the Charing Cross Road towards Centrepoint, they could talk of nothing at first except the extraordinary change in Culpepper's appearance.

"I can't *believe* it," Philip kept saying. "The man was a dynamo at school, whatever else you thought about him."

"So what happened? Years of four-course business lunches taken their toll, d'you think?"

"Must've done. He seems to be on the board of about a dozen companies, so I suppose that means twelve times as much food. Anyway," he said, in a gently accusing voice, "you could have asked him yourself, if you hadn't spent the entire hour locked in conversation with the captain of industry. What were you talking about, all that time?"

"I thought he was a nice guy," said Claire. "Bit of a smoothie, but nothing too obvious. He was telling me all sorts of stuff. He's had some really bad luck recently. Hasn't even got a job at the moment."

"Claire, do you realize who Michael Usborne *is*? Don't you ever read the business pages?"

"Of course I don't read the business pages. Who reads the business pages? My cat poos on them."

"Michael Usborne," said Philip, as they dodged a trio of drunken teenagers gesturing noisily at the driver of a vacant black cab, who clearly had no intention of picking them up, "was CEO of Pantechnicon until earlier this year. He was responsible for half the railway track in the south-east. It was the second job he'd had running one of the privatized railway companies: his speciality is to cut the workforce, economize on safety procedures and then usually get the hell out of the boardroom before the shit hits the fan, which it usually does a few months later. He ran that company into the ground and I think they paid about three and a half million to get rid of him. Before that he was in telecommunications and he did exactly the same thing. And before that it was a distillery. The man's a serial wrecker of companies."

Claire said nothing in reply to this. She stopped outside the window of an electrical shop and looked at the gleaming racks of stereo systems, laptops and DVD players. It was still open, even at this hour, and a young guy in denims—he looked as though he might still be a teenager—was loading himself up with cardboard boxes while his friend signed a credit card slip. The consumer boom was still in full swing, then.

"Why do they have all these shops next to each other, selling the same things?" she wondered aloud. "It can't be good for business."

Philip sighed and asked: "He wasn't coming on to you, was he?"

"What does it matter to you?" she said. "Are you my guardian angel all of a sudden?"

"He's had about four wives as well, you know."

"He's been married twice," she corrected him. "And he told me that he was always on the lookout for good technical translators, so I gave him my business card." Something else occurred to her. "Oh—and he asked me up to his hotel room. But I told him I wasn't in the mood."

"Dirty old man," Philip muttered. "Still, at least he can't pester you much in Malvern."

"Funnily enough, he's got a house near there—in Ledbury," said Claire. "He invited me down next weekend."

"You're not going, are you?"

They had reached the lobby of their hotel. Claire headed for the lift, pressed the button for the third floor and turned to Philip, with a kind of weary resolution in her voice: "I'm forty-one, you know, and I can make my own decisions. I'm also single, and to be perfectly honest, I don't get hit on much any more. Perhaps you've forgotten what that's like. So if some good-looking guy—who also appears to be good company—and also happens to have a house near me with not one but *two* indoor swimming pools—wants to invite me there, for whatever reason, it's up to me whether I go or not.

On top of which, I haven't had a shag for . . . well . . ." She tailed off as the lift arrived. They both stepped inside, and Claire didn't finish that particular sentence. She just said: "Well, there are some things you don't even tell your ex-husband."

Philip smiled at her then, fondly and apologetically, and they made their way in silence to their adjacent rooms. Claire's was a double, which she was sharing with Patrick.

"Anyway," she said, fumbling in her handbag for the electronic card. "That was a very nice evening. Thank you."

"I enjoyed it too. Say hi to Patrick for me. I'll see him at breakfast."

"Will do. If he's still up."

It was later than they had both thought: almost 1:30.

"Shit," said Philip. "I meant to phone Carol tonight. Find out how Benjamin was." And then, at the mention of this name, he remembered something. "By the way—when you saw him a few weeks ago, did Benjamin say anything to you about a hairdresser?"

Claire stopped in the act of opening her door.

"Yes, he did. Why, has he mentioned her to you?"

"Only in the sense that . . . Well, he told me that he went to see her last week and tried to get talking, and it all went horribly wrong. Apparently, not only did he *not* manage to ask her out, and not only did he *not* get his hair cut, but the manager's banned him from going within a hundred yards of the place."

"*Banned* him?" said Claire, disbelieving. "Why, what happened?"

"He just got nervous, I suppose," Philip said. "And sometimes, you know, when you get nervous—the wrong words come out."

"But all he was going to ask for was a cut and blow dry."

"The 'cut' bit came out OK," Philip told her, deadpan. "It was 'blow dry' he had some difficulty with." He shook his head and unlocked the door. "I suppose he just had something else on his mind at the time."

And for the next half hour, he and Claire lay listening to each other's laughter on either side of the dividing wall.

7

—— Original Message ——
From: P_Chase
To: Claire
Sent: Thursday, August 9, 2001 10:27 a.m.
Subject: Déjà vu

Great to see you last week. We must celebrate the painful and devastating severance of our marital bond more often. And what a weird surprise that we should run into Culpepper that night. He seemed so pleased to see us that, for a moment there, I'd got him marked down as nothing more than a harmless old bore—until I remembered what a bastard he'd been at school, and how he had made life hell for Steve, apart from anything else. Shows how dangerous nostalgia can be, blurring the sharp outlines of fact into something more palatable, more soft-focus . . .

Anyway: I was emailing for a slightly odd reason, namely that I just this morning remembered what it was that I *couldn't* remember the other night re. Paul Trotter and Miriam. And now that I have remembered it, it seems a bit embarrassing—too insubstantial, in a way, to be worth passing on. Also, I'm not sure that I should encourage you (or Patrick) to keep obsessing over this business. Some things simply have to be laid to rest, and a firm line drawn under them.

Anyway. This is what it was. One day at school, Benjamin and I were out with the Walking Option and we got lost pretty badly—as we did most weeks, I seem to remember. I can't say we tried very hard to get back to the others—my memory is that we'd taken some food with us, and possibly some beer as well, and we ended up just sitting down and making a picnic of it. That was when Paul came by, riding his bicycle. He was off sick that day—allegedly—though that didn't seem to stop him practising for the *Tour de France* up and down the Lickey hills, as far as I could see.

Benjamin and I were having one of those laddish (I'm not sure the word existed then, or was used much, at any rate) conversations about women. We were both rather ruefully admitting that neither of us had ever seen a naked woman except on the telly. And that (at least, this is how I remember it) was when Paul chipped in and reduced us both to silence by saying that he *had* seen someone naked—and then he mentioned your sister.

Now, I wouldn't attach any significance to this at all—because he could have been making it up, or he could have been referring to some pervy glimpse of her he got when spying on the girls' school showers one day (I wouldn't have put anything past him, at that age)—if it wasn't for one peculiar detail. Remember that we're talking about a conversation that took place probably about twenty-five years ago, so my memory of it is hardly going to be very clear; but on the other hand, I haven't thought about it since then—not once—which means that it hasn't had the chance to get distorted and rewritten in my head. And my recollection is that he said he had seen her down by a reservoir—a reservoir near Cofton Park. I suppose that means the one off Barnt Green Road.

Now—that would be a pretty strange thing to make up, wouldn't it? Ben and I just thought he was bullshitting us—took absolutely no notice of what he was saying, really, whereas if he had not been such a comprehensive pain in the arse we would at least have *registered,* I suppose, that this was a curious tale he was spinning. What I'm trying to sort out now, in my mind, is the date of this event. I mean, I have no way at all of knowing how recently Paul had had this experience (if it was a real experience); but I think I can say, with some certainty, when he told us about it. When he waylaid us on his bicycle he was singing "Anarchy in the UK"—I remember that, with complete clarity—so it can't have been any earlier than autumn 1976. Two years after Miriam disappeared. And it may even have been a few months later than that because I've got a feeling that Benjamin was already into his on-off-and-on-again thing with Cicely by then—which would date it after his famous "Othello" review came out at the beginning of the spring term, 1977.

Benjamin himself might remember more about this. I'll ask him when he gets in from work tonight. (Mind you, it's hard to get him to talk about anything other than the miserable state of his life at the moment.) Alternatively, you could contact Paul directly—get it from the horse's mouth, as it were. Rather you than me, on that one.

Look, I'm probably making a big deal out of nothing, here. I can't help feeling guilty even about sending this message off to you. I hope it doesn't start you off on some sort of false trail and just re-open all the stuff you tried so hard to put a lid on years ago. Don't rush into this, Claire, OK? Think about what you're getting into. Take a few days and try to decide whether you really want to start off on that road again.

Take care, anyway, and big love from
Phil XX.

—— Original Message ——
From: Claire
To: P_Chase
Sent: Thursday, August 9, 2001 11:10 a.m.
Subject: Re: Déjà vu

Hi Phil, thanks for that.

Can you let me have Paul Trotter's number please?
Much love Claire x

—Hello?
—Hello—am I speaking to Claire Newman?
—Yes, you are.
—It's Paul Trotter here.
—Oh. Hello.
—Is this a good time to call? Are you alone?
—Um . . . yes, this is a good time. And yes, I'm alone.
—I received your message on my answering machine.
—Good. Well . . . that was where I left it.
—Quite.
—It was nice to see you again, the other day.
—I'm sorry?
—In London—a couple of weeks ago—at the restaurant? It was nice to see you again.
—Ah, yes. You too. We'd . . . met before, then, had we?

—Well—at school, obviously.

—Ah! School! Of course. I thought you might have been . . .

—We haven't met since then, I don't think. I've been out of the country a lot—

—The message you left on my machine was rather extraordinary.

—Um . . . Yes, I'm sorry about that. It might have been a good idea . . . Maybe it would have been a better idea to explain things in person.

—I'm not at all sure that I can help you.

—No. Well, I understand that, of course.

—Your husband, Philip—

—Ex. He's my ex-husband.

—Ah. Ex-husband. I hadn't appreciated that. I was under the impression that you were celebrating your anniversary.

—We were—after a fashion. It's a long story. Not really relevant.

—Your husband is a journalist, isn't he?

—I'm not married.

—I mean your ex-husband.

—Yes. That's right. He is.

—And he was the one who gave you my number?

—Yes, that's right.

—Is he there with you now?

—There's nobody with me now. I'm alone. I'm not married any more. Philip lives in Birmingham, I live in Malvern. There's nobody else here.

—Forgive me if I sound paranoid. I've had a lot of difficulty with journalists.

—This is nothing to do with Philip. I'm trying to find something out purely for my own personal . . . interest.

—I see.

—Does that make things any easier for you?

—It might do. Possibly. But, as I said, I really don't think I'm going to be of much help to you.

—You remember my sister, I take it? You remember the story of her disappearing?

—Of course.

—It was just that Philip had this memory of something you'd said to him. Something about seeing her—

—Yes, I heard your message. I have no recollection of having said that. None whatsoever.

—No. Of course not. It was a very long time ago.

—But I do remember the . . . incident itself.

—You do? I mean—which incident?

—I remember seeing your sister . . . at the reservoir.

—Can you tell me anything—?

—I must ask you to clarify this, Claire. You have no intention of putting any of this into the public domain?

—None whatsoever.

—I have your sworn undertaking on that point?

—Absolutely. I'm doing this for myself. That's the only reason.

—Well then. It's true—I believe—that I did see your sister early one evening. It was getting dark and I was cycling alone down by Cofton Park. It was after school and I was on my way home.

—Were you at King William's then?

—I believe not. I believe I was still at primary school.

—What sort of . . . state was she in?

—She had no clothes on.

—None at all?

—None—that I remember.

—When was this? What time of year?

—It was winter.

—Was she alone?

—No. There was a man with her.

—A man?

—Yes. It was getting dark, as I said, and I couldn't see very well. The paleness of her body was what caught my attention through the bushes. I got off my bike and came nearer. As I got closer I realized that there was a man with her and he turned and stared at me. I became frightened and I ran back to my bicycle and then I cycled home.

—You didn't tell anybody about this? Why not?

—I was frightened.

—Was my sister . . . Was she alive?

—I don't know. At the time I thought that she was. I thought that she and the man were having sex—that that's what they were doing by the reservoir.

—Was he undressed as well?

—No. I don't think so.

—Why didn't you tell anybody about this, after my sister disappeared?

—I didn't hear about your sister's disappearance for some time. Two or three years, at least, I should think. It wasn't talked about in our household. Round about the same time, we had our own tragedy to contend with.

—Do you remember meeting Miriam and me one morning at the café in Rednal, down by the number 62 terminus? You and your brother had just been to church.

—No, I don't believe that I do.

—I was wondering if that was before or after you saw her at the reservoir.

—I never spoke to her after seeing her at the reservoir.

—Are you sure of that?

—Quite sure.

—So it must have been before.

—Yes. I would think so.

—OK. OK, there's a lot I need to think about . . .

—I've now told you everything that I know.

—Yes. Thank you.

—I can't see any need to continue this conversation. Can you?

—No. No, there's no need. Thank you. You've been very—

—It has all taken place in the strictest confidence. You understand that, don't you?

—Yes, of course.

—Good. I shall remember you said that. Goodbye then.

—Goodbye. Have you—?

—— Original Message ——
From: Doug Anderton
To: Claire
Sent: Monday, August 20, 2001 20:53 p.m.
Subject: Papers

Dear Claire

Well, that one came out of left-field. Hearing from you at all, never mind with such an unexpected request.

I'm sorry it's taken me a few days to reply. Funnily enough I have been up at my mother's. Well, actually there's nothing funny about it. About ten days ago she had a stroke—quite a bad one. We were on holiday in Umbria at the time and I had to fly straight back. The whole of one side of her body went and she couldn't speak or move. She lay on the living room floor in her house for eighteen hours. Luckily her neighbour had arranged to come round the next afternoon. Mum's a tough old thing—a real fighter—but she was shit scared, as you can imagine.

She came out of hospital four days ago (they can't wait to get you out these days) and I've been staying with her at home since then. Just got back to London a few hours ago and have only just read my emails. Mum is not really in a state to see anyone at the moment. Maybe in a couple of weeks she'll be able to have visitors. Meanwhile she's got this care worker coming round in the afternoons and I'll be going up myself every few days.

I'll let you know when she's ready to see people. But I should also warn you that the papers you're talking about haven't been sorted since my dad died—they're all upstairs, in what used to be my bedroom. (Did you ever go there? No, I don't think so. Never did manage to entice you into that particular den of iniquity. Ah, the chances let slip!) And I very much doubt that there's anything about your sister up there. I didn't know that she and my dad had been on a charity committee together. There might be a bit of paperwork relating to that, I suppose. I'm not sure exactly what you're looking for—but then, maybe you're not either. I suppose anything you come across might turn out to be a clue, in the most unexpected of ways.

Anyway, keep your curiosity under control for a little bit longer and I'll get back in touch as soon as it seems OK for you to go round. In the meantime—do you ever come down to London? It'd be great to have a drink. I'm a happily married man these days as you know, so there would be no funny business unless you specifically requested it.

Kiss kiss
Doug.

—— Original Message ——
From: Doug Anderton
To: Claire
Sent: Friday, September 7, 2001, 22:09 p.m.
Subject: Visiting Rednal

Dear Claire

Just got back from a few days with my mum this afternoon. She is still in a sorry old state, but quite a lot stronger than when I wrote to you last. I told her you were interested in coming to visit and she said (insofar as I could tell—it's bloody hard to understand a word she's saying at the moment) that she would like to see you. I told her you wanted to look through Dad's papers and she said that you were going to have your work cut out, which is true. I went up there myself and it's a nightmare. About fifty cardboard boxes full of stuff. Go and have a look if you want but you'll have a terrible job—none of it's in any order. For years I've been meaning to donate it all to the Modern Records Center at Warwick University—they already have a big archive of trade union papers there—and this has given me an incentive to get on with it. I rang them up and there's a bloke going to come and check it all out at the end of next week.

If you wanted to take a look before he does, why not go round at the beginning of the week? Mum has a doctor coming round on Monday so Tuesday would be a good bet. Any time in the afternoon would be fine.

Let me know how you get on. And how you think she's doing!

Lots of love
Doug xx

——Original Message ——
From: Claire
To: Doug Anderton
Sent: Tuesday, September 11, 2001 23:18 p.m.
Subject: Re: Visiting Rednal

Dear Doug

You're right—there's no way I'm going to find anything in those boxes; not the way they're currently arranged. Needles and haystacks don't come into it. I was only in there for about fifteen minutes and I could tell straight away that it was going to be hopeless. Thanks for letting me go there all the same. I'll just have to wait till they've all been sorted and archived, and then I'll have another look, if that's OK.

Anyway, it doesn't seem very important, now. Nothing else seems very important, all of a sudden, does it? Have you been glued to the telly all evening like me?

Your mother seemed to be in good spirits. Considering what you told me, I think she's made an amazing recovery. Sometimes she seemed a little bit confused. When

I got down from your bedroom, at about four o'clock, the first pictures were just coming through and at first she thought it was one of those crappy TV movies they put on in the afternoons. She saw the people throwing themselves out of the windows and tutted and said that they shouldn't show that kind of thing before the nine o'clock watershed. But after a while she worked out that it was for real.

We sat and watched the news together for about two hours. I have to say she was much calmer about it than I was. For some reason I kept breaking down and crying. But all your mum said was that she was so sorry for the people who had died, and that America was now going to take some terrible revenge for this. I asked her what she meant and she didn't answer. In the end she just said she was glad she wouldn't be around to see what happened next.

I told her not to be so silly. What else can you say?

Incredible times.

Love
Claire.

6

Perhaps the secret was to live in the moment. Or try to find a way of doing that. Hadn't he once managed to convince himself, after all, that "there are moments in life worth purchasing with worlds"? And wasn't this just such a moment, when you looked at it from a certain angle? The sun was shining. It was a bright, crisp, late-October morning. Sunlight sparkled off the water, sending shards of light dancing in the air in fantastic patterns as the waves crashed against the shingle. It was only ten o'clock, with the prospect of a whole, leisurely day in front of him. And, to top it all, he was sitting at this wooden table, overlooking the beach, cradling a cappuccino in his hands, in the company of a beautiful, stylish, eighteen-year-old woman who for the last few days had been hanging on to his every word and even now was looking at him with unfeigned love and admiration. He could feel the envious glances of every other middle-aged man at the café. It was unfortunate—from one point of view—that she was his niece, rather than his girlfriend. But then, you couldn't have everything; and life was never perfect. Benjamin had learned these simple truths long ago.

It was autumn, 2002, and he had been separated from Emily for fifteen months.

"Three weeks, was all it took her," Benjamin was complaining to Sophie. "Three weeks, and she starts going out with the bloody church warden. Next thing I know, he's moved in with her. Living in *my* house."

Sophie sipped her cappuccino and said nothing, merely smiled at him with her warm hazel eyes in a way that immediately—and inexplicably—made him feel better.

"I know, she's entitled to be happy," Benjamin said, half to himself, looking out over the ocean. "God knows, I don't begrudge her that. I certainly wasn't making her happy. Not towards the end, anyway."

"And you're happy too, aren't you?" Sophie asked. "You like being alone. It's what you always wanted."

"Yes," said Benjamin, dolefully. "Yes, that's true."

"Of course it is," Sophie insisted, responding to the lack of conviction in his voice. "People have always said that about you. It's one of the things they've always envied in you. Even when you were at school. Didn't Cicely say that once? Something about not wanting to be stuck on a train with you, because you never said anything much, but being convinced that you were a genius and the world was going to recognize you one day."

"Yes," said Benjamin, for whom the memory of that conversation had never faded. "That's true too."

It had ceased to surprise him, by now, Sophie's exhaustive knowledge, and apparently effortless recall, of just about everything that had ever happened to him at school. At first he had found it astonishing; now he was used to it, and considered it to be just one more remarkable facet of a personality which turned out, the more he got to know her, to be remarkable in every other way as well. She had explained to him, some time ago, how she had become so well acquainted with these childhood stories. She had heard them from her mother, when she was only nine or ten years old. Lois had just started working at York university; her husband Christopher was still practising law in Birmingham. For more than a year they had maintained separate households, and almost every Friday during that time, Lois and her daughter had driven down to Birmingham, returning to York on Sunday evening so that Sophie could go to school the next morning. And it was on these three-hour drives, to and from Birmingham, that Lois used to fill the time by telling her daughter everything she could remember about Benjamin and his schooldays.

"But how did *Lois* manage to know so much?" Benjamin had wanted to know. "I mean, she wasn't even there. She was in hospital for ages."

"Exactly!" Sophie had replied, her eyes gleaming. "Don't you remember? She heard it all from *you*. Every Saturday you used to come and visit her, and take her for a walk, and tell her everything that had happened at school that week."

"You mean—she heard all that? She took it all in? I didn't even think she was listening. She never said a word to me on any of those walks."

"She heard it all. And she remembered it all, too."

Benjamin had often pondered these words, during the long, wakeful nights that had become one of the many depressing features of his new bachelor lifestyle. He was ashamed to have forgotten that he and Lois had been so close, in those days. It was the oddest paradox of all: when his sister was still in post-traumatic shock, forever silent, seemingly insensate—that was when the bond between them had been strongest. However remote she had seemed, however unreachable, she had in fact never been more devoted to him, never more dependent. The Rotters' Club, they had called themselves: Bent and Lowest Rotter. But once she started to recover, they had drifted apart; and as soon as she met Christopher, the drift accelerated, until they had become as formal and distant with each other as . . . well, things were never as bad as they were between him and Paul, obviously. But still, he felt no particular kinship with his sister any more; could not recover that sense of nearness, however hard he tried to will himself towards it. Perhaps some sly process of transference had taken place, unnoticed, and the affinity he had once felt for Lois was being replaced, gradually, by his growing and deepening fondness for Sophie. That would be satisfying, on some level; would have about it something of the symmetry he tended to spend much of his life vainly hunting for: the sense of a circle being closed . . .

"It's amazing, how you remember all that stuff," he said to her, now. "You're a walking encyclopedia of my past."

"Someone has to keep the records," she said, smiling enigmatically.

They finished their coffees and began to walk towards the sea. They were at Hive Beach, in Dorset, a few miles south of Bridport. Benjamin had spotted this beach, and this café, yesterday afternoon as the whole family—including Lois and his parents—had driven along the coast. "Great place for breakfast," he had remarked—to no one in particular; but it was Sophie who had woken him at eight o'clock the next morning and said, "Come on then: breakfast at the beach!"; and so the two of them had come here together—fugitives, *compadres*—while the others were left to struggle at their rented property, bleary-eyed, with unfamiliar toasters and recalcitrant plumbing systems.

"Do you ever visit *FriendsReunited*?" Sophie asked, while Benjamin—an inveterate skimmer—combed the beach for suitably flat stones.

"Now and again," he said, casually. In fact he checked it at least once a week—sometimes daily—to see if Cicely had registered. "Why do you ask?"

"Oh, I just wondered if you knew what became of some of those people. Like Dickie—the one whose bag you all used to have sex with every morning."

"Richard Campbell . . ." Benjamin recalled, aloud, as he approached the water's edge and achieved a satisfying score of twelve with his first stone. "He's probably been in and out of counselling a dozen times by now." He turned to Sophie, who was hunched up against the autumn wind in a full-length scarlet overcoat, a blue cashmere scarf wrapped around her throat. "You know what—I reckon you'll turn out to be the writer in the family. I've never known someone with such an interest in stories. You have . . ." (he skimmed again) ". . . a very advanced sense of narrative."

Sophie laughed. "I bet you say that to all the girls."

"I meant it as a compliment, actually."

"And coming from you, Benjamin, I'm sure it is." She took a stone from his outstretched palm and attempted to skim it. It sank promptly into the water with a resounding slap. "Anyway, it's not true. I'm just interested in people, that's all. Who isn't?"

"No—it's more than that. I mean, how long did you spend reading those log-books last night? We couldn't tear you away from them."

Benjamin, Lois and Sophie were staying with his parents for a week at a fifteenth-century castle a few miles east of Dorchester, rented out by the Landmark Trust. On arrival they had found in a drawer, among the old jigsaw puzzles, packs of cards and tourist leaflets, four substantial log-books, running to several hundred pages each, bound in green vellum, recording the experiences of every visitor to the castle for the last twenty years. The people who had stayed here seemed to conform, on the whole, to a very particular type: conservative in their values, intellectual even in their leisure pursuits.

Sophie had picked up the log books out of nothing more than passing curiosity, but had soon started to find them fascinating, as social documents if nothing else.

"If I ever do become a therapist," she said, "I'm going to use that stuff as source material. What you've got there is a record of decades of systematic abuse. Powerless children subjected to the whims of parents who won't let them do anything for a whole week except . . . make tapestries and sing madrigals. I mean, can you imagine? Or that one who says that he got his eight-year-old son to dress up in Tudor costume and spend four days trying to learn how to play 'Greensleeves' on the sackbut. What do you think *he's* going to be like when he grows up? Whatever happened to Game Boys and Playstations? Don't any of these people do anything normal, like watch television or go to McDonald's?"

"What about that couple—the one you read out to me last night?"

"The bondage guy? The one who complained that there wasn't a proper dungeon, and left the address of a place in Weymouth that sold chain mail and branding irons?"

"And his wife sounded so sweet. She put all those pressed flowers into the log-book, and wrote that little poem: 'Sonnet to the Castle.' The one with twenty-three lines."

"It takes all sorts, Benjamin. All human life is in those books."

"I bloody hope not. God help us if that's true."

He waited for a lull between two of the foaming breakers, then skimmed the last of the stones across the water; after which they walked on, westwards, away from the café and the car park, in the direction of the crumbling, striated cliff face. Walking erratically, buffeted by the occasional wind, stumbling on the uneven shingle, they sometimes fell against each other, and it would have felt natural to Benjamin, at those moments, to take Sophie in his arms and clasp her in a hug. A neutral, avuncular hug, would that be? Could he trust himself to keep it that way? He had to keep reminding himself that his niece—who seemed like a full-grown and very sophisticated woman, to him—was still in her last year at school. This was her half-term holiday. He must remember these facts. And remember, too, that Sophie and Lois would be leaving, driving back up to York on Friday, in two days' time. In the meantime, he should just try to savour the luxury—the fleeting luxury—of her company. That was the important thing. To savor the moment.

The castle they had rented for the week was dominated by a cavernous sitting room, which never seemed to get properly light or warm. Here Benjamin's father Colin would pass much of the day reading newspapers or playing Scrabble or Monopoly with Lois, while Sheila would busy herself in the kitchen, washing up, boiling the kettle, making tea, preparing meals, and generally allowing the time to pass exactly as she had allowed it to pass for the last fifty years. Sometimes they would go out for a walk, get extremely cold, and come back again; then they would stoke up the fire, drink tea, get extremely hot, and go out for another walk. It often seemed to Benjamin that his parents had purposely devised a life for themselves which involved nothing more dramatic than regular changes in body temperature.

Of the six bedrooms, two had already been colonized by Benjamin himself: one for sleeping in, and one to accommodate his papers and his recording equipment. His parents had merely stared, incredulous, when he arrived on the Monday afternoon with a car filled to the roof with cardboard boxes and instrument cases. He had brought with him an Apple iBook, a sixteen-track Yamaha digital mixing desk, two microphones, accoustic and electric guitars and four separate Midi keyboards and control devices. "I thought you were writing a book," Colin had said. "What else do you need, apart from a pen and some paper?" Benjamin had answered, "It's a bit more complicated than that, Dad," but didn't bother to explain any further. He had given up trying to make them understand.

Late in the afternoon after their walk on the beach, Sophie came up to his workroom, sat down on the bed, and announced: "I'm halfway through the second log-book. I can't take any more at the moment. Those people are doing my head in."

"Hold on a sec," Benjamin said. He was clicking repeatedly on his mouse, his eyes fixed on the sequencing software on his monitor. "There's a funny little 'pop' sound on this flute sample. I'm just trying to find it and get rid of it." He scrolled along the screen a few more times, then sat back with a sigh. "Ah well. It can wait."

"So," Sophie began, "are you going to tell me what you're up to in here? Rather like Grandad, I was under the impression that you were working on a book."

"It is a book," said Benjamin. "Look—there it is if you don't believe me."

He pointed to a corner of the room, where two large cardboard boxes overflowed with manuscript. Sophie squatted down beside them and, seeking and obtaining permission from his eyes, she picked up a bundle of papers and began to glance through them.

"There must be about ten thousand pages here altogether," she said, wonderingly.

"Well, that's because I've kept all the drafts," said Benjamin. "Though it is going to be pretty long. Also, all my source material's there—stuff I wrote when I was a student, diaries from the last few years. Even some of the things I wrote at school."

"So it's about you, is it, this book? It's a kind of autobiography."

"No, not really. At least I hope not."

"Then—" (she laughed) "—I mean, this is a really stupid question—you must hate it when people ask you this—but what *is* it about?"

Normally, Benjamin did hate it when people asked him this question. (Not that many people asked it any more.) But for some reason, he was quite happy to attempt an explanation for Sophie.

"Well . . ." he said, "well, it's called *Unrest*, and it's about some of the political events from the last thirty years or so, and how they relate to . . . events in my own life, I suppose."

Sophie nodded, uncertainly.

"It's easier to talk about the form, in a way. I mean, what I'm trying to achieve, formally—this sounds very ambitious, I know—crazy, really—is a new way of combining text—printed text—with the spoken word. It's a novel with music, you see."

"How's that going to work?" Sophie asked.

"Well, in addition to this," Benjamin said, flicking through the pages of the manuscript, "there's going to be a CD-ROM. And some passages you have to read on the screen; on your computer. The text scrolls down at intervals that I've programmed myself—sometimes it's normal reading speed, sometimes there'll only be one or two words on the screen at a time—and certain passages of text trigger bits of music, which will also play on the computer."

"Which you've written yourself?"

"That's right." Unnerved by her silence, by the solemnity with which she was staring at him, he said: "It sounds mad, doesn't it? I know it does. Maybe it *is* mad. Maybe *I'm* mad."

"No, no, not at all. It sounds absolutely fascinating. It's just hard to get any sense of it, without . . . reading some of it, I suppose."

"I'm not ready to show it to anyone yet," said Benjamin, reaching out instinctively, self-protectively for the fragment of manuscript, which she handed to him.

"No. I can believe that."

But she looked so disappointed; and Benjamin could not bear to disappoint her. It was years since anyone had shown such interest in him. He felt hugely grateful and indebted to her, and knew that he would have to repay her somehow.

"You can hear some of the music, if you like," he said, tentatively.

"Really? I'd love to."

"OK, then."

With a few clicks he had brought up a folder of .wav files. He scrolled through the titles, highlighted one and double-clicked. He turned up the volume on the computer's speaker system, then sat back in his chair, arms folded, tense. He remembered the time he had played Cicely some of his music and all she had noticed was that you could hear a cat on the tape, miaowing in the background.

But Sophie was a better listener. "This is lovely," she said, after a minute or two. The music was complex and repetitive, owing something to systems music, but with more chord changes. There was no melodic line: fragments of melody peeped out occasionally, on guitar or sampled strings or woodwinds, before submerging themselves again, absorbed into the densely contrapuntal texture. These undeveloped tunes were modal, like extracts from half-remembered folk songs. Harmonically, there was an emphasis on minor sevenths and ninths, giving the piece a melancholy undertow; but at the same time, an underlying pattern of ascending chords suggested optimism, a hopeful eye fixed on to the distant future.

After a while Sophie said: "It sounds a little bit like the record you gave Mum all those years ago."

"Hatfield and the North, you mean? Yes, it probably does. Not the most up-to-date musical genre I could have chosen to imitate, really."

"No, but it works. It works for you. It sounds sort of . . . sad and cheerful at the same time." Then a new melodic idea was introduced, and she said: "Now I recognize that. You've stolen a famous song there, haven't you?"

"It's Cole Porter, 'I Get A Kick Out Of You.'" Turning the volume down slightly, he explained: "This is meant to go with a passage about the Birmingham pub bombings. I don't know if your mum ever told you, but . . . this was the tune that was playing. When the bomb went off."

"No," said Sophie, looking down. "No, she never told me that."

"For years she couldn't bear to hear it. It used to completely freak her out. She's probably over that now." Benjamin reached for the mouse and switched the music off. "Well, that's probably enough to give you an idea."

He knelt down by the boxes of manuscript, and tidied the papers away. While his back was turned, Sophie said: "It's going to be fantastic, Ben. I know it is. It'll blow people away. I'm just worried that it's so . . . big. Are you ever going to finish it?"

"I don't know. I thought that when I moved into my own place there wouldn't be so many distractions. But all I seem to do now is mess around on the internet and watch TV. And in the summer I finally left my job, but that hasn't helped, either. It just seems to have taken all the structure out of my life."

"Can you carry on much longer, with no money coming in?"

"A few more months."

"You *must* finish it. How long have you been doing this, now? You *must.*"

"What if nobody wants to publish it?" Benjamin said, flopping back into his chair. "Anyway, should I be sending it to a publisher, or to a record company? Is anyone going to be interested? Does anyone want to know? I'm a middle-aged, middle-class, white, public-school-, Oxbridge-educated male. Isn't the world sick of hearing from people like me now? Haven't we had our say? Isn't it about time we shut up and moved over and made way for somebody else? Am I kidding myself that I'm doing something important? Am I not just raking over the embers of my little life and trying to blow it up into something significant by sticking a whole lot of politics in there as well? And what about September the eleventh? How do I find room for *that* kind of stuff in there? I didn't write a word for months after it happened, or after the Americans went into Afghanistan. Suddenly everything I was doing seemed even smaller, even less important. And now it looks like we'll be going into Iraq soon. The thing is . . ." (he leaned forward, his hands clasping and unclasping) ". . . I've got to try and *remember*. I've got to try and remember how I felt about this when I first started it. Recapture some of that energy. I had so much conviction then, so much self-belief. I thought that I was putting together words and music—literature and history, the personal and the political—in ways that no one had thought of before. I felt like a pioneer."

"That's what you are," said Sophie; and he could tell that she meant it. "A pioneer. Remember that, Benjamin. It doesn't need to make you pompous, or up yourself. It's just the truth. Nobody else has done anything like this."

"Yes. You're right," he said, when her words had sunk in. "I'm not going to lose faith in it. I'm not getting clapped out. The work's only getting slower and harder because it's getting better. I know more, and I understand more. Even what's happened between me and Emily is something I can learn from. Everything—everything that happens to me is going to feed into this book and make it richer and stronger. It's good that it's taken me so long. I'm ready to finish it now. I'm not callow any more. I'm mature. I'm in my prime."

He might have said more in this vein; but just then, there was a knock on the door. It was his mother, carrying a tea towel over her arm and wearing an expression of mingled reproof and solicitude.

"You haven't eaten for ages, have you?" she said to her son. "Come on downstairs—I've made you a boiled egg and some Marmite soldiers."

Benjamin's eyes met Sophie's briefly. She smiled at him, a secret smile. His heart melted.

He lay awake, at two o'clock in the morning. Outside, the wind howled, and the castle's walls and flagstones did nothing but reflect the cold back at him, but still Benjamin felt sweaty and feverish. His pubic hair, through which his hand roamed restlessly, was moist. He had an erection which seemed to have nothing to do with desire, and everything to do with habit, of the most dismal and wearying sort. The prospect of masturbating—even though it was probably his only chance of getting to sleep—seemed impossibly bleak. His eyes were wide open. He picked up the mobile phone from his bedside table, turned on the backlight and learned that it was now 2:04. He groaned, and switched on the radio. It was the second movement of Bruckner's fourth symphony: his least favourite movement from his least favourite work by his least favorite composer. He switched the radio off again. In the next bedroom, he could hear his father coughing. His mother got up to fetch a glass of water from the adjacent bathroom. There were fragments of conversation. Lois was asleep, in a far-off wing of the castle. Sophie, so far as he knew, was still in the sitting room, in her pyjamas and dressing gown, freshly bathed, reading the third of the log-books by the light of a standard lamp, the fire having dwindled to a mound of flickering ashes. Benjamin had left her to it, feeling tired, and imagining, for once, that he might be able to get off to sleep quite easily, but no . . . It was the same old story. He still couldn't get used to sleeping alone.

He closed his eyes, screwed them tight shut, clenched his fist into a ball, and tried to summon up some plausible fantasy to get himself started. In desperation, he pictured the new anchorwoman on the BBC *Six O'Clock News*, and began to prepare himself for the labour involved in bringing himself to climax, but then became distracted by the image of those thousands of joyless sperm about to be left stranded on the bedsheets, expiring, gasping for breath, their destinies unfulfilled. Where had *that* mental picture come from, for Christ's sake? What did it matter anyway? Millions of the poor little sods had spent their energies on futile encounters with his wife's eggs in the last twenty years, and in the end they had fuck all to show for it. He was hopeless, in that respect. He had failed, failed. The bedsheet was the best place for them. It was the only destiny they deserved.

In any case, five minutes of mechanical exercise got him nowhere. He was about to give it up as a lost cause and turn the radio on again, when he heard footsteps on the stone staircase outside his bedroom.

Then there was a voice outside his door.

"Benjamin?" It was Sophie. "Are you awake?"

"Yes," he called, turning over on to his side. "Come on in."

The handle was turned and Sophie stood framed in the doorway. She was still wearing her dressing gown, and carrying one of the log-books under her arm. She came inside and sat down on the bed beside him. She was breathing fast and heavily, either with excitement, or with the exertion of running up the stairs, or both.

Benjamin switched on his bedside light.

"What is it?"

"Your friend Sean," Sophie panted. "Sean Harding. He had a pen-name, didn't he?"

"What?" said Benjamin, rubbing his eyes now, trying to adjust to this sudden change of direction.

"Was it Pusey-Hamilton?" Sophie asked. "Sir Arthur Pusey-Hamilton?"

"That's right," Benjamin said. "He used to write these mad articles for *The Bill Board.* That was the name he used."

"Well," said Sophie, beaming in triumph. "Here you are. Take a look at *that.*"

She handed him the log-book, and pointed to an entry which began half way down one of the pages. And Benjamin reached for his reading glasses, and then gasped aloud when he saw the once-familiar handwriting; and began to read.

5

Claire had been seeing Michael Usborne for more than a year, and still she didn't quite understand the nature of their relationship. But in the end, she decided that this didn't matter; that it might even be one of the things she liked about it. Certainly, it bore no resemblance to any of her previous relationships. It was extremely sporadic; it was hardly passionate (although there had been a fair amount of decent sex); and neither of the parties involved seemed to have any idea where it was heading, or indeed any interest in deciding such a thing. She knew that he saw other women (younger ones), she knew that he had sex with them, she even suspected that he paid for this service occasionally. So what? If she had been in love with him, it would have bothered her: but she wasn't, so it didn't. She also knew that he didn't regard her as wife material (not quite young enough, not quite pretty enough, not quite posh enough, not quite skinny enough): but he *was* on the look-out for a wife, and when she materialized, Claire's own period of tenure would presumably be over. That was a slightly more dampening thought. She would miss him. A little. At first. But then, she could hardly describe herself as being in too deep: this wasn't a Stefano situation, or anything like it. She liked seeing Michael, on those (rare) occasions when he was not out of the country, not down in London, not working late, not tied up for the weekend. She liked being taken out by him, she liked using his gym and his swimming pool, she liked sharing his bed. She enjoyed teasing him and arguing with him about politics and playing up to the stereotype of the left-leaning, *Guardian*-reading feminist, which was how he had chosen to classify her. (And which seemed to make him think that by spending any time with her at all he was doing something very daring and unconventional and amusing.) There were, in other words, a good many perks attached to the job of being Michael Usborne's temporary girlfriend—if that's what she was—and best of all, he made it possible for her to enjoy them without feeling cheap, without feeling that she was being used, without feeling that she was selling her soul. That at least, she thought, reflected well upon him, and for that at least she would always be grateful.

So where had this new feeling of dissatisfaction recently sprung from? She was aware of it even now, sitting in what should by all accounts have been very agreeable surroundings—the BA executive lounge at Heathrow Airport—watching Michael searching through the papers in his attaché case (open on the seat next to him) while conducting a conversation on the mobile phone clamped between his shoulder and his ear. A few weeks ago, this scene would have inspired affectionate amusement, nothing more: crazy Michael, she would have thought, always on the go, always driven, never able to sit still for a moment while there was money to be made. And yet this morning, his behaviour simply annoyed her. Was it because this was supposed to be the beginning of a holiday—their first holiday together—and so far he had shown not the slightest interest in relaxing? Was it because Patrick was there, too, and it was the first time they had met and Michael had not managed to address more than three words to him since being introduced? Or did it (as she suspected, in her heart) actually go deeper than that?

The basic problem was this. It was almost three years, now, since she had walked out on Stefano in Lucca; almost three years since she had stood on the chalk cliffs above Etretat and looked across the grey waters of the English Channel towards the country to which she had reluctantly decided to turn her defeated footsteps. She had convinced herself, that day, that it was better to be alone than to be unhappy in love; but now, three years on, that conviction was fading. Her relationship with Michael had been fun for a while. It had been a novelty, at the very least, and a way of easing herself gently back into the practice (so easily forgotten) of being intimate with another person. But she was forty-two, and she could not afford to waste much more time on someone whose interest in her seemed to be so casual. She wanted something else, now, something that was not superficial, and not part-time: she wanted a partner. Banal as it might seem, she wanted someone who would go to the supermarket with her, help her choose salad dressing, decide between different brands of washing powder and shampoo. (How jealous her glances had become, these days, when she spotted couples having precisely those bland conversations in the aisles of Tesco and Safeway.)

Did Michael ever go to the supermarket, she wondered? Had he ever set foot in one, in the last twenty years? She had noticed, whenever she was round at his house near Ledbury, that his fridge (which was about the size of her own spare bedroom) was always filled with fresh vegetables, organic red meat, freshly squeezed orange juice, bottles of champagne. Where did it all come from? Since his most recent divorce—perhaps even before it—he'd employed at least two housekeepers, and presumably it fell to one of them to ensure that stocks never ran low. She could not imagine sharing her life with someone who lived like that. Real though it obviously felt to him, she could not stop herself from regarding his entire mode of being as a kind of preposterous fantasy. This holiday, for instance: a week in Grand Cayman, first-class travel there and back, and a beachfront villa—owned, apparently, by a business associate from America—at their disposal for a whole week, complete with gardener, housekeeper, chauffeur and cook. People just didn't *live* this way. It was unreal. But he refused to see it like that. Took it all in his stride, insisted it was nothing special. Extended the invitation to Patrick without even thinking about it. (The place slept fifteen, after all.) Even said that he could bring his girlfriend: Rowena, his girlfriend of six weeks' standing, who now sat reading *Vanity Fair* and drinking chilled white wine in the executive lounge and looked as though she couldn't believe her luck.

Claire sighed as the weight of all this pressed down upon her. The incompatibility between them—their absurdly polarized lifestyles and value systems—struck her that morning with dizzying clarity. Could he not see it as well? Did it not bother him, or was he just choosing to ignore it? Maybe they would get a chance to talk about these things on holiday. But the holiday had already started; and the omens, so far, didn't appear to be good.

"What about just pointing out that this is the fastest-growing area of our business and the one that offers the most sustainable margins?" Michael was saying, into his mobile. If there was any urgency or irritation in his voice, it was hard to detect. He always seemed to speak in the same way—gentle, mellifluous, persuasive—whether he was ordering food in a restaurant or (as now, it appeared) giving a dressing-down to a subordinate.

"Well, those are exceptional charges. No one is trying to hide the fact that there will be exceptional charges . . ."

Patrick stood up and wandered over to a coffee-dispensing machine. Claire's eyes followed him.

"'Synergies' is a good word, yes. I don't have a problem with that. As long as we make it crystal clear that this is not about cost-savings, it's about growth." He sighed. "I mean, is Martin really on the ball with this one? Because it feels to me that I'm writing the thing myself."

Claire joined Patrick by the coffee machine and gave him an empty cup to fill.

"You don't have to serve yourself here, you know," she pointed out. "That waitress over there would have brought us a refill."

"This is quicker," he said, shortly.

Claire tried to keep the nervous edge out of her voice as she asked: "What's your impression of Michael, then?"

Patrick thought for a moment. "He's everything that I expected him to be."

"What does that mean?"

Handing her the coffee, he said: "How well do you know this guy, Mum? This is the last kind of person I would have thought you'd have any time for."

She took a sip. It was scalding hot. "You're not seeing him at his best. He's very preoccupied." As they walked back towards their seats, she added, "You've got to learn to see beyond the surface of people, Patrick. It's not about what people do. It's about their human qualities."

Patrick didn't answer; and even to her, it sounded as though she was trying to convince herself of something that was hard to believe.

Patrick sat down next to Rowena and refilled her wine glass. She had finished with *Vanity Fair* by now and had moved on to *Condé Nast Traveller*. He leaned across and looked at the feature she was reading, illustrated with a full-colour photograph of some idyllically pastoral French scene, with what seemed to be a large château at the center.

"That looks cool," he said. "Who lives there?"

"It's a monastery," she answered. "Somewhere in Normandy. You can stay in places like that, you know. The monks will take anybody in. It's part of their philosophy—providing hospitality to anyone who needs it."

"Bloody hell, so now they're touting spiritual retreats as holiday options for the stressed executive, are they? Capitalism really has conquered everything."

"I don't see any reason why we have to put a figure on it," Michael was now saying. "I've seen different estimates and it could be anything between nine and twenty-four. Alan's guess is nearer twenty-four and that's the one I'd be inclined to go with."

"Our flight's being called," Patrick said, looking up at the departures screen.

"We can't rely on an upturn in market conditions. Everybody knows that. Put it down to 'global uncertainty.' That's the buzz word at the moment."

"I can't believe we're flying first class," said Rowena, slipping the magazine into her bag. "It's so exciting."

"Are we going, then?" Patrick asked, standing up. He started collecting some of the free newspapers from a nearby table, hoovering up the *Times, Independent* and *Guardian*. Claire noticed that one of the pictures above the masthead on the *Guardian* today showed a familiar face. The tagline next to it said: "*Paul Trotter—My grave doubts over war with Iraq.*"

"It doesn't sound to me like anyone's on top of this situation," Michael continued. Claire was trying to catch his eye. He glanced at her and held up a finger, telling her to wait for a minute. "We're trying to restore profitability—is that such a difficult message to get across?" Now, at last, there was an audible undertone of irritation.

"You go on ahead," Claire said to her son. "We'll meet you at the gate." She walked with them to the door of the executive lounge, and before seeing them off she assured Patrick: "Don't worry—he won't be like this all through the holiday."

"How do you know?" he asked.

"Because I'm going to tell him not to be."

Patrick smiled when he heard that, pleased to see that his mother was feeling combative again. That was the best part of her, he sometimes thought: the part that had not been much in evidence for the last few years, since her return to Britain.

"She means it, as well," he said to Rowena, as they walked down the corridor together. "She's going to give him one of her bollockings."

"What does Michael do, anyway?" Rowena asked. "I couldn't understand a word he was saying on the phone."

"I'm not sure what kind of company he's running at the moment. They're called Meniscus. Something to do with plastics, I think." Patrick searched his pockets, suddenly anxious, until his fingers lighted upon his passport. "Sounded like they were trying to draft a press release, didn't it? I heard him saying something about consolidation and rationalizing. That's management-speak for closing down factories and putting people on the dole. I expect they're trying to find a gentle way of breaking it to the papers."

While Michael continued his latest telephone call, accompanied by ever more impatient searches through the papers in his attaché case, and occasional calculations tapped out briskly on his palmtop, Claire kept one eye on the departures screen (which showed that the last call for their flight had come up five minutes ago) and rehearsed what she was going to say to him.

This is ludicrous, she would begin. How are we ever going to get to know each other, how are we ever going to *relate* to each other in a meaningful way, if you can't even put your work aside on holiday, if you can't even make the time to spend a few minutes talking to my son when you first meet him? And she would attempt to extract, as a condition of their continuing to see each other when this week was over, some sort of undertaking: that he would not spend this holiday on the telephone, that he would not hide himself away in some study for the next seven days, sending faxes and tinkering with balance sheets, while the rest of them were out scuba diving. She would present him with an ultimatum, confident that this was the sort of language he would understand. And confident, too—though she didn't know where this confidence came from, apart from her own instincts, which were usually sound—that he would not be angered or frightened off by this approach. There was a core of genuine feeling between them which he appreciated, even if it was at some deep level that he wasn't used to recognizing. She was sure of that.

"So how did it go?" Patrick asked a few minutes later, when she arrived at the check-in desk.

Claire was alone.

"I didn't get the chance to say anything," she said. "He's gone back to the office. Said that the next few days were make or break and he couldn't trust anybody else to look after it. He's going to join us on Tuesday."

"Promises, promises," said Patrick. "Anyway, Rowena and I will be gone by then." (They were not coming for the whole week, just the first three days.) He put his arm around Claire, and said: "Never mind, Mum."

She returned the hug, and smiled an effortful smile. "Ah well, *c'est la vie*. Let's just get out there and enjoy ourselves, yeah? Get some of that Caribbean sunshine on our faces."

4

Having decided that what he wanted to write was not an article, but a whole book about the British far right and their rise in popularity during Blair's second term, Philip spent almost fifteen months collecting material. Then, one morning in September, 2002, he sat down to start work on the first chapter, and three days later—having written 243 words and played 168 games of Freecell on his computer—he resigned himself to a dismal fact: he was never going to do it. For two decades he had produced nothing longer than 2,000 words; had never bothered with any argument so complicated that it couldn't be pitched to the features editor in a few seconds. "About Town with Philip Chase" might have become a tired old formula from which he was desperate to break free, but it was also—unfortunately—all he was capable of. A man must work within his limits, he concluded.

After abandoning this project, he did not look at the notes he had amassed towards it for almost two months: not until he received a letter from Benjamin, in the second week of November. That was what prompted him to boot up his computer at work one morning, and reopen the folder labelled *BNP Book*.

What chaos he found there! How had he ever hoped to fashion something coherent out of this random selection of press cuttings, photographs and taped interviews? There were three sub-folders, labelled *Neoliberalism*, *Fundamentalism* and *Nationalism*. These, he seemed to remember, had been the three strands he was trying to weave together in the course of his treatise. He had been hoping to argue that they could all be traced back to the same source: that the proponents of each system were driven by the essentially primitive impulse to inhabit a self-contained world, insulated from anyone with whose beliefs or way of life they felt uncomfortable.

The neoliberals [he had written] *are seekers after purity just as much as the fundamentalists or the neo-Nazis. The only difference is that they are not setting out to create a nation state based on religious or genetic principles. The state they are building (which is rising up all around us, even as I write) is supra-national: global travel being one of its defining characteristics. Its geographical features are exclusive hotels, exclusive resorts, gated communities of wildly expensive houses. Its inhabitants will not travel by public transport, and will only use private hospitals. The impulse which drives these people is fear of contact with, and contamination from, the great mass of humanity. They wish to live among them (or rather, they have no choice in the matter) but use their money to put up as many screens as possible, as many boundaries as possible, in order that they need only come into meaningful contact with people of their own economic and cultural type. The way that New Labour has got into bed with these people—domestically, through things like the Private Finance Initiatives—and in foreign policy, through their support of Bush and the neo-cons in America—shows that it basically supports them in their elitist and divisive objectives. Small-scale, social democratic initiatives in health and education are a smoke-screen, a sort of lip-service paid to old style Leftism, in order to camouflage the real nature of the New Labour project.*

After this, he had added a note to himself: *Ask Claire why her boyfriend was having dinner with Paul Trotter!!*

Philip sighed as he looked over this material again. That last paragraph was all well and good, he thought, but it was meant to be the conclusion of the book, and he could never remember quite how he was supposed to arrive at it. What was the path he had hoped to trace, leading from those terrible letters Steve had been sent, to this damning indictment of current mainstream politics? It was to do with the nature of modern fascism, the way the nationalist movement in Britain had splintered, and now based itself not just upon old-fashioned race hatred but a far more tangled, far more slippery matrix of beliefs. The way that the battle-lines, which had seemed so stark and simple back in the 1970s, were now almost impossible to define with any clarity. Among the new British fascists, for instance, he had found that there were a number of thinkers (using the term in a fairly loose sense) who no longer advocated violence against the black or Asian population, and no longer talked about forced repatriation or tighter immigration controls, but who argued, instead, that white racists should form themselves into small, close-knit, rural communities, become self-sufficient, develop a quasi-mystical relationship with nature and "the land," and generally have nothing to do with a decadent, urbanized, multicultural modern society. None of which, admittedly, was likely to appeal much to the young skinheads who still made up a large part of the movement, whose *milieu* was the inner city and whose liking for violence and hooliganism was queasily romanticized by these theoreticians as a modern version of the "warrior" spirit inherent among the Aryan people. It did, however, mean that strange, uncomfortable affinities were beginning to emerge between elements of neo-Nazi thinking and aspects of the Green movement.

Similarly, the gulf between British fascism and militant Islam no longer seemed to be as wide as Phil had expected to find it. Hatred of black, Asian and Arabic people now seemed to take second place to anti-Semitism: all the talk was of overthrowing the Zionist Occupational Government, a conspiracy of powerful Jews which was alleged to rule the world with American (and British) corporate and military backing. Perhaps it was no surprise, therefore, to discover that white racists were prepared to make common cause with revolutionary groups from other cultures committed to the same idea, and that Osama bin Laden had been a hero to these people long before the September 11th bombings. And so it was now being argued in some quarters (mainly on the internet, in nationalist discussion forums), that true National Socialism had nothing to do with racism, but was simply a political system which allowed all peoples to return to their (separate) cultural roots and live in harmony with nature and God; and the only thing holding it back—the current "established world-order" based on capitalism, decadence and Godless materialism—therefore had to be overthrown by violent or subversive means.

Philip found that following the logic of these conspiracy theories was deeply treacherous and disorientating. He kept finding himself arriving at conclusions he agreed with (that Western society was decadent and valueless, for instance) and then having to retrace his steps and anchor himself in simple facts, concrete objects eliciting a gut response in which he could trust: the foul, racist language used in the anonymous letters to Steve, or the hate-filled lyrics on the *Auschwitz Carnival* CD. In the absolute incompatibility between these things and the mystical, almost poetical outpourings of the more articulate neo-Nazis, with their talk of Folk Culture, Soil and Honour, Philip struggled to find a moral position of his own. His overriding sense was that every system of values seemed to be in a state of flux, of meltdown, and that somehow New Labour itself was symptomatic of this, constantly talking a language of beliefs and idealism but in fact behaving with as much ruthless pragmatism as anybody else, and as deeply in thrall to its own

God (the free market economy) as any Muslim fanatic. The figure of Paul Trotter kept coming to mind.

But it was all far too complicated to put into words. Sometimes he would draft a paragraph or two, and read it back only to discover that he himself had started to sound like a far-right sympathizer; and then half an hour later he would look at it again and find that it now seemed to be coming from the radical left. There didn't seem to be a difference between the two perspectives any more; between anybody's perspectives. At other times, what he had been attempting looked so massive and all-encompassing that he had started to feel like Benjamin, with his ever-evolving, never-completed masterwork: which, if its fusion of words and music had any precedent at all, harked back to Wagner's notion of the *Gesamtkunstwerk*, a concept which had also turned out to sit far too comfortably with Nazi ideology. More complications! Philip couldn't get a grip on this. He was much better off doing "About Town" again. He had it in mind to write some pieces about the Gas Street Basin, how its network of interlocking canals bore witness to the bitter rivalries between the controlling companies at the beginning of the nineteenth century. These, at least, were the kinds of complexities he could handle. He would take refuge in what he understood; in what was knowable.

One evening, during the time when he was most deeply mired in his research on the book, Carol had said something interesting.

"Why are you so fascinated by all this stuff?" she asked.

And Philip explained, not for the first time, about the warmth and good feeling he had observed between Steve and his family, and how sickened he had felt when he saw the things that had been anonymously written about them.

"Yes, but what's the point in dwelling on any of that? The people who do these things are just scum—lowlife. By writing about them you're just glamourizing them."

"Well, racism is a continuing problem. These letters prove it. The case of Errol McGowan proves it. So somebody should be writing about it."

"But in a way, what you're investigating isn't racism. I mean, racism is everywhere, but it doesn't *announce* itself. If you want to find racism, take a look inside Middle England and gatecrash a Rotary Club dinner, or something. There's a whole lot of white, middle-class British people out there who basically don't *like* black people—don't like *anybody* who's different to themselves—but they're comfortably off and they're in control of their own lives so they don't have to do anything about it: except maybe read the *Daily Mail* and sound off about it among themselves at the golf club bar. *That's* racism. Whereas the people you're talking about, the people who organize, the people who go on demos and get into fights, the ones who talk about it openly—that's about something different. These people are damaged. Their fear and their sense of powerlessness are so strong that they can't hide it. In fact, that's why they're doing it—*they want people to see their fear.*"

"So what are you saying—that Combat 18 is a cry for help?"

"What I'm saying, Phil," Carol answered, laying a hand on his shoulder as he sat chewing a pencil at his desk, "is that I know you. You can't write about politics, you can't write about ideas. It's too abstract for you. You're interested in *people.* That's what this book ought to be about, if you're ever going to write it: what drives people to these positions? And I think that maybe it's started to fascinate you because in the middle of all this you think you're going to find something out."

"Something? What sort of something?"

"I don't know. The answer to some riddle. The answer to something that's been puzzling you for years. That's why it's started to take you over, this book."

He had frowned at her, not really understanding what she meant; but her words had stayed with him, for many months, and they came back to him that November morning when he opened Benjamin's letter and saw what he had discovered in Dorset.

Dear Phil [*Benjamin wrote*],

Harding is alive and well!

Or at least, he was nine years ago.

Last week I was staying down in Dorset with Mum and Dad, and Lois and her daughter Sophie. We were staying in an old castle which had lots of log-books which previous visitors had written in. And Sophie was reading them one night when she discovered this! What do you reckon. Is it our man, do you think?

All the best
Benjamin.

The photocopied log-book entry was on four separate sheets of paper. It said:

13–17 March 1995

They say that an Englishman's home is his castle, and I very much wish that this were true. Unfortunately, at the time of writing, my home (to which I must return, heavy-hearted, in only a few hours) is an almost derelict caravan in the bleak north-east of England, permanently sited in a windswept field only twenty yards from a nuclear reactor and with the most physically and psychologically challenging sanitary facilities that I think I have ever encountered in seventy-five years of—in retrospect—futile and utterly miserable existence.

O, that the last of the Pusey-Hamiltons should have come to this!

It has been a joy, by contrast, to occupy this noble establishment for the last three days. If only I could have shared them with Gladys, my late and so very much lamented good lady wife! My late ex-wife, I should say. Not because she was fond of dressing up in latex (although there were, I must admit, two or three happy occasions when I persuaded her to do so, during my halcyon and fondly remembered days as secretary of the Sutton Coldfield Bondage and Rubber Fetishists Group, a circle of respectable citizens and taxpayers engaged in entirely consensual activities, which was nevertheless scandalously closed down by the West Midlands Vice Squad, despite its chief officer being, at that time, one of our most enthusiastic members. O tempora, O mores!). Now—where was I? Yes—I refer to Gladys as my late ex-wife not for that reason, but for two others: firstly, because she is now deceased (she died, I regret to say, within a few days of her 67th birthday, after being struck on the head by a falling Maypole during a pagan fertility rite that got seriously out of hand); and secondly, because—and even now I can hardly bear to commit these words to paper—she also chose to leave me, to walk out on her loyal companion of almost forty years, shortly before our ruby wedding anniversary.

The circumstances surrounding this abandonment were widely reported in the newspapers at the time. Our marital dispute centred on a trifling misunderstanding. That summer, during an otherwise idyllic badger-baiting holiday in north Cornwall, I had taken her to visit a secluded cove (actually a good friend of mine, Major Harry "Grapeshot" Huntingdon-Down, then engaged in putting a private army together in a remote Cornish farmhouse), after which we took a stroll down to the beach together. There, I persuaded her to remove most of her clothing—not that it took much persuading: she had always, to be frank, been anybody's for a half-pint of Old Peculiar and a couple of pickled onions; her virtue was not so much loose as falling apart at the seams—and to pose for a series of tasteful and artistic photographs which I took using my trusty old Brownie (whose name I temporarily forget).

Now, it was Gladys's belief that these photographs were taken entirely for my own entertainment, and would not be made public in any way—except, perhaps, for framing one or two and putting them on the mantelpiece back at Hamilton Towers, to provide a talking-point when friends came round for an evening of bridge and conversation dried up over the saddled hare canapés. However, having inspected the results, I took a different decision. It would be stretching a point, admittedly, to describe her as an attractive woman at this advanced stage in her arduous and dissipated life, when the ravages of time had wreaked a terrible vengeance on a body which, even in the prime of her youth, had always inspired in me feelings of awestruck medical curiosity rather than sexual arousal. It did occur to me, nonetheless, that there were some sad and twisted individuals—long-term inmates of high-security penal institutions, for instance, or ageing Benedictine monks with severe visual impairments—who might, after a couple of strong drinks, find in Gladys's naked form something to titivate their starving palates at the end of a long day. Accordingly, I decided to publish the photographs: and made them the centerpiece, soon afterwards, of the first edition of my new publishing venture—a magazine called <u>Aryan Babes</u>, *which aimed to combine the finest in hardcore pornography with the most up-to-the-minute neo-Nazi news, features and comment, and which for some reason (a mystery to me to this very day) never caught the imagination of the reading public.*

The magazine folded after three issues, and there was, I seem to remember, some nasty business involving police raids and the seizure of computer equipment and floppy disks. And then, after I had served out my three-year sentence (plus another four or five months added on for minor sexual offences committed while incarcerated), I emerged from my confinement only to find that Gladys had left me. Yes!—Flown the nest, and stripped the house of all its contents. Taken even my most prized possession—the framed photograph of Gladys and I shaking hands with "Benny" Mussolini. (People told me that we had been duped—that we couldn't possibly have met him at the Eastbourne Winter Gardens in 1972—but it was envy, that's all—sheer envy.)

Happily, I am pleased to report that towards the end of her life Gladys saw the error of her ways and came back to live with me. Our twilight years were perhaps the most joyous of all (she always did look at her best in the twilight—or perhaps better still, in complete darkness). But this has made my subsequent bereavement even harder to bear and it has, I will be the first to admit, been a desolate time here without her. For many weeks after she died, I could not get used to the feeling of coldness and lifelessness on her side of the bed—and it was even worse when they took the body away and buried her. Of course, I never travel these days without my ouija board, and I communicate with her by this means every night. Sometimes we have the odd game of ghostly Scrabble together, the midnight candle flames flickering as she transmits her words to me from the other side of great River Lethe. I try to keep my spirits up by joking ("That was a dead heat!" I will quip, or "I'm facing stiff competition tonight"), but it's not the same, not the same . . .

O Gladys. Life is so very hard without you.

I have passed the rest of my time here as productively as I can, making notes towards my great work, The Decline of the West, which I intend to publish privately in four volumes, bound in moleskin. In fact I have made great progress towards that aim this week, because the grounds here are overrun with moles and I managed to go out and brain more than thirty of the little buggers with the poker at dawn on Wednesday morning, after a particularly restless and unhappy night. When completed, I shall donate the work to the fine private library at this castle—along with my brief autobiographical sketch of childhood, a little memoir of the days I spent as a young stripling in Equatorial Africa, in the care of my father: a good and honorable man—firm but fair—as the title, Birched Before Breakfast, makes clear. Finally I will add a literary product of my later years, a small but useful handbook called The Accidental Onanist: an Illustrated Guide to 100 Solo Sexual Positions for the Divorced, Widowed or Quite Frankly Unattractive Male. All of which I hope will be of use and interest to future occupants.

It has been a pleasure—albeit a lonely one—to spend some time in this fine old corner of England; a pleasure to fly the flag of St. George above those ancient battlements; a pleasure to feel, for a few fleeting days, that it might one day again be possible to live in this country as our ancestors did, in a land that can and will be free, unsullied, as all men of truth and honour desire it to be.

Arthur Pusey-Hamilton, MBE.

"ALBION RESURGENS!"

SEALED WITH THE ANCIENT AND NOBLE SEAL OF THE PUSEY-HAMILTONS

Philip read this passage with mixed feelings. It brought back many memories of his schooldays, of the increasingly outrageous articles that Harding used to submit anonymously to *The Bill Board.* Sometimes, the arguments over whether it was possible to publish them had been long and vociferous: but they had always succumbed, in the end, to Harding's humour, and to the conviction that no one could mistake the tone of these pieces for anything other than calculated irony. Often that irony had been almost too dark for comfort; often the milieu he wrote about—the lonely fantasy world of the Pusey-Hamiltons, with their traumatized son and their lunatic political beliefs—had seemed to be underscored by a real and unaffected sadness. But neither Philip nor any of the others had ever doubted one thing: that Harding was only doing it for a laugh.

Had he still been doing it for a laugh, nearly twenty years later?

As for the phrase "Albion resurgens"—well, that caused Philip a shiver of unease as well. He supposed it was a phrase that any literate British nationalist might be expected to use, and so would come naturally enough to the pen of someone who was satirizing the movement. But it was also, he realized now, the name of the record label that had released the "Unrepentant" CD.

Just a coincidence? Probably. But he wasn't going to be able to stop himself from making sure. After reading Harding's words for the second time, he went straight into his email program, and sent a message. He sent it to the editors of the anti-fascist magazine who had already helped him with much of his research. Philip told them that he needed to come down to London and look through their photo archives again.

3

For once, the roles were reversed, and it was Doug who had come to Benjamin for comfort. He was in Birmingham to visit his mother, and one Thursday evening they drove into town together and went to a Japanese restaurant in Brindley Place. Benjamin sat mesmerized as the bowls of food revolved slowly on a little conveyor belt before his eyes, while they sat perched on chrome stools and drank chilled Gewurtztraminer from fine, fluted glasses.

"Can you imagine what life would have been like in the 1970s, if we'd had places like this to come to?" he said, dousing his king prawn *tempura* with soy sauce. "I would probably have ended up marrying Jennifer Hawkins. It's no wonder that she dumped me. I remember for one date I took her to the chip shop and then for the rest of the evening we just sat on platform eleven at New Street Station. I couldn't think of anywhere else to go. There *wasn't* anywhere else, in those days."

"As far as I remember," said Doug, "she didn't dump you. *You* dumped *her*. In order to stay with Cicely. Interesting rewriting of history, though. I don't know quite what to make of it." He noticed Benjamin hesitating over a plate of *maguro maki*. "I'm paying for tonight, by the way—if that's what you're worried about."

"Oh. Thanks." Slightly shamefaced, Benjamin took the plate from the revolving belt and added it to the collection already in front of him. "I'll do the same for you some time."

"No hurry."

Benjamin spent some time attempting to pick up his rice roll with the chopsticks provided. It kept slipping out of their grip, and fell back on the plate so often that it was threatening to disintegrate altogether. Hunger getting the better of him, he used his fingers and polished it off in one go. "So what's all this about you and Claire?" he tried to say, through the mouthful of food.

"Well . . ." Doug leaned in closer. The stools in the restaurant were packed densely around the central table, so that the other customers were well within earshot. It had perhaps not been the best place to come for a confidential chat. "It's not that we've fallen out or anything. It's just that she said something last night that . . . shocked me, I suppose. Or maybe it was what she didn't say."

Benjamin's eyes were tracking a bowl of *tori nambazuki.* He wondered if there was going to be any left by the time it got round to them. "Go on," he said.

"I suppose it started a couple of years ago. Mum came down to London for the weekend and we went out to Starbucks one afternoon—rather strangely, I know—and we were talking about all sorts of stuff. About your brother, among other things."

Benjamin, half way through a chicken wing, grunted his surprise.

"It was when he was seeing Malvina. I was thinking of writing something about it."

The grunts became more expressive, culminating in a swallow and the words: "You wouldn't have done that, would you?"

"No, probably not." Doug decided not to say any more on that subject. Now that Malvina seemed to have disappeared, and no longer figured in any of their lives, there didn't seem to be much point. Hastily, he went on: "Mum advised me not to. She told me that nobody was perfect and people shouldn't always be judged by what they did in their personal lives."

Benjamin nodded. There were some mixed vegetable dumplings coming their way now.

"And that was when she told me—by way of illustration—that Dad had been unfaithful to her."

"God," said Benjamin, scooping up a couple of the dumplings and reaching for the soy sauce again. "Had you never suspected anything?"

"Not a thing."

"Did she tell you . . . who it had been?"

"Nope. She gave the impression there'd been more than one, actually. But I didn't ask who. It never really occurred to me that it might have been someone I knew. Anyway, last night I spoke to Claire and I found out."

"Don't tell me," said Benjamin, pausing in the act of taking another mouthful. "It was Claire's mother."

"It wasn't, actually."

"Not *Phil's* mother, surely?"

"No."

Benjamin went a little pale, and put his chopsticks down. "*My* mother?"

Doug shook his head impatiently. "This isn't twenty questions, you know, Benjamin. Will you just listen to the rest of the story? Now, last year—just after Mum had her stroke—Claire sent me an email. She asked if she could go round to Mum's house and look through Dad's old papers. Which I believe she did, although they were in such a state that she didn't manage to find anything."

"What was she looking for?"

"I don't know, exactly—but I think she's started wondering about Miriam again."

Benjamin was sorry to hear this. "That way madness lies," he said, shaking his head. "I mean, God knows what that must feel like—to lose your sister that way, and never know what's happened to her—but it was . . . how long ago? More than twenty-five years, isn't it? She's never going to find anything out about it now. She's got to let it go."

"Easier said than done, I should think," Doug reflected. "Anyway—" (he took a deep breath) "—you can guess what's coming, I suppose."

But Benjamin, apparently, couldn't.

"Well, the reason she wanted to look through Dad's papers," Doug said, spelling it out, "is that *she* was the one. It was Miriam he was having the affair with."

"Jesus . . ." Benjamin put down his wine glass and said nothing for a while, shocked beyond words. "When did she tell you?"

"Last night." Doug pushed some food around his plate distractedly. He had hardly eaten anything. "Dad's papers have all been taken away now. I gave them to Warwick university and they've put them in a proper archive. Last week I phoned them up and asked if they were accessible yet and they said yes, and then I emailed Claire, because I promised to tell her as soon as this had happened. Well, I didn't get any answer to the email so last night I phoned her up. Seems she'd been on holiday and had only just got back." He frowned. "Do you know anything about this new boyfriend of hers? Do you know who he is?"

"Not really. Phil said he was a businessman of some sort. A high-flyer. Absolutely loaded, by the sound of it."

"Well, that figures, because he took her on holiday to the Cayman Islands, of all places. And it can't have gone very well because Claire told me that she'd come home early, by herself. She'd only just got in when I phoned so she hadn't read the email. Anyway, I told her she could go to Warwick now and look through the archive if she was still interested and obviously she is, because right away she said she was going to go this week some time." He fell silent, and waited while Benjamin filled up his wine glass. Then drank deeply. "She sounded really excited about it: so I said, 'What's this all about, Claire? Are you ever going to tell me?' and she went quiet for a bit at the other end of the line, and then she said, 'What do *you* think it's about, Doug?' And I suppose I already knew, by that stage. So I said: 'It's my Dad, isn't it? He was sleeping with your sister.' And she said: 'Yeah, that's right . . .' "

In the long pause that followed, Benjamin noticed how noisy the restaurant was: how loud the music rippling in the background, restless with the thump and tick of drum machines and the wash of synthesizer chords; how boisterously all the other diners were enjoying themselves, laughing together, shouting jokes at each other, living in the present, living for the future: not locked in the past, as he always seemed to be, as his friends always seemed to be; the past that kept reaching out to them with subtle tendrils whenever they tried to break away and move forwards. Unfinished business.

"That's not all, though," Doug continued, slowly. "She said she'd made up her mind about something."

Benjamin waited. "Yes?"

"She says she knows that Miriam's dead. She doesn't have any doubt about that any more. She's not hoping to find her or anything. She just wants to know the truth."

Hesitantly, Benjamin asked: "What does that have to do with looking at your dad's papers?"

"That's what I wanted to know. What I asked her, in fact."

"And what did she say?"

"Nothing, for a while. So I said to her, 'I'm presuming that you don't think your sister died of natural causes. You think she was . . . murdered.' And she just sort of said, 'Yes,' in a very quiet voice. Very distant. I wondered if . . . you know, I wondered if she'd actually used that word before. In that context. Even when she was just thinking about it."

"Maybe she hadn't," said Benjamin, not knowing what else to say.

"So anyway—" Doug looked down at his wine glass, and swilled the golden liquid around slowly, unthinkingly "—so I had to ask her, didn't I? I had to say to her: 'Claire, you don't think my father did it, do you? You *can't* think that. You can't possibly.' " He put the glass down, rested his face on his hands for a moment. When he looked up, Benjamin noticed how tired his eyes were. "And do you know what she said to that?"

Benjamin shook his head; though he could already guess the answer, by now.

"Nothing." Doug smiled, the hardest and grimmest of smiles. "She did not say . . . a bloody word."

Just behind him, a young man with spiked hair and a business suit reached the punchline of a joke and was rewarded with explosions of laughter from his two companions. They looked like sales reps, staying away from home and ready to make a night of it. Benjamin winced at the noise, could almost feel it knocking him backwards.

"Shit," he said to Doug, feelingly, and put a hand on his arm.

"I hung up, then," Doug told him. "I just said, 'Bye-bye, Claire,' and put the phone down." He looked up at Benjamin and, although he attempted a smile again, there was a sadness in it this time. He seemed to be looking back, back across the years to the schooldays which kept tugging at them: the past that wouldn't let go. "I always knew Claire hated me," he said. "Now I know why."

They decided that the best solution was to get drunk. Doug had driven them both to Brindley Place, but his car was now safely tucked away in a 24-hour car park and they could easily share a taxi home. Doug reckoned he could claim it back on expenses anyway. So they abandoned their stools, and the endlessly revolving circle of food, sat down on square, unyielding cushions on opposite sides of a low table, with their knees wedged up almost as high as their faces, and ordered another bottle of wine to get themselves started.

Benjamin told Doug about the discovery he had made in Dorset. He had read the log-book entry so many times by now that he could recite most of it from memory. A lot of it made Doug laugh; but it was uncomfortable laughter. He reminded Benjamin of how Harding had once taken part in a mock by-election at school, and put himself forward as the candidate for the National Front.

"He always thought it was hilarious to take the piss out of those guys," he said. "It started to become a little bit obsessive. Now it sounds even worse."

"Even this was seven years ago," Benjamin pointed out. "We still don't know what he's doing now, or where he is."

"As I've said a hundred times—it could only be a disappointment to find out. But look," he said, taking Benjamin by the shoulder, his speech beginning to slur, "you're not seriously telling me that you've started to fancy your niece, are you? We're all getting worried about you, mate. It's been a long time now since you left Emily. It's about time you found somebody new. Somebody your *own age*. And preferably not a blood relation."

"I don't *fancy* Sophie. Not in that way. We hit it off, that's all. She takes me on my own terms. She makes an effort to understand what I'm trying to do, and she doesn't pity me or think I'm some kind of weirdo. Besides, I can't help it if all the nicest and most interesting people I meet are younger than me. I like young people—I find them easier to empathize with."

Doug chuckled derisively. "Yeah, right."

"It was the same with Malvina." (At the mention of whose name, Doug merely raised his eyes to the ceiling.) "I don't care what you think—I had a rapport with that woman, an amazing rapport. I don't think I've ever felt such a strong connection with someone. A real, immediate emotional connection. Not since—"

"Please." Doug held up his hand. "Do you think we could possibly get through the rest of this evening without mentioning the C-word?" Benjamin went quiet, at this point, and Doug started to think back to the evening a couple of years ago, when he had taken Malvina out for a drink in Chelsea, and had begun to realize how unhappy she was. It was a real, deep-seated unhappiness, too, the kind you probably need years of therapy to fathom. He felt suddenly cold at the thought of it. "I wonder what happened to her, anyway? Where she ended up after your brother had finished with her."

And Benjamin said, surprisingly: "We're still in touch."

Doug looked up. "You are?"

"Well . . . sort of. I haven't seen her or anything. But every so often I send her a text message."

"And? Does she text back?"

"Sometimes," said Benjamin, and left it at that. In all honesty, he had no idea where Malvina was living at the moment, or what she was doing. All he knew was that her mobile number hadn't changed in the last two years. For a while he had tried calling her, but usually he just got the answering service, and on the two or three occasions when they had actually spoken, Malvina had been monosyllabic and evasive, and the conversation was impossibly stilted. Since then, he had got into the habit of texting her every two or three weeks. He tried to make the messages pithy, and amusing, and to tell her a little bit about what was happening in his life, and he liked the discipline of trying to accomplish all this in only 149 characters. It was like writing in some highly economic and constraining verse form. Sometimes she replied, sometimes she didn't. Sometimes the replies would come at the oddest hours of the night. He had noticed that she was more likely to reply if he finished his own message with a question, even something bland and formulaic like *How r things with u?* or *What r u up 2 now?*, to which she would more often that not furnish some even more generalized and unenlightening answer. But at least it was contact, of a sort. At least this way he knew that she was still alive. And it was more than his brother had: this, to Benjamin, was a very important point. *He* was the one who had found Malvina; she had been *his* friend, until Paul had stolen her away from him. But Paul had blown it. Paul was never going to see her again. Benjamin had scored a victory, in that particular contest. A tiny victory, maybe, to some people: but to him, a momentous one.

"I'm probably going to go away for a few days soon," he announced now: and added (although at heart he knew that this was pure fantasy), "I was thinking of asking her to come along with me."

"Really? Where are you going?"

And Benjamin told Doug about the Abbaye St. Wandrille in Normandy; how he had been there with Emily, and how he had known, from the moment he had set foot inside the chapel and listened to the monks singing their *Complies*, that it was a place where he might one day feel completely and blissfully at home.

Doug was puzzled. "But Malvina's a woman."

"There's a dormitory there for women," Benjamin said. "It's outside the walls, and the female guests aren't allowed inside to eat with the monks or anything like that. But, you know—it's still a pretty nice place to stay."

Doug looked at him for a while, amazement and amusement struggling for precedence on his face. "Benjamin," he said at last, "I don't know how you do it. Even when I think that nothing you say could surprise me, you still manage to pull something out of the hat."

"How do you mean?"

"Only you, Benjamin—only *you*—could invite a woman to spend a dirty weekend with you at a fucking monastery!"

He laughed so hard that he fell backwards off his cushion and cracked his head against an adjoining table, while Benjamin just sat there sipping his wine and looking offended. He didn't think it was that funny, personally. But he was glad that something had cheered his friend up.

2

After Claire had been shown to her desk, she sat there for several minutes, with the first of the dozens of folders lying in front of her, unopened. She had laid two sharpened pencils next to it, and an A5 notebook, with a silky blue hardback cover and thick, roughly cut pages, which she had bought in Venice some years ago, and which contained, so far, only one piece of writing: the long letter she had composed to Miriam, describing her return to England in the winter of 1999. As for the folder, she didn't touch it. Not yet. It wasn't that she lacked the will, more that she was waiting for her head to clear. She wanted to be alert when reading this material, she didn't want the smallest detail to pass her by, and at the moment she felt anything but alert. The drive from Malvern to Coventry had been hellish: an hour and three-quarters, in the driving rain. The Warwick campus had been far busier than she was expecting, and she had struggled to find a parking space even in the biggest of the multi-storey car parks. She had arrived at the Modern Records Center fifty minutes later than the time agreed with the librarian over the telephone. Not that anybody seemed to mind: but Claire herself was flustered, disorientated. Right now, she didn't feel up to the task.

Maybe some coffee would help.

It was less than a minute's walk from Modern Records to the Arts Centre, but even in that time the rain managed to drench her. She asked for a double espresso and bought a hot chocolate as well, mainly so that she could keep her hands warm on the mug. She sat in a corner and watched the life of the university straggle before her on this Tuesday late-morning. Not many students in here, she noticed: it was more of a place where the academics and other staff came to eat. The air smelt heavily of wet, steaming clothes and dripping hair. Young, whey-faced lecturers split open packets of crisps and shared them with female postgraduates in ceremonies of would-be flirtation. Single women in their mid-fifties sat looking through their Filofaxes, and pulled dripping tea bags out of paper cups, holding them aloft uncertainly before depositing them to spread hot brown tea stains on their paper napkins.

She was back in England again: no mistaking it now. No wonder she was disorientated, then, given that forty-eight hours ago she had been sitting on a private beach near Bodden Town, beneath a tropical sun. Two days ago she had also been in a relationship (of sorts); this morning, she was single.

And probably all the happier for it, on the whole.

The holiday had got off to a good, if somewhat surreal, start. Never having flown first class before, Claire, Patrick and Rowena had over-indulged themselves wildly, drinking more than one bottle of champagne each, gorging themselves on Beluga caviar and Italian truffles, and then watching seven or eight hours' worth of movies on their personal video screens. As a result, they arrived drunk, bloated and exhausted while the other, more experienced travellers, who had spent most of the flight asleep, stepped off the plane looking in excellent shape. They were then met at the airport by George, the driver employed by Michael's business associate (whose name they never discovered), and were driven the fifteen miles or so to his villa, *Proserpina*, on the south side of the island.

Maybe it was the alcohol, or maybe it was the tiredness, but when they first stepped inside the villa, and when their cases had been taken away by the butler, and their coats by the maid, they all three simply burst into laughter. Opulence on this kind of scale was comical: they could not summon up any other response to it.

The very size of the rooms was staggering. The main reception room was as big as a hotel lobby, with six sofas, two bars, innumerable concealed speakers connected to a central Bang and Olufsen stereo system and French windows opening on to 500 yards of private beach. The smallest of the bedrooms contained a bed that could easily have slept five, raised—like all the other beds in the house—on a dais beneath a high ceiling with individual, hand-crafted oak mouldings. There were televisions everywhere, and bars everywhere (even, paradoxically, in the gymnasium). The study boasted a desk as wide as a snooker table, which faced a bank of twenty-four television screens which could be used either to provide surveillance of every room in the house, from every conceivable angle, or to watch all the satellite news and business channels simultaneously. For those who couldn't cope with the arduous twenty-yard walk to the beach, there were swimming pools indoors and out. The sunken bath in the master bathroom was, in itself, a swimming pool by any ordinary standards.

Claire spent most of the next two days on the beach, in the water, or sitting on one of the sun terraces reading. There were no books in the house, apart from a locked and alarmed glass-fronted display cabinet containing modern first editions (Thornton Wilder, Scott Fitzgerald, Steinbeck) and some eighteenth- and seventeenth-century volumes, none of which looked as though they were intended to be read; however, she had brought plenty of her own. She saw little of Patrick and Rowena, who would disappear to go diving and snorkelling for hours at a time. They met only at mealtimes, which proved to be fraught with problems of etiquette. The first night, their dinner was prepared for them by the resident cook. They felt so uncomfortable with this arrangement, and the staff who served the food appeared, in turn, to feel so uncomfortable about the guests' attempts to be friendly with them, engage them in conversation and generally treat them as living, breathing human beings rather than items of household furniture, that Claire decided she couldn't go through with it again. For the next two nights, they ate out at restaurants in Bodden Town. Even then, George insisted on driving them to their destination, and waiting for them in the car outside until they were ready to go home. Claire did her best to draw Rowena out on these occasions, but she found her cold and remote, almost to the point of rudeness. She and Patrick seemed to have almost nothing in common; there seemed to be no rapport between them except for the obvious physical one. Claire gave the relationship until Christmas at the latest.

By the end of the third day, Michael had still not appeared; and it was already time for Patrick and Rowena to fly home. They were both in their gap years between school and university, and in two days' time Rowena would be starting a temporary job at her uncle's architectural practice in Edinburgh. Patrick, chivalrously, had offered to drive her all the way there. Claire waved goodbye as George swept them off to the airport, and then spent thirty-six even more bizarre hours alone in the house, with no one for company but half a dozen servants who appeared to be under written instructions not to talk to her, although they were endlessly hovering on the edges of whichever room she happened to be in, ready to refill her glass or clear away her plate as soon as it was done with.

She began to feel more than slightly strange. She could not reconcile her sense of being entirely alone with the knowledge that she was always under surveillance (whether by the wordlessly vigilant servants, or the security cameras which switched themselves on with a click and a whirr and began tracking her progress as soon as she entered a room). She did not know what she was doing here. She felt more like a prisoner than a guest. Her sense of identity was starting to fracture. She had begun to feel like the Catherine Deneuve character in a big-budget, full-colour Hollywood remake of *Repulsion*.

Michael's long-delayed arrival made a certain amount of difference, but not as much as she had been expecting. They went diving together, they swam together, they ate meals together in the evening by the side of the swimming pool. One night he took her out in a speedboat and they had dinner with a friend who had a yacht moored a few miles along the coast towards Long Coconut Point. They made love on the beach, in the bedroom and even (once, rather precariously and disastrously) on the rowing machine in the gymnasium. The only thing they didn't do, in fact, was talk. All of Claire's resolutions about confronting Michael with her growing despair about the future of the relationship were thwarted by his constant air of preoccupation, his magnificent unreachability. He could be talkative when he wanted to be: they had their usual, half-serious, half-facetious political arguments; he would discuss current affairs, the state of the economy, the looming war with Iraq (which he opposed) and even, occasionally, more trivial things like Caribbean cuisine or the education of his children (who were all at boarding school). But every attempt to shift the conversations on to an emotional level met with blankness.

Claire began to ask herself, again, why she had come to this place. In the main reception room, she watched Michael pressing a button on the remote control so that a widescreen plasma TV rose up from beneath the floor like something on the console of the Starship *Enterprise*, watched him flicking between Bloomberg and the other satellite business channels, and kept asking herself, over and over: what am I doing here?

It was not that he spent the whole time working. Whatever crisis had delayed him back in London seemed to have been successfully resolved. He only spent an hour or two every day in the study. When a call came through on his mobile, he would check the number first, and only answer about one in four. Sometimes, if Claire asked him what the call had been about, he would even try to tell her. She did not really understand business jargon, and she always got the sense that he was being fairly selective with the information he chose to share with her, but all the same, she felt that he was making a decent effort to help her understand what was on his mind. She did not feel that she was being deceived, or kept out of a loop. She knew that the company was in the process of disposing of some of its surplus land and plant: there were repeated references to premises near Solihull, just outside Birmingham. The deal seemed to be in its final stages. It appeared to be going well, and that, for Claire, was the important thing. It meant that Michael was in a good mood.

At about ten o'clock one morning, she came out of the shower and saw that Michael was sitting on the balcony outside their bedroom, overlooking the beach. Breakfast had been served and he was talking on his mobile while drinking coffee and picking with his fork at some eggs benedict. Still wearing only her dressing gown, she sat down at the table opposite him, poured some coffee into a bone china cup, and carried on reading the novel she had started the night before. Michael glanced at her, telling her with his eyes that he would not be on the phone for much longer. She lost interest in the novel after a sentence or two, and sat admiring the view instead, sundrunk and mesmerized by the subtle movements of palm trees against an azure sky as the morning breeze rustled their leaves.

"So that's definite, is it?" Michael was saying. "One hundred and forty-six is the final figure?" There were some words of confirmation at the other end of the line, and he nodded approvingly, looking very pleased with this development. "Excellent. OK. Well I think we can release that in a few weeks and there won't be much fall-out. No—after Christmas, definitely. Just after."

Shortly afterwards he clicked the phone shut, smiled at Claire, and leaned across the table to kiss her good morning.

"Good news?" she asked, filling his coffee cup.

"Very satisfactory."

She waited for him to elaborate, but it seemed he had no intention of doing so. Claire was annoyed by this, for some reason, but managed to keep her tone of voice airy as she asked: "So—a hundred and forty-six, eh? Is that million?"

He looked up from his breakfast plate. "Mm?"

"Is that how much you're going to get—for selling the Solihull buildings?"

"Oh." He laughed, dismissively. "No. Not at all."

"Don't tell me, then: it's going to be your Christmas bonus this year?"

He laughed again. It was perfectly relaxed laughter. Whatever it was that he had just confirmed over the telephone, it was nothing that caused him any embarrassment, or he felt obliged to conceal from her.

"Hardly," he said. "Sorry not to tell you anything more dramatic, but it's just plain one hundred and forty-six, I'm afraid. We're closing down the R&D department completely. Not paying its way. We're shutting it down and selling off the plant. That means we'll be making a hundred and forty-six people redundant."

"Oh," said Claire. "I see. And why's that good news?"

"Because I was afraid it was going to have to be more than that. Anything over two hundred would have been a PR disaster. But a hundred and forty-six is nothing, really, is it? People are barely going to notice."

"No," said Claire, thoughtfully. "I suppose they won't."

Not long afterwards, Michael disappeared inside to have a shower, leaving Claire to ponder these words. She made no attempt, this time, to pick up her novel again. Instead, she could feel a kind of numbness spreading over her. It was not new, this feeling: she realized now that it had been growing inside her all week. And what she had just heard from Michael made no difference, in a way: it was not as if this was a turning point, or a moment of revelation. Perhaps the numbness was now, at least, beginning to assume a shape; or perhaps it had become so pressing that she knew she could not ignore it for much longer. Whatever the reason, all at once she felt deeply, oppressively unhappy to be sitting there on this sundrenched balcony, the sparkle of ocean laid out before her, thousands of miles from the world she knew, the world she understood. She felt a pang of almost unbearable longing for her little terraced house on the slopes of Great Malvern.

A few minutes later she went inside, changed into her bathing costume and left the house without saying anything to Michael. She walked to the beach.

She was not outraged by anything she had heard; she was not naive; she knew what it was that Michael did for a living. People lost their jobs all the time; and this inevitably meant that somebody, somewhere, had to make the decisions which led to those job losses. It just so happened that this particular decision had been made this morning, just across the table from her, on a Caribbean island, by a man she had chosen to become intimate with, on a balcony outside the bedroom she was sharing with him. What difference did that make? It shouldn't make any difference at all. And he was right. One hundred and forty-six wasn't such a big number. You regularly saw stories in the newspapers about thousands of people losing their jobs.

So why did she suddenly feel sick to the stomach?

Perhaps that was precisely the problem. Five thousand would have been an unimaginable figure. It would have seemed meaningless. Whereas, there was something obscenely specific and graspable about the number one hundred and forty-six. As Claire dropped her towel on the scorching white sand at the water's edge, and waded out to the point where the waves would break against her, she thought about the one hundred and forty-six families who would be receiving that news shortly after Christmas. Doubtless Michael was right to have done what he did. And it was thoughtful of him, too, to wait until Christmas was over before telling them. He wasn't a bad man, she could see that: but she couldn't love him, either. She couldn't love the man who made those decisions and took satisfaction in them. Perhaps somebody else could. She hoped so.

The warm water foamed around her thighs, her waist. She took a breath and dived into a breaking wave. The shock of it stung her face, set her ears ringing, and when she surfaced a few seconds later the sunshine all around her was almost too much to bear. She shielded her eyes against the dazzle and glimmer, then dived again, repeatedly, hurling herself into each oncoming wave, and every time she dived, it was like a slap in the face, a wake-up call from an unforgiving but well-intentioned friend.

Soon afterwards, she walked back to the house. Thankfully, Michael was nowhere to be found. She packed her bag and left a simple note, saying "Thanks for all the good times, but better make that 147." Then asked the ever-dependable George to drive her to the airport.

Claire finished her coffee, gave up on the hot chocolate, and ran back to the Modern Records Centre with her raincoat pulled up over her head. The rain was starting to ease off anyway.

The coffee had revived her. She knew that she was strong enough to look through the folders now, and was ready for anything that they might reveal. (The only thing that scared her, in fact, was the thought that they might reveal nothing.) Reflecting on the holiday had only made her understand, with more clarity than ever before, who she was and why she had come here. This rain, these grey English skies, this scurrying, preoccupied mass of dour and dampened humanity: these were the things that defined her. If her life for the last twenty-eight years had been leading anywhere meaningful at all, it was here: to this campus, and this library. Anything else, she knew now, was an irrelevance. She would never be able to move on, until she had confronted whatever it was that this place was now ready to disclose to her.

She began reading.

. . .

Whatever else she had been expecting from Bill Anderton's papers, she had never thought that they would be so involving. She had assumed they would be dry and guarded, written only so as to preserve the tersest and most official of records. Instead, she found a whole world, and a whole era, summoned up for her.

As Convenor of the Works Committee, it seemed that Bill had been something more than just the spokesman for his workforce. He had been agony aunt, political agitator, resolver of disputes and keeper of secrets. People had written to him on almost every conceivable subject: from a fellow shop steward in the forging factory, who had complained that his men's pay was being docked for time spent washing down in the showers after their shift (a complaint that had ended in a walk-out), to a distraught father who had penned a closely written, five-page letter claiming that his daughter was being tortured and held prisoner by nuns at a convent in Gloucestershire. It was not clear whether Bill had replied to all of these letters. Certainly he had replied to many of them, and the work must have kept him extremely busy. Claire had never thought of the 1970s as being a distant era, but she found that the tone and the discourse of the correspondence now seemed touchingly archaic. She was struck by Bill's unironic use of the word "Brother" when writing to the other union members, and by the way he signed off each letter with "Yours fraternally." She was struck, too, by how much of his paperwork related to the National Front, and to the ways in which various elements from the far right had attempted to infiltrate the Longbridge factory in those days. There was a letter frostily refusing a member of the National Front permission to use union facilities for one of their meetings; a copy of an almost illiterate message inviting workers (incredibly, it seemed to Claire) to a party in Birmingham celebrating Hitler's birthday on April 20th, 1974; and a statement from the Works Committee which condemned

> . . . the outrages that occurred in Birmingham on Thursday night the 21st November 1974. We urge our members to exercise restraint, and not to allow the instigators of these acts to create divisions among working people. The most positive manner to help and express our sympathies is to contribute to a massive collection in this factory, and not to participate in demonstrations called by outside organizations.

But where was Miriam in all of this?

Claire did not imagine that she would find any love letters. There would be nothing as obvious as that, surely: personal documents would have been sifted out by the archivist, she supposed, and discreetly returned to the Anderton family. If there was to be any direct reference to her sister, the likelihood was that it came in the folder marked "Charity Fund Committee." Bill had been the Chairman of this committee, and Miriam had been its secretary. That was how they had met in the first place, she seemed to remember. But she had not opened this folder yet. She had placed it carefully to one side, intending to leave it to last. She had been determined to go through this material in sequence, patiently.

But that resolve did not last for very long. The Charity Committee folder was the second that she opened, after only twenty minutes.

The papers here were not arranged chronologically. At the top of the pile was a thick sheaf of legal documents relating to one Victor Gibbs, who appeared to have been the treasurer of the committee, and who had been caught out by Bill in the act of forging cheques and embezzling funds. He had been dismissed from the company, according to Bill's notes, in February 1975, although no criminal proceedings had been brought against him.

Claire recognized this name; or thought that she did. Hadn't Miriam once referred, in one of her diaries, to somebody called "Vile Victor?" It must be the same person. She tried to remember what she had written about him, but nothing surfaced. Why had she called him "Vile"? His forging and embezzling didn't imply an especially attractive personality, of course: but was it something more than that? Had he done something to Miriam—victimized her in some way—to make her write about him with such repugnance?

The minutes of the Committee followed next, at considerable length. The chief interest of these, for Claire, lay in the fact that her sister must have typed them. Otherwise, they were not especially revealing. None of the names of the other committee members was female, she noticed. Women were still barely getting a look-in, in those days. Claire tried to imagine what the atmosphere must have been like in the committee room, on those wintry weekday evenings. She pictured cigarette smoke, curling in the light of a naked sixty-watt bulb or fluorescent tube. A group of men sitting around the table, the sweat and grime of a nine-hour shift at the factory still thick upon their bodies. Miriam, sitting next to Bill, scribbling everything down in her haphazard Pitman shorthand. They would all have been looking at her. She had been beautiful. She had always found it easy to attract men, and had always enjoyed the power she exerted over them. What a focus of rapt, furtive attention she would have been! Had Victor Gibbs been one of that circle, resentfully captivated, unable to take his eyes off her, and had she made it clear that she wasn't interested? Was that the cause of the animosity between them?

The next document Claire found did not answer that question. But it gave her such a shock that, after her first glance at it, she pushed back her seat with a crash that shattered the silence of the library, and rushed outside to stand on the steps for a few minutes, gasping for breath, unmindful of the rain that drizzled thinly on to her hair and began to trickle down her neck in tiny streams.

It was a letter from Victor Gibbs to Bill Anderton. A letter about Miriam. But it wasn't the content of the letter that had shocked her. It wasn't what it said. It was the way it had been typed.

Claire thought about photocopying the letter; but she didn't want to have a photocopy. She wanted to have the letter itself. So she stole it. She had no scruple about this at all. If it righfully belonged to anyone, it belonged to her. She folded it and placed it in her handbag and carried it out of the library without anybody noticing. She knew that it was the right thing to do.

When she arrived home that afternoon, she laid the letter out on the kitchen table and read it again. These were the words that Victor Gibbs had typed to Bill Anderton nearly three decades ago:

Dear Brother Anderton,

I am writing to complain to you about the work of Miss Newman in her capacity as Charity Committee Secretary.

Miss Newman is not a good Secretary. She does not perform her duties well.

There is a lack of attention on the part of Miss Newman. At meetings of the Charity Committee, you can often see her attention wandering. I sometimes think she has other things on her mind than performing her duties as Secretary. I would prefer not to say what these other things might be.

I have made many important remarks, and addressed many observations, which have not been recorded in the minutes of the Charity Committee, due to Miss Newman. This is true of other Committee Members, but especially of me. I think she is discharging her duties with total inefficiency.

I draw this matter to your urgent attention, Brother Anderton, and personally suggest that Miss Newman be removed as Secretary of the Charity Committee forthwith. Whether or not she continues in the Design Typing Pool is of course at the firm's discretion. But I do not think she is a good typist either.

Yours fraternally,
Victor Gibbs.

After reading it one more time, Claire ran upstairs, and unlocked the desk in the spare bedroom where she kept all her most precious souvenirs of Miriam. She took out the most precious of all—the letter her parents had received early in December, 1974, two weeks after her sister had disappeared—the last news they had ever heard of her—and ran back downstairs with it. She placed it on the kitchen table, next to the letter from Victor Gibbs. It said:

Dear Mum and Dad,

This letter is to tell you that I have left home and will not be coming back. I have found a man and I have gone to live with him and I am very happy. I am expecting his baby and will probably have it.

Please do not try to look for me.

Your loving daughter.

It was signed by Miriam herself—or so, until today, Claire had always believed. But hadn't Victor Gibbs proved himself to be an expert forger of signatures? She could only speculate about that, for now; and in the meantime, there was no need to speculate about the letters themselves. They both had the same typographical oddity—a defective letter "k" that fell slightly above the line. They must have been typed on the same typewriter.

What did this mean? That Miriam's final letter was a forgery? Or that she had still been alive, two weeks after she vanished, and had been with Victor Gibbs when she wrote it?

Either way, Claire was going to have to find him.

I

Benjamin's neighbour, Munir, was a vocal opponent of the war. The war hadn't started yet, but everybody talked as though it was inevitable, and you were either for it or against it. Actually, almost everybody seemed to be against it, except for the Americans, Tony Blair, most of his cabinet, most of his MPs, and the Conservatives. Everybody else thought that it was a disastrous idea, and could not understand why it was suddenly being talked about as if it was inevitable.

The only person who didn't seem to have a definite opinion about the war, either for or against, was Paul Trotter. This was ironic, because he was regularly being paid large sums of money, by several of the national newspapers, to express his opinion about it. The first of these pieces, headed "My Grave Doubts over War with Iraq," had appeared in the *Guardian* in November. It was followed by similar pieces for the *Times*, the *Telegraph* and the *Independent*, all expressing further doubts, of equal gravity, over the moral justification for the war, its legality, and its political wisdom. These articles would find Paul wrestling with his conscience in language of the most anguished sort, while somehow managing to stop short of actually telling his readers the very thing that they wanted to know, viz., whether he thought that the war was a good idea or not. He was careful not to include any attacks on Tony Blair himself, or to portray him as anything other than a man of principle and a potentially fine war leader. It had also not gone unnoticed, by most commentators (including Doug Anderton) that on the two occasions so far when there had been a vote on this subject in the House of Commons, Paul had done the bidding of the party whips and voted with the government. And yet his doubts, it would seem, remained grave. The reading public was never allowed to forget this fact.

"Have you seen this?" said Munir, walking through the open doorway into Benjamin's flat one evening early in December. He waved a copy of that day's *Telegraph*, which had called Paul back for a repeat performance. "Your brother is sitting on the fence again. I don't know how he gets away with it. It's a joke."

"I'm on the phone, Munir," Benjamin said, covering the mouthpiece. "It's not a good time."

"That's all right," said Munir, sitting himself down on the sofa, the cheapest and most uncomfortable in the Ikea range. "I can wait."

Benjamin sighed and walked through into his bedroom. He liked his neighbour and didn't want to antagonize him. A middle-aged Pakistani who worked as an informations officer for the City Council, Munir—like Benjamin—was single, and had got into the habit of coming upstairs from the ground floor flat most evenings to drink tea and to discuss politics, of which he was an avid follower. Sometimes the two of them would also sit and watch television together: Munir didn't own a set—claiming that British television was corrupting and decadent—which meant that he frequently had to come and watch Benjamin's for hours at a time. Theirs were the only flats in this small terraced house (where Benjamin had been living now for eight months) and the two men had come to value each other's company.

"Sorry about that, Susan," Benjamin now murmured into the telephone, closing the bedroom door behind him.

"That's all right—I'd better go now anyway," Susan said. "I haven't given the girls their bath yet and it's nearly eight. Thanks for listening, anyway, Ben. You must get sick of this sad old cow calling you every night."

"You're not sad, you're not a cow, and *no way* are you old," Benjamin insisted.

Susan laughed at the other end of the line. "Yeah, I know—it's just how your brother makes me feel, sometimes."

"He's just busy, Susan. I know you've heard that before—from me and everybody else, probably—but I'm sure that's what it is."

He hung up and went back into the living room.

"Hi, Munir. I was just going out, actually."

"Oh. Oh well, never mind. I was just hoping for a little chat. Perhaps you wouldn't mind if I stayed and watched the news for half an hour?"

"No problem," said Benjamin, scooping up his keys and wriggling into his winter coat. "Just don't go flicking channels. I know how easily shocked you are."

This advice failed to elicit a smile. Munir didn't like being teased. Looking around for the remote control, he asked:

"Was that Susan on the telephone again?"

"Yes," said Benjamin, buttoning his coat.

"That's a bad situation," said Munir. "Your brother is neglecting her. She's going to have an affair if he's not careful."

"I don't think she's got the time or the inclination, to be honest," Benjamin answered. "Not with two little kids running around. All she wants is a bit of grown-up conversation every now and again."

Munir shook his head disapprovingly and turned on the television. Within a few seconds he was absorbed in the recital of closing headlines on *Channel 4 News*, and might almost have forgotten that Benjamin was there. Benjamin smiled and made his way downstairs, out into the freezing streets of Moseley to wait for a 50A bus into town.

Philip was late, but Steve Richards was already waiting for Benjamin at The Glass and Bottle, a pint of lager on the table before him. It was the third time they had all met up since Steve and his family had moved back to Birmingham. The arrangement had quickly become formalized, and they now met on the second Thursday of every month. It was something they all looked forward to.

"I did something really stupid a couple of weeks ago," Steve said, returning from the bar with a Guinness for Benjamin. "I saw Valerie again."

"Valerie?" said Benjamin. "Wow. That's going back a bit, isn't it? How did you find her?"

"*FriendsReunited*, of course."

They touched glasses, and Benjamin drank deeply of the black, creamy liquid.

"I don't know . . ." Steve began. "It was one of those things where you know you shouldn't be doing it, but you can't stop yourself. Each step seems innocent enough at the time, but it takes you further down the path. The worst thing, when I look back at it, is how many times I lied to Kate. Lied to her for no reason at all, really. Just think about it: I was upstairs on the computer one evening, looking at *FriendsReunited*, when I'd told her that I'd got lots of work to do—that was lie number one. Then I got an email from Val a couple of days later, and I was reading it when Kate came into the room, so I deleted it straight away and told her it was spam—lie number two. Then I told Kate I was going out for a meal with some of the new guys from work—

lie number three. Then, when I got home, she was asking me questions about them, and I had to make everything up: their names, their life histories, all the things we were supposed to have talked about—lies number four to twenty-seven. And what was the point? Me and Valerie just sat in a pub for an hour and a half and told each other how happily married we were and how much we loved our partners. And for *that*, I had to deceive my wife? Crazy. Crazy. A complete waste of time."

"You're not going to see her again?"

"I shouldn't think so."

Benjamin sipped his Guinness, and thought about those secret meetings with Malvina which had started three years ago, and which had spelled the beginning of the end of his marriage. But he knew that Steve's situation was different.

"Look," he said, "I wouldn't beat yourself up about this. I know what Valerie meant to you. She was the first one, wasn't she? Stuff like that never goes away, it never leaves you. So if you get the chance—or you can *give* yourself the chance—to revisit that place, and take a look at it, and realize that you don't belong there any more, no one's going to blame you for doing that. You need closure. Everybody needs closure. That's what it's all about, I reckon."

"What about you and Cicely? Have you got closure on that one?"

Benjamin thought long and hard before answering. "Put it this way," he said at last. "I don't think about it any more."

"That's not quite the same thing."

But Benjamin wasn't to be drawn any further on that subject. Instead, he started asking Steve about his move to Birmingham: how the family were settling into their new home, whether Kate was starting to feel comfortable yet in this unfamiliar city, whether the girls liked their new school. He asked how it felt to return to the city of his birth, and Steve said: "You know what, Ben? It feels so good to be back in Birmingham. That's all I can say. Don't ask me why, but it feels *so . . . damn . . . good.*" They touched glasses again, and Steve started telling him how sad it had been to leave behind that little outfit in Telford, whose bosses had given him so much leeway to pursue his research. But he didn't regret the decision. You had to move onwards and upwards. The firm he had now joined, Meniscus Plastics, had a large and thriving R&D department, with excellent lab facilities, housed in premises just outside Solihull. And it also had a new, dynamic CEO, appointed only last year, who promised to take the company on to even bigger and better things. All in all, the future had never looked brighter.

. . .

Philip arrived just after half past nine, straight off the London train, his face flushed with excitement. He had his briefcase with him, and insisted on sitting with it perched on his lap, as if the contents were unusually precious and he was afraid that somebody would steal it if he laid it on the floor.

"There was something I wanted to ask you, Steve," he said, having downed most of his first pint of lager in one thirsty draught. "Do you still have that St. Christopher's medal? The one that Valerie gave you."

Benjamin and Steve exchanged surprised, rather conspiratorial glances.

"We were talking about her before you arrived," Benjamin explained. "We've been going back in time a bit this evening."

"Sure, I've still got it," said Steve. "Stashed away in a drawer somewhere. It's not the kind of thing you parade in front of your wife and kids. Why do you ask?"

"Because I've been thinking about what happened at school. When we all thought Culpepper must have pinched it, to put you off your stroke on sports day."

"Well, he probably did. He was a nasty piece of work, wasn't he?"

The three of them drank in silence for a moment. Both Steve and Benjamin were waiting to see where this was leading. Eventually, Philip said:

"Do you remember what happened the year after that?"

"When do you mean?"

"When we were doing our A-levels."

"Of course I do. The bastard drugged me. Made me drink something just before my physics exam."

"That's right. We were all locked in a room together. Me, you . . . Doug . . . Anyone else that you can remember?"

Steve shook his head. "It was years ago, wasn't it? I can't even remember the names of half of those kids." He made for his glass, but then paused in mid-sip. "Oh yeah—Sean was there, I remember that. Sean Harding."

"Exactly." Philip leaned forward. "Now think about this, Steve. Remember what happened. Culpepper found your medal in the lost property box, and we all crowded round to have a look at it. And we always assumed he'd done that on purpose, to create a diversion, so he could spike your drink. Right? But think about what happened *after* that."

Steve's expression was blank. "No. It's gone."

"Sean played one of his jokes. Remember? He got one of the little kids to throw a piece of paper through the window. You and Culpepper both thought it was the exam paper for that afternoon, and you had a fight over it.

A real scuffle on the floor. And of course it wasn't. Sean had set up the whole thing, and while you were scrapping about it he just sat there, with this big grin on his face. Tapping away on the side of his tea cup, with—"

"With that *ring* of his! The signet ring. Yeah, I remember now." But he didn't smile at the recollection of it. He had fallen out of love with Harding's mischief-making long before most of the other pupils at King William's. He had never really forgiven him for playing the part of a National Front spokesman, even as a joke. "What about it, anyway?"

"Well," said Philip, "supposing *that* was the real diversion? Supposing Culpepper had nothing to do with it?"

"What—and Sean was the one who doped me up? Why would he want to do that?"

"OK." Philip clicked open his briefcase, and took out a manila envelope, A4 size. He put it on the table between them. "I'm going to show you something now. It's to do with the CD you gave me."

He took two black and white photographs out of the envelope, and pushed the first one forward for Steve's inspection—without revealing the second, which lay hidden beneath it.

"There's a magazine down in London that keeps tabs on the activities of the far right. When I was thinking of doing that book, they gave me a lot of help. Offered to let me have copies of all these pictures. I never took them up on it, but then Benjamin found this thing down in Dorset—did he tell you about that?"

Steve shook his head.

"Well, he can explain later . . . Anyway, it set me thinking. I thought I'd go down and have another look. That's where I've been today. Now: what do you make of this?"

The picture showed four skinheads, standing around a desk in some anonymous, sparsely furnished office, staring at the camera with dead eyes, as if they were challenging it to a fight. At the desk sat an overweight man in T-shirt and bomber jacket, leering cheesily and brandishing a pen.

"Who are these guys?" Steve asked.

"These are the four talented musicians in question. Unrepentant—the original line-up, now sadly defunct. And this is Andy Watson, one-time owner of the fine independent record label, *Albion Resurgens*—currently putting himself up for election as a BNP councillor, somewhere in the East End, I believe. The question is: who's the *sixth* man?"

Steve looked more closely at the picture. "There isn't anybody else."

"Look again."

He picked up the photograph and held it just an inch or two from his eyes.

"I suppose this could be somebody's arm."

"You've got it." Philip took the photograph back, and showed it to Benjamin. "See? Just here. There's someone else standing on the edge of the picture. He's leaning against the desk."

Philip paused, theatrically, relishing their state of suspense.

"Who is it?" Steve asked at last.

"I can't say for certain," said Philip. "But I got the photo blown up as much as I could. And this might give us a little clue."

He uncovered the second photograph, which showed just a small detail from the first—a man's disembodied arm—magnified to about ten or twelve times its original size. Steve and Benjamin leaned in, looked at the arm, the slightly scruffy black sleeve which suggested a well-worn suit, the pale flesh at the back of the hand, the thin, slender fingers; and on the middle finger, a ring. A ring which they both recognized at once. It was the ring that Harding had once bought at a Birmingham antiques market, countless years ago: the signet ring with which he had stamped, at the foot of any number of scurrilous letters and articles written for *The Bill Board*, the supposedly ancient and noble seal of the Pusey-Hamiltons.

NORFOLK RHAPSODY NO. I

Winter

10

"'Norfolk Rhapsody Number One,' it's called," said the taxi driver. "By Ralph Vaughan Williams. Lovely, isn't it? I heard it on Classic FM and went out and bought the CD. Do you want me to turn it up a bit?"

"No thanks," said Paul. He had only asked the question because, last week, a waspish young woman from the *Independent* had come to interview him, and one of her comments in the resulting profile had been that, "He seems to live within an absolutely impermeable bubble of self-absorption, incapable of taking any real interest in other people."

Anyway, he had got the driver talking now, and there was going to be no stopping him, by the sound of it.

"Do you know his music, at all? Beautiful stuff, it is. They play a lot of it on Classic FM. He did this piece called 'The Lark Ascending,' which is totally fantastic. Actually it's on this CD—coming up the track after this. You can *see* the bird taking off into the sky when the violin starts playing—you know, you can really see it. When that's playing, I just have to close my eyes and I'm back on the South Downs. My mum's old cottage. That's where I'm from, originally, you see. 'Course, I don't actually close my eyes when I'm driving, that'd be lethal, wouldn't it? I just mean metaphorically. But I need something to calm me down when I'm driving around London these days. Fucking unbelievable it is, the traffic. I need something to help me relax or I just get too fucking wound up. If I was at home I'd have a glass or two of Australian Shiraz, you know, something fruity and mellow. But I mean, I can't get pissed when I'm driving, can I?"

49

PAUL TROTTER, MP

His career has been on the up since returning to the backbenches two years ago. Frequent TV and radio appearances have made him one of the best-known New Labour faces, and his suits just seem to get sharper and sharper every time he pops up on screen. His Commission for Business and Social Initiatives has yet to report, but its findings are likely to confirm his position as a leading figure on the right wing of the party.

Paul Trotter wears: Bespoke special made suit by Kilgour (from £2,300), white harness cotton shirt by Alexander McQueen (£170).

(Extracted from magazine feature, "The 50 Sharpest Men in Britain," December, 2002)

Paul stepped out of the taxi to find that there were two rows of photographers lined up outside the restaurant, and he was going to have to walk down the aisle formed between them. There wasn't actually a red carpet, but it did rather feel as though there should have been. As the taxi pulled away, he straightened his tie and patted his hair into shape. Then he stepped forward, feeling suddenly self-conscious, trying to move with the feline grace of a catwalk model but convinced, for some reason, that his arms and legs had started to swing in some weird, uncoordinated parody of the way he normally walked. He smiled to his left, and smiled to his right, not wanting to look as though he were unaccustomed to this kind of attention. But he needn't have worried. None of the dozen or so paparazzi bothered to raise their cameras as he passed, and the expected barrage of flashlights never materialized. Just as he was reaching the door of the restaurant a white stretch limo pulled up behind him, and a couple in their early twenties emerged: the man had designer stubble and wrap-around shades, the woman a virtually non-existent dress which seemed to consist of three tiny muslin handkerchiefs held approximately together by some pieces of string. Paul had no idea who they were, but all hell broke loose among the photographers, and he was almost knocked to the ground as they stormed past him, flashbulbs popping. He rubbed his elbow where it had been knocked out of joint by one of the stampeding crowd, and smiled an embarrassed greeting at the tall, supercilious doorman who now swung the glass door open for him and waved him inside.

Paul had been to this restaurant before: it was at the corner of Kingsway and the Aldwych, and he regularly met journalists here to talk off the record over steak and oyster pie or pressed guinea fowl terrine. Tonight, however, it had been transformed. The tables had been cleared away and the walls covered with posters emblazoned with the logo of the magazine and messages of welcome to "Britain's 50 Sharpest Men." The lights had been dimmed to the point where guests had to grope their way towards the bar through a crepuscular gloom. The speaker system had been cranked up to top volume, but for all the racket it was making, it could have been playing anything: all Paul could hear was a pounding bass drum and a lurching, robotic bass line that throbbed so fiercely it rattled his bones. He had been hoping, irrationally enough, that it would not be long before he saw someone he knew at this party. But as soon as he began to push his way through the clusters of shouting people, he realized not only that no one from his social or political circle was likely to be there, but he wouldn't even be able to spot them if they were. If he was not going to pass the evening in humiliating isolation, he would somehow have to break in to one of the small, exclusive, tightly knit groups that already seemed to have formed all around him. But how was he supposed to do that? Who were all these people, anyway? Most of them looked at least ten years younger than him. The men were more at ease than Paul, and more handsome, and the women had blonde hair and tight black dresses and all looked bored and beautiful. Presumably most of the people here worked for the magazine, in some capacity or another. Was one of them the editor? The editor had written to Paul personally, congratulating him on making the list. It was a prestigious, glossy men's magazine, with an affluent young readership, and Paul would have liked to thank the editor for the letter, and used it as a lever to get into conversation with him. But he had no idea what he looked like.

Paul had a contingency plan, which he had been hoping he would not have to fall back on: he could always talk to Doug Anderton. Doug was also on the list—a good deal higher than Paul, at number twenty-three, gallingly. But at the moment, Paul couldn't see him anywhere. Perhaps he hadn't bothered to come.

He went to the bar and armed himself with a glass of champagne. The champagne was free, tonight, and someone had had the bright idea that it should be served in tumblers, and drunk through straws. It tasted horrible that way. Paul tossed his straw on to the floor and began to look around him with something approaching desperation.

Finally he homed in upon a middle-aged man with wavy grey hair and horn-rimmed spectacles, standing in a corner with a woman who was almost certainly his wife. She had a tight perm and was wearing a suit that looked as though it came from Marks and Spencers, and they both gave the impression of being lost and more than slightly horrified by the situation in which they found themselves. Surely, Paul thought, this couldn't be one of the fifty sharpest men in Britain? He looked like a rural sub-postmaster on a day out with his wife in the big city, after they had both drifted away from the rest of their tour group and wandered by mistake into this party when they should really have been watching *Cats*.

Paul decided to give them a try anyway.

"Paul Trotter," he said, approaching the grey-haired man and holding out his hand. "Number forty-nine."

"Ah! Very pleased to meet you." The man shook his hand warmly. "Professor John Copland. Edinburgh university. Number seventeen."

Seventeen? Paul was astonished.

"Thank goodness you came to talk to us," said Professor Copland's wife. "We feel like fish out of water here."

It turned out that Professor Copland was one of the country's leading geneticists, and the author of several best-selling books on the subject. Paul, unfortunately, had never heard of him, and knew next to nothing about genetics, so the conversation—which they managed to stretch out for nearly half an hour, with some considerable effort on all three sides—was confined to generalities. The professor and his wife were interested to hear Paul's views on the impending invasion of Iraq; they seemed to be in some confusion, even after reading many of his newspaper articles, as to whether he was in the pro- or anti-war camp. He wasn't able to enlighten them much. This was, in truth, the first issue over which his loyalty to the party leadership had started to fracture, but he found it impossible to say so, either in public or in private. On the one hand, he felt an absolute debt of allegiance to the party which had swept him to office in 1997; on the other, his most basic political (and moral) instincts told him that this adventure was ill-advised and dangerous, that the justifications being offered for it were disingenuous, that it skirted the limits of international law and was more likely to provoke terrorism than to prevent it. He could not understand why the Prime Minister, whose judgment he trusted wholeheartedly on every other issue, was so fiercely wedded to this course of action. It puzzled him; and that was perhaps the most unsettling thing of all, as far as Paul was concerned. He did not like being puzzled. He liked to deal in certainties.

"Well, lovely talking to you," said Professor Copland's wife, after a longer than usual silence between them had signalled that all the possible conversational avenues had now been explored. Her husband's eyes had started to glaze over. "We'd better be getting along. This isn't really our scene."

"Nice to meet you," said Paul, waving goodbye, and when they had gone and he was once again reduced to solitary eavesdropping on the fringes of the unwelcoming young groups, he felt genuinely bereft.

He was rescued a few seconds later by an unexpected greeting.

"Paul Trotter, isn't it?"

Paul turned to see a man he didn't recognize; or at least, recognized only vaguely. He met hundreds of people in the course of his working week, and this could have been any one of them. He seemed to be in his early thirties and had a goatee beard and a shaved head, perhaps to hide incipient baldness.

"Hello," Paul said, uncertainly. "I'm sorry, but I'm not sure I . . ."

The man introduced himself, reminding Paul that they had met almost three years previously, when he had been one of the producers on a television comedy quiz show. It had been Paul's first television appearance, and not an outstanding success; but in any case, they had both moved on since those days. For his own part, he now ran an independent production company and currently had two hit sitcoms to his credit—one on Channel 4, one on BBC 2—with another half dozen in development. On the basis of these achievements, the magazine had decided that he was the fourteenth sharpest man in Britain.

"I'm number forty-nine," said Paul, glumly. It was beginning to feel like a less impressive statistic by the moment. It would have helped if he could meet number fifty, but he couldn't remember who it was.

"All by yourself tonight?" the producer asked him.

"Yes," said Paul. "Susan would have loved to be here—that's my wife—but . . . you know. Kids."

The producer nodded. He didn't know, having no kids of his own. Besides, Paul was lying: he had not mentioned to Susan that he was attending this party. Instead, he had invited the waspish young journalist from the *Independent* to come with him, but she hadn't answered any of his emails.

"Bit loud, isn't it?" the producer said. "God knows who all these people are."

"Dreadful," Paul agreed. "I think I'm going to slope off in a minute. Grab something to eat." Clutching at a straw—because he couldn't face the prospect, now that it lay before him, of going to a restaurant alone, or returning to his flat and ordering a takeaway—he asked awkwardly: "I don't suppose you'd care to join me? We seem to be the only two single blokes at this party. No harm in sticking together."

"Thanks all the same," said the producer, "but I'm with someone, actually."

And just then, his companion returned from the ladies' toilet, and appeared at his side.

Paul would not have thought it possible that Malvina should be even more slender than he remembered her. And even paler. She had added red streaks to her black hair, and there were dark moons of mascara under her eyes, which gave her a look of sleeplessness. She was wearing a black chiffon dress which allowed glimpses of the milky thinness underneath. In her eyes, in the split second when she first glimpsed him, he saw a wild flare of panic; but it was subdued immediately. Instead, she cleared her throat and adopted a formal pose, clutching her handbag to her waist with both hands.

"Hello," she said, with not the smallest emotion in her voice; and then turned to the producer, who was regarding them both with some curiosity. "Paul and I worked together for a while. Remember?"

"Oh yes," he said. "Of course."

"I'd like some more champagne, please," Malvina now said, bluntly.

The producer nodded, and after asking Paul if he would like some too, went to the bar to get three glasses. It looked as though he was used to obeying such orders.

"So," said Malvina, when they were left alone in the centre of the ever-noisier, ever-drunker crowd. "How have you been?" Her voice was still drained of any feeling.

"Fine," said Paul. "Things have been fine." Then he asked: "Did you know I was going to be here tonight?"

Malvina shook her head. "You're on the list, are you?"

Paul nodded.

"Well done."

"Thank you."

There was a longish pause. "You've got another daughter now, I see."

"Yes, that's right. She'll be two in April. Time just seems to whizz by."

"Is Susan here?"

"No. No, she's not." Paul looked at her closely, trying to read the expression in her eyes. It was impossible. "I've thought about you a lot," he said.

She looked at him directly for the first time. "Have you?"

He nodded.

"You never got in touch," she said, quietly accusing.

"You told me not to. I took you at your word. You told me," he reminded her, "that we couldn't be friends again until we were . . . over each other." Malvina looked away. "Has that happened, do you think?"

She shook her head. "No. I don't think it has."

Paul thought about this for a moment: it wasn't what he had been expecting to hear, and it seemed to leave them with little else to say to each other.

"Anyway," he muttered, "this event's been a bit of a let-down, to be honest. I was just on my way out."

And now Malvina said something even more unexpected. "I'll come with you."

The noise of the party seemed to die away, leaving Paul and Malvina alone together: as if suddenly transported back to the same isolation, the same absolute stillness, as the day they had last seen each other, standing at the centre of the ancient circle formed by the Rollright Stones.

"What about . . . ?" Paul looked across at the producer. He was hemmed in at the bar, deep in flirty conversation now with two of the young women who may or may not have worked for the magazine.

"He'll be OK," said Malvina and, taking Paul's arm, propelled him in the direction of the cloakroom.

As he helped her on with her winter coat he allowed himself briefly to caress her fleshless shoulders, and when he touched her, even fleetingly, he could feel her leaning in towards him, as if impelled. He knew at once that the long silence between them had been an aberration, a foolish mistake. And he knew it was an absolute certainty that they would sleep together that night.

The only person who saw Paul and Malvina leaving the party together was Doug Anderton. He was standing by himself, leaning against a wall, composing in his head the first few sentences of an article for Sunday's paper.

He had not been looking out for Paul, although he knew he was probably in the room. His gaze was fixed, instead, on a scene unfolding in the corner of the restaurant nearest to the entrance, where the young couple who had arrived just behind Paul in a white stretch limo were enjoying the attentions of a crowd of journalists and photographers. This couple, whom Paul had not recognized, had last year been two of the contestants on

Britain's most popular primetime reality TV show. For weeks they had kept the public guessing as to whether or not they were going to have sex with each other on camera. The tabloid papers had devoted hundreds of column inches to the subject. Neither of them had talent, or wisdom, or education, or even much personality to speak of. But they were young and good-looking, and they dressed well, and they had been on television, and that was enough. And so the photographers kept taking pictures, and the journalists kept trying to make them say something quotable or amusing (which was difficult, because they had no wit, either). Meanwhile, Doug could not help noticing, right next to them, waiting for his wife to emerge from the ladies', the figure of Professor John Copland: Britain's leading geneticist, one of its better-selling science writers, and regularly mentioned as a potential Nobel prizewinner. But no one was taking his photograph, or asking him to say anything. He could have been a cab driver, waiting to drive one of the guests home, as far as anybody else was concerned. And for Doug, this situation encapsulated so perfectly everything he wanted to say about Britain in 2002—the obscene *weightlessness* of its cultural life, the grotesque triumph of sheen over substance, all the clichés which were only clichés, as it happened, because they were true—that he was, perversely, pleased to be witnessing it.

Doug watched the distinguished professor standing patiently with two coats over his arm, and watched the celebrity couple, basking in their tenuous fame, and he was as hypnotized, in his own way, as the tabloid journalists who were desperately trying to coax an interesting remark out of them. As he tried to commit every detail of the scene to memory, it was only out of the corner of his eye that he noticed Paul Trotter leaving the restaurant with his arm around Malvina, their heads together in a halo of self-absorbed intimacy. Though that, when he thought about it, was interesting too.

9

Munir was, by nature, a man who worried about things. The list of things he would worry about at any given time was endless: the well-being of his brothers and sisters, for instance, or the inadequacy of his pension plan, or the threatened cutbacks at work, or the damp patch above his bathroom window, or the creaking of his joints whenever he stood up after prayer, or the overdue library book he couldn't find any more, or global warming. But at this particular time—in the third week of December, 2002—there were two things that gave him extra cause for concern: the looming certainty of war, and the state of Benjamin's mental health.

"This country is going mad," he said to Benjamin one evening, during the commercial break in the middle of the ITN news. "And so are you, if you ask me. Why did you sell all of that equipment? It was your pride and joy."

"Because I need the money," said Benjamin.

He went into the kitchen to put the kettle on. Munir followed him.

"But you'll never finish the book now."

"I'll finish the *book*," Benjamin corrected him. "I'm just getting rid of the music. It was all getting far too complicated anyway."

"But I thought that was the whole point!"

Benjamin paused in the act of turning the kettle on, looking ahead of him while he searched for the *mots justes*. "I've decided to go for radical simplicity," he said.

They returned to the living room. The coffee table in front of the sofa was strewn with travel guidebooks, covering every part of the globe from

Thailand to Alaska. Benjamin was planning a trip. The trouble was, he couldn't decide where he should go first, and there was too much choice.

"Do you realize," he said, "that just by selling that reverb unit I've got enough money to pay for a ticket on the Trans-Siberian railway? First class!"

Munir snorted. "What are you going to do on the Trans-Siberian railway?"

"Look out of the window."

"At what?"

"I don't know . . . Trans-Siberia, I suppose. Or there's Bali. South America. The Cape Verde Islands. The world's my oyster."

Munir wasn't convinced. "Well, I only ever ate an oyster once, and it made me sick. Forgive me for saying so, Benjamin, but you are trying to run away from yourself. And it won't work."

"I'm not trying to run away from myself. I'm trying to run away from . . . this!" He gestured around him at the flat, its sparse furnishings, ancient wallpaper and grubby paintwork. "I'm running away from Birmingham. From boredom. From failure. What's wrong with that? It's about time, isn't it?"

Munir sat down and turned up the volume on the television again. "Start small, Benjamin, that's all I would say. Don't bite off more than you can chew this time."

They watched the special report on Iraq's Weapons of Mass Destruction and then muted the volume when the sports news came on. Neither of them had the slightest interest in football.

"Ha!" said Munir contemptuously, "So now the Americans have got a 12,000-page document to go through and *still* they admit that they can't find any proof that these ridiculous weapons exist. Is there anyone in the world who can't see that this is just an imperial adventure, that they are determined to establish a power base in the Middle East and these weapons are just a trumped-up excuse for doing it?"

Benjamin agreed, but said: "What can we do, though? Once these people are voted in, they can do anything they like. We're stuck with them."

This seemed to infuriate Munir more than anything. "I hear that on every side, nowadays! Defeatism. Apathy. It's not good enough, I'm telling you. What about mobilizing ourselves, demonstrating, writing letters to parliament, signing petitions?"

"What about it?"

"Well, it worked for Longbridge, didn't it? You were in Cannon Hill Park that day. So was I. Didn't it inspire us? Didn't it change the course of events?"

Benjamin shrugged. "Who knows whether the government took any notice, really? Maybe things would have turned out that way even without the rally."

He picked up the remote control again and flicked channels. For a few minutes he and Munir watched an American comedy show. It was about four rich single women who lived in Manhattan, and met regularly over lunch to discuss the most intimate details of their sex lives. Benjamin liked this programme. He had never met women like this in his life, and suspected they were little more than some screenwriter's fantasy, but he craved the lifestyle they enjoyed and was grateful for these voyeuristic glimpses into their louche, privileged milieu. Besides which, he fancied two of the stars.

Within a few seconds, however, Munir was tutting over the bad language and the brazenly provocative frankness of the dialogue. Soon he had to stand up and pace the room, unable to listen any more.

"Turn it off," he said. "This programme is a disgrace."

"Oh, come on," said Benjamin. "It's only a bit of escapist fun."

"No, I find this unbelievable," Munir insisted. "These women are sitting down in a public place, talking to each other about ways of giving oral pleasure to their men, as if they were discussing knitting patterns or recipe books. One of them—that one there—has openly admitted to having sex with five different partners in one week! What respect, what *respect* are these women meant to feel for themselves, for their own bodies? What is happening to society, when this kind of thing is allowed on our screens? What goes through the minds of the people who make it? Look at this, Benjamin!" He walked right up to the screen and pointed at it, as one of the characters gave a practical demonstration of her technique, using the neck of a wine bottle. "*This* is America today. A land of degenerates! Is it any wonder that the rest of the world has started to despise them? What kind of . . . *probity* can we expect from a nation that conducts itself in such a way? This is a country that professes one thing and then does the opposite—but in full view of everybody! It preaches religion and morality but then its women behave like whores. It forces other countries to disarm but then it spends all of its money building up the most terrifying arsenal of nuclear and conventional weapons on the planet. It spits in the face of the Muslim world and stampedes through the Middle East in its thirst for the oil to fill its petrol-guzzling cars and then it professes astonishment that a man like Osama bin Laden can exist and believe what he believes. And this—*this* is where our Prime Minister tells us our allegiance lies. With a nation of cowboys and call-girls!" He sat down on the sofa, exhausted by his own rhetoric, and ran a distracted hand through his hair before concluding: "I'm not a man who likes swearing, Benjamin—you know that—but this country is screwed. This whole world is bloody well screwed, as far as I can see."

Benjamin struggled for something to say. For some reason the phrase, "It's a point of view" hovered on his lips. But in the end he just muttered—to himself more than Munir—"I've got to get away from here, you know. I've got to get away soon."

He decided to take his friend's advice, and make his escape in small, manageable steps. A good way to begin, he thought, would be to spend a few days down in London. He didn't want to stay with Doug and Frankie this time, however. He wanted to get away from all of that, from everything associated with his past life. He wanted to be alone.

Susan's brother Mark had a flat in the Barbican Centre, which stood empty during his frequent absences from Britain. His work for Reuters meant that he spent most of the year abroad: currently he was in Bali, reporting on the authorities' attempts to track down the terrorists responsible for the recent night-club bombing. Susan and her daughters sometimes used the flat when they went down to London, and she had often suggested to Benjamin that he should take advantage of it too. Now, he thought, might be a good time to take her up on the offer. He could stay there over Christmas, for a start. Anything would be better than Christmas alone with his parents.

He went to visit Susan the following afternoon. He thought it would be better to ask her in person, and besides, he liked spending time with his little nieces. He arrived late in the afternoon, and found that both girls were preparing to help their mother decorate the Christmas tree. It was so heavy that Susan could barely lift it, and the foot of the tree needed to be sawn off before it would fit into its stand. Even Benjamin, the world's worst handyman, believed he could help with that one. He laid the tree out on the floor of the high, vaulted sitting room and set to work with a saw while the two girls looked on. He felt himself swell with pride beneath their admiring gaze.

"There was . . . something . . . I wanted to ask you," he said to Susan, surprised to find himself gasping for breath after only about thirty seconds' work. "I was . . . wondering if . . . Mark's flat was free . . . at the moment."

"As far as I know," she answered. "Why, did you want to use it?"

"I think I need . . . a break," Benjamin panted. "Thought I might go down to London . . . for Christmas."

He felt something cool and moist on his forehead. Antonia, thoughtfully, had run off to the kitchen and returned with a wet wipe, which she was using to dab the beads of sweat away from his crimson face.

"That ought to be fine. I mean, you never really know from one day to the next where he's going to be. He told me that if the war starts they'll call him back and he'll be going off with British troops to Iraq. But anyway, the flat's empty now. The only thing is, I don't have a key. Paul's got it."

"Paul?"

"Yes—Mark gave him the key, in case there was an emergency, or something. I don't think he ever goes there. Do you want me to call him about it?"

"That would be great . . . when you've . . . got a minute."

"I'll do it right now."

Susan made for the kitchen, and after a few more strokes with the saw, Benjamin decided to down tools and join her. He was ready for a break, even though he had only sawn through about half of the trunk. The girls stayed behind, laying their Christmas decorations carefully out on the carpet in readiness for the great moment when they could start hanging them on the tree.

"He's not answering," said Susan, putting the receiver down with a sigh. "God knows why I thought that he would, actually. I can only ever get through to him about one time in ten."

(Paul heard the mobile ring, in fact, but didn't answer it. As it happened, he was in Mark's flat at the time, his fingers working neatly to unbutton Malvina's blouse.)

Susan looked at Benjamin and her face was suddenly twisted with pain. "I've become a single mother, Ben. How did that happen?"

"It's not that bad, is it? Is that how it really feels?"

(Paul lay back on Mark's bed and Malvina kneeled over him. She undid the last of the buttons herself and slid the blouse from her shoulders.)

"It's worse than that, in a way. If I was a single mother at least I could be looking for somebody else—terrifying though that would be. But I'm stuck in this no man's land at the moment."

"Perhaps you should leave him," Benjamin ventured; conscious, as he said it, that it was not his place to be making this suggestion.

"I don't *want* to leave him," said Susan. "I don't want to be out there again. I don't want the girls to lose their father when they're still so young. And I did choose to marry your brother, after all. Because I loved him—for some stupid, unfathomable reason. In fact I still do."

She sniffed and blew her nose, turning away so that Benjamin would not see the tears in her eyes, as Paul, one hundred miles away, reached up to touch Malvina's shallow, naked breasts, and caressed her nipples until they were hard and standing.

"He's not seeing anyone else again, is he?" Benjamin asked.

"How would I know? I don't think so. He's been quite attentive, the last few weeks, by his standards. I sort of . . . dread it happening, and yet another part of me wants it. It would force the issue, I suppose. It would set me free, in a way." She blew her nose again. "But I don't know if I *want* to be set free. What would come after that?"

Antonia appeared in the kitchen doorway.

"Come on, you two," she said. "We're all ready to start decorating now."

She took Benjamin's hand entreatingly and led him back to the Christmas tree, while Malvina pulled off Paul's shirt and started to unbuckle the belt on his trousers.

Benjamin found the rest of the trunk easier to saw through, and within a few minutes the tree was raised into place. Next came the difficult process of threading the string of fairy lights around the branches. Ruth had already trodden on one of them by mistake, and cracked the bulb.

Malvina helped Paul to wriggle out of his trousers and tossed them aside, then pulled down his boxer shorts in a greedy movement. Now naked except for her panties, she lowered herself towards him and let the rough lace come into contact with his straining, impatient penis, rotating her hips, resting herself against him heavily.

"What do you think should go on first, love?" Susan said to Antonia, ruffling her hair. "Father Christmas?"

"No, let's do the baubles first." She took a silver one and a golden one, and hung them from two of the branches, frowning with concentration, her tongue peeping out from between her lips. As she did so her father groaned with pleasure at the first touch of Malvina's mouth on his penis, her tongue running wetly along the shaft.

"What about you, Ruthie? Are you going to put something on?" Ruth looked doubtful, so Benjamin passed her a little angel, its glittering wings slightly askew, and she did her best to balance it on one of the branches. She jumped back in shock when her finger was pricked by the pine needles.

"Careful, love!" Susan said. "Those things are sharp, remember?"

Ruth looked seriously at her index finger and sucked it until the pain went away. She kept throwing her mother solemn glances, as if rebuking her for not having told her, already, that the world was such a dangerous place. Her mouth quivered and she was on the verge of tears but she blinked them back. Benjamin took her in his arms and squeezed her tightly, kissing the top of her head and breathing in the warm, almondy odour of her hair.

Paul parted the lips of Malvina's vagina and inserted his tongue. He savored the hot, salty tang as her juices leaked into his mouth. He took her engorged clitoris between his teeth and bit it gently, teasingly. Her back arched and she cried out with tormented pleasure.

The telephone rang.

Susan went to the kitchen to answer it. "Take it in turns now, you girls," she called back to them. "And watch out for those sharp needles!"

She was away for a few minutes. Benjamin and the girls managed to hang up several more baubles in the meantime, and then Antonia and Ruth lost interest and started wrapping each other in tinsel instead. Then they wrapped Benjamin in tinsel and laughed when they saw how funny he looked, and Malvina lay spreadeagled on the bed like a starfish as Paul lay between her legs and entered her, and Susan appeared in the kitchen doorway again and said, "Ben—can I have a word with you?"

"Sure," he said, and sashayed towards her, expecting her to laugh at the sight of his head wrapped in tinsel, with a plastic reindeer perched on top, the way Ruth had arranged it. But Susan was looking serious, almost apprehensive.

"Is everything all right?" he asked.

"Yes, everything's fine." She turned and led him back into the kitchen.

"Who was that?"

"That was Emily."

"Emily? What did she want?"

"Well, it's good news, actually. At least, I hope you'll think it's good news."

Benjamin waited, in expectant silence, until Susan told him:

"She's pregnant."

He had no idea what to say. The radio in Susan's kitchen, he noticed, was playing the third of Poulenc's Christmas motets. Slowly, he removed the reindeer from the top of his head, and began to unwind the tinsel.

8

Benjamin vanished shortly before Christmas. He gave no explanation to his friend and neighbour, leading Munir to wonder whether he had caused offence that night, by launching into his diatribe against Western values. But he couldn't believe that this was the real reason for Benjamin's departure, since they had had so many similar conversations before. Something else must have done it. It remained a mystery.

It had happened very suddenly. The morning after visiting his sister-in-law, Benjamin borrowed a car from somewhere, and spent more than an hour filling the boot, the back seats and the passenger seat with cardboard boxes crammed full of papers. He drove away at nine o'clock in the morning and did not return until late at night. He came back on foot, having apparently returned the car to its owner. It was after midnight when he knocked on Munir's door and presented him with the keys to his flat.

"I'm catching an early flight in the morning," he said. "I don't know when I'll be back. Look after the place for me."

"Where are you going?" Munir asked.

Benjamin hesitated, before telling him: "My ticket's to Paris. But I'm not going to stay there long. After that, I don't know."

And that was all he would say. When Munir came home from work that night, he went upstairs to Benjamin's flat and found that it was far from empty. Benjamin had left most of his clothes, most of his books, most of his CDs. His computer was still there, although all of his papers had gone. It looked as though he was intending to come back, but it was impossible to guess when.

But Benjamin had made no arrangement with their landlord to keep paying the rent. One Saturday morning early in January, 2003, Munir heard noises in the hallway and discovered that the landlord had appeared, with two of his sidekicks, and was in the process of changing the locks on Benjamin's flat and removing all his remaining possessions. Munir protested, but to no avail: the lease had expired at the end of December, letters had gone unanswered, and the flat was going to be made available for reletting immediately. Munir managed to salvage some of the books, most of the CDs, the computer, the television, and some of Benjamin's clothes. Everything else—including the furniture—was taken away.

But the flat was not relet. It was not even redecorated, as the landlord had promised. It remained empty, and became the site of strange meetings, mysterious comings and goings. It was the start of an uneasy, fearful time for Munir. Where had Benjamin gone? If he had taken his mobile phone with him, it never seemed to be switched on. His parents phoned for information and Munir was unable to provide any. Meanwhile, upstairs, there were footsteps late at night, voices in the small hours, cars and motorbikes pulling up outside the front gate after most decent folk had gone to bed. Once there was the sound of a fight and once, at three o'clock in the morning, Munir was convinced that he'd heard a woman screaming, waking him out of a deep sleep. He found himself lying awake, now, most nights, listening for these sounds, his heart thudding in the darkness. When he grew weary of lying there, alert and wakeful, his mind racing with speculations about what might have happened to his friend and what nefarious business his landlord might be conducting on the premises, he would turn on the radio and listen to the World Service. Whatever he heard just fuelled his anxiety. The news was getting worse and worse. The British government seemed to be expressing nothing but ever more slavish support for President Bush and his bellicose rhetoric. More and more troops were being sent to the Gulf in readiness for an invasion. Besides his weekly attendance at *salat al-jama'ah*, Munir would now often get up and pray in the middle of the night, in the spare bedroom where he had put down a mat expressly for this purpose. In his *du'a* he would ask Allah to have mercy upon the world and not to plunge it into a terrible war. He would say these prayers aloud, feeling more alone and friendless than ever as the words tumbled from his mouth and slipped away unheard into the darkness of the Birmingham night.

Munir knew that he was not the only person who opposed this war. Knew, in fact, that the majority of British people were on his side. He took some comfort in the great rallies that were held, in every major city, on

February 15th. He stood side by side with his fellow citizens and listened to rousing speeches and clapped and cheered, and when he got home late that afternoon he watched the news on Benjamin's television and saw that an even greater crowd, a vast crowd, had gathered in Hyde Park in London. But in his heart he knew that the Prime Minister would not listen to any of these protests. An unstoppable process had begun. History—whose end had been announced, prematurely, by some writers more than a decade earlier with the defeat of Communism—was gathering terrible momentum, swelling into a pitiless, fast-flowing river which would soon burst its banks, and millions of people, Munir feared, were going to be swept along in its current towards an unknown fate over which they had no control.

Strangers continued to arrive at the house after dark; footsteps continued to be heard, thumping dully up and down the staircase. Munir thought about phoning the police, but knew that he had nothing definite to tell them, and believed that they would not take him seriously. Instead, he positioned a chair near to the window of his ground-floor flat, and spent many evenings sitting there, with an eye half on the television, half on the street outside. It was a sorry state of affairs. He had become a curtain-twitcher, and it made him feel very old.

One night, a few days after the February peace marches, a great fog descended on the city. Munir, sitting at his window and periodically peeping out through a crack between the curtains, could not even see as far as the garden gate, a mere five or six yards from the front door. He could, however, hear footsteps in the street outside. Somebody had been loitering there for five minutes or more. Whoever it was had a peculiar gait, halting and irregular. It was even possible that he had heard more than one pair of footsteps, although there had been no voices this time. After a few more minutes he decided to investigate. He took his roll-up umbrella from the coat rack—it was quite heavy, and perhaps not completely useless as a weapon—and stepped out into the murky winter darkness.

Fog wrapped itself around the amber street lamps in drifting spirals. Munir lived on a quiet street: there was no traffic noise tonight, and as soon as he opened and closed his front door, he could hear the person who had been lingering outside turn and walk away. He hurried down to the garden gate and listened more closely. The receding footsteps did not sound fast; they sounded effortful, and—again—somehow irregular. After a few seconds they faded to nothingness, and the invisible stranger had gone.

Munir was not satisfied. He decided to wait by the garden gate for a while. He stepped out on to the street and sat down on the low wall that bordered his scrap of front garden. The brickwork was freezing: a sharp pang of cold transmitted itself instantly through the thin serge of his trousers and spread across his buttocks. This is how you get piles, he reminded himself; but after a while the pain subsided, and he remained sitting there, shivering somewhat but none the less enjoying the raw freshness of the misty outdoors. He tended to overheat his sitting room, and realized now that it had been too close and airless in there.

Before long he heard footsteps again.

He knew it was the same person. The steps were heavy, slow and careful: the sort of steps you would associate with an old man. Whoever it was had been scared off, apparently, by Munir's arrival, but had now changed his mind and was coming back towards the house. Munir stiffened and rose to his feet and peered out into the gloom, tightening his grip on the umbrella. After a few seconds, he caught a glimpse of a human figure, still half-obscured by the shifting fog, little more at first than a blur of denser blackness, its outline fuzzy and ill-defined. Then, as the shape came closer, he realized that it was not a man at all.

It was a woman, walking slowly but with fixed, inexorable purpose, leaning heavily on a walking stick and looking ahead of her with eyes that gazed forward with bulbous intensity—like the eyes of some startled, nocturnal creature—but appeared to see nothing. She was wearing a dark brown overcoat in fake fur which came just below the knee, revealing strong calves and ankles sheathed in woollen flesh-coloured tights. Her head was wrapped in a scarf, knotted beneath her chin. Her face was pale, thick with powder, and her swollen lips glistened with ample coatings of dark red lipstick. The face was bloated and sickly, and the woman's figure was stout, but there was about her, at the same time, something formidable and imperious. The heaviness of her body suggested strength of character; so too did the unrelenting evenness with which she stared ahead of her. As Munir rose slowly to his feet, and watched this massy apparition emerge from the coils of fog, he felt apprehensive, intimidated.

The woman stopped a few feet away from him and placed her whole weight on the stick, breathing heavily. Her fishy, protuberant eyes rested on Munir and she gathered the breath to speak.

"Do you live here?" she said.

"Yes," Munir answered.

"Does Benjamin live here?"

Because the answer to that question was complicated, and because he thought that she might want to rest, and because he was curious to find out more about her, Munir said: "You seem a little tired. Would you like to come inside for a moment?"

The woman shook her head. She repeated her question, and Munir explained that Benjamin had lived at this address until recently, but that he had disappeared two months ago, and nobody knew where he had gone. He apologized for not being able to tell her more.

Something inside the woman seemed to shrivel at this information. Her body curled in upon itself. She seemed to dwindle in stature before Munir's eyes.

"Thank you," she said.

"I'm trying to make contact with him all the time," he added. "If I manage to speak to him, would you like me to pass on a message?"

"Just tell him," said the woman, turning to leave, "that Cicely was asking after him."

Munir did not recognize the name. It meant nothing to him. In bewildered silence he watched the cumbersome body recede, laboriously, until the blankets of fog swirled around it and carried it away from view, like curtains closing upon the final act of a long-enduring drama.

7

Soon enough, for Paul and Malvina, Mark's flat became more than the place where they had sex. They began to think of it as home; their shared home. Which is not to say that they started going out and choosing new wallpaper or buying toasters and coffee-makers. But it was where they met, every day, for hours at a time, not just to make love but to talk, to eat together, to drink wine, to watch television. It was the place where they began to invent themselves as a couple.

It had never been Paul's intention to come here in the first place. That night in early December, they had left the "Sharpest Men in Britain" party and gone for a quick meal at Joe Allen's, a restaurant just a few streets away, much favored by actors and minor celebrities. Before they had even ordered, Paul's mobile beeped and a text message came through: it was from Doug Anderton.

> Old habits die hard, eh Paul? I thought you were sharper than that. Take care Doug

"Oh, shit," Paul said, after reading the message.

"What's wrong?" Malvina asked.

"Someone spotted us leaving together."

He closed his eyes and screwed them tight shut, willing himself to believe that this wasn't happening. Were they going to have to go through all this again? He looked at Malvina, who was gazing at him worriedly, trustingly, and he was helpless in the grip of the desire that coursed through him; his sense of all the time they had wasted, all the time they had to make up. And then his hand had closed on the keys in his pocket—the keys to Mark's flat in the Barbican—and at once he knew that this was the solution. It was miles from Kennington; the press knew nothing about it, and would never find him there. It was convenient, and it was safe, and it was empty.

They had taken a taxi there just an hour later, and stayed the whole night.

The pattern they quickly evolved for themselves—Monday, Tuesday and Wednesday nights spent at the flat, and some lunchtimes when Paul's timetable allowed it—was disrupted too soon by Christmas and the New Year. Malvina stayed at the Barbican for most of that time, but Paul was obliged, for decency's sake, to spend at least two or three days in the Midlands with his wife and daughters. He even had to endure an evening in Rubery with his sister and parents, which turned into a crisis meeting about the disappearance of Benjamin. Paul, personally, couldn't see what the fuss was about. His brother was a grown man of forty-two. He could look after himself. He didn't buy the notion that he was having some kind of nervous breakdown, brought on by the fact that his wife (from whom he had been separated for more than a year) was pregnant by her new boyfriend. Lois seemed to consider it significant that he had driven up to York, shortly before leaving the country, and left all his papers with her daughter Sophie—whose bedroom was far too small to accommodate them all. But again, Paul couldn't see what was meant to be so ominous about that. It had always been obvious to him that Benjamin was wasting his time writing this never-ending novel. Now, at last, he had woken up to the fact. Wasn't that a cause for celebration? Nobody else seemed to think so. The rest of the family told him he was being heartless; but he wasn't, really. He was just feeling impatient because he missed Malvina's naked body so much.

January was an idyllic month. There was little parliamentary business to distract him, and they were able to spend long days and nights together. At the same time, Paul was helping to draft the final pages of the report from his Commission for Social and Business Initiatives, which would, he was convinced, be well received by the leadership and generate considerable attention in the press. The report was prefaced by a quotation from Gordon Brown, taken from the *Financial Times* of March 28th, 2002: "The Labour Party is more pro-business, pro-wealth creation, pro-competition than ever before." It strongly recommended that the role of private firms in the public sector be extended still further, with special emphasis on health and education. It advised that GPs' surgeries, for instance, should be encouraged to contract out their payrolls and support services to the private sector. Likewise, the governing bodies of state schools should start hiring privately run management teams. "The vital ingredient that the public sector continues to lack, and the private sector is well equipped to provide [Ronald Culpepper had written] can be summed up in one word: management." The objection that such initiatives had notably failed in the recent past—in the case of the privatized railways, for instance—was firmly rejected as "defeatist."

The completion of the report was celebrated at a special meeting of The Closed Circle in the first week of February, 2003. The only absentee, on this occasion, had been Michael Usborne, who was caught up in crisis talks with the board of Meniscus Plastics. Since his appointment as CEO, despite his radical programme of rationalization and forced redundancies, which had already involved closing down an entire R&D department at the Solihull plant, the company's share price had started to fall and operating costs appeared to be soaring. It seemed likely that he would have to resign again, and he was in the process of renegotiating the finer points of his compensation package. Paul had phoned him about it earlier that afternoon and it sounded as though he was in good spirits. And so was Paul himself, when he left Rules Restaurant shortly after eleven o'clock. He texted Malvina from his taxi and asked if she could be at the Barbican flat by midnight.

But when he arrived there himself, at about 11:30, he got a nasty surprise. He turned the key in the lock only to find that the lights were already on, and his brother-in-law Mark was sitting on the sofa watching CNN.

"Paul?" he said, rising to his feet. "What are you doing here?"

Paul mumbled some excuse about being on his way home from a dinner in the City, and deciding to check up on the flat because it was such a long time since he'd been there. Then he asked if he could use the toilet and once inside the bathroom he looked around for traces of Malvina and frantically tried to remember if she had left anything of hers in the bedroom. He knew there were some condoms in the drawer of the bedside table. He would have to try and remove those as soon as possible. In the meantime he sent her a quick text telling her that she should turn around and go home immediately.

"So, what brings you home?" he asked Mark, returning to the sitting room. "A few days' holiday?"

"No—Reuters have decided that they don't need two people out in Indonesia any more. One of the Bali bombers has confessed now but apart from that there's nothing much else going on. They're pulling a lot of us back in case we all need to be sent out to the Middle East."

"I see," said Paul. "So you're going to be here for a while?"

"All depends on President Bush, really. And your own much-esteemed party leader, of course."

"Then, how long . . ." (Paul tried to make the question sound casual) ". . . how long do you think it'll be?"

Mark looked at him curiously, and laughed. "I rather thought *you* might be able to tell me that, Paul. Aren't you supposed to be voting on it soon?"

In the next few weeks, it seemed that everybody wanted to know which way Paul was going to vote on the war. The Commons debate was due to be held on February 26th. A bland motion had been tabled, reaffirming endorsement of UN Security Council Resolution 1441, and expressing support for "the government's continuing efforts in the UN to disarm Iraq of its weapons of mass destruction"; but of much more interest was the moderate cross-party amendment, tabled by Labour's Chris Smith and the Conservatives' Douglas Hogg, which insisted that the House "finds the case for military action against Iraq as yet unproven." There was no prospect of the government being defeated; but people were talking about a substantial backbench rebellion, which would significantly weaken Tony Blair's authority and might even cause him to rethink his apparently uncritical support for President Bush. Of course, it was well known who the diehard anti-war campaigners were; but there were also dozens of Labour backbenchers who had yet to express a definite opinion either for or against an American-led invasion of Iraq, and Paul was one of the most high-profile of these. Journalists would waylay him whenever he got near the Palace of Westminster, anxious to know if he had made up his mind yet; the government whips would buttonhole him in the Palace corridors, dropping none-too-subtle hints that a vote for the amendment would be bad for his parliamentary career; while, back in the Midlands, the members of his constituency party—who were solidly anti-war—pressed him to vote in their interests and muttered about possible deselection if he failed to do so.

As far as Paul was concerned, however, the single most persuasive voice in the anti-war camp came from much closer to home. It was Malvina's.

Losing their access to Mark's flat had been a serious blow. Malvina no longer had a place of her own in London; her mother's relationship with her boyfriend in Sardinia had—like all her mother's relationships—ended badly, and Malvina had been told to leave the Pimlico apartment as a result. For her own part, she didn't seem especially upset about it. Now that she was seeing Paul again, nothing seemed capable of puncturing her happiness. Two of her poems had recently been accepted by a little-read but prestigious literary magazine, and this had simply added to her euphoria. On the downside, her mother was back in London too, but Malvina seemed to be taking a robust approach to that situation.

"Perhaps you could move in with her for a while," Paul had suggested.

"You've got to be kidding. I don't even know where she lives."

"What?" he said, incredulous. "Don't you ever see her?"

"Not if I can help it. If she wants to see me, she can call my mobile, and we can go for a coffee. That's as close as I want to get."

"Have you told her about us?"

"No way. Maybe when things are a bit less . . . complicated between us. But there's no hurry. It makes no difference to me what she thinks of me any more."

In the meantime, Malvina had moved into a house in Mile End, which she shared with three other ex-students. There was absolutely no prospect of Paul visiting her in that environment, and in the face of continued enigmatic emails and text messages from Doug Anderton, he remained paranoid about taking her back to the flat in Kennington. Instead, they found an out-of-the-way hotel near Regent's Park that was not too expensive, and not too depressing, and began meeting there. Malvina would make the bookings, and pay with her credit card, and Paul would reimburse her in cash. It was all right as a stopgap, but soon they would need to find a more permanent arrangement. Neither of them had any ideas. And after more than two weeks of this, Paul was beginning to despair.

The hotel was hardly stylish, and seemed to be about thirty years overdue for a refurbishment, but one advantage was that every ensuite room boasted an enormous bath, and it was in one of these that they lay together on the evening of February 25th, 2003. Malvina was at the end with the taps. They were drinking Prosecco, and while Malvina reclined with her feet propped up against Paul, one foot on each shoulder, he stroked her gently between the legs, his soapy fingers creating a soft lather amidst her pubic hair. It was not done in a sexual way, to bring her to orgasm; there was something friendly and easy-going about it, although judging from the way that Malvina stirred sometimes, and shifted her weight, and every so often let out a small sigh or moan, it did seem to be having a pleasurable effect.

"I can't understand," she was saying, "what's holding you back. You know what you *believe*. So there's only one way you can possibly vote tomorrow, isn't there?"

"It's a huge thing, to vote against your own party. It's not something you do lightly."

"But—'the case for military action is as yet unproven.' It's just a simple statement of fact, isn't it?"

Paul fell silent. "Did you notice the way the guy on the desk looked at us tonight?" he said, after a while. "I wonder what he thinks is going on."

"Pretty bloody obvious what's going on, I would have thought," said Malvina, with a satisfied chuckle.

Paul said, almost querulously: "You're very *relaxed* about all this."

"All what?"

"All this . . . deception. Booking into a hotel, signing in under a different name, all the paraphernalia of having an affair. It doesn't seem to faze you."

"Why should it?"

"I was just thinking . . . All that time ago, that day in Oxfordshire: you told me then that you'd never have an affair with me."

"Times change," said Malvina. She sat up and took a sip from her Prosecco. "So do people. And besides, the alternative's worse."

"What alternative?"

"Not seeing you."

Paul said, "That's not the only alternative." He paused now, choosing his words carefully. "I think I've made my decision, you know."

Malvina smiled, and leaned forward, and kissed him tenderly with her open mouth. "That sounds good. Is it one I'm going to like?"

"I think so. I think I'm going to leave Susan."

She drew back again, surprised. "What?"

"I'm leaving her. I want to be with you all the time. It's the only way. Aren't you pleased?"

Malvina struggled for words. "Well . . . yes, but . . . you don't have to do that, Paul. I'm happy with what we've got at the moment."

"Why? Why are you happy with it?"

"I don't know, I just am. It's working. I've never asked you to leave Susan, have I?" She laughed uncomfortably, and to fill the wounded silence her words seemed to have provoked in Paul, she said: "I thought you were talking about the war."

Paul continued to say nothing; just drank his Prosecco in resentful sips.

"When were you thinking of telling her?" Malvina asked.

He shook his head. "I don't know."

After that, she could only think of one way of improving his mood. It involved raising Paul's hips until they were out of the water, leaning forward, taking the tip of his at first flaccid penis into her mouth, and then one minute's vigorous exercise with her head and neck. It seemed to do the trick.

Hours later, Malvina awoke with a start to find that Paul was lying sleepless beside her, his eyes wide open, staring into the semi-dark of their hotel room.

"Hey," she said, stroking his hair. "What's up?"

"The debate starts in a few hours," Paul answered. "What am I going to *do*?"

"Follow your heart," said Malvina, and nestled against him as the noises of the waking city began to drift upwards to their window.

Paul sat through the whole debate next day. It lasted for six hours. The back benches and the members' side galleries were overflowing. The public gallery was packed.

Paul himself did not speak. He listened as Kenneth Clarke said:

If we ask ourselves today whether the case for war has now been established, I think this house ought to say not, and there is still a case for giving more time to other peaceful alternatives for enforcing our objectives . . . I have the feeling there is a little blue pencil around a date some time before it gets too hot in Iraq.

Paul agreed with this. Any reasonable person would agree with it, he thought. He listened as Chris Smith said:

There may well be a time for military action . . . but at the moment the timetable appears to be determined by the President of the United States.

He joined in with the cries of "Hear, hear!," then looked around, having forgotten himself, to see whether any of the whips had been watching him.

He listened as Tony Blair said:

I think the case we have set out in respect of Iraq is a good case. I hope that if people listen to it and study it in detail they will accept that if we do have to act and go to war, it will not be because we want to, but because of the breaches by Saddam Hussein of UN resolutions.

Paul was not convinced by this argument. He had never been convinced by it. And still he remained puzzled by the way this man, this apparently principled man, clung to his half-truths and would not be swayed—either by public opinion or by the words of his colleagues—from the path he had chosen, this narrow, unswerving path. It made no sense. *Why were we doing this?* Why were we trying to talk ourselves into seeing a threat from a small, impoverished country thousands of miles away, with no proven links to terrorism and a clapped-out arsenal that had been dismantled years ago under the scrutiny of UN inspectors?

Six hours was too long to sit in the same spot listening to speeches. Even as the debate grew more impassioned, Paul's attention started to wander. He thought about Malvina and he thought about the practicalities of leaving Susan and he thought about that dowdy hotel in Regent's Park, and the insolent glare of the young man behind the reception desk. And then another thought popped into his mind. It had been lurking there for days, actually, waiting in the shadows, but this evening it marched out boldly to the forefront and assumed center stage. It was an outrageous thought, but one which he could no longer suppress.

He thought: *If we go to war against Iraq, Mark will be sent there too and we can start using his flat again.*

And this was what he wanted more than anything else in the world.

One hundred and twenty-one Labour MPs defied the government that night, and voted in favor of the rebel amendment. But Paul was not one of them. At the end of the debate, he walked into the No lobby, and then made his escape from Westminster as fast as he could, dodging the journalists and his fellow MPs.

He had followed his heart, and in response it pounded unremittingly as he walked home through the empty streets.

Spring

6

It took Claire almost three months to find Victor Gibbs. It was not an easy thing to do. Thirty years ago, back in those unimaginable, pre-computer, pre-internet days, it might have been impossible.

Even now, she had been obliged to enlist somebody's help, against her better judgment. But there had been no alternative. Her first computer search had turned up thousands of people called Gibbs, and writing to those with the initial "V" had produced no results apart from letters returned or short, polite assurances that she had found the wrong person. But then eventually, after a few weeks of these disappointments, she remembered that Colin Trotter used to work as a personnel officer at Longbridge, and made a reluctant decision to take him into her confidence.

She had been nervous about speaking to Benjamin's father on the telephone, but found him far more sympathetic than she had been expecting. Now that Benjamin himself had disappeared, he told her, he felt that he understood a little of what Claire and her family must have gone through. She assured him that the two cases were very different: that Benjamin was a mature (or at least middle-aged) man, that he knew what he was doing, that he could look after himself, that he had left of his own accord, and so on. Had they not heard anything at all from him, in the last two months, she wanted to know. Colin said that they hadn't, and seemed to have nothing more to add on the subject. But he agreed that he would go back to his old office at Longbridge in the next few days, and look through the files to see if they had any record of Gibbs's employment there.

He was as good as his word. A few days later, he called Claire and told her that Gibbs was still listed on the old card index system, and that in 1972 he had given an address in Sheffield for his next of kin. Claire checked the address against her computer listings and found that a member of the Gibbs family still lived there. It turned out to be Victor's brother. She wrote to him, posing as a fund manager from Longbridge and spinning some story about the firm having decided to pay out extra pension money to former employees. Two weeks went by before she was rewarded with a reply telling her Victor Gibbs's current address: he lived on the North Sea coast in Cromer, in the county of Norfolk.

On the last day of February, 2003, she drove out to see him.

The weather was worse even than on the day she had visited the Warwick university library, and the journey took much longer. She set out from Malvern at nine o'clock in the morning and arrived more than five hours later. Already exhausted and frazzled, she parked the car in a pay and display car park and walked to the seafront. Rain, made skittish by the buffeting wind, slapped into her face and stung her eyes. The waves rolled grey and lacklustre on to the pebble shore, and a vaporous mist had closed in, dampening everything. Soon, Claire was chilled to the bone.

It was a Friday afternoon, and the town felt dead. A couple of amusement arcades were open, sending a neurotic medley of electronic noises out into the street—partly the jittering of the games machines themselves, partly the thunder of dance music from merciless speaker systems—but there were few punters inside, and the shops and cafés weren't doing much business. Claire pulled her fleecy raincoat tightly around herself, and found that she was by now shivering uncontrollably: not just with the cold, but with fear at the prospect of the encounter she was about to inflict upon herself. She had thought that perhaps, during the long drive, she might have been able to devise a strategy for this meeting, or at least think of something to say—an opening line if nothing else. But her mind remained blank. She was in a panic. She had no idea what this man was going to be like, how he would react to her unannounced appearance, so she would have to improvise. Her worst fear was that he would turn violent. But she had to be prepared even for that.

She had committed the address to memory, and after a few minutes' walk found herself standing outside a narrow, three-storeyed terraced house some streets away from the seafront. The doorbells suggested that it had been divided into three flats; Victor Gibbs supposedly lived in Flat B, although there was no namecard under that particular bell. She pressed the button and heard a distant ring and waited. Nothing happened.

Claire pushed the bell a few more times. She noticed a lace curtain move on the ground floor, and soon a shadow appeared behind the frosted glass of the front door. A woman opened the door and said:

"Are you looking for him upstairs?"

"Yes," said Claire. "My name's—"

The woman wasn't interested. "He'll be in the pub. The Wellington, probably. You can't miss it—round the corner and half way down the next street."

"How will I know him?" Claire asked.

"Black hair—he dyes it, I reckon—leather jacket, always sits in the same corner, next to the dartboard. Reads the *Express*. You'll see him all right."

Claire mumbled a few words of thanks. The woman nodded and the door was closed.

The pub—like the whole town, it seemed—was more than half empty. A juke box was playing some terrible song by Simply Red and there was no one behind the bar. Claire spotted Victor Gibbs almost immediately, and at once a current of apprehension ran through her, even though he looked perfectly ordinary—just as his neighbour had described him, right down to the newspaper. Finally she managed to get served. She asked for a glass of fizzy water, and took it over to the corner, where she sat at the table next to Gibbs. She drank in silence next to him for a few minutes, glancing across at him occasionally, not bothering to make the glances surreptitious, wanting to be noticed. She began to feel a little calmer. He was in his late fifties, she reckoned. Not terrible looking, not as bad as her sister had long ago implied by calling him "Vile Victor." He was reading the sports pages, and the next time he looked up, she smiled at him. He held her gaze for a moment, wary, slightly incredulous. He did not look like a man who was used to having women smile at him in pubs. He probably thought she was on the game, which was not the impression she wanted to give. Perhaps she should go to the bar and buy some cigarettes, so she could ask him for a light: but she hadn't smoked since the night of Benjamin's concert, back in December 1999. The taste of it would probably bring on a coughing fit.

Gibbs was looking at the racing results and writing notes against them in blue biro. This was what gave Claire the idea. She took her diary out from her handbag, opened it, and then pretended to fumble in the bag, as if she had forgotten something. After which, she sighed pointedly, and leaned across to Gibbs.

"Excuse me," she said, indicating his pen. "Is there any way I could borrow that for a minute?"

He gave her the same wary, disbelieving look, and handed her the pen without a word. She scribbled some nonsense in her diary, then sat back for a moment, affecting to think, while she put the pen in her mouth absently.

"Oh—I'm sorry," she said, as if coming to her senses, and offered to hand the pen back to him.

Gibbs smiled. "It's all right. You keep it. Plenty more where that came from."

Claire smiled back. "Thanks."

"You look tired," he said then, laying down his newspaper.

"I've just had a long drive."

"Oh?" He folded the newspaper carefully, smoothing the creases with firm movements of his hand. "Where've you come from?"

"Birmingham," Claire lied.

"Ah, good old Brum," he said. "I know it well. Lived there for years."

"Really?"

"Going back a bit now, mind you."

"Which part? I'm from Harborne."

"Oh, I wasn't far from there. Bournville. I used to work at the Longbridge factory."

"Small world," said Claire, sipping her water.

"What brings you to Cromer?"

She hadn't even thought of an answer to that: but an obvious one quickly presented itself.

"I'm here to see my sister."

"I see. Waiting for her now, are you?"

Claire shook her head. "She's a doctor. She was supposed to have the day off today but . . . some emergency came up." (Her invention had failed her, but he didn't seem to notice.) "Had to go into the surgery and won't be free till the evening now." She looked across at Gibbs and could see that already he was almost hooked. "So," she concluded, "what on earth can you do in Cromer when you've got a wet Friday afternoon to spare?"

Gibbs rose to his feet. "Well you can start," he said, "by having another drink."

. . .

Claire realized that she had never actually done this before—come on to someone, flirted with them—and was amazed by how easy it was. All she had to do was listen, for the most part. Gibbs was not talkative at first, but after another pint of bitter and a whisky or two he became positively chatty. Claire found herself almost touched by how eager he became: eager to impress her, to put on a good show. He talked a lot about the races and the system he had devised to beat the bookies and how it averaged out that he was clearing about twenty pounds a week. Gambling seemed to be his passion, these days. He also did the pools and bought more than fifty pounds' worth of Lottery tickets every Wednesday and Saturday, and once they'd had enough to drink he took Claire out to demonstrate his expertise in the arcades. They played the game where piles of 10p coins appeared to be teetering on the edge of a shelf that moved slowly backwards and forwards, giving the impression that if only you could drop another 10p coin in at exactly the right moment, a waterfall of loose change would cascade out of the machine and into your hands. Gibbs explained how it was all a fix and more than half of the coins were glued to the shelf, but you could sometimes make a profit if you won some coins at your first half dozen attempts and then moved straight on to another shelf or another machine. He showed Claire how it was done, and she stood beside the machine, watching him with admiring eyes as he played on, now and again leaning towards him to throw in some crassly complimentary remark. Once or twice he let her drop the coins in herself. The second time she tried it she won £1.80, and Gibbs laughed and clapped his hands delightedly and touched her on the shoulder.

When they left and walked to the nearest café she wondered whether to take his arm but decided that would be too forward.

They sat opposite each other at a formica-topped table and ordered two cappuccinos. "Frothy coffees," Gibbs called them. It was getting on for four o'clock and outside the light was starting to fade. Rain flung itself angrily against the café windows.

Claire had chosen this table herself. It was in a tight corner of the café, and Gibbs was sitting with his back against the wall. To get out, he would have to squeeze past her. If she pushed the table further towards him, he would be boxed in completely. He was trapped, in effect. Which meant that her moment of opportunity was now presenting itself, and the confrontation could not be put off for much longer.

She could tell that Gibbs, too, was getting anxious to move things forward. He looked at his watch and said, "After we've had these you should really come back to my flat. We could watch television or something. I've a pack of cards."

Claire nodded, non-commitally.

"What time d'you think you'll be going to see your sister?"

"Well, actually . . ." She looked him in the eye, and gave a shamefaced sort of smile. "The thing is, Victor—I wasn't telling the truth about that."

He stared back at her blankly. "Your sister doesn't live here?"

"I don't have a sister," said Claire, in a quiet voice. "My sister's dead."

"Oh." Clearly, he had no idea what to make of this. "I'm sorry to hear that, Claire."

"At least . . . I'm pretty sure she's dead. She disappeared a long time ago. Almost thirty years. I never heard from her again."

Gibbs was watching her carefully, perhaps beginning to think that she was deranged. "Well then," he said. "So . . . so what are you doing in Cromer? You told me it was your sister you came to visit."

"Do you mind if we talk about her for a minute?"

"No, no. Of course not. Whatever you want." He shifted in his chair—suddenly noticing, at some subconscious level, that he was hemmed in by the table. His whole manner was starting to change.

"Actually, Victor," she said, "I've got a feeling you may have known her."

"Known her?" He laughed. "What are you on about? You and I only met a couple of hours ago."

"I've got a letter here," said Claire; and she took a folded piece of paper from her handbag. It was a colour photocopy of the original, the best her local library could provide. "It's the last letter my sister ever wrote to her parents. Would you like to have a look at it?"

Gibbs took the letter from her and spread it open on the table. He looked down at it, elbows apart, resting his chin on his hands. He stayed that way for a long time. He didn't move, didn't look up. Claire waited for him to say something. She was conscious of a murmured conversation at the table behind her, and the periodic noisy spluttering of the cappuccino machine.

Finally Gibbs looked up, and slid the letter back to her. His expression gave nothing away, but his face had lost some of its blood, now, and there was the slightest of tremors in his hand.

"What do you make of that?" Claire asked, when there was even more silence between them.

Gibbs shrugged. "What's it to do with me? I don't bother much with other people's business."

"This is your business," said Claire. And added: "I think you wrote that letter."

After a second or two, Gibbs tried to get up. "I think you must be potty," he said. But his legs were trapped by the edge of the table. "Let me out, will you?"

"Sit down, Victor. We're going to talk about this."

"There's nothing to bloody talk about!" he said, raising his voice. "I've never met you or your bloody sister and I reckon you must be mental or something. I reckon you belong in a mental home."

"I've got another letter," Claire told him. "A letter you wrote to Bill Anderton."

For a moment that wrongfooted him, and he sat down again, just long enough for her to say: "You remember *that* name, don't you? And I can prove they're from the same person. They were written on the same typewriter."

Gibbs tried to get up one more time, pressing with more force than ever against the table's edge. "I've never heard of him," he hissed. "You've got the wrong bloke."

"Sit down, you lying bastard," Claire heard herself saying. And all at once, she was the one whose whole body was shaking, whose voice was out of control, who felt her grip on the situation beginning to slip away. She was terrified, now, by the look of levelled hatred on his face. "Please sit down. *Please.* I'm not going to go to the police or anything like that. I haven't come here to hunt you down."

"Then what the fucking hell have you come here for?"

He was pushing the table up against her until it hurt. She could feel the sharp edge of it digging into her belly.

"Stop that!" she shouted. "Stop!" Furious with herself, she realized that tears were welling up in her eyes. "I just want to *know,* Victor. I just want to know what happened to my sister. I was just a girl. She was twenty-one. I just want to *know.*"

He glared at her for the last time, the malevolence concentrated, unbending.

"Well you won't get it from *me,*" he said, and on the last word he gave the table such a powerful shove that Claire was thrown backwards, spinning off her seat, colliding at first with the woman sitting behind her and then ending up sprawled on the floor. Gibbs pushed his way out from the corner and stepped over her. As he did so a mug flew off the table and lukewarm coffee was thrown into Claire's face, down the front of her raincoat, on to her hands. Gibbs rushed onwards and was out of the café in an instant. The other customers looked on. Someone came over and pulled Claire to her feet. She was sobbing.

"Did he hurt you, the rotten bastard?" a man was saying.

The girl from behind the counter sat Claire down in a chair and began cleaning up her coat with kitchen towel.

"Don't cry," she repeated, over and over. "Don't cry. A little sod like that isn't worth it."

The town was cloaked in darkness. Claire sat hunched on the seafront, her limbs aching with the cold, her body numbed from sitting on the same concrete bench for more than an hour. Behind her, on the main road, occasional cars swished past wetly. Ahead of her, a few yards away across the beach, the ocean rolled in as it always would, a regular, monotonous whisper of waves against shingle. There was a bruise on Claire's cheek, just beneath her left eye, where she had caught it against a chair as she fell to the ground. She touched it now, exploring it with her fingers, and winced at the raw tenderness. A wilder than usual gust of wind blew in from the sea and set her shivering again: she would need to drink something hot before she went back to the car. Another five-hour drive lay ahead of her, in the darkness this time. And she was so tired. Maybe she should find a hotel to check into: but the prospect was too depressing. She knew what it would be like: tea bags and sachets of instant coffee on a bedside tray, a battered old portable TV, the ghosts of a thousand previous guests. She should drive home. The long journey would do her good, take her mind off things.

But she didn't move. Something held her to this bench, in spite of the cold, in spite of the loathing for this town that had been building up inside her. She continued to sit there, no longer crying, no longer thinking, no longer even hearing the changeless background noise of the waves and the cars. Far out to sea, deep in the cloudy blackness, mysterious lights were winking. And meanwhile, Claire was paralysed. Freezing cold and soaked to the skin, she couldn't imagine what it would take to make her leave this spot.

Some minutes later—she couldn't have said when, the passing of time had become unmeasurable, meaningless—she heard footsteps approaching, and then the voice of a man addressing her. He said: "You'll catch your death, sitting there."

Claire glanced up. It was Victor Gibbs. The mist and the rain made him look scrawny and bedraggled. She turned away again.

Uninvited, he sat down beside her. He leaned forward and was silent at first.

"You've got some of the look of her," Gibbs said, finally. "I should have noticed that, the first time I saw you."

Without moving, her voice almost toneless, Claire said: "You remember what my sister looked like?"

"Oh, yes. I remember her, well enough."

Claire shifted on the bench, moving an inch or two further away from him. She pulled her raincoat up around her throat.

"I don't know much," Gibbs said hoarsely, after a long pause. "What I know, I'll tell you."

To all outward appearances, Claire made no response. But she had stiffened. Her whole body was rigid with expectation.

"There was a guy in the factory," Gibbs began. "A kind of a friend of mine. Name of Roy Slater. We didn't work together or anything. I was in the accounts department, he was on the shop floor. But we got to know each other, I forget how. I think it may have been at some kind of political meeting. We had a few things in common like that. We saw eye-to-eye, politically."

"I read about him in Bill Anderton's files," said Claire, flatly, distantly. "He was a fascist, wasn't he?"

"Times were different then," said Gibbs. "You had more freedom to say what you thought. Anyway. I won't deny that Slater was a villain. So was I, in those days. I stole some money out of a charity committee account—forged some signatures, I was pretty good at it, still am as a matter of fact—and ended up getting the push. Got caught doing the same thing with another firm a few years later and did some time for it, then. That pulled me up sharp. I was pretty straight after that."

He took a pack of cigarettes from his pocket and offered Claire one. She shook her head.

"I don't think Slater had anything against your sister. I don't know if he even knew who she was. She just happened to be in the wrong place at the wrong time. She got caught up in events.

"This was how it went. You remember the Birmingham pub bombings? When the IRA blew up those two pubs in the middle of town and there were loads of people killed? Well, there was a bad atmosphere after that. All over the city, but in the factory as well. A lot of anti-Irish feeling. A hell of a lot. Not just things being said, but . . . things being done. There were Micks being beaten up all over the place. There'd been anti-Irish stuff going on in the factory before, but this was in a different league. And Slater was always prepared to go one better than anyone else. He hated the Micks. Fucking hated them. I suppose it was only a matter of time before he did something about it.

"Well, it could only have been a week or so after the bombings, when they picked on someone. There was this block where the blokes used to shower off after the shift, and they took this lad there—he was only a young lad, mid-twenties maybe—and three or four of them dragged him off to this block, with Slater in tow, and they gave him a hell of a going-over. They never meant just to rough him up, those guys, that was never the plan. They meant to kill him. And that's what they did. Cracked him over the head with a hammer or something and finished the poor fucker off. It was a professional piece of work. They did a good job of making it look like an accident. That was how it was reported in the papers a few days later."

"Jim Corrigan," said Claire suddenly—as a name slipped back into her consciousness after an absence of more than twenty-five years.

"What?"

"I read about it. That was his name. It was in our school magazine." She remembered the day clearly now. She had been in the old Ikon Gallery in John Bright Street, looking through back issues of *The Bill Board*, when she had come across this story. While she was reading it, she had spied on Phil's mother as she enjoyed a surreptitious date with Miles Plumb the art teacher. "I remember thinking at the time what a terrible story it was. He had a wife and a kid. They said that a big piece of machinery had fallen on him."

"Most probably, yeah. That was the one."

Gibbs fell silent. In the distance came the sudden boom of a ship's foghorn.

"I don't get it," Claire said at last. "Where does Miriam fit into this story?"

"Like I said," Gibbs continued, "she was in the wrong place at the wrong time. She was *there*, when they did it, you see. She was there in the shower block. She saw the whole bloody thing." He drew on his cigarette, and tapped ash on to the pavement. "God knows what she was doing there. That I never *did* understand."

Claire knew. "She would have gone there to meet Bill," she said. "It was one of the places they used to meet." She sat back and closed her eyes, trying to remember every detail, everything that might turn out to be a clue. Had her sister's relationship with Bill reached a crisis by then? She thought it probably had. "So what happened next?"

"That," said Gibbs, "I don't know. I think Slater must have had a word with her and told her to keep her mouth shut. But that wasn't good enough for him. She was a witness to what they'd done, so somebody had to get rid of her. Slater told me afterwards that he'd done it himself. He was always a boastful little swine, but I think he was telling the truth. I believe she tried to go straight home and he followed her but . . . well, I don't know where he did it, exactly. He told me he'd left her by a reservoir. Then later that night he came back and tied weights to the body and chucked her in."

"And then," said Claire, her voice shaking, "then he asked you to write that letter? And you *did it*?"

Gibbs stubbed out his cigarette and sat for what seemed like an age, staring impassively out to sea. At last he said, very slowly, slurring the words: "I wished your sister ill. Don't ask me why. But I did."

He had no more to say. And Claire had nothing more to ask him. After a few more minutes he rose to his feet stiffly.

"There. Now I've told you. Go to the police if you want, I don't care any more."

He turned and walked away. Claire heard his footsteps receding. She did not watch him go.

Twenty minutes later, when she had slowly absorbed everything that Victor Gibbs had told her, Claire realized that there was another question she wanted to ask: what had happened to Roy Slater? Was he still alive? She hurried round to Gibbs's flat, half-running, with a premonition, already, that she was going to be too late. When she arrived, she found the front door open and his neighbour from the ground-floor flat standing in the hallway.

"I don't know what you said to him," the woman said. "But he's gone. Drove off a few minutes ago, with two suitcases. He's taken everything he owns." She started sorting through a pile of free newspapers on the hall table, throwing most of them into a black bin liner. "No great loss," she added, sourly. "He hadn't paid his rent for months anyway."

5

One evening, many years later, when Philip was paying a visit to Claire and Stefano in Lucca, she told him about the events of that day, and said: "And then, when I was driving home, I started to think about the pub bombings and how they'd messed up Lois's life, of course, because of what happened to her when she was in The Tavern in the Town with Malcolm that night, but not just hers, how they'd messed up Miriam's, as well, indirectly, because of what she saw happening at Longbridge and what that made them do to her, and how that means that they also messed up my life, because for years I couldn't really think straight or get on with anything because of wondering what had happened to Miriam, and in a way how they'd also messed up Patrick's, because he ended up obsessing over Miriam too, to compensate for something, to compensate for the pain we'd put him through by splitting up when he was little. And I started thinking of all the other families, all the other people, whose lives must have been touched by that event, and how you could go mad trying to trace the thing back to its source, trying to point the finger of blame at someone, you know, going right back to the beginnings of the Irish problem until you end up saying something like, Is Oliver Cromwell to blame for the fact that Lois had to spend so many years in hospital? Or is he to blame for the fact that Miriam was killed? And in a way, you know, although it's a terrible thing to say, the Birmingham bombing was a small atrocity if you look at it statistically, compared to Lockerbie, or compared to the Bali bombings, or compared to September the eleventh, or compared to the number of civilians who died in the 2003 Iraq war. So what would happen if you tried to explain all those deaths, all those messed-up lives, tried to trace those events back to the source? Would you go mad? I mean, is it a mad thing to try and do, or is it really the only sane thing to try and do, to face up to the fact that in big ways and small ways perfectly ordinary, perfectly innocent people continually have their lives fucked up by forces outside their control, whether they're historical events or just the shitty luck of stepping outside your house on the day a drunk driver goes past at seventy miles an hour, but even then you can start blaming the culture, the culture that's told him it's cool to drive at seventy miles an hour or the culture that's turned him into an alcoholic, and like I said maybe that's the *sane* thing to try and do, to stop shrugging our shoulders and just saying 'Life is random' or 'These things happen,' because when you get right down to it *everything* has a cause. Everything that one human being does to another is the result of a human decision that's been taken some time in the past, either by that person or by somebody else, twenty or thirty or two hundred or two thousand years ago or maybe just last Wednesday."

And Philip said: "Are you pissed, or something, Claire? Because I've never heard you talk so much rubbish."

To which Claire said: "I have drunk about two-thirds of this very excellent bottle of Bardolino in the last half hour, that's true."

Philip said: "At the end of the day, if someone you love has been a victim of terrorism—has been killed in a terrorist attack, let's say—it makes no difference to them whether the terrorist has done it because he's psychotic or because he feels his country or his religion or something has been hard done by. The fact is that the person you love is dead and the person who did it is the person who planted the bomb or flew the aeroplane or whatever. You don't care about their motives. *They shouldn't have done it.* Roy Slater killed your sister because he was an evil man. Sorry to be so blunt about it, but that's that."

Claire said: "Yes, but it *wouldn't have happened* if it wasn't for the pub bombings."

Philip said: "Maybe not to that person, at that time. But he would have found other reasons for doing it to somebody else. And whatever became of him, by the way?"

Claire said: "It was weird, I had no curiosity about Slater, after that. It was as if I'd been bled dry of all those feelings. Patrick made some inquiries, a couple of years later. Found out that he'd died a while ago. Died in prison. Emphysema."

Philip said: "That's funny. Patrick never mentioned doing that."

Claire said: "What that day in Norfolk made me realize—this is all I'm saying—is that there are patterns. You have to look hard for them but when you see them you can cut your way through all the chaos and randomness and coincidence and follow the path back to its source and say, 'Ah, *that's* where it started.'"

Philip said: "You'd be crazy to do that. There are individuals. There are *bad individuals*—it's as simple as that—and they're the people you have to watch out for, and even if there are reasons for the way they behave, nine times out of ten they're not to do with history, and not to do with culture. It's to do with psychology and human relationships. *Other people* have made them the way they are. Parents, most of the time."

Claire said: "So then you have to ask what made the *parents* the way they were."

Philip said: "But that's impossible! Then you'll just keep going further and further back and there'll be no end to it."

Claire said: "No, not impossible. Difficult, yes. Very difficult. But that's what we have to do."

Stefano came out on to the balcony. He was carrying a bottle of red wine from which he refilled both of their glasses.

Claire said: "Smells fantastic in there. How long's it going to be?"

Stefano said: "Another half an hour or so. You can't rush risotto."

He went back inside. Claire and Philip sipped their wine, and the mournful late sunlight of a September evening threw long shadows and burnished the ancient stones of the piazza beneath them.

Philip said: "People have to accept responsibility for themselves, that's all. Look at Harding. Maybe he was damaged by his parents, I don't know. But lots of people are damaged by their parents and end up living more or less harmless lives. He *chose* to become the person he became."

Claire said: "You never really told me what happened when you went to meet him."

Philip said: "I'll tell you now."

"Harding was in Norfolk, too. Nowhere near where you went, though. Right at the other end of the county—the western end. The address I'd been given was some farm in the middle of nowhere, a few miles south of King's Lynn. The beginnings of the fen country.

"I don't remember the date exactly but it must have been some time late in March because I was listening to the radio on the way up and the Americans had been bombing Iraq for a couple of days by then. 'Shock and awe,' that was the expression. You couldn't listen to the radio for five bloody minutes without some military strategist banging on about 'shock and awe.' It felt strange after I'd left the main roads and I was driving through this empty landscape—things get very quiet in Norfolk very quickly, you can leave civilization behind in no time—and all I was hearing on the radio was descriptions of carnage and destruction, and all these American guys talking proudly about how much bloody *awe* the rest of us must be feeling. I suppose it's not hard to inspire awe in someone if you're the richest country in the world and you spend half of it on machines designed to bomb the living shit out of people. Anyway, there are different kinds of awe, aren't there? Sometimes it can be a landscape that gives you that feeling. It's so beautiful around there, so still. Miles and miles of watery flatness. Just you and the birds. And those Norfolk skies! In the summer they can be amazing. That afternoon it was just grey, silvery grey. But . . . the *silence* of it. That's what was so awesome, I suppose, coming from the city. I turned the radio off and before going to find the farmhouse I pulled the car over and turned the engine off and for a while I just got out and listened to the silence.

"I could see why he'd chosen to come and live here.

"You could see the house from miles away. There was no woodland round there, and the land was completely flat. Just reed beds for as far as you could see, and those strange-looking waterways which were made hundreds of years ago but still run absolutely straight, and feel very man-made. An odd kind of landscape. Not like anywhere else I know. Very exposed, in a way, but at the same time, so remote, you couldn't imagine anyone coming to find him there. I wondered if that was the idea. I wondered if he was hiding from something, or someone. I think the police had been after him more than once in the last few years, because of things he'd said and things he'd posted on the internet and of course the CDs, as well. I thought perhaps he was just lying low for a while, to give whatever trouble he was in the chance to blow over.

"I could see smoke coming from the direction of the house but when I got there I realized it wasn't coming from the main building. It was coming from the chimney of this old caravan he'd parked in the yard. There were a couple of women living there—or girls, actually—I don't know what you'd call them, they looked like they were in their early twenties. He called them Scylla and Charybdis and I never found out what they were doing there apart from helping him out with some of the farm-work. They were very good looking. I don't know where he'd found them or how he'd persuaded them to come there.

"Anyway, I parked the car next to this caravan and sat there for a while trying to get my thoughts straight. I had no idea what I was going to say to him, or even what I was there for, really. I suppose it was curiosity, mostly. I wanted to know how the person we'd known at school—or thought we knew, at any rate—could possibly have turned out like this. I suppose that learning what Harding had become had knocked my whole past—our shared past—out of shape, and I was hoping to put that right, somehow, to make it seem that there was some logic behind it all. Keeping that chaos at bay, again. But there was another reason, too. I wanted to ask him about Steve. What he'd done to Steve at school. I wanted to know how he could ever justify that, even to himself.

"I sat there for about five minutes and then I went to the front door and I knocked as loudly as I could.

"There was no way I would ever have recognized him. In fact for a second or two I was sure that I must have got the wrong house. He was wearing a flat cap—I found out later this was because he'd gone almost completely bald—and had little round steel-rimmed glasses and an incredible bushy beard that came down practically to his chest. He was dressed in tweeds, a mustard-yellow waistcoat, neckerchief, the lot—he'd reinvented himself as an English gentleman farmer, although judging from the state of the fields I'd just driven through, he hadn't quite got the hang of the farming part of it yet. I can't say that he looked very strong, physically—he'd begun to walk with quite a stoop, and there wasn't much flesh on him—but the thing that really struck me about him was his eyes. There was real aggression there. Was he always like that, at school, can you remember? I mean, he knew who I was, he remembered me, and he was expecting to see me, but there was terrific hostility, terrific *suspicion* in those eyes. As if he was just waiting for me to say a word out of place and then he'd explode. And it was like that from the minute I appeared. No trust. You could tell he didn't trust me, didn't trust anything for that matter. He didn't trust the world.

"Of course, the first problem was, I didn't know what to call him. I'd already found out that he didn't like to be called Sean any more. He'd anglicized it to John. John Harding. I suppose it had a good, solid, English sound to it. I remembered that his dad was Irish, but later on, whenever I mentioned that, he'd ignore it. At one point he said that his father was only Irish going back a generation. Made quite an issue out of that. But on the whole he hardly talked about his father anyway. He said his mother was far more important to him, and there were pictures of her everywhere—on the shelves, on the mantelpiece, on the piano. She was a scary-looking woman, I must say. Looked like someone from the 1930s, not the 1970s. Like the kind of headmistress who'd give you nightmares. In a couple of the pictures she was wearing a monocle.

"I have to say the place was fairly tidy, and clean. I've got a feeling that Scylla and Charybdis had something to do with that. Not that there was much to clean, or tidy, when it came down to it. I don't think he had many possessions. There was hardly any furniture, just a table to eat off and a table to work at—one of the rooms was set up as his study, and he had a computer in there. But there were books everywhere: not just in the study, but all over the place, in the kitchen, the hallway, the bathroom. Great piles of them. Books on every subject. A lot of stuff on local history and topography, but also weird things like occultism, witchcraft, paganism. A lot of classical texts. Novels, hundreds of novels—not modern stuff, but lots of eighteenth- and nineteenth-century writers. Some politics, history. *Mein Kampf,* inevitably. A lot of books on the eastern religions. A lot about Islam. Very eclectic, I had to admit. Quite impressive. I don't remember him being that much of a reader at school.

"The silly thing was, we had nothing to say to each other. At least, he clearly had no desire to make conversation, and nothing that I said seemed to interest him very much. You know, the routine questions like 'How are you?' and 'What have you been up to?' didn't seem to get us anywhere. I tried telling him what the people from school had been doing, but he didn't want to know. Didn't even try to be polite about it. 'I don't remember any of those people,' he would say. Didn't remember Doug—didn't remember you, either. He just said, 'You were all earthbound. You were all of the earth.' I'm not sure what that was supposed to mean. The only exception, seemingly, was Benjamin. Something lit up for a minute in his eyes when I mentioned Benjamin. He asked whether Benjamin had ever got his book published and I said no, he never managed to finish it. He seemed to think that was a pity. He said Benjamin had potential, or something.

"I told him how it was Benjamin who had rediscovered him, how he'd come across that entry he'd written in the log-book in Dorset, and I asked him if he'd remembered writing it. And he said, oh yes, that was him all right, but he didn't write those kinds of things any more. He said Arthur Pusey-Hamilton was dead and buried. I asked him how closely he'd identified with the character and he said very closely: he had this theory that in order to satirize something, or in order to parody it properly, you really had to be in love with it, on some level. He told me that he'd developed this theory in a big book he'd been working on, a history of English humour, starting with Chaucer and coming up to P. G. Wodehouse. He talked a lot about all the books he'd written. None of them had been published. But then he said that he'd 'renounced' humour, like someone would say they'd given up smoking or converted to a different religion. Apparently he'd spent some time in a monastery—there you are, another link with Benjamin—and he told me about this saint called Saint Benoit and how the monks tried to live according to his rules, and one of them was not to make jokes, and another was not to laugh too often. He said that laughter wasn't holy, wasn't dignified. Those kinds of words—holiness, dignity—seemed to have become important to him. He used them a lot.

"So I took him up on that. I said that I couldn't see there was anything holy about drugging Steve Richards to make sure he didn't pass his physics exam, or that there was much dignity in victimizing one of the teachers—we had this maths teacher for a while, called Mr. Silverman—just because he was a Jew. And as for working with a bunch of Nazi thugs like Combat 18, or putting money into bands who wrote songs celebrating the Holocaust—well, I couldn't see how any of that could be justified with the kinds of words he was using. But that argument didn't seem to worry him. He said that he'd made mistakes in the past, he didn't deny that. But he said that he actually admired the skinheads and the people who took 'race war' seriously—that was the phrase he used, race war—people who took it to the streets. He said he didn't call them thugs, he called them warriors, and the Warrior Spirit was part of our heritage, part of our folklore. So I said to him, 'What about the riots in Bradford and Burnley and Oldham a couple of years ago, when these people were out of control and were beating people up, Pakistani and Bangladeshi guys in their sixties and seventies—grandfathers! What was so great about that?' And he said that violence was terrible but if it was the only way to reach your goal then it was justified. He said that he approved of those riots and thought they were a positive step and that was when I began to think that he was a little bit delusional because he started claiming that he'd helped to provoke them, that some of the things he'd written on the internet had been influential in getting them started.

"And I said, 'Well what is this goal, anyway? I don't understand. What is it you're trying to achieve?' And he said that the only thing the Aryan people had ever hoped for was to be able to live the way they wanted, in peace, and in harmony with nature. So I said, 'What's stopping you, then?' And he said that it couldn't happen while the land was suffering. He said the land was suffering because it was being raped and polluted by the big corporations, and it was overrun with aliens, people who had no respect for the land and no right to be here, and it was the big corporations and the political establishment who were in collusion to keep things this way, because this was what their power was based on. The usual conspiracy theory nonsense. He said it was a way of perpetuating an evil, materialist culture and it was all based on usury, and of course he reckoned the Jews were behind it all.

"And that, apparently, was why he had become so interested in Islam and had convinced himself that *jihad* was the new way forward. Not that he seemed to be learning how to fly an aeroplane or taking part in any suicide bombing missions or anything. But he did claim to have met Osama bin Laden, who he called 'Usama,' for some reason. I suppose to prove that he was on better terms than the rest of us. That was the point I decided he must have gone completely mad. He said that al-Qaeda and the Aryan warriors were basically on the same side because the real enemy was America and the Zionists who ruled the world but I'd sort of stopped listening by that stage. But he was in favour of the war in Iraq, apparently because he thought it would inspire more terrorist attacks on the West and this was a good thing.

"I had one last crack at it and said, 'But what about all the Iraqi civilians who are being killed in the war?' and again he just said that this was very sad, but war was a tragic necessity and much more blood would flow before things were put right again. And he told me to read an essay he'd written called 'Violence and Melancholy.' It was on the internet with all his other stuff, he said, on some website that his friends had set up for him. I was glad to hear that he had some friends, all things considered.

"Well, we didn't talk much after that. He went off to make me some tea and I looked at his record collection. That was pretty impressive too. A few thousand albums, all in alphabetical order, all on vinyl. I think he'd got most of Western classical music pretty well covered. When he came back in I remarked on this and I pointed out, 'Not much "Oi!" music here then, is there?' He put on the record that was already on the turntable—it was Vaughan Williams, 'Norfolk Rhapsody Number One'—and he listened to it in silence while we were drinking our tea, and his face changed while he was listening to it, he stopped looking aggressive and paranoid, and this kind of beauty came over him, he came closer to smiling, for a few minutes, than I'd seen him all afternoon. But when it finished he looked very sad and he told me that he must have listened to that music thousands of times, tens of thousands of times, but he never grew tired of it. It was one of his mother's favourites, he said. So I reminded him that Vaughan Williams was a socialist and would have hated him and everything that he believed. But he said that politics like that were superficial, and you could tell that the composer's real beliefs were in his music. There didn't really seem to be any answer to that.

"Just before I left I told him what had happened to Steve Richards, how he'd landed this great new job and moved his family to Birmingham and then just a few months later the whole department had been closed down. (Which I believe, Claire, was the work of an ex-boyfriend of yours—am I right?) And Harding said he was sorry about that but the real trouble was, Steve didn't really belong in this country, he'd be happier if he went back to where his own people were. His 'folk,' as he liked to call them. I lost my temper when he said that and just told him he was a fucking idiot. And I remembered something that Doug had said about Harding once, that it would be depressing to meet him again because he'd probably have turned into a quantity surveyor, but nothing could have been more depressing than this, to think of all that cleverness, all that humour, all that mischief, and see the place it had led him to, in the end. So sad. I asked him if there was a Mrs. Harding, and he said there had been, for a while, but she'd died. And I took one more look around the house and shuddered to think what a mean and bitter and *lonely* little life he'd made for himself—you know?—but I couldn't manage to feel sorry for him. You couldn't *reach* him, that was the problem, so how could you feel sorry for him? He'd put himself beyond that. I didn't shake his hand, I just said goodbye, and on the way out I said, 'Give my regards to Usama, won't you? Ask him if he'll do an interview for the *Birmingham Post* one of these days.' And he said something back to me in Arabic. I asked him what it meant and he translated it for me and said it was from the *Qu'ran*. It meant, 'Show us the Straight Way, the way of those on whom You have bestowed Your grace, whose portion is not wrath, and who do not go astray.'"

"Then I drove off. He didn't wave or anything, but he stood there in the doorway, watching me go. That was the last I saw of him."

The warm evening drew on. They lit candles on the balcony, and after their meal they sat there, Claire, Philip and Stefano, until the sun had gone down and the bars had started to close and the city of Lucca had fallen almost silent. Just a few voices, raised in farewell, and passing footsteps on the cobbled streets. Already the events of spring 2003 seemed to have taken place aeons ago.

It was long after midnight when Claire said: "I don't know what we can learn from Sean's story. I don't think it makes what I was saying any less true. If there is an exception to what I was saying, it's not Sean, it's Benjamin. *That* I would probably admit. You can't blame anyone for what happened to him. There's no chain of cause and effect there. Nobody forced him to fall in love with Cicely and waste twenty years of his life obsessing over her. He's entirely responsible for that."

Philip said: "But the thing is—Benjamin's happy now. He's got Cicely again, hasn't he? And that's all he ever wanted."

"I don't believe he's really happy."

"Have you seen them together?"

"I went round there once. I couldn't handle it. She was sitting there in her wheelchair, ordering him around like a fucking dog. The *temper* on her . . ."

"It does that to you. That's one of the things that MS does."

"Well, I couldn't handle it."

"But you see, he's *happy*, Claire. He's writing again—did you know that? And playing music. I think that's great. I mean, if you'd seen him a few years ago . . . Or think about the time when he disappeared, and went to Germany, and nobody heard from him for months."

"Maybe . . ."

"That's the thing, you see. We've all ended up with what we wanted, in our different ways. You, me, Doug, Emily. Think about it. We've all lived happily ever after."

4

The Munich Train

In the foothills
Snow streaks the black fields.
Dusk steals over empty balconies, shuttered houses solemn
With mystery, where children
(I am forced to think) grow and parents love
In terrible privacy.

Augsburg. Ulm.
Already in my head
These names throw dark blue shadows
Sad as Sunday afternoons.

Parallel to the track, now
A liquid channel runs. Sheets of ice
Hover on its greygreen, and beside it the grass
Is the beige of carpet in a done-up flat
Someone has been
Trying too hard to sell.

Köln. Mannheim. Stuttgart.
In any of these places
A home could be found

Or made. But equally,
Pale, hinting light glimmers still
Behind the distant Alps, and that sun soon will
Brush its lips across the downy shoulders
Of towns I've not imagined yet:

No choice at all
When choice is infinite.

Benjamin stood in a corner of the *Drogerie* and held up the two packs of condoms, one in each hand, trying to decipher the German instructions. There was clearly some important difference between them, but he couldn't imagine what it was. Size? Texture? Flavouring? He had no idea.

He had never used a condom before. Incredible, when he thought about it, but true. He and Cicely had not used any protection at all, that day—somewhat recklessly, in retrospect—while Emily had been on the pill to start with and after that . . . well, there had been no need in the first place, as it turned out. So it would be a new experience for him. All the more important, then, that he made the right choice.

Still he hesitated. He remembered an embarrassing incident, back in the 1980s, after Saps at Sea had played a successful gig at an arts centre near Cheltenham. In the van on the way back to Birmingham the five of them had played a game called "Deprivations." The challenge of this game was to name supposedly widespread activities which you yourself—to your shame, perhaps—had never performed. For every other member of the group who *had* performed them, you were awarded a point: which meant that the more points you were awarded, the more freakish you were likely to appear to the other players. Benjamin had won the first round, scoring a maximum of four points by admitting—to howls of incredulity—that he had never had sex while wearing a condom. Furthermore, he went on to win the next ten rounds, each one again with a maximum score, by confessing that he had never used cocaine, never smoked cannabis, never smoked a cigarette, never had sex outdoors, never driven a car at more than eighty miles an hour, never had a one-night stand, never played cards for money, never played truant from school, never drunk more than three pints of beer in one night and never forgotten his mother's birthday. In addition, none of the other players ever managed to score the maximum of four points, because no matter what they admitted to never having done, Benjamin hadn't done it either. There had been only one moment when it seemed there might be an exception to this rule—when Ralph, the drummer, confessed dolefully that he'd never had sex with two women. "Ah!" Benjamin had exclaimed in triumph. "Now—I've done that." But then it had to be explained that Ralph was referring to having sex with *two women at the same time*. For which he only won three points.

Benjamin looked at the two packs again, and realized, with a sinking heart, that it probably didn't matter which one he bought. He'd been in Munich for three weeks now, and had hardly spoken to a living soul, let alone a woman who might want to go to bed with him. He tried again to deduce the meaning of the unfamiliar words, and ended up putting them both in his shopping basket anyway. He had a German dictionary back in his flat, after all.

The English Garden in Winter

The English Garden in winter
Stands almost empty. Beneath my feet,
A slushy mix of ice and mud.
The river here is Alpine,
And even in July it's mountain-cold.
A solitary bird skims the surface, wary.
What sort of bird? I'm not quite sure.

Hard to see, amidst these greys,
These leafless trees (the names of which
Escape me) how, in the summer, flowers might bloom,
And women lie, along this bank,
Naked—so I'm told—
While full-clothed businessmen snatch lunch
And furtive glimpses, hungry-eyed.

What flowers would those be, then?
The ones that plan to bud among the spikes
Of this squat bush I can't identify?
Shivering, I wonder where's the rain
Long threatened by this Munich sky,
And feel my ignorance.

I must move on, from this unlucky town,
Hung low with clouds I might describe
In detail if I had the terminology.
The beauty of those sundrunk girls
Is real enough, in my imaginings.
But winter in the English Garden
Freezes me today with two brown certainties

I won't be here,
When they arrive to show it,
And I shall never make a nature poet.

Benjamin had not written poetry since he was at school. He knew that he was out of practice at it, as at so many other things. But after the twenty-year debacle of *Unrest*—the mound of paperwork it had generated, the hundreds of wasted hours spent wrestling with MIDI interfaces and sequencing software—he had no appetite for anything more technologically advanced than a biro and an exercise book, or any literary form more complex than a sonnet. Every day, after hauling himself out of bed at about ten or eleven o'clock, he would go to one of the bars or coffee shops near the university, and settle down to write. Most days he wrote nothing. Usually he had a hangover from the night before. In the evenings he would find a cinema showing English-language films and then he would go back to his flat and drink most of a bottle of wine and try to write again. When the poetry wouldn't come, he would try to write something else—prose reminiscences, often, of episodes from earlier in his life—but he never kept any of these outpourings. Often he could scarcely be bothered to read them through in the morning. The paucity of his own experience had started to disgust him. He had nothing to write about. And whenever this realization hit him hardest, late at night, he would drink more than one bottle of wine. He developed a taste for spirits: Islay malts in particular, although they weren't easy to find in Munich, and cost a fortune. One memorable night (or rather, one night about which he could remember nothing afterwards) he drank three-quarters of a bottle of Talisker and was sick into his shoes: a fact he did not discover until he tried to put them on the next morning. He knew it was time to stop. But didn't.

His German failed to improve. His social life failed to materialize. His money started to run out. He began to feel nostalgic for Morley Jackson

Gray, for the office banter and the comfortable routines of the working day. He had his mobile phone with him. The battery had been flat for weeks but he could easily have charged it up. He could have phoned Adrian or Tim or Juliet at the office; he could have phoned his parents or his sister or his niece; he could have phoned Philip or Doug; he could have phoned Munir. But the battery stayed flat. Benjamin was determined to reinvent himself before any of these people saw him again. He would return in some kind of triumph.

Sexyland

My gaze is fixed upon her breasts
Because there is less shame in that
Than looking in her eyes.

They're cobalt-blue (her eyes, that is)
And glazed with sadness, anger, boredom—
Something, anyway, that makes of her
A human being. Which isn't what we want—
Not me, nor any of the men (all young, I note)
Who watch her from the shadows,
As they sip the foul red wine that's priced
At thirty euros. (By the glass.)

In laudable conformity, perhaps, to EC laws,
She's democratic, scrupulous and fair.
Divested, now, she leaves the stage
And offers up an eyeful of her ample charms
To each of us in turn.

I'm seventh in the queue.
The music having pumelled through
Another sixteen bars, she crash-lands
On my lap, or thereabouts.
Her pelvis sways, not quite in touch with mine,
And not quite mechanistically, though I've no doubt
Her mind is somewhere else.
(Somnambulant. Yes, that could be the word.)

And in my face—a nipple. Which
The bard in me feels honour-bound to sketch.

And yet, there isn't much to say, about this thing
With which she fills my field of vision.
It's round, and pink,
One of a perfect pair unless I'm much mistaken,
And has (on this I'd lay a bet) been sucked on
Fervently, not many hours ago,
With closed eyes and liquid, greedy lips,
By the infant son whose crumpled face
Already she must long to kiss again.

The visit to the lapdancing club made him realize that he was getting close to rock bottom. Most days now he was finding it hard to get out of bed at all. He reckoned that he had put on about a stone in weight. He had given up shaving and proved to himself conclusively that he looked even worse with a beard than he did without one. He developed an addiction for internet pornography and began to indulge in strange auto-erotic practices which involved plastic coathangers, Ben & Jerry's ice cream, the leather belt of his trousers and a spatula. He noticed that the female students who frequented the cafés in Schellingstrasse, singly and in groups, had started to recognize him and would never sit at a table next to him if they could help it. He was doing well if he produced more than six lines of poetry in a week.

He was astonished to find how much he missed Emily. That was the most unexpected thing of all. Increasingly he was fantasizing not about romantic encounters with topless undergraduate sunbathers in the English Garden, but evenings spent at home with Emily, side-by-side on the sofa, reading or watching television. He discovered that the very thing he had once wanted to escape was now the thing he most fiercely desired. The knowledge of this broke upon him one morning before dawn, as he lay in bed, wide awake, tangled up in bedsheets that had not been washed for weeks, and suddenly, without warning, he found himself howling with loneliness in the middle of the night, sobbing as he could not remember sobbing since he was a child. He cried so much he thought that he would never stop, cried until daybreak, until his chest ached with the unending force of the convulsions.

Benjamin left his flat that morning, and checked into a hotel for one night while he decided what to do next. At breakfast the following day he read the English newspapers—it was ages since he had read a newspaper—and learned not only that America and Britain had invaded Iraq without the legal sanction of a UN resolution, but that Baghdad was already on the point of falling to the allied troops. The indifference with which he received the news alarmed him. He wanted to be feeling something. He realized that he was at a turning point: was it time to reconnect himself with the rest of humanity, or was it time to isolate himself still further? Which in turn prompted another question, one that he had been carefully avoiding: why, in more than three months of joyless travelling, had he so far refrained from doing the obvious and visiting the Abbaye St. Wandrille? The answer to that was simple, if he was brave enough to look it in the eye. He could not bear the thought of going there because it would remind him of Emily; remind him of the time they had visited it together, and walked along the riverbank in the late afternoon, and attended *Complies* at nightfall. It would reek of her absence.

But that was where he had to go.

Checking Out

When I checked out of the Hotel Olympic,
I said to the receptionist in my still-halting
German, "I'd like to check out please,"
But being tired forgot—at just that moment—
That I must return the key, which was in a trouser pocket.

Well. Groucho Marx, Stan Laurel and Buster Keaton,
Performing a unique triple act at the height of their powers,
For one night only,
Could not have had the same effect.
She laughed and laughed.
She laughed and laughed and laughed and laughed.
She laughed and laughed and laughed.

Asking whether I had used the minibar,
She could barely speak for laughing.
I had given her the key by now, but all the same,
As she counted my banknotes, she was hard pressed
To work the till for laughing at this funny Englishman

Who had left it in his pocket while checking out.
She would dine out on this story for weeks,
And even now she laughed while giving me my change,
And as she took my suitcase to the store
Behind her desk, she laughed and laughed,
And laughed and laughed and laughed.

And they say the Germans have no sense of humour.

3

The train pulled into Yvetot shortly before dark. Benjamin found a taxi easily enough, and hugged his suitcase close as he was driven along the valley, through a landscape which he had been expecting to recognize but which seemed, on this misty April evening, spectral and unfamiliar.

The taxi driver left him at the monastery gates. The whole village appeared to be deserted, and although the door of the *hôtellerie* was open, it was no surprise to find that there was no one to receive him at the reception desk. Benjamin waited anxiously for some minutes, unsure now whether his telephone message had been passed on. Finally he walked the hundred yards or so to the rear of the grounds, where the well-stocked shop selling monastic souvenirs was just closing for business, and asked the *frère* behind the counter if he might be able to help. Benjamin's French was creaky, but after some misunderstanding the obliging monk directed him to a wide metal gate in the monastery walls, painted pale green, and pressed a button somewhere beneath his counter which caused the gate to slide mysteriously open. After Benjamin had passed through, it slid back automatically, and closed with a decisive clang. The noise seemed final, ominous. He was inside.

Benjamin found himself faced with a wide expanse of well-cut lawn, which swelled towards a path leading to a bridge over a silently flowing brook. Beyond that was an orchard and what seemed to be a walled *jardin potager.* To the right of these grounds, the ancient mass of the abbey itself rose up, stern, indifferent, shadowy in the gathering dusk. Benjamin walked nervously towards it, drawn and to a certain extent comforted by the warm squares of lamplight which glowed from some of the windows. He followed a gravelled path that guided him towards two solid oak doors, both of which were open, and both of which turned out to lead into the same ill-lit hallway.

His footsteps echoing on the flagstones, Benjamin peered closely at the door on his right and saw that it bore the nameplate "*Salle des hôtes.*" This, at least, seemed to be a good sign. He knocked on the door, received no answer, and pushed it heavily open.

He found himself in a high-ceilinged room, lit brightly by an electric chandelier, but still there was no one there to receive him. Religious brochures and leaflets were scattered on the wide table which almost filled the space, and a clock ticked loudly on the wall, staring fixedly and unresponsively at the crucifix which hung opposite: its iconography of pain, suffering and bondage as usual sending a chill through Benjamin rather than inspiring him to thoughts of worship.

Not knowing what else to do, he put down his suitcase, sat in a high-backed armchair—upholstered with a tapestry faded beyond recognition—and waited, listening to the ticking of the clock, the seemingly random peals of bells near and distant, and the occasional murmur of footsteps and voices in some far-off corner of the building. In this manner, time slowly began to pass.

Then, after fifteen minutes or so, during which his unease began to swell into something like panic, rapid and decisive footsteps outside the door announced an arrival. A tall, sallow young man in a monk's habit, his hair shaved to a crew-cut, eyes smiling keenly behind his wire-rimmed spectacles, swept into the room, came to a halt before Benjamin's chair and held out an apologetic hand.

"*Monsieur Trotter? Benjamin? Je suis désolé . . .*"

It was Father Antoine, the *Père hôtelier.* And without another word, he took Benjamin's case, and escorted him out of the room and across a courtyard to the doorway which led to his first-floor cell, in a low, finely proportioned tower from which you could even now breathe in the scent of the sweet-smelling newmown lawn.

It turned out that there were three other guests at the monastery at this time, none of whom spoke much English. Benjamin only saw them at mealtimes, when conversation was forbidden, so the likelihood of striking up any friendships seemed remote. The monks themselves were courteous and welcoming, but not talkative. None the less, the relief of finding himself surrounded by other people again was indescribable.

Benjamin soon discovered that life at the abbey was highly formalized, and after the dreary shapelessness of his days in Munich, he was grateful to have a routine mapped out for him. The first service of the day, *Vigiles*, took place at 5:25. He rarely attended this. If he had slept well the night before, he might feel himself capable of turning up for *Laudes*, at 7:30. After that came breakfast: some slices of bread and marmalade, a bowl of chocolate made with boiling water, Nesquik and powdered milk, taken in a small, low vaulted chamber beneath the *hôtellerie* itself. Breakfast was eaten in the company of his fellow-guests, and usually in silence—although silence was not compulsory here, as it was at other meals. Once or twice Benjamin would try to get a conversation going, but his efforts tended to meet with politely monosyllabic replies—either in French or in English—which he took as a rebuke.

Messe was the great event of the morning, and started at 9:45. It was attended by large numbers of people from the village, and was held, like the other services, in that same magnificently austere chapel—converted from an old tithe barn, its roof a dazzling criss-cross of beams and wooden vaulting—where he and Emily had sat almost two long years ago, and listened to the same chanting. (Not knowing that it was the last evening they would ever spend together.) Then came *Sexte*, at 12:45, and soon after that, lunch. Benjamin and the other guests would file into the vast, brightly sunlit refectory, watched over on either side by rows of monks, of ages ranging, it seemed, from about twenty-five to ninety. Impossible to gauge their thoughts from their faces, however richly expressive the older ones seemed. Grace was sung, calm and mellifluous, and then the guests would take their seats and be waited on by two or three of the monks, serving with a briskness and cheerful efficiency that would have been the envy of the diners in many a Michelin-starred Parisian restaurant. Aromatically dressed salad was followed by meat, and vegetables from the monastery garden, and then a dessert which might be no more than warm crème anglaise topped with a raspberry or blackcurrant purée. Since conversation was forbidden in the refectory, instead of having to cope with the awkwardness of small-talk the guests listened while a young, angel-faced monk read—or rather sang—to them, chanting from the pages of what appeared, during Benjamin's stay at least, to be a book of seventeenth-century French history. Reflecting on the exquisite monotony of the novice's performance, Benjamin saw that here he might have stumbled, at last, on the key to the attainment of his lifelong artistic goal: finding new ways of combining music and the written word. Had these monks not solved this very problem, and in fact (as seemed almost annoyingly typical of them) done so in the simplest and most obvious fashion?

The afternoons stretched long and languorous before him, punctuated only by *None* (straight after lunch) and *Vêpres*, which took place as dusk fell. Sometimes he took part in these services, sometimes not. No one seemed to mind one way or the other: he could never tell whether his behaviour was being noticed, his movements monitored. In any case the monks seemed so tolerant, it was hard to imagine anything he could do with his time that might discompose them. (He sometimes thought that boring them, failing to arouse their interest, would be the worst offence he could commit.) And then, after dinner came the final service of the day, and Benjamin's favourite: *Complies*. This was held at 8:35, in the pitch dark. The old barn was illuminated only by two dimly glowing electric lights, mounted on to vertical beams on either side of the altar, which did little to dispel the dense shadows of those cold April nights. In the obscured recesses of their stalls, the monks ranged themselves as before, their cowled figures seeming ever more Gothic, ever more other-worldly, the clean lines of their melancholy chant sending out a dying, ethereal fall into the black stillness, and the measured silences interleaved between them seeming longer, calmer, more profound than ever.

As his stay extended, Benjamin began to recognize the different characters of his hosts. At first he had found it difficult to tell them apart, even physically: the standard uniform of closely shaved heads, wire-rimmed spectacles and seemingly identical habits had made them all but indistinguishable to him. But gradually, peeping through the screen of daily ritual and apparent conformity, he began to get glimpses of different quirks and personality traits. He found garrulous monks, playful monks and arrogant monks; gossipers, thinkers, dreamers and misfits; jogging, vegetable-growing and cycling monks. In Père Antoine, rather to his surprise, he found a fellow-writer: one with an advantage over Benjamin, in fact, for Antoine's works of "religious sociology" on the politics of the family had actually been published. "*Quand votre recueil de poèmes sera publié,*" Antoine said to him kindly one day, "*vous devrez nous en envoyer un exemplaire.*" Benjamin, embarrassed to think of his work being scrutinized by readers so pure in heart, had answered: "*Ah, je ne sais pas: ils sont un peu trop profanes pour votre bibilothèque, je crois.*" At which the monk had laughed delightedly: "*Trop profanes! Ah—vous vous faites des illusions sur notre compte!*"

One day, at the end of lunch, when a basket of fruit was passed among the assembled diners, Benjamin found himself faced with a row of contented monks, some youthful, some near-senile, all sucking or chewing abstractedly on a half-peeled banana. Their eyes were locked into the middle distance, as if in all-too fleeting acceptance of the pleasures of this earthly life, and for once he felt an intense, incongruous bond with them. It made him want to laugh, but in a joyous way, with no hint of mockery. There seemed a good deal of laughter to be had at the Abbaye, despite the warnings against it which were inscribed in the rulebook of Saint Benoit (a copy of which was deposited in his cell): "*54: Ne pas dire de paroles vaines ou qui ne portent qu'à rire. 55: Ne pas aimer le rire trop fréquent ou trop bruyant.*" Sometimes, he would even find groups of monks gathered together on one of the bridges spanning the Fontenelle as it flowed silently through the grounds, feeding crusts of bread to the ducks clustered there, with expressions of such child-like glee transforming their scholarly faces that for a moment it seemed possible—an old, once-familiar feeling—that the whole of life might one day be composed of these fragments of blissful simplicity, and a sense of fugitive gladness stole over him, just as it had done long ago on one or two priceless occasions, during his schooldays.

It was the routine, Benjamin realized after a few days, that was doing most to restore him. What had seemed at first like a death-like sequence of repetitions came to feel perversely liberating, and he gradually slipped into his own pattern, attending four out of the day's seven services, and filling the interstices with reading, walking and contemplation. (Though daydreaming, he sometimes thought, might have been a better word for it.) He became reluctant to vary this pattern, even to the point of wanting always to sit on the same bench at the same hour of the day. Even when gentle rain began to fall from the steel-grey skies over St. Wandrille, then, he was still to be found, at three o'clock every afternoon, at rest in the orchard, an object of no apparent curiosity to the working monks, chasing the tail of his own antic reflections. He was contented, now, up to a point: certainly glad to have escaped the miserable solitude of Germany. But he knew that beneath the surface, everything remained chaotic in his mind. He had no sense of religion; nothing returned to him, there, however many *Laudes* and *Vêpres* he sat through. He had nurtured a vague hope that by coming here he might start to feel holy, whatever that meant. Instead, the more his body felt rested, the more dreamless and pellucid his sleep became, the more his rogue brain whirred into anarchic overdrive. He thought about the past; his failed marriage; Emily; Malvina; Cicely; any others who happened to visit his consciousness. He thought about his lost faith, and his wasted years. Tried to decide whether they really had been wasted. Tried to decide all sorts of things, big and small. And invariably failed.

On the eighth day of Benjamin's retreat, a new guest from England arrived at St. Wandrille, and moved into the cell next door. From the very beginning, he seemed to differ slightly from the other retreatants. Not in outward appearance, perhaps: he was grey-haired, in late middle age, possibly a little more athletic-looking than most people the monkish life seemed to attract. The real difference lay in his manner. He appeared profoundly ill at ease within the abbey walls. He seemed to speak no French and was constantly looking to Benjamin for guidance on matters of protocol: when to stand, when to kneel, how to address the abbot, and so on. At mealtimes, when the other guests would be withdrawn, contemplative, this man's eyes would dart around the room, anxiously, as if he was trying to make sure that his behaviour was not betraying him in any way. He rarely attended the services, and when he did, he looked even more uncomfortable. Benjamin became convinced that he had some secret to hide.

He resented this man's presence, at first. He had enjoyed being the only other British guest at St. Wandrille. Of course, staying there (he realized this now) was not going to solve any of his problems; but it would, at least, give him the will to start solving them as soon as he got home. Meanwhile, he had begun to feel as though he had been elected to the membership of a more than usually exclusive club, and this notion had always appealed to Benjamin, ever since his membership of the Carlton Club at school. Perhaps that was to demean, slightly, the experience that St. Wandrille had afforded him. It felt less like a club, maybe, than a glorious secret garden, unknown to the outside world, to which Benjamin had been magically offered the key. He could imagine going back to Birmingham, now, and drawing strength from his awareness that this place would always be waiting for him; sitting next to someone on a bus, or standing next to someone in the queue for a sandwich, and taking immeasurable comfort in the thought that these people knew nothing of Benjamin's little paradise-on-earth; that he, *he alone*, knew that it existed, and where it could be found. He felt that there would be no end to what he could achieve, no limits to the vigour with which he could bounce back, if he kept this private knowledge clutched tightly to himself.

Thinking these thoughts late one morning, shortly before lunch, as he sat on a hillside bench high above the valley with the milk-white splendour of the abbey stretched out beneath him, Benjamin found himself being approached by the mysterious guest.

"All right if I join you?" the man asked, breathing fairly heavily from the exertion of having strode up the hill.

"By all means. My name's Benjamin, by the way."

"Good to meet you, Benjamin," said the man, shaking him by the hand as he sat beside him. "And do you mind if I ask you something I've been meaning to ask ever since I arrived?"

"Feel free."

"What on *earth* has brought you to this Godforsaken hole?"

This was not what Benjamin had been expecting to hear; and for a moment he could think of nothing to say in reply.

"That seems . . . an odd phrase to use," he stammered, in the end, "about a monastery."

"Well, it's very pretty here," said the man. "I'll give it that." Belatedly, he held out his hand in return. "Michael's the name: Michael Usborne. Pleased to meet you. Did you read about this place in *Condé Nast Traveller* too?"

It was time to go home. Benjamin was sure of that now. Not just because of the new arrival, although that was reason enough in itself. Usborne had chosen to come to St. Wandrille, apparently, because the press were hounding him following the revelation of the pension scheme he had negotiated for himself after bringing yet another once-successful company almost to the point of liquidation. Benjamin had never heard of Michael Usborne, and was not really interested in the details, but it seemed that he had made something of a career out of this kind of thing. His latest pay-off, all the same, was considered so outrageous that the news had spread beyond the ghetto of the financial pages and made it on to the front of three of the national broadsheets on the day it was announced.

"I've had bloody journalists camped on my doorstep ever since," he said. "How do these people find out where you live? Well, they're not likely to track me down here, at any rate. My spiritual side has been a well-kept secret up till now, and long may it stay that way. Thank Christ for monks! What would we do without them, eh?"

Even before this development, however, Benjamin had been starting to feel a growing sense of confidence, a growing resolve, and the beginnings of an impatience to rejoin the world at large. The symptoms, at first, were not dramatic. He had started walking into the village every day to buy a newspaper and read more about the progress of the war. He had gone to the shop at the rear of the monastery grounds and browsed through the large CD selection; and instead of just buying (as had been his intention) recordings made by the monks themselves, he had bought half a dozen classical CDs as well. He was ready to listen to music again.

One of the albums he bought was a new recording of Honegger's oratorio *Judith*. Benjamin still remembered how it had been playing on the radio when he drove away from Claire's house in Malvern in the summer of 2001, how he had turned the radio on just in time to hear the "Cantique des Vierges," and how moved he had been by it, by the memories it rekindled. Claire had been so kind to him that evening, given him such good advice. She had always been kind to him, now that he thought about it, and he'd never given her much in return. How blind he had been, for so many years, where Claire was concerned! He had always been a little frightened of her, he realized now. She was very much his equal—more than his equal, in most respects—and he had never really been brave enough, perhaps, to enter into a relationship with a woman like that. He and Emily had huddled together behind the screen of their religion, and if she'd never had much to say about his writing or his music, well, that had suited him, in many respects. He didn't like to be challenged. Claire would challenge him, every step of the way. If he wrote something that was no good, she would tell him. But surely that was what he needed. Surely that was what a real friend—a loving friend—would want to do for him. Was he big enough, yet, to cope with it?

He would go to see Claire, as soon as he got back to the Midlands. Pay her a friendly visit, and see what came of it, see where it led them. Listening, now, to the music which he had come to associate with her, and which he had found so serendipitously in the monastery shop, he knew that it was absolutely the right thing to do.

But then . . . then there was also Malvina.

Benjamin sighed, and rolled over in bed. Moonlight peeped in around the edges of his threadbare curtains. How could he compare Claire and Malvina? Well of course, he couldn't. And it was ludicrous, by any rational standard, to suppose that Malvina might make a suitable partner for him. She was twenty years younger than him, for a start. And he hadn't actually seen her for almost three years—although he'd had a text message from her as recently as last October. He could imagine the contempt of his friends and family, if they were ever to become lovers; the sad shaking of heads over silly old Benjamin and his nervous breakdown and his mid-life crisis. (The same contempt *he* had felt for his brother, in fact, during the nightmarish episode—thankfully long over—when Paul and Malvina had themselves been on the point of having an affair.) And indeed, he couldn't explain to *himself*—had never been able to explain—why he had always felt so close to Malvina, from the very first time he saw her. It had little to do with desire, although that came into it. He just felt helplessly, irresistibly drawn to her, as if by some elemental force. Feelings like that couldn't, and shouldn't be ignored. He had never felt anything like that for Claire. Never.

Thinking of text messages stung Benjamin into action. He got out of bed and, for the first time in more than three months, he plugged his mobile phone into the mains and recharged the battery. As soon as it was turned on and the recharging icon started flashing, he waited for it to beep. But, anti-climactically, it remained silent. If any messages had been sent since his disappearance, they must have been deleted by his server some time ago.

He climbed back into bed, and pulled the coarse blankets tight under his chin. Claire and Malvina . . . Malvina and Claire . . . The two names, the two faces, spun around inside his head as he sank into sleep.

The next day, as Benjamin said his farewells to Père Antoine, they talked at some length about books, about poetry, about music. Benjamin told him about the CD he had bought the day before.

"Arthur Honegger," said the brisk, friendly, academic-looking young monk, "was an interesting man. Before I came here, I used to listen to his music a lot. Not the big oratorios so much, but the symphonies. The five symphonies. Do you know them? There is a very . . . *religious* spirit behind that cycle of symphonies. Number three, the *Liturgique*, never failed to move me. It used to shake me to the core, actually. And you know, although his parents were Swiss, he was born very close to here."

"Really?" Benjamin liked to hear about coincidences of this sort. It made him feel that he was on the right path, that he could start to see the patterns behind things.

"Yes, he was born in Le Havre. You can probably still see the house. I expect there is a plaque or something. Are you going back that way?"

"I was going to go to Paris," said Benjamin, "and take the Eurostar."

"Take the ferry," Père Antoine advised. "You'll be able to walk straight on to it this evening, no need to book. And on your way, you can stop for a little while, and pay your respects to a great composer." He put his arm around Benjamin, and clasped him affectionately as he said goodbye. "Good luck, then, Mr. Trotter. And remember, when your poems are published, don't forget St. Wandrille!"

"I won't," said Benjamin. And meant it.

. . .

Benjamin stood on the cliffs above Etretat. High on the chalk. It was a clear evening, and the ocean lay smooth and somnolent. A windless evening, on which it seemed possible to believe that the whole world was at rest. He was not to know that thousands of miles away, in Baghdad, statues of Saddam Hussein were being toppled by cheering crowds as the Americans declared the invasion to have been a success, or that hundreds of miles away in the other direction, on another clifftop above the Irish Sea, on the Llŷn peninsula in North Wales, Paul and Malvina were making plans to escape together while Susan Trotter, in the kitchen of a barn conversion on the rural outskirts of Birmingham, wept over the collapse of her marriage. It's not possible to know everything, after all.

It was half past six in France—half past five across the Channel—and apart from an elderly couple who had walked past him a few minutes ago, arm in arm, Benjamin had seen no one else on the cliff path. He was alone, and free to think: as indeed he had been free to think for the last few weeks and months. But he was bored with this freedom, by now: or rather, worn down by the responsibilities it conferred. Freedom, he was starting to believe—or absolute freedom, at least—was overrated.

He thought, once again, about Claire, and about Malvina. Benjamin found it hard to retain a strong visual memory of people, even the women he was drawn to. When he thought of Malvina he thought of their long confidential meetings at the Waterstone's café—of a time when he had been employed, and married and (he realized now) happy. His feelings for Malvina were infused with the memory of that happiness. When he thought of Claire he thought of a time late at night when he was driving away from her house, and had listened to Honegger's "Cantique des Vierges" on the radio, and had seen the reflection of a yellow full moon in the rear-view mirror of his car. For Benjamin, this was a primal image, an archetype: only by keeping it always in his sights did he feel that he could successfully navigate, from now on, the treacherous waters of his life. And yet somehow, between these two very different, irreconcilable options, a choice now had to be made. Claire and Malvina. Malvina and Claire. How could it ever be done?

He would stand by the decision he had reached earlier that day, on the bus from Yvetot to Etretat.

He took out his mobile, and wrote a quick text message.

U'll probably think I'm mad, but have just realized something: we belong together! Why fight it any longer? Am coming back 2 c u NOW. Ben xxx

Then he sent the message, and walked down the chalk path into Etretat, ready to catch a bus to Le Havre; hoping as he did so that he would have some time to spare before the ferry departed, so that he could stand a while outside the house where Honegger was born, and pay his *hommage.*

2

8 April 2003

Dear Prime Minister,

It is with great regret that I feel I must tender my resignation as a Member of Parliament.

I am doing so entirely for personal, rather than political reasons. Almost three years ago, as you may recall, certain rumours about my private life appeared in the newspapers. I acted swiftly to stop them, and deeply regretted any embarrassment they may have caused to the party. More recently, I am sorry to say, my private life has again become difficult: and this time, rather than let the newspapers get there first, I have resolved to take pre-emptive action. (A concept with which you will be familiar, I'm sure!)

In short, I have decided to leave my wife, Susan, and our two young daughters. Such a step, as you must imagine—being a husband and father yourself—cannot be taken lightly. I have no doubt that, when the press comes to hear about it, I shall be vilified. So be it: this is the media culture we choose to live in. But I am not prepared to let the party suffer as a consequence.

It goes without saying that it has been an honor to serve the Labour party, and you personally, over the last seven years. I truly believe that yours has been, and will continue to be, a great radical and reforming government. History will look back on your achievements in health, public services and education with unqualified admiration. If I may add a more personal judgment relating to New Labour's first years in office, I would say that our crowning glory has been to release the party from the deadening clutch of the trades unions, and to start earning the trust and respect of the business community. It was your genius to recognize that these difficult tasks must be begun, and your courage that has inspired us all never to waver from the chosen path.

As you know, I have never been disloyal to the party, in any parliamentary vote. Six weeks ago, I voted against the rebel amendment on the Iraq war. At the time of my writing this letter, the American-led invasion of Iraq seems on the point of achieving its aim of dislodging Saddam Hussein from power. If this does indeed happen, in the next few hours or days, I would like to congratulate you, again, for holding fast to your principles. The military campaign seems to have been swift, efficient and responsible.

None the less, I feel greater unease about this war than about anything else you have led the party into during your period of office. Was toppling Saddam Hussein indeed the aim? That was not how we presented the matter to the British people. And once he is toppled, what will follow? There seems to be an assumption that the Iraqis, having been bombed to pieces by us, will turn around and welcome us as heroes and saviours as soon as Saddam is gone. Am I alone in considering this an unlikely scenario? My great fear is that we have not even begun to imagine the possible consequences of this Middle Eastern adventure.

I think that I have, in the time since making my decision to resign, acquired a certain clarity which was somehow difficult to attain while I was committed to forging a career in the hothouse atmosphere of Westminster. And the main consequence of this, so far, has been a growing sense that our war with Iraq is impossible to justify. Saddam's Iraq posed no imminent or direct threat to the British people; he had no proven links to international terrorism or the September 11th attacks; we have broken international law; we have weakened the authority of the UN; we have alienated many of our European partners; and, most seriously of all, we have confirmed the worst prejudices of the Muslim world as to the contempt and indifference which they believe the Western people feel towards their beliefs and their way of life. Further terrorist attacks on the West—and on Britain in particular—which before this war were merely likely, are now inevitable.

Voting against the rebel amendment, and for the invasion of Iraq, was the only political act of my career on which I look back with shame. It was such a huge misjudgment, in fact, that it forced me to look hard at my motives for making it; and when I did so, I realized that a complete revolution had taken place in the relationship between my political and personal priorities. It was this realization that led directly to the decision to leave my wife, and so, unavoidably, to the decision to resign.

Please forgive me, Prime Minister, for any distress, embarrassment or polit-

ical damage which my actions might cause. You will read this letter, I suspect, with mounting disbelief and anger. But after giving all of these matters much thought, I am convinced, finally, that I have done the right and honorable thing.

In continuing friendship and admiration.
Yours truly,
Paul Trotter.

From: Paul Trotter
To: Susan
Sent: Tuesday, April 8, 2003 11:07 p.m.
Subject: <None>

Dear Susan

There is no kind way of saying this, so I might as well be direct. I am still in love with Malvina and I have decided to leave home and be with her. I have sent a letter of resignation to Tony. She and I are going to leave the country for a while and then I shall be back in touch. In the meantime of course you must continue to use our joint bank account and credit cards.

Tell the girls that their father loves them and will see them soon.

I'm so sorry.

Paul.

Malvina buzzed the entryphone of Paul's Kennington flat at a quarter to twelve that night.

"What are you doing here?" he said from the doorway, as she reached the top of the staircase. "I said I was going to pick you up in the morning. You're not supposed to come anywhere near this place." Then he saw that she was crying, and put his arms around her trembling frame. "What's happened? What's the matter?"

"My mother," sobbed Malvina. "My stupid, lying, fucking mother."

"What about her? What did she do now?"

In a daze, Malvina walked towards the sitting room and said: "Did you send your letter to Tony?"

"Yes. I did it this afternoon."

"Fuck," she murmured. "What about Susan? Have you said anything to her?"

"I promised you," said Paul, "I was going to tell her today. I sent her an email about half an hour ago."

"Fuck," said Malvina again, more forcefully this time. "*Fuck.*"

She collapsed on to the sofa, and smothered her face in her hands, and her whole body shuddered with weeping.

"Darling," said Paul, sitting beside her, stroking her hair. "What is it? Just tell me."

"We can't be together any more," said Malvina. "It's over. I can't see you again."

"What are you talking about? Why not?"

It took Malvina several minutes to compose herself, to dry her eyes and wipe away the watery snot that was leaking from her reddened nostrils, to reach a point where she felt able to tell her story. She rested her head on Paul's shoulder for a while and then she sat up and faced him, taking hold of both his hands, locking him into her gaze.

"I told my mother about us," she said. "It was the first time I'd told her. She went crazy. Ballistic."

Paul sighed. "But you knew that was going to happen. You always said she'd react that way."

"I know, but this was different. It wasn't just . . . the fact of what's happened between us. It's worse than that. It was when I mentioned *you.*"

"What do you mean?"

"It was when I told her your name."

Paul said nothing; unable to imagine, at this moment, what Malvina could be trying to tell him.

"Paul," she said at last. "She's been lying to me. My mad bitch of a mother has been lying to me, the whole of my life."

He stared back at her. "About what?"

"About me," said Malvina. "About who I am."

Susan picked Ruth up from nursery, and picked Antonia up from school half an hour later. Back at home, she plonked them both in front of the television and started to prepare their dinner. She put three sausages in the oven, along with some fried potatoes shaped like smiley faces, and left some frozen peas in a bowl of shallow water ready for microwaving. When the sausages seemed to be cooking nicely, and the girls were uncomplainingly watching a wildlife programme fronted by a slightly manic young woman with spiky hair, she realized she had a few minutes to spare and popped into the study to check emails.

There was only one message. It was from Paul. She read it once, quickly, and then shut the computer down.

Antonia heard a crash of glass and came running into the study.

"What happened, Mummy, what happened?"

"Nothing, darling," Susan said, her hands and voice shaking. A large Stuart Crystal vase lay shattered next to the far wall—where Susan had thrown it, with all her strength—and the lilies it had contained were strewn among the fragments, in a spreading pool of water. "I knocked it off the shelf by accident, that's all."

"Can I help you clear up?"

"And me!" said Ruth, joining her elder sister in the doorway.

"No, it's all right." Susan knelt down beside them and hugged them fervently. "You go back and watch the television. I'll see to this mess. It's my fault. It's dangerous for you with all this glass around."

The girls disappeared and Susan stood quite still in the middle of the study for a while, waiting for the trembling to stop. She made no attempt to gather up the fragments of glass, or to mop up the water which was sinking deeply into the carpet.

Ten minutes later the smell of burning sausages sent her rushing into the kitchen. The room was filled with smoke and the alarm had gone off, beeping with an obscene insistence that had the girls smothering their ears and shouting, "Too loud, too loud!" Susan turned off the oven and pulled out the grill pan containing the charred sausages. She didn't know how to stop the alarm so she climbed up on to one of the work surfaces, ripped it from the ceiling and pulled the battery out.

"Mummy, are you all right?" Antonia said, when Susan had dropped back down to the floor with the neutralized smoke alarm in her hand. "You keep doing silly things."

"I'm fine, darling, fine." She put her arm around her elder daughter and guided her back towards the sitting room. "I've just got a lot to think about today, that's all. Never mind. I'll do you some fish fingers instead." She glanced at the television screen, in front of which sat Ruth, transfixed by a children's news programme which was broadcasting images of a statue being pulled to the ground by a jubilant mob. "What's all this about?"

"There's been a big war," Antonia said, knowledgeably. "In Iraq. But it's over now, and everything's going to get better."

Susan looked at the faces of the crowd and wasn't so sure. So this was how it was going to end. Or perhaps start. The Iraqis looked exhilarated, to her, but also stunned. And there was a kind of mania in their eyes. A kind of fury: the fury of a people who had been granted freedom, of sorts, but not on their own terms; a people whose liberation had come too brutally, too swiftly; a people who would never feel kindly towards those who had freed them; would never trust their motives. A people who did not know what to do with their freedom, yet, and would soon turn their energies into hatred against those who had bestowed it on them, uninvited, unasked.

Watching the cloudy television screen through tear-filled eyes, Susan knew, at that moment, exactly how they felt.

"No, nothing," said Paul. "More than thirty messages about my resignation, but nothing from her."

He switched off his laptop, disconnected his mobile from the USB port and locked the doors of his car. It seemed that you had to come to this point—the highest point on the peninsula—to get any mobile reception at all. He had been checking his emails every half hour, waiting to see if there was a message from Susan. But she had made no attempt to contact him so far.

"Perhaps she never got it," Malvina suggested.

"I'll check again in a little while," Paul said. "Come on—we might as well go for a walk while we're up here."

It was half past five on the evening of Wednesday, April 9th, 2003: an evening of impossible stillness, where the buzzing of a fly amongst the heather could seem like an event of consequence. Paul and Malvina were walking on the headland above Rhîw, at the westernmost tip of the Llŷn peninsula in North Wales. It was the remotest place he could think of: no one would be likely to recognize him here. Besides which, he had been seized, unexpectedly, by a pressing desire to revisit the places he had last seen as a child, on the caravanning holidays he had enjoyed (or rather endured) with his family back in the 1970s. These places were part of his history. Part of Malvina's, too, he now realized. They had driven up from London the night before, starting from Kennington at two o'clock in the morning, and arriving in time for breakfast at a café in Pwllheli. After that they drove on and a few hours later checked into an otherwise deserted bed and breakfast, in the tiny, inaccessible seaside village of Aberdaron.

Now, they scrambled up towards the ragged escarpment of Creigiau Gwineu until they reached the summit and were rewarded with a view of Porth Neigwl—Hell's Mouth—the bay that stretched beneath them for more than five miles, enclosed by two great mounds of headland, thrusting out from the coastline like vampire's teeth. Benjamin had looked down on this view once, almost twenty-five years ago. In fact, as they stumbled along the descent to the clifftops, Paul and Malvina, unknowingly, were following the same path taken by Benjamin and Cicely one equally still and silent afternoon in the late summer of 1978. Like his brother before him, Paul took his partner's hand and guided her along a sheep-path through the bristling gorse. Before reaching the edge of the cliffs they came upon a broad and well-worn path which clung low to the headland. Here they turned left and walked in the direction of Porth Neigwl. Just as the path started to curve inland, a wide, flat rock jutted out from the bracken. It was the perfect place to sit. There was just room for two people, provided that they wanted to sit as close to each other as possible.

Paul spread his overcoat over the cold surface of the rock, and Malvina nestled beside him.

They sat for some minutes in silence. There is not much point in talking, when confronted with a landscape of almost indescribable beauty.

"Amazing spot, isn't it?" said Paul, in the end, conscious of the inadequacy of his own words. "I didn't really notice it when I was little. Sort of took it for granted. My nose was always in a book, in those days. I used to lie in my tent reading up on economic theory."

"I love it here," said Malvina quietly. "It feels like home." Then she sighed. "How much longer can we stay, do you think? A few more days?"

"We'd better move on tomorrow, or the day after. I think if we can get to Holyhead we should cross over to Dublin, and we must be able to get a flight to Germany from there."

Their ultimate destination was Binz, on the island of Rügen, where Rolf Baumann had a holiday home. Paul had phoned him shortly before they set out on their journey, and Rolf—his voice thick with sleep—had assured him that the house was at their disposal. He asked how long they would be staying, but didn't seem to mind when Paul admitted that he didn't know. And it was true: he and Malvina had no plans, at this stage, no real sense of how long they would have to go into hiding. They only knew that what she had learned from her mother, yesterday, made no difference to their feelings for each other. They had to be together: that was beyond doubt; their only constant.

Malvina closed her eyes and took deep breaths. She felt light-headed from lack of sleep. "This is crazy," she said. "It feels so crazy. I still can't believe it's happening."

"We have to get away," Paul insisted. "We have no choice."

"I don't mean that, so much. I mean what *you're* doing. You've given everything up. You've lost everything."

"It doesn't feel like that," said Paul. "It feels exactly the opposite."

Malvina kissed him. It was a kiss of gratitude, at first, but like all their kisses, it soon turned into something else. Before it got out of hand, she broke away and said: "This ought to feel bad. Really bad, what we're doing. But it doesn't."

They huddled closer together after that, and when it grew cold Paul pulled his overcoat from beneath them and they draped it around their shoulders, and the silence was unbroken again, apart from the mournful cries of the gulls as they wheeled around the cliffs. Paul and Malvina felt a great calm, and a great certainty, which seemed to make all the risks they were taking seem small and unimportant. The sun, sinking into a coppery haze behind Ynys Enlli, Bardsey Island, shone its dying light upon them, filling them with both sadness and hope. The luminous immensity of the early-evening sky made Paul think of Skagen, and he realized now that the two places, Skagen and Llŷn, were linked, somehow. These were the places that had pointed him towards his destiny; staging posts on the same long, inevitable journey.

The sudden electronic beep of Malvina's mobile sounded unimaginably loud and intrusive. She fished it from her pocket and glanced at the screen.

"Text message," she said, and quickly called up her Inbox. She blinked with surprise when she saw who it was from; and was even more surprised when she saw the message itself.

> U'll probably think I'm mad, but have just realized something: we belong together! Why fight it any longer? Am coming back 2 c u NOW. Ben xxx

"Oh," she said, simply, and clipped the phone shut. She stared out to sea for a second or two, trying to take in the implications of what she had just read.

"Who was it from?" Paul asked.

Malvina turned to him and answered: "Well, believe it or not, it was from Benjamin, of all people." Paul appeared stunned. "Your brother," she added, as if it needed any further explanation. "My father."

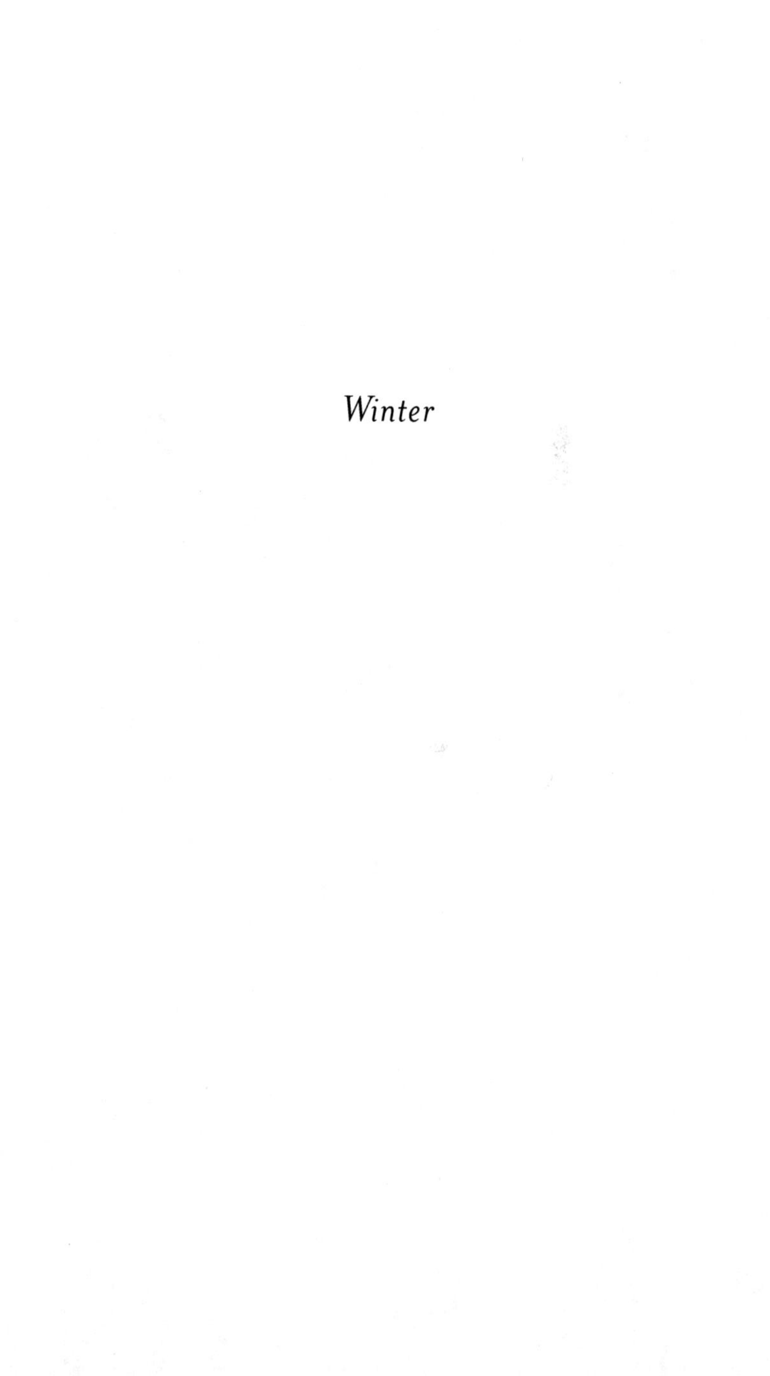

Winter

I

The afternoon of Friday, November 21st, 2003 was cold, crisp and clear. Even at this time of year, Berlin hummed with tourists, and by three o'clock the lobby of the Hotel Adlon on Unter den Linden was as busy as ever. Groups of hotel guests and sightseers were sprawled in various stages of exhaustion, while waiters drifted smoothly between the richly upholstered sofas, bearing silver platters loaded with tea pots and bone china cups and gargantuan slices of cake. Patrick stared with some apprehension at the cream-laden strawberry cheesecake that had just been placed before him, and Phil poked uncertainly with his spoon at a wedge of glazed tart smothered in blackberries, cherries and blueberries, unable to find a suitable angle of entry to scoop out his first mouthful. Water spilled from a fountain in the center of the lobby, its liquid susurrations blending seamlessly with the music drifting down from the upper terrace, where a pianist was working his way discreetly through a repertoire of standards: "Night and Day," "Some Other Time," "All the Things You Are." Everything was part of a serious, expensively mounted effort to evoke an atmosphere of Middle European elegance; and it was almost working. But the hotel had been destroyed during the Communist era, and rebuilt in the 1990s, and to Philip it all felt too clean, and too new. You couldn't manufacture old-world charm from scratch in a matter of years.

"I've just remembered," he said, taking the plunge and carving out a bite-sized chunk from his cake. "I bought a record once, by Henry Cow—on Benjamin's recommendation, of course. And there was a track on that called 'Upon Entering the Hotel Adlon.' It starts with a drum roll and this primal scream, and then for the next three minutes everyone just bangs away on their instruments like maniacs. It was the kind of thing we liked listening to, in those days."

"Uh-huh," said Patrick, yawning.

"Come to think of it," Phil continued, thinking aloud, "the title of that album was *Unrest.* That's probably where he stole it from. The title of his unfinished masterpiece."

It had been Carol's idea, that Philip and his son should go away for a few days together by themselves. Patrick had been reading biology at University College, London for just two months now. He wasn't good at replying to emails, or returning phone calls, and they had little sense of how he was settling in. He rarely mentioned the names of any new friends, male or female. (His relationship with Rowena—as Claire had predicted—had not lasted more than a few weeks after their visit to Grand Cayman last year.) And so Philip had decided on Berlin (having always wanted to go there), had spent an hour or two on the internet, and found a flight that was so cheap that it freed up enough money to fulfil a long-held fantasy and stay for two nights in the city's most expensive and famous hotel. They had flown out from Stansted the day before. It meant that Patrick would miss a lecture or two, but nothing serious. Now, after a gruelling morning's visit to the Kulturforum, they had nothing more strenuous planned for the afternoon than finishing these cakes and perhaps spending an hour or two burning off the accumulated calories in the hotel spa.

"Ah—'The Night Has A Thousand Eyes,'" said Phil, recognizing the pianist's latest tune. "Stéphane Grappelli used to do a nice version of this. You've probably never heard of him."

"I have, actually, Dad. I'm not a complete ignoramus, you know."

Philip watched his son as he took a museum catalogue out of a plastic bag and started to flick through it. The nervousness, the wary self-consciousness that Claire had once identified in him was starting to slip away. Something of his mother's strength of character was beginning to emerge in his face, now. Philip had been vaguely hoping that, during this trip, they would get a chance to talk about some of the things that had happened in the last year—the discovery of the truth about Miriam, first of all, and then the reappearance of Stefano in Claire's life, and her decision to return to Italy—but he realized now that there was no need. He would certainly not try to force a conversation on these subjects. From what he could tell, Patrick seemed contented in London, and optimistic about the future. He glanced at his face one more time, then took up the history of Berlin he had brought with him from Birmingham central library, and for a while, father and son read together in silence.

A few minutes later, there was a commotion on the other side of the lobby. Philip had noticed that there was an English couple sitting there: a young, attractive woman of about Patrick's age, and another woman Philip assumed must be her mother. The mother was sitting with her back to them, so he had not seen her face. Now, suddenly, she appeared to be in some distress. There was a clatter of crockery as she stumbled to her feet, clipping the edge of her tray as she did so, and then as her daughter stood up beside her, the mother swooned and fell, landing heavily in her daughter's arms. She had not fainted, exactly, but she seemed to be having a mild fit of some sort. "It's all right, Mum, it's all right," her daughter was saying. And as she walked her towards the revolving door at the entrance to the hotel—saying to the concerned staff who swarmed around them, "It's OK, she'll be fine, she just needs some air"—Philip caught a glimpse of a deathly white face, and eyes swimming with tears, and this face triggered off a long-lost memory.

"What's up with those two?" Patrick asked, looking up without much interest.

"I don't know . . ." Philip stared after them, trying to remember where he had seen the mother before. Then he noticed something: the piano music wafting down to them from the upper terrace. "Wait a minute. This song—do you recognize it?"

Patrick sighed. "We're not going to spend the whole trip playing 'Name That Tune,' are we?"

"It's Cole Porter—'I Get A Kick Out Of You.'" He jumped to his feet. "I know who that woman is—it's Lois Trotter."

Philip hurried towards the door, with Patrick following him.

"How do you know that, Dad?" he was asking.

"Because Benjamin told me once that she can't bear to hear that song. It always has a terrible effect on her."

They pushed their way through the revolving door and felt a slap of cold air as they came out on to the broad boulevard of Unter den Linden. Lois and her daughter Sophie were standing by the wall of the hotel. Lois was leaning against the wall, taking deep breaths, and Sophie was trying to allay the fears of the liveried doorman, who was addressing her in tones of great concern and apparently trying to persuade her to call an ambulance.

"It's all right, really," Sophie was saying. "I've seen this happen before. It only lasts for a few moments."

Philip stepped forward. Mother and daughter regarded him with equal suspicion.

"It's Lois, isn't it? Lois Trotter?" He turned to Sophie. "We've never met, but I'm a friend of your uncle Benjamin's. Philip Chase. This is my son, Patrick."

"Oh—hello." Sophie shook their hands, uncertainly. She seemed taken aback by this development; and Philip had to admit that his timing wasn't great.

"Is your mother all right?" he asked.

"I think we should just get into a taxi," said Sophie, "and go back to our hotel. We were only having tea at the Adlon. She needs to rest for a while."

"Hello, Philip," Lois now said, unexpectedly. She was no longer leaning against the wall, and some of the colour was beginning to return to her face. "That bloody music. It gets me every bloody time . . ." She leaned forward, and kissed him on the cheek. "Good to see you again. It's been ages, hasn't it?"

"Come on, Mum," Sophie tugged on her sleeve. "There's a taxi waiting."

"What are you doing in Berlin?" Lois asked.

"We're just visiting," said Philip. "Maybe we could meet up later."

"That would be lovely."

"I'm sorry," Sophie said, glancing back at Philip and Patrick, as she led her mother away. "She has to rest. It's very important."

"Of course. I understand." Philip watched Sophie ease her mother gently into the back seat of the taxi, and had the presence of mind to ask, just as she was closing the door: "Where are you staying?"

"The Dietrich!" Sophie called back; and then they were gone.

Two hours later, Philip called their hotel and spoke to Sophie. Lois was feeling much better, apparently, and they were on the point of going out to do some late shopping. Philip told them that he had booked a table for two, that night, at the revolving restaurant at the top of the Fernsehturm—the old television tower overlooking Alexanderplatz, in former East Berlin. Would Lois and Sophie like to join them? Sophie wasn't sure that it was the kind of thing her mother would feel comfortable with. Maybe they could talk about it later. The shops they were planning to visit were in Kurfürstendamm, not far from their hotel. They would only be an hour or so. Perhaps Sophie and Lois could come for a drink at the Adlon afterwards? It was settled: they agreed to meet in the lobby bar at seven o'clock.

. . .

Lois didn't like the idea of the Fernsehturm. Too high. She didn't like lifts. And she didn't like revolving restaurants. Sophie, on the other hand, was intrigued. So was Patrick. Philip told them that the food there wasn't meant to be very good, and suggested that they cancel the booking and go somewhere else. Sophie and Patrick seemed disappointed. Lois, who had had some cocktails by now, and was thoroughly entering into the spirit of the reunion, apologized for being a killjoy. The others told her not to be silly. They bought more cocktails. Lois had been stuck in an international conference on university librarianship for the last three days. It had finished at lunchtime, and she was feeling high on her new-found freedom. But still she didn't want to travel up in a lift to a revolving restaurant.

Finally it was decided that Sophie and Patrick should have the table at the Fernsehturm, while Philip and Lois should look for somewhere else to eat. They would all meet back at the Adlon for a final drink at the end of the evening. It was an arrangement that seemed to please everyone.

The Fernsehturm was approached, unprepossessingly, through a concrete precinct powerfully evocative of everything that had been disastrous about the architecture of the 1960s, whether in Eastern or Western Europe. Even at 8:30 on this cold and wintry night, tourists were still pouring in. Patrick and Sophie had to stand in a queue for the lift, in a crowd mainly of schoolchildren and backpackers. They felt somewhat overdressed. The lift was much smaller than they had been expecting: they were crammed in with a dozen other visitors, and an attendant who recited toneless statistics about the tower as the elevator car shot skyward with a velocity that made their ears pop.

Already late for their table, they didn't linger on the observation floor, but made directly for the curved stairway that led to the restaurant. A waitress, beaming at them intimidatingly, as if it was a racing certainty that they were about to have one of the best evenings of their lives, led them to an empty table and turned the table-lamp on. She explained that if they wanted to look at the view, it was better to have the lamp switched off; but they might find this a little gloomy. They each managed a shy "*Danke schön,*" and took immediate refuge in their menus, which seemed designed to appeal to hearty rather than gourmet appetites. Sophie ordered duck breast with almond broccoli and boiled potatoes; Patrick took a chance on pork fillet with *spätzle.* They sipped their glasses of dry Riesling and watched as the vast, brightly lit glass-and-concrete extravagance of the new Reichstag revolved into distant view.

"I didn't think the platform would go round quite so quickly," said Patrick, watching the cityscape skim past, surreally, behind the reflection of Sophie's face in the slanted windowpane.

"It takes half an hour to do a complete turn, apparently," said Sophie. "Look—there's the moon. Every time we see it, we'll know half an hour's gone by."

A full moon was hanging over the Reichstag and the Tiergarten, further illuminating the features of this glimmering, electrified city. Patrick thought of his mother, and the two nights he knew she had spent alone, a few years ago, on the twenty-third floor of the Hyatt Regency in Birmingham, looking down on a probably not dissimilar view. He missed her suddenly, fiercely, with an ache that had not become any easier to live with over the years.

It was an odd situation Sophie and Patrick had been thrown into, this evening. There had seemed to be a spontaneous intimacy between their parents, even though it was so long since they had known each other. They had flung themselves into their reunion with a sort of joyous relief, as if this chance encounter in a Berlin tea-room could somehow erase the intervening decades, heal the pain of their passing. That had left Sophie and Patrick floundering in a different, more awkward kind of intimacy. They had nothing in common, they realized, except their parents' histories.

"Where do you think they've gone?" Sophie asked.

"Clubbing, probably. Checking out the techno places."

"Are you serious?"

"Of course not. My dad's never been to a club in his life. The last album he bought was by Barclay James Harvest."

"Who?"

"Exactly."

Sophie asked Patrick if his father ever talked much about his schooldays. Patrick said that just recently he had started to talk about them more. Earlier in the year he had been to Norfolk to visit an old friend called Sean Harding. The visit had seemed to affect him profoundly, but Patrick wasn't sure why. He didn't really know who Sean Harding was.

"I can tell you," said Sophie. "I can tell you that whole story, if you like. I've heard it all from my mother, you see. She has perfect recall of those days."

"How come?"

"Well . . ."

And then Sophie began to explain. It was hard to know where to start. The era they were discussing seemed to belong to the dimmest recesses of history. She said to Patrick: "Do you ever try to imagine what it was like before you were born?"

And so Sophie and Patrick spent that evening telling each other stories. Sophie told the story of Harding and his anarchic schoolboy jokes; the rivalry between Richards and Culpepper; the teenage love affair between Benjamin and Cicely. And Patrick told her the story of how Benjamin and Cicely's daughter, Malvina, conceived on the morning of May 2nd, 1979—the only time they had ever made love—had unknowingly sought out her father twenty years later, only to find herself falling in love, instead, with his younger brother Paul. And he told her, too, the story of his mother, Claire, and how she had finally uncovered the truth about her sister's disappearance in the winter of 1974.

As they told these stories, the platform of the restaurant revolved, and they saw the full moon go by six times, until it was almost midnight, and the smiling waiters and waitresses were standing by the doors to the observation floor, waiting for them to leave. And when the full moon was hanging again over the Reichstag and the Tiergarten, they knew that it was time to go, and that the circle had closed for the last time.

It was a clear, blueblack, starry night, in the city of Berlin, in the year 2003. Patrick and Sophie walked together through the now quiet streets, along Karl-Liebknecht-Strasse and Unter den Linden until they had almost reached Pariser Platz and the Hotel Adlon. As they crossed the wide boulevard, a taxi pulled out quickly behind them from a side street, and they had to run across the final stretch of road. Patrick grabbed Sophie's hand to pull her after him, and when they reached the safety of the pavement, he did not let go.

As they passed the hotel, they saw there were only two people still sitting in the windows of the Restaurant Quarré on the ground floor: Philip and Lois. Patrick and Sophie waved to them, and gestured silently ahead in the direction of the Brandenburg Gate, to let them know that they had not quite done with walking yet.

Philip and Lois had not ventured far that evening. They had moved only a few yards, in fact, from the lobby bar to the Restaurant Quarré, where they were given a window table without a reservation because the *maitre d'* recognized Lois from her fainting fit a few hours earlier.

They could hardly avoid talking about Lois's brothers, for most of the meal. It was some weeks since Philip had heard any news of Benjamin. He knew that he was down in London, and reunited with Cicely. Lois also said that he'd got another job, now, with a big firm of City accountants.

"The thing nobody ever really explained to me," she said, "was how Cicely managed to find him again in the first place."

"Oh, that was simple," Philip answered. "We have Doug to thank for that. When she finally came back to London—having been in Sardinia for a few years, I think—one of the first things she did was to email Doug at the paper. He puts his address at the bottom of every column, you see. So he was the one who gave her Ben's address in Birmingham. And then, of course, when Benjamin got back from his travels, he couldn't believe it when Doug told him that she'd been trying to get back in touch. He probably went out and found her that afternoon."

To which Lois said, surprisingly: "Poor Malvina. That would have been the last thing she wanted to happen."

"Why do you say that?"

"Because she's always wanted to keep them apart. She's always wanted that, more than anything. For Benjamin's sake." Philip seemed puzzled, so she asked: "Did you ever meet her?"

"Only once—very briefly, a few years ago, at the rally for Longbridge."

"I spent a whole day with her," said Lois, quietly, reflectively. "And I'm glad that I did. I understand things better now. And I'm not angry with her any more."

"When was this?" said Philip.

"A couple of months ago. In Germany. Only a few hundred miles from here, as it happens—up on the coast. That's where she and Paul have been . . . hiding out. I went to see them both—actually it was Paul I really wanted to see, to ask him what the hell he thought he was doing—but he miraculously disappeared that day. I never got to see him at all. It was Malvina I spoke to."

Then, slowly, she began to tell Philip everything she had learned that day.

"I think about four years ago, Malvina must have been starting to despair. I mean, imagine it. She's been born in some Godforsaken town in the middle of America to a twenty-year-old mother who's going through a lesbian phase. When that falls apart, she gets shunted from man to man, from father-figure to father-figure. As for her *real* father, Cicely thinks so little of him that she won't even tell her daughter who it is. Builds up this fantasy, instead, of some genius set designer who's supposed to have died of AIDS in the eighties. So Malvina has this huge . . . *absence* to contend with all her life, and on top of that, Cicely herself. For twenty years! Twenty years of Cicely, having a nervous breakdown every time one of these guys leaves her and crying endlessly on her little daughter's shoulder and telling her what a terrible terrible person she is. What must *that* do to you, after a while? And then the latest relationship starts looking rocky, and for the first time ever, Cicely is starting to look ill—I mean, *really* ill this time, no play-acting—and suddenly Malvina realizes that she can't do this any more. She can't do it alone. But she can't bring herself just to walk out on her mother, either.

"And then, she discovers something, something that gives her an idea. She finds an old tape someone made for Cicely, when she was still at school. It has a little piece of music on it, written for piano and guitar, called *Seascape No. 4*. The playing isn't very good and the recording quality's dreadful—half way through the piece she can even hear a cat miaowing in the background—but even that gives it a kind of charm, and it makes no difference to the really important thing, the thing she realizes as soon as she hears it: that the person who wrote this music must really have loved her mother. She becomes obsessed with this tape and starts listening to it over and over. And she starts asking her mother questions about the person who wrote the music, but all Cicely will tell her is that it was someone she knew at school called Benjamin. It's not much to go on but in the end it's all that Malvina needs. A few hours on the internet and she's worked out that his name must have been Benjamin Trotter and nowadays he works for a firm of accountants in Birmingham. So up to Birmingham she goes, some time in the winter of 1999.

"She gets talking to the receptionist at Benjamin's office, and before long she knows who to look out for. She follows him to a bookshop and follows him into the café and waits for her moment, and soon enough it comes. But of course, she doesn't have any kind of game plan. Somewhere at the back of her mind is the thought that here's somebody who might be able to come to her rescue, one day, to take Cicely off her hands. But she only has to talk to him for a few minutes to know that it's not going to work, that she can't go through with it. Not because he's forgotten her—oh no. Quite the opposite, as it happens. He talks about Cicely the very first time he and Malvina meet, because he tells her about this epic novel-with-music that he's writing, and admits that one of the things that's driving him on—the main thing, in a way—is the thought that he's still writing it for her, to prove something to her, that it's a kind of present that one day he wants to lay at her feet. He doesn't know *how* this is going to happen, exactly, he doesn't seem to have thought it through, but he seems to have no doubt that once this thing is published, or released, once it's *out there*, anyway, Cicely will know about it and . . . what? Come running back to him? God only knows." Lois looked down, wincing, her brow furrowed with pity. "Well—whatever. Malvina's in no doubt that he's still in thrall to her, at any rate. But this is exactly what makes her realize, after a while, that she can't go through with the plan. There's a big problem, you see, something she hadn't anticipated. She *likes* Benjamin. Really, really likes him. And she feels so sorry for him, too, for the way he's locked himself inside this obsession and it's ruined everything for him, in the end—his work, his marriage, his whole life up to that point. She knows that seeing Cicely again is the thing he wants most of all; and she also knows that it would be the very worst thing that could happen to him. So she keeps quiet. In no time at all she's learned to do what all of Benjamin's friends learn to do, sooner or later. You don't mention the C-word.

"No doubt the sensible thing would have been to get straight on the train to London and never come back. But she's drawn to Benjamin, for reasons she can't explain. She feels incredibly close to him. And he senses this too, and feels the same way, but because he doesn't know what's going on, he gets confused, and starts to wonder whether really she fancies him, whether there's some kind of attraction building up here. Of course, being Benjamin, he doesn't act upon this, doesn't do anything crass like jumping on her or trying to start an affair, but still, when they see each other again, and the time after that, and the time after that, he makes the mistake of keeping it a secret from Emily, and before long, for him, it's started to *feel* like an affair, even if there's nothing like that really happening. So he gets into a bit of a muddle over it. And all Malvina's thinking, in the meantime, is how comfortable she feels with this person, how nice he is to be around, how *kind* he's being to her. Because he *is* kind, Benjamin. Nobody would deny him that. And Malvina notices that he listens to what she has to say—not many people listen to her, it's an unusual experience, at first—and he takes an interest in the fact that she wants to write, and he takes an interest in what she's doing at university in London. And that's where his kindness leads him to make a big mistake.

"Malvina's doing media studies, and she's doing a project that year on politics and the media, with specific reference to New Labour. So what does Benjamin suggest, with that big heart of his? 'Oh, you should really have a word with my brother.' And of course, Malvina jumps at this idea. Paul's not very keen, at first, but then Benjamin tells him how pretty she is, and that seems to do the trick, and—well, the rest you know . . ." She gazed out of the window, looking back over this train of events, trying to make sense of it. "It all started," she realized, "with that piece of music. Recorded in my grandparents' house. Decades ago. That's where it all began . . ."

She looked up, suddenly aware that a waiter was hovering over her. It was late in the evening, now, and he had come to offer them coffee.

When he had left, Philip asked: "How much of this do your parents know?"

Lois shook her head. "Almost nothing. Well, they know that Paul and Malvina are together now, obviously . . ."

"But they don't know . . . who she is?"

"We've got to keep it from them," Lois said. "They couldn't handle it. The only thing I can hope is that it doesn't last much longer. Malvina's coming back to London more and more. She sees Cicely. Benjamin won't see her. Not while she's living with Paul. But I wonder if she'll realize, soon, what a terrible mistake she's making. I think she might." She looked up and smiled; a brittle, unhappy smile. "Her writing's coming on, apparently. Did you ever see anything of hers?"

"No, I can't say I have."

"Well, I don't suppose I would've done, either, except that I was shelving the new periodicals last week, and I saw that she had something in one of them. A poem."

"Did you read it?"

Lois nodded.

"What was it about?"

"Fathers. Fathers and daughters. Ironic, isn't it—that Benjamin's daughter, of all people, should make it into print before he does? I wonder how he'll feel about that, if he ever finds out." She sipped her coffee. "Anyway: that's why I try not to blame Malvina, too much. Her motives were good—some of them. Paul's the one I blame. He's the one I can never forgive. None of us can. The fucking . . . *idiot.*" The word suddenly came out with terrible force, terrible venom. Philip would never have imagined that Lois could speak like this. "Abandoning Susan and the girls. Giving it all up, giving up *everything*. I mean, what does he think he's going to do? What's he going to do when it all falls apart?"

"Oh, you'd be surprised," said Philip, wearily. "Paul will be back. Sooner rather than later."

"I don't see how. His political career's finished."

"He's got a lot of contacts in the business community. A lot of good friends. They'll find something for him. The thing is, people like Paul always bounce back. Always. Look at Michael Usborne. After he ran that last company into the ground and parachuted out with a couple of million, everyone said he was finished. But now he's back and he's running a bloody electricity company. These people aren't like the rest of us. They're invincible."

Lois didn't know who Michael Usborne was. Philip explained, as well as he could, the story of his involvement with Paul—and the even stranger story of his brief, unsuccessful relationship with Claire, which had ended this time last year with their holiday in the Cayman Islands.

"And is Claire OK?" Lois wanted to know. "How's she managing, these days?"

"Claire," said Philip, with undisguised delight, "could not be happier. She's gone back to Italy and she's with the man she loves and the last time I saw her she was looking about ten years younger."

"Benjamin told me something about this," said Lois, remembering a conversation they'd had in Dorset last year. "He was married, wasn't he?"

"To a woman who was cheating on him. Claire was convinced he'd never find it in him to leave her. But he did, in the end. And he flew all the way to England to tell her about it. *And* he sued for custody of his daughter. *And* he won."

"I'm glad about that," said Lois. "Very glad. If anybody deserves to be happy, it's Claire."

Philip stirred his coffee, slowly, thoughtfully, and said: "And then there's you, of course."

"Me?"

"You. The quiet one. The one that nobody really talks about. You deserve to be happy, too, Lois. Are you?"

There was a gentle bravery in Lois's voice as she looked at Philip and said: "Of course I am. I've got a job I like. A husband who loves me. A wonderful daughter. What more could I want?"

Philip met her eyes, and smiled quickly. After which he looked away, and said something she could not possibly have been anticipating. "'What is the name of your goldfish?'"

Lois frowned. "I beg your pardon?"

"'What is the name of your goldfish?' That was the last thing I ever said to you. Don't you remember?"

"No—when was this?"

"Twenty-nine years ago. I was round at your parents' house. They threw a dinner party, for my mum and dad. You were wearing an incredibly low-cut dress. I couldn't take my eyes off your cleavage."

"I don't remember this *at all*," Lois said. "Anyway, I never even had a goldfish."

"I know. You were talking to my dad about *Colditz*, the television programme. I misheard what you were saying. Then I asked that question and it reduced the whole table to silence. Seriously, Lois, I was so consumed with lust for you that I couldn't even make myself understood in the English language that night."

"I wish I'd known," said Lois. "You weren't a bad-looking little thing in those days. History might have been very different."

"It would never have happened. You were already spoken for."

"Ah, yes. Of course I was." She looked down at the table, remembering that evening now; and also remembering Malcolm, her first boyfriend, who was never out of her thoughts for more than a few hours. There was a long silence. Philip wondered if he had done the wrong thing, reminiscing about an occasion which touched upon that charged, bitterly sad episode, however obliquely. When Lois finally spoke again, her voice seemed far off, tiny. "You never forget," she told him. "Just when you think you've forgotten, something comes back. Something like that tune, that Cole Porter song. You think it's over and done with, but it never is. It's always there. Those images . . ." She sighed, closed her eyes, withdrew into herself for a second or two. "You just have to go on. That's all there is to do, isn't it? What else is there? What other choice? You just have to go on, and you try to forget about it, but you can't, because even if it's not a piece of music there's always something else, something else that brings it all back to you. Christ, you only have to turn on the television. Lockerbie. September the 11th. Bali. I've watched them all. I can't keep away from them, in a terrible kind of way. And the worst of it is, it never stops. It never stops, and it gets worse and worse. Mombasa, this time last year. Sixteen people killed. Riyadh. Forty-six people killed. Casablanca. Thirty-three people. Jakarta. Fourteen people.

And now Istanbul. Have you heard the news since you've been here? Thirty people killed, yesterday, by a suicide bomber at the British consulate. Have you seen what they're doing to the embassy here, just around the corner? Great concrete blocks in the middle of the road, to stop anyone driving a truck full of explosives into it? And that's nothing, Philip—*nothing*—compared to the people the Americans killed in Iraq this year. Every one of those people meant something. Every one of them was like Malcolm, to somebody. Fathers killed, mothers killed, children killed. The *rage* that's building up in the world, Philip, because of all this! The rage!"

She looked away, out of the window, her cheeks glistening. Philip said: "I hadn't heard about Istanbul. That's bad. Really bad."

"There are going to be more," said Lois. "I'm sure of it. It's only a matter of time before something worse happens. Something *huge* . . ."

She tailed off, and soon afterwards caught sight of Sophie and Patrick, walking together towards Pariser Platz. The young couple waved at them, and their parents waved back.

"Well, they seem to have had a good evening," said Philip, pouring more coffee for Lois and himself.

"I thought something like that might happen," she murmured. "Maybe our dynasties are going to be joining up after all."

"Maybe," said Philip. "It's a little bit early to say."

"Yes," Lois agreed. "You're right. It's a little bit early to say."

And they watched in silence as Patrick and Sophie walked beneath the great arch of the Brandenburg Gate, hand in hand; the two of them wanting nothing more from life, at that moment, than the chance to repeat the mistakes their parents had made, in a world which was still trying to decide whether to allow them even that luxury.

Synopsis of
The Rotters' Club

Birmingham, England, 1973. LOIS TROTTER (aged seventeen) answers a lonely hearts advertisement and starts going out with MALCOLM, a man in his early twenties, also known as The Hairy Guy. Meanwhile her younger brother BENJAMIN TROTTER (aged thirteen) attends King William's School and converts to Christianity after a bizarre, quasi-religious experience: having forgotten to take his swimming trunks to school one day, terrified that the PE master will make him swim in the nude in front of his classmates, Benjamin prays to be saved from this humiliation and his prayer is answered when he immediately discovers a spare pair of swimming trunks in an empty locker.

Benjamin's best friends at school are SEAN HARDING (an anarchic prankster), the quiet and conscientious PHILIP CHASE, and DOUG ANDERTON. Doug's father BILL ANDERTON is a leading shop steward at the British Leyland car factory in Longbridge. He is having an affair with MIRIAM NEWMAN, an attractive young secretary. But the affair is making Miriam miserable, and she threatens to bring it to an end.

On 21st November, 1974, Malcolm takes Lois to a pub in central Birmingham called The Tavern in the Town, intending to propose marriage to her. An IRA bomb explodes in the pub and Malcolm is killed. A wave of anti-Irish feeling spreads through Birmingham in the subsequent days and weeks; and, shortly afterwards, Miriam Newman disappears without trace. Nobody knows whether she has run off with another man, or something more sinister has happened.

. . .

Two years later, in the summer of 1976, the Trotter family go on holiday to Skagen in Denmark, with the family of Gunther Baumann, a friend and business associate of Benjamin's father. Lois remains in England: she has not yet recovered from the shock of seeing Malcolm die, and is still hospitalized. During this holiday, Gunther's fourteen-year-old son ROLF BAUMANN makes enemies of the two Danish boys in the house next door, and they try to drown him at the treacherous meeting point of the Kattegat and Skaggerak seas. Benjamin's younger brother PAUL, now aged twelve, dives in and saves Rolf's life.

Back in England, Benjamin joins the editorial staff of the school magazine, *The Bill Board.* His colleagues include Doug, Philip, EMILY SANDYS and Miriam's younger sister, CLAIRE NEWMAN. One of the stories they cover concerns the deadly athletic and personal rivalry between RONALD CULPEPPER and STEVE RICHARDS—the only black boy in the school, popularly known as "Rastus." Culpepper is disliked by almost everyone at King William's, with the exception of Paul Trotter, who is beginning to show a precocious interest in politics, and who persuades Culpepper to let him join a secretive school discussion group known as The Closed Circle.

Benjamin writes a review of the school production of *Othello*, savaging the performance of CICELY BOYD even though he is hopelessly in love with her. However, Cicely is grateful for the review, and becomes his friend. The rivalry between Culpepper and Richards intensifies, Lois slowly begins to recover, and Harding's humour becomes increasingly provocative and uncomfortable: in a mock by-election held at the school Debating Society, he puts himself forward as a candidate for the National Front, causing Steve Richards to walk out in disgust.

Steve Richards beats Culpepper to the school sporting trophy, and incurs his lasting hatred. Later, when Richards comes to sit his A-levels, someone doses him with a sedative beforehand and he fails a crucial physics exam. He is obliged to take a year out before resitting the paper.

Meanwhile Benjamin abandons a rainswept family summer holiday on the Llŷn peninsula in North Wales, and makes his way instead to the house where Cicely is recovering from an illness with her uncle and aunt. He and Cicely declare their love for each other, but they do not sleep together for many more months.

Not, in fact, until May 1979. Benjamin is now working for a bank in central Birmingham, prior to attending Oxford university in the autumn.

Cicely has been living with her mother in New York. One morning after her return to England, she and Benjamin make love for the first and last time in Paul's bedroom. Ecstatically happy, Benjamin takes her for a drink that lunchtime in a Birmingham pub called The Grapevine. There, he meets Philip's father, SAM CHASE, who makes two predictions: that Benjamin and Cicely will have a long and happy life together, and that Margaret Thatcher will never be Prime Minister. Cicely leaves the pub, after being told that a letter has just arrived for her, from her friend Helen in New York. Later that day, Mrs. Thatcher sweeps to her first election victory.

Printed in the United States
by Baker & Taylor Publisher Services